A Biologically Male Magical White Kid

A Biologically Male Magical White Kid

and the

Book You Thought You'd Already Read

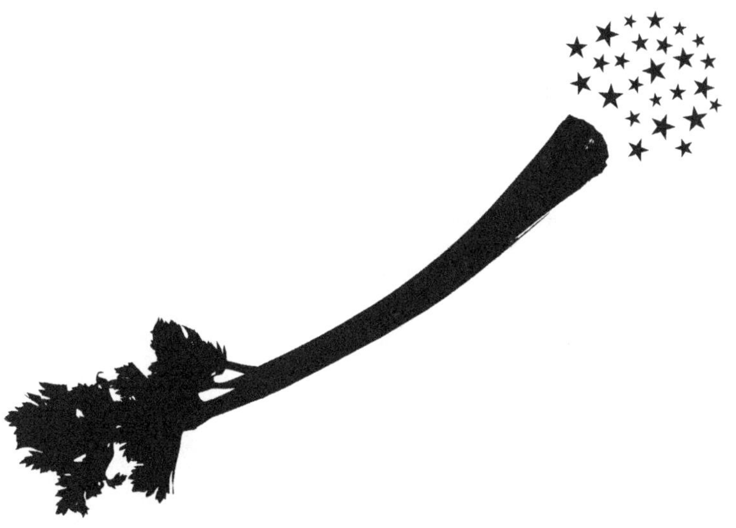

a parody by

Ben Fletcher

First published in 2021 by Enchanted Celery
Enchanted Celery is an imprint of Enchanted Celery Limited

Enchanted Celery Limited
85 Great Portland Street (1st Floor)
Marylebone, London, W1W 7LT
United Kingdom

A CIP Catalogue record for this book is available from the British Library

enchantedcelery.com

ISBN 978 1 7399320 2 2
3 5 7 9 11 10 8 6 4 2

Typeset by Enchanted Celery Limited
The printer and binder of this book may vary between territories of production and sale

for

Clemi

for always standing proud and unapologetic in the face of hate

Elliott

for being proud to be who they are and never who anyone else wants them to be

Sydny

for always caring about the faceless and nameless when no one else will

This book is a work of satirical parody and pastiche fiction, and makes use of copyrighted works and trademarks for the purposes of satire, criticism, review, and commenting on current events. Such uses are permitted under Section 30A(1) of the Copyright, Designs and Patents Act 1988 (as amended) in the United Kingdom, Section 107 of the Copyright Act in the United States, and Article 5(3) of European Union Directive 2001/29/EC, as incorporated into the law of member states.

Commentary, criticism, and review contained within this book, while based on true facts, events and quotations, may be dramatised for the purpose of continuity and narrative, and may therefore not portray a fully accurate representation of timing or context.

The content of this book is the sole responsibility of the author and the publisher, and has not been reviewed or endorsed by any third party distributor, printer, binder, or retailer.

The mention of any business, brand, or individual in this book is purely for entertainment purposes or for the purpose of satire, commentary, and criticism. No such mention should be taken to imply any relationship or partnership with, or an endorsement from, that business, brand, or individual.

Contents

Chapter One

Of Course, the Boy Is White

Mr and Mrs Moustache were a rather ordinary husband and wife, really.

Though, it could certainly in future be suggested by some that in certain specific circumstances, Mr Moustache could be interpreted to have displayed a subtle, yet on reflection actually perceptible, degree of toxic masculinity, which means upon reaching an appropriate age or the subject being topical in the news of the day, readers should assume there had been a hidden campaign of emotional abuse from him towards his wife the whole time, and that such a campaign is not a series of actions which any reasonable person should ever engage in themselves.

Mr Moustache was the sort of man who took daily both a copy of *The Sun* and the *Daily Mail*. It was very much the highlight of his daily routine to take a seat at the kitchen table around seven o'clock each morning and compare how the two, as he called them, *esteemed publications*, each undertook their own unique approach towards realising their joint ambition of ensuing that everything bad that ever happened in the world – from the gloomy weather last Thursday afternoon to the twelve-minute delay on the nine twenty-nine departure from Slough the next day – was blamed on immigrants. And vegan sausage rolls. Vegan sausage rolls simply had to be part of the radical left's liberal agenda imported into British society by European migrants. Mr Moustache was sure of that.

Mr Moustache approved very much of the *Duchess of Cambridge*, but not at all of *Megan Markle*, the *Duchess of Sussex*, who he refused to even acknowledge as having ties to royalty. "*The Duchess of Cambridge*, she knows exactly how to act with grace and with dignity," he would always be the first in the room to say whenever the opportunity arose to do so. Most often, that opportunity came during an evening news report on the television, when there would be a piece about the royal family presented by a royal correspondent who Mr Moustache would always refer to as "not British enough for the job."

"But that Megan," Mr Moustache would then go on to explain. "It's not that I don't like her. I just think our royal family should be all British, that's what I'm saying. I mean, what would the Australians or Canadians think if they found out that we had started letting foreign people into their royal family simply for the sake of diversity, or whatever they call it these days? Did anybody think of that? No. I didn't think so."

It would be reasonable to assume that, like many others who consider religiously supporting the royal family a personality trait to list proudly alongside casual racism and an irrational hated of anyone who looks even the slightest bit different from themselves, or be from a village, town, city or country which they fail to possess the intellect to spell, let alone locate on any map, Mr Moustache was unaware that the current royal family were once known as the house of *Saxe-Coburg and Gotha*, but made the decision in 1917 to adopt the surname *Windsor*, after the castle, in an attempt to avoid any sort of anti-German sentiment towards them during the later years of the First World War and subsequent decades.

You may at this moment wonder how it can be possible for a person such as Megan Markle to be relevant in a book clearly set some years before her rise to prominence, and also in an entirely different, and entirely fictional universe. But this is where readers learn the first rule of magical universe club: just because something was never mentioned in magical universe club, it doesn't mean it didn't actually happen in magical universe club. Sometimes, it is important to understand, things happen simply because magic, and never should you trouble yourself too much with such trivialities as sense, continuity, or whether future comments directly contradict what was actually in the book. No, not when there's an entire world of harm and hate to exploit in the name of convenience, topicality, and of course, a deep burning desire to remain relevant at all costs.

Mrs Moustache agreed with Mr Moustache's opinions on the royal family. In fact, Mrs Moustache agreed with Mr Moustache's opinions on almost any subject. This wasn't necessarily because she believed everything her husband said was always right — though often it was far right — but because in her view of the world, it was simply her job as Mr Moustache's wife to support and agree with any of the opinions he voiced. You see, Mrs Moustache had internalised misogyny, which is where a woman believes it's their place in society not to have their own views or ambitions, but to submit themselves to be controlled and suppressed by all the men who uphold the centuries old patriarchy.

While Mrs Moustache didn't believe in women having their own opinions, she was, to think of no better word, a fan of the works of various biologically female professional agitators who had all made their names and fortunes by crisis acting their way to a perceived impression among the gullible, racist, and simply fatuous members of society, that they were being oppressed despite being rich, white, and very privileged — and that is nothing to say of the larger than average platforms they all enjoyed, which if not being used to incite hate and discrimination without any real or meaningful consequences, could be put to good use sharing messages of unity, love, compassion, and understanding.

However much she found solace and solidarity with the voices of the aforementioned bigots, Mrs Moustache would have wanted you to know that never on a single occasion did she actually refer to herself as being a fan of them, for being a fan of anything made you a lower class of person than what Mrs Moustache believed herself to be. She was, nevertheless, permitted to admire the opinions of these particular owners of naturally occurring vaginas, for her husband approved of all their viewpoints. "They are a real man's woman," Mr Moustache would say if any of them appeared on the television.

It would also have been important to Mrs Moustache for you to know she never felt any sort of affection towards these women. After all, that would be quite unnatural. No, it was the true alpha males who sought to gain high office by holding rallies for the hate-filled and easily influenced, all while claiming to be telling people things exactly as they were, that made Mrs Moustache's body temperature rise. They were real men who always knew exactly what women like her were thinking, thought Mrs Moustache, and in her Mr Moustache-approved opinion, there were no finer men to speak on behalf of women everywhere – except perhaps Mr Moustache himself, of course.

Mr Moustache will be described first by his job and contribution to society, because he is the owner of a penis grown naturally in the wild. As the head of the household, Mr Moustache earned his living by working as a director of a large company, which paid him a handsome enough salary to afford him and his family a comfortable life. Though, not so large as to make any of them ever realise they didn't actually belong to an oppressed demographic.

It would be natural to assume that in a fictional world of the writer's own creation, where many risk their lives in the pursuit of eradicating all forms of profiling, that body shaming simply wouldn't exist. The reality is, however, that society had ingrained within each member a subliminal negative connotation that anyone whose body is of a larger size than average must most likely be a very bad person. And for this reason, and because it's an easy and lazy way to describe a character, Mr Moustache not only had an enormous black moustache on his top lip, but he was also rather short and very fat.

As though to reinforce society's belief that all women should be reduced to their appearance, Mrs Moustache will be described first by the way she looked. In deliberate contrast to Mr Moustache, Mrs Moustache was both tall and very thin. And to manipulate you into having a subconscious understanding that she was not an especially intelligent woman by employing the use of yet another stereotype, she was also blonde.

Intrusive would have been an accurate adjective for someone to deploy if describing Mrs Moustache's personality to an outsider. She enjoyed spending her time stalking the neighbours and clearly led an unfulfilling life of such hate, dullness, and frustration that she had become obsessed with the personal affairs of others – she would, for example, only be too interested to know the intimate details regarding the genitalia another might use when going to the toilet.

On one single occasion, Mr and Mrs Moustache had – solely for reproductive purposes, you must understand – scheduled an evening of affectionate activities between the two of them. It wasn't fun, so much, because fun wasn't for people in the middle to upper classes, but Mr Moustache had dimmed the lights a little and the two of them had looked away from one another while they engaged momentarily in synchronised missionary. The end result of this night of raucous behaviour, which, if it had been anyone else, Mr Moustache would have referred to as being both filthy and degrading, was that nine months later, Mrs Moustache had given birth to their son, Yate.

As a well-to-do family living under a right-wing government, the Moustache family were perfectly satisfied with their lives, but they also had a secret. Their greatest fear was that not only would their dinner party guests discover they reserved a cheaper cut of meat for them, but also that someone, anyone, found out about the Smiths. Mrs Smith was Mrs Moustache's sister, but they hadn't seen each other for many years. In fact, Mrs Moustache acted as though she didn't even have a sister, because her superiority complex meant she could never just be happy for someone else. Mr and Mrs Moustache knew the Smiths had their own son, but they had never met him.

When Mr and Mrs Moustache were woken early one morning by a thunderstorm that Mr Moustache would later attempt to somehow blame on immigration, our story begins.

There was nothing except a desire to cash in on a debut fluke to suggest that many strange, mysterious, and incredibly drawn-out things would soon be happening all over the country, and when that dries up, a couple of theme parks, a two-part live theatrical show, and a five-part spinoff film series as well. Upstairs, Mr Moustache whistled the tune to Rule Britannia as he picked out his tie for work, skipping over any which had red on them in case anyone mistook him for a communist, while Mrs Moustache argued with herself in the kitchen as she made breakfast.

Neither of them noticed the large pigeon flying past the window in an unsubtle sign of things to come.

At eight twenty-two precisely, Mr Moustache pulled on his suit jacket, kissed Mrs Moustache goodbye in a way that suggested neither of them had their hearts in the marriage anymore, and attempted to give Yate a hearty pat on the shoulder — because kissing wasn't an acceptable father-son activity in Mr Moustache's mind — but missed, because Yate was too busy throwing anything he could reach at his mother. "Boys will be boys," Mr Moustache laughed to himself as he left the kitchen.

A moment later, as the front door slammed shut, Mrs Moustache breathed a sigh of relief. It would be a whole eleven hours until Mr Moustache would be home, and that meant she had time to devote to hobbies, such as internet poker. Mr Moustache didn't know his wife was a problem gambler, and even if he did, there was little he'd do to help her overcome the problem. Mr Moustache just wasn't the sort of man who supported anyone through any sort of difficult time or situation.

Mr Moustache was also not a man who approved of women doing anything which might give them some independence. For this reason, he didn't know that during the day while he was at work, Mrs Moustache would also secretly spend time working on her debut novel. She knew that if Mr Moustache ever found out about this, it would damage his fragile masculinity to discover he wasn't as talented a writer as she was. To protect Mr Moustache's ego, she had fought an internal battle inside her head and came to the conclusion that when it would be convenient for her – and only when it would be convenient for her – she was actually perfectly comfortable with the idea of people choosing how to identify. So she had decided that should her novel ever be published, it would be published under a male pseudonym. She had already chosen the name she would use. It was a nice name, or at least she thought so. Mrs Moustache was also certain that if it ever transpired its namesake just happened to be a homophobic psychiatrist who believes all mental illnesses are caused by genetic defects, and that conversion therapy is an acceptable idea, no one would make a big deal out of it and just accept it was all nothing more than a coincidence.

Outside the front of the house, Mr Moustache got into his car and gazed up at the dull, grey sky above. "Bloody immigrants," he muttered to himself, xenophobically. Shaking his head, Mr Moustache turned the key to start the car, then reversed out of the driveway.

It was as he reached the corner of the street that he first noticed something unusual: a white rabbit was reading what appeared at first glance to be the local telephone book. For a moment, Mr Moustache wasn't sure what he had just witnessed. He swung his head around to check again. There was a white rabbit there, but there was no telephone book in sight. What could he have been thinking of? It must have been a trick of the light. Mr Moustache shook his head again, then proceeded to drive around the corner and up the next road. As he began pulling away, he watched the rabbit getting smaller in his mirror. It was now campaigning for Scottish independence. He gave his head a final shake and put the rabbit out his mind so that as he drove towards the centre of town, he thought of nothing except how his secretary was starting to get a little too old for his liking.

But on the edge of town, any thought of replacing his secretary with someone younger was driven out of his mind by something else entirely. As he sat in the usual morning traffic jam — something which was a direct result of the country being too full, he was sure — he couldn't help but notice a lot of strangely dressed people about. People wearing dressing gowns. Mr Moustache was far too judgmental not to be bothered by people dressing however they chose. He supposed this was just some phase a bunch of weirdo young people must be going through, because it was the popular thing to do. Yes, he thought, they'd grow out of it soon enough. He drummed his fingers on the steering wheel as a group of these "fruitcakes" standing nearby caught his eye.

Huddled close together so no one could hear what they were saying, they were talking in excited whispers. Mr Moustache was furious to notice that a couple of the group weren't young at all: why, that man had to be eligible for one of those free TV licences he was in full support of the government scrapping, and he was wearing a bright blue dressing gown.

As his eyes narrowed on the group, Mr Moustache suddenly remembered that just like physical appearance and the way a person chose to dress, mental health was also a perfectly acceptable thing to mock or make light of, and so in his mind, this group was probably just a bunch of people not right in the head. All these people were obviously just too lazy to get over whatever it was. "They all need to man up, dress properly, and start contributing something to society," Mr Moustache said to himself. The traffic started moving again, and a short while later, Mr Moustache arrived in the carpark outside his office, his mind back on the idea of promoting the blonde receptionist to be his new secretary.

Mr Moustache always faced away from the window in his top floor office. If he didn't, he might have found it a lot harder to concentrate that morning. He never saw any of the pigeons flying past the window. Though he did think he heard something when an especially large and clumsy pigeon misjudged their flight path and ploughed themselves into the glass at high velocity, before bouncing back and falling to the ground as people in the street gazed open-mouthed as another did the same thing moments later — pigeons weren't intelligent. Mr Moustache, however, had a perfectly ordinary and pigeon-free morning. He screamed at many people. He sexually harassed a few more. And he called the company's legal department to discuss a couple of unfair dismissal cases after firing two women in marketing in retaliation for them making a formal complaint about his behaviour. After being advised he could settle the cases out of court in a way that any civilised society would consider inadequate justice for his actions, Mr Moustache was in a good mood by the time lunch came around, when he decided to stretch his legs and walk across the road to buy himself a soft drink from the fast-food chain opposite.

The people in dressing gowns had completely slipped his mind until he passed a small huddle of them stood by the doors to the restaurant. He eyed them suspiciously as he passed. This group were also whispering with a sense of joy, and he couldn't see a single sign that even one of them had escaped from somewhere. It was on his way back past them, as he was angrily muttering to himself about having to pay extra for his soft drink because of the government's latest attempts to curb his freedoms by imposing a sugar tax, that he overheard a few words of what the group were saying.

"The Smiths — Billy, that's right — that's what I heard."

Mr Moustache came to an immediate stop. If it wasn't for the fact he didn't believe in anxiety, it would have flooded his entire body. He turned back the group as though he wanted to tell them all to get a grip on their lives and stop living off the backs of hardworking members of the community like himself, but he thought better of it.

Instead, he ran back across the road, rushed up the stairs to his office, screamed at his secretary that she should just get over his comments about her looking plump that morning, sat down at his desk before the office wall stopped shaking from his slamming shut of the door, grabbed the telephone off the receiver, dialled his home number, pressed the call button, and was just wondering what he was going to say to his wife when a voice answered. "Hello, Nice Slice Pizza — we cut it that way just to annoy you. What's your order?"

Mr Moustache swore loudly as he slammed the phone back down on the receiver. He was reaching once more to dial when he changed his mind. He tapped the top of his desk with his fingers and reclined in his chair so far he fell back and hit the floor. He got to his feet, righted his chair, and sat back down thinking… no, he wasn't the one being stupid, it was everyone else. Smith wasn't that unusual a name. He was quite sure there were many couples called Smith, who had a son called Billy. When he thought about it, he wasn't even sure his nephew was called Billy. He'd never met the boy. For all he knew, he might have been one of those weird people who chose to identify by a different name or as some sort of inanimate object; perhaps a lemon. There was no point in bringing it up with Mrs Moustache, not when it took her a whole evening of munching on edibles to calm down after any mention of her sister. He didn't blame her. If he'd been related to anyone like that… but all the same, those people wearing dressing gowns…

Mr Moustache found it a lot harder to concentrate on harassing and bullying his staff that afternoon, and by the time he left the office at close of business, he was still so worked up about what he had overheard that he walked straight into someone who was stood just outside the door.

"Will you look where you're going?" he asserted as the old man fell to the ground. It took a moment for Mr Moustache to notice that the man he'd just knocked over clearly wasn't as important as he was, and that he was wearing a long dressing gown. The man didn't seem at all bothered by being knocked to the pavement. He got to his feet and smiled broadly at Mr Moustache, before proclaiming in a squeaky voice, "My dear sir, I offer you all my most humble apologies for I was too distracted by my joy to see you there. Rejoice for That-Evil-One has finally gone and disappeared from our lives!"

Out of nowhere, a small grey cloud appeared above Mr Moustache. There was a bolt of lighting and a crash of thunder, and then, as Mr Moustache looked up at it, the cloud spat a small amount of water onto his face, then disappeared quite as suddenly.

"Even the commoners like yourself should be celebrating this joyful, joyful day, sir!" said the old man. And with that, he stepped forward to hug Mr Moustache around the middle, and then strolled off down the street.

Mr Moustache stood momentarily frozen where he was. He had just been touched by a complete stranger without his consent; he had always thought only powerful white men like himself could get away with doing that. He also thought he had just been called a commoner, whatever one of those was. He felt irritated. He forcefully shook himself into moving again, and then quickened to his car, so he could set off home, furious that some stranger on the street had exercised their right to free speech as though it was somehow equal to his own.

The problem wasn't that Mr Moustache was not a fan of free speech. On the contrary, he was quite the supporter of the concept when he was the one speaking or another was sharing views he agreed with. But he simply could not abide by free speech which made him feel uncomfortable or targeted his obstinate beliefs and narrow-minded view of the world. He would, for example, only be too willing to defend anyone who'd lost their job for speaking their mind — no matter how much scientific evidence existed to disprove their attempts to grab attention and be little more than as harmful and hurtful as possible towards an already marginalised and persecuted demographic. But at the same time, he would almost certainly be the first to hypocritically claim he was being harassed and start threatening legal action should anyone ever dare to point out the flaws or make a mockery of anything he had ever put his name to.

When he pulled into the driveway at home a short while later, the first thing he noticed – and it only served to increase his irrational feelings of rage – was the rabbit he'd seen earlier that morning. It was now sitting on the grass in the middle of his front garden. He was certain it was the same one. It was wearing a rosette in the colours of the *Scottish National Party*.

"Bugger off," he bellowed with sufficient volume for the neighbours to be concerned enough about the welfare of the rabbit to be promoted into looking up the number to report animal cruelty. The rabbit didn't move. It gave Mr Moustache a look that made him feel sure it knew how little he knew about the benefits an independent Scotland and its people might enjoy as a member of the European Union in its own right. Was this behaviour normal for a rabbit? Mr Moustache wondered. Striving to retain some dignity, he let himself into the house. He was still determined not to mention anything to his wife.

Mrs Moustache had had a pleasant and rather ordinary day. She spent dinner telling Mr Moustache about how she had spent a few hours stalking the next door neighbour in the morning, and then spent the afternoon writing a furious letter to *OFCOM*, the country's communications regulator, after a woman from the television appeared on one of the many magazine programmes she watched each day, to discuss matters surrounding woman's sexual health while Yate was in the room.

Mr Moustache attempted to act normally. After Yate had been put to bed, he joined his wife in the living room as the local evening news presenter brought his show to a close: "And finally, people everywhere have been reporting that the nation's pigeons have been behaving abnormally today. Although pigeons normally spend the day annoying members of the public by defecating on their lunches and diving at them unexpectedly in open places, there have been hundreds of reports that today, they have been flying in every direction as though on a joint mission – certainly no drone sighting grounding flights here. Experts have been unable to explain this sudden change in their behavioural patterns." The presenter allowed himself a smile.

"Most strange. And now, it's over to Sonny Gale with the weather. What's your take on all these pigeons, Sonny?"

"Well," said the weatherman, "if I was to take a guess, I'd say that all this mention of pigeons is simply an attempt to avoid any potential copyright infringement. But legal experts as far apart as Exeter, Warwick, and Inverness have been phoning in to tell me that the choice of bird is unlikely to be the main complaint anyone has in this situation. Some of our most loyal and bored viewers with not much else to do during the day have also been in touch to say that instead of the rain I promised them yesterday, they've been seeing strange lights up in the sky. Perhaps the Russian military are conducting secretive surveillance missions under the cover of darkness in violation of international laws, treaties, and sanctions – remember, the Cold War was over decades ago, Mr Putin! But I can promise you all freak hailstones as a direct impact of global warming tonight."

Mr Moustache sat glued to his armchair. Covert operations by the Russian Military? Pigeons acting in strange ways? Weird people in dressing gowns all over the place? Global warming creating freak weather phenomena because society had ignored the issue for far too long?... well, he didn't believe in that one so much, but still, there was that mention of the Smiths too...

He glanced across at Mrs Moustache, who was concentrating on the television. It was no good. He'd have to bring it up. He coughed as though attempting to assert his position at the top of the household hierarchy. "Er – Jennifer, dear – you haven't heard from your sister lately, have you?"

As Mr Moustache had expected, Mrs Moustache reached straight for a small tin underneath her chair, and within a moment, she was chewing furiously on an edible she had taken from it.

"No," she answered bluntly. "Why would you ask such a question? Do you think she's better than me? Do you wish you'd married her instead of me?"

"No, no, that's not what I'm saying at all. But, you know, bizarre things on the news and all that," Mr Moustache mumbled. "Pigeons… climate change… and there were a lot of weird-looking people around town earlier…"

"So? What does that have to do with anything?" Mrs Moustache said at such speed Mr Moustache could barely understand a word she was saying. "You think I'm weird-looking, don't you? I already know you do. Just admit it."

"No, I was just wondering if… perhaps… all these things had something to do with… you know… her bunch of pathetic losers."

Mrs Moustache chewed ever more ferociously as she stared at her husband unblinkingly. Mr Moustache deliberated about whether he should tell her he'd overheard people talking about the name "*Smith*." He decided against it. Instead, he said, with an attempt to sound as casual as possible, "Their son – how old would he be these days? He'd be about the same age as Yate, wouldn't he?"

"Why are you asking about *their* son? Is our son not good enough for you? Would you rather we all swapped sons so you could have their son, and they could have our son? Would that make you happy? Would it? Would it?" asked Mrs Moustache frantically.

"No. I'm just asking. What was his name again?"

"Why do you want to know his name? You do want their son. Well, why don't you just leave me and Yate here and go live with my sister if we're not good enough for you?" said Mrs Moustache, before nearly choking as she swallowed the remainder of her edible.

"I wish you wouldn't keep eating those," said Mr Moustache as he watched her reach for another. "They make you all paranoid."

"Who's paranoid? Do you think I'm paranoid? I'm not paranoid? You're the one who's paranoid. You're paranoid about whether I'm paranoid."

Mr Moustache decided not to say another word on either subject for the rest of the night. A short while later, when they had gone upstairs to bed, as Mrs Moustache brushed her teeth in the bathroom, Mr Moustache went over to the bedroom window and looked out into the front garden; something which was considerably more intricate than you'd imagine as their bedroom looked out over the back of the house. The rabbit was still there.

It was gazing down the street with eyes that pierced the darkness as though they were electric torches powered by the sort of batteries another of its kind might advertise for a living.

Was he imagining all this? Could any of it really have anything to do with the Smiths? And if it did… if it got out he and Mrs Moustache were both judgmental morons? — Well, he thought, they were at least powerful enough to avoid any real consequences.

Mr and Mrs Moustache got into bed. Mrs Moustache fell asleep quickly – one of the side effects of her edibles – but Mr Moustache lay on his back long into the early hours of the morning, the day's events running through his mind. His last, reassuring thought before he too fell asleep was that even if the Smiths were involved, everyone else was sure to share he and Mrs Moustache's opinion and believe the Smiths were the most unnatural of people and the very definition of freaks of nature. The Smiths knew very well that they both thought of them and anyone like them… he couldn't comprehend the idea that he and Mrs Moustache could ever not be regarded as the victims in this situation – he yawned and turned over onto his side – they knew better than everyone else…

How very wrong they both were.

Mr Moustache might have been drifting into a disturbed sleep, but outside in the garden, the lone white rabbit showed little sign it too was weary. It was still quite as unmoving as the average baby boomer when confronted with the reality that they aren't always the most important or knowledgeable person in the room, its eyes fixed on a point in the middle of the road that was quite as unremarkable as the city of Hull. It didn't so much as start when a loud explosion shook the ground beneath it as the night shift got to work on fracking the local area, nor when an aeroplane flew low overhead despite curfews designed to reduce noise pollution. In fact, it was several more hours before the rabbit moved at all.

A man appeared in the middle of the road exactly at the spot where the rabbit had been watching, and almost immediately, he fell over and hit the surface with a dull thud. The rabbit's nose twitched as it watched.

The man pulled himself up and looked down to see what had

caused him to fall. "Bloody potholes," he muttered to himself irritably as he straightened out his clothes. "The local council really should be doing more to fix these. I mean, we pay enough in taxes, don't we?"

This man was quite the unusual sight for this street. He was very tall, quite thin, and looked as though he could have once been the lead singer of some rock band, judging by the length of his greying hair, which just about reached down far enough for him to be able to tuck it into his belt. His beard was the same length as his hair, though more a sign of his shortcomings in personal hygiene than one he had a long-lost past which he refused to let go of. He was wearing a long purple dressing gown, which reached far below any normal dressing gown, and covered his heavy, bucked boots.

His eyes were of a light blue shade and bright enough that they could reflect the light coming from the headlights of a small car parked on the street ahead. The owner of the car had been forced to live in it ever since a change in government policy had made them homeless, and leaving the engine running was the only way to keep warm during the cold nights.

This man's name was Professor Richard Crumbleceiling.

Richard Crumbleceiling didn't seem to know he was as welcome in this neighbourhood as an asylum seeker was in Britain under a right wing government who had appointed a heartless bigoted hypocrite as Home Secretary — though she did have eyebrows which Mr Moustache said didn't make her quite look a million dollars, but more in the region of seventy-seven thousand pounds. Crumbleceiling was busy feeling around the inside of his pockets looking for something. He wasn't so distracted by his search, however, that he didn't notice the pair of eyes watching him from nearby. He stared at the rabbit momentarily and then laughed to himself. "To be expected," he said.

He looked away from the rabbit as he pulled what he was looking for out of his pocket. It appeared to be a small hairpin. He glanced around to check that no one except the rabbit was watching him, then walked over to a telephone exchange box close by on the pavement. Kneeling down in front of it, he took the hairpin and began using it to pick at the lock. With a click, the lock came loose, and the door it kept shut swung open on its hinges. Crumbleceiling reached inside and began ripping out and pocketing any wire he could reach. Once he had scavenged as much as possible, he made his way over to where the rabbit was still watching him and sat down on the grass next to it.

"Copper wiring," he said smugly as he held up a small piece of what he'd just stolen from the telephone exchange box. "It is most valuable on the black market, and with us teachers facing another pay freeze, Professor McDouglass."

He turned to smile at the rabbit, but it had gone. Instead, he was smiling at a stern-looking woman who was wearing the sort of glasses you'd expect to see on the face of an especially strict librarian. She too was wearing a dressing gown: a green one. Her hair was almost as long as Crumbleceiling's, but rather than let it fall down, she had worked it into a neat bun that sat atop her head. On her face, she wore a distinctly frustrated expression.

"How did you know it was me?" asked Professor McDouglass.

"My dear Professor, how could I not? I've never seen a rabbit sit so still. Incidentally, why were you a rabbit?"

"I figured that if every other stereotype is going to be used and overused in this world, I might as well introduce one that might actually be relevant. If you turn away for a moment, then I can pop out of a top hat and really complete the image. I've been practicing that trick all day."

"All day? But what about the celebrations? I must have passed by tens of gatherings on my way here."

Professor McDouglass tutted angrily.

"Oh yes, that's right, everybody's certainly celebrating," she said frustratedly.

"You'd think they'd all show just a little more caution, but no – they've spent all day drinking and now they're going to be making their way home while intoxicated. Did you know hundreds of people are killed by drink-driving each year in this country alone? And then there are the thousands more who are seriously injured by such stupidity."

"You shouldn't be too surprised by their actions," said Crumbleceiling. "People have had so little to celebrate for so long."

"I know that," said Professor McDouglass impatiently. "But that's no reason for us all to start acting so irresponsibly now. Some people aren't even trying to be careful. Out speeding on the roads all day and not even bothering to stop for any red lights. Swapping stories with one another as though the news can't wait for even a moment."

She glanced across at Crumbleceiling with a concerned yet expectant expression, as though she herself couldn't wait another moment to hear the news from him, but he said nothing, and so she continued. "Very great it would be if on the same day That-Evil-One…" – Crumbleceiling pulled out a small umbrella as a dark cloud appeared above his head with a flash of lighting. Once it had stopped raining, he put the umbrella away – "As I was saying," Professor

McDouglass went on, "very great it would be if on the same day that, you know, appears to have finally disappeared, hundreds of us cause the police to waste valuable time and resources on dealing with drunk drivers and speeding, rather than their real responsibilities of assaulting peaceful protesters and arresting anybody who looks at them funny or is wearing a hooded jumper. I am right in saying that he's gone, aren't I, Crumbleceiling?"

"That appears to be what has happened, yes," Crumbleceiling replied. "We certainly have much to be grateful for. Now, would you like a bon-bon?"

"A what?"

"A bon-bon, Professor. They're a sweet that the commoners eat, and they really are quite nice."

"No, I would not like a bon-bon, thank you very much," said Professor McDouglass with disgust. "Have you even stopped to consider the damage all that sugar is doing to your health – not to mention your teeth? Don't you think our public health system is under enough strain as it already is, Crumbleceiling?"

"My dear Professor –"

"I'm just saying. I do hope you're brushing your teeth regularly, that's all."

"After every meal," Crumbleceiling reassured her as he began sucking on a bon-bon, as though he was a grandmother who'd misplaced her false teeth at a family gathering.

"Anyway, even if That-Evil-One..." – Crumbleceiling had his umbrella ready – "...has disappeared –"

"Professor, surely you are not so scared of a person that you will not even call him by his name? All this That-Evil-One stuff..."

Professor McDouglass was not so prepared as Crumbleceiling as to have an umbrella with her. As the cloud appeared above her head, she waited with apprehension, as first came the flash of lighting and wave of thunder, and then sure enough, a stream of water began trickling onto her head and running down her face.

Crumbleceiling continued, "...year after year I have been telling people to just call him by his name – Steven." Professor McDouglass' whole body shook as though it had actually been hit by the lighting, but Crumbleceiling, who was busy holding up a bon-bon to his eye-line and admiring how it looked in the moonlight, didn't notice. "It's all very confusing when everybody keeps saying That-Evil-One..." – more water streamed down the side of Professor McDouglass' face – "...I mean, people might end up confusing them with somebody else like, say, a popular author, if we aren't more specific about it. And anyway, I have never seen any reason to be frightened of saying Steven's name."

Professor McDouglass expelled the water that had gathered in her mouth by letting it dribble out in a half-sarcastic manner. "Everybody knows that, Crumbleceiling," she said. "But you're different to the rest of us. And we all know that you're the only one That-Evil-One..." Crumbleceiling pulled out his umbrella, but Professor McDouglass was ready for him. She grabbed the umbrella and held it out of reach before he could put it up. The cloud appeared above Crumbleceiling's head, but it seemed to hesitate for a moment. And then, as though it held a personal grudge against Professor McDouglass, it flew across from above Crumbleceiling's head and rained atop her own instead. "...that Steven was ever afraid of," she finished with little enthusiasm in her words.

"You really do flatter me, Professor," said Crumbleceiling, as he began chewing on another bon-bon. "But Steven has many powers that I shall never possess. His name for one — he is called Steven."

"There are rumours, too, Crumbleceiling. The drinking and the celebrations are nothing compared to all the rumours people are sharing with each other. Have you heard what people are saying? About why Steven has finally gone? And what it is that stopped him?"

It appeared Professor McDouglass had finally brought the conversation around to what he wanted to discuss. She stared at Crumbleceiling piercingly. It was clear she wasn't going to let him avoid the subject. She wanted to hear the truth directly from him.

"What everybody is saying," she went on, "is that late last night, Steven turned up in Nempnett Thrubwell. He went to find the Smiths. People are saying that he — that he killed them. It can't be true, can it, Crumbleceiling?"

Crumbleceiling nodded gently and bowed his head as Professor McDouglass looked on in shock.

"But… I can't believe it… I don't want to believe it… Not Phalaenopsis and Keith."

"Oh, Richard…"

Crumbleceiling reached his arm around Professor McDouglass' shoulder to comfort her. "I know… I —"

"Please do not touch me without my consent," Professor McDouglass interrupted as she pushed his arm away. "Just because we work together and have known each other a long time, it doesn't mean it's okay for you to touch me without me saying you can just because I'm upset."

"I'm sorry if I offended you," said Crumbleceiling.

"Sorry if you offended me? You're not sorry for what you did, only that I might be offended by it?"

"I — I offer you my deepest regret and unreserved apologies."

There was a moment's silence. "Unwanted physical contact and sexual harassment is simply not acceptable, Crumbleceiling. I'd have thought you might have known better. But it just goes to show that even those closest to you who you think you know best can still surprise you and ignore your boundaries.

"Never do it again, please." Professor McDouglass shook her head. "Anyway, that's not all people have been saying. They're saying that Steven tried to kill Billy, the Smith's young son, too. But he couldn't kill him. He couldn't kill a small defenceless child. No one seems to know why, but they're saying when he tried to kill Billy Smith but couldn't, Steven's power broke somehow — they're saying that's why he's gone."

Crumbleceiling nodded. "It can happen like that sometimes. A powerful person can spend so much time going after others without consequence or challenge that eventually, when they do finally face some unexpected opposition, they are so shocked by the experience that they themselves are destroyed."

"So — it's true then?" said Professor McDouglass with surprise. "After everything he's done… everybody he's killed… he wasn't able to kill a baby? How does that happen? Of all the things to stop him… but how did Billy survive?"

"My dear Professor, if I were to answer that now, a much more convenient answer would only come along sometime in the future."

Professor McDouglass pulled a tissue from her pocket and dabbed at the tears collecting below her eyes. Crumbleceiling cleared his throat and took from his own pocket a small golden pocket watch which he opened and examined. "Barry's late. I assume he was the one who told you I'd be coming here?"

"Yes," answered Professor McDouglass. "But why here of all places? It's hardly somewhere out kind frequent."

"I'm here to deliver Billy to the only remaining family he has. His aunt and uncle live just here," said Crumbleceiling as he gestured towards the house behind them.

"You mean — you can't mean the people who live here?" Professor McDouglass exclaimed. "You can't. You just can't. I've been watching them all day, and they're just the most awful of people. They voted for Nigel Farage in a parliamentary election, Crumbleceiling. And they've got their own son — I was watching him earlier as his mother dragged him down the street. He was crying all the way. They aren't good parents. Billy Smith come and live here?"

"I can assure you, this will not be the most damaging thing I was ever do to the boy," said Crumbleceiling schemingly. "He is much safer here with his aunt and uncle, and they will be able to tell him everything when he's older. I've written them a letter to explain it all."

"A letter? You've written them a letter?" Professor McDouglass looked shocked. "Really, Crumbleceiling, how can you begin to explain any of this in a letter? And besides that, by the time the boy is old enough to understand, the situation could be completely different."

"You don't have to tell me that, Professor. Why, in just a few years time, I may discover I have been gay all along."

"Well, I don't see what's wrong with that. You're allowed to do things at your own pace. No one should be forcing you to come out."

"You misunderstand me, Professor. I don't mean I may discover I am gay for the first time. I mean I may find out that I already know I'm gay and have been for decades, and even that I've had a relationship with another man."

"But surely you'd already know if you'd ever had a relationship with another man?"

"You'd think so, wouldn't you? But perhaps certain people feel that information can wait for another time. At least until they've had the chance to work out if revealing it would be beneficial to their career and relevance anyway."

"You'll be able to be openly proud of your sexuality once that has happened, though? You can be a role model for young people unsure of their own sexuality who are looking to see themselves represented in popular culture?"

"Many would hope, but alas, higher powers may worry about money and alienating certain groups far too much to actually choose to show that love is indeed love."

"It won't just be that things are different when he's older, though. These people will never understand him. With them, he'll be an outcast. Among our kind, he'll be famous — I wouldn't be surprised if there's an entire day named after him in the future. People will write books about the boy. He'll be on postage stamps and overpriced collectables. People will use him as a shield to get away with saying awful things. Everybody will know his name and reference him in situations where he is completely irrelevant to what is actually going on, and it will never, ever end."

"That is precisely my point," said Crumbleceiling as he looked at her over the top of the spectacles balanced on the end of his nose.

"Can't you see he'll be much better off if he grows up away from all that? Can't you understand it's much better if he returns to our world with absolutely no idea of who any of us are, who his parents were or what he is? In my view, it's much better if he grows up misunderstood, isolated, and bullied, and that he never has any real friends until he reaches the age of eleven."

"Crumbleceiling, that's complete madness, and it's cruel."

Professor McDouglass swallowed hard. "Well, I guess you're going to do it your way no matter what anybody else says. But how exactly are you going to deliver the boy to his family? You don't have him with you now, do you?"

"Barry is bringing him here."

"Barry? You think it... wise? Can Barry be trusted with something as important as this?"

"I think so."

"But Barry is an alcoholic. He drinks more than anybody else I've ever known – hold on... did you say the boy's parents were murdered last night?"

"That's right."

"Then why are you only bringing the boy here now? What have you been doing for the past twenty-four hours?"

"Oh, well... I was distracted..."

To Crumbleceiling's relief, before Professor McDouglass could question him further, their conversation was interrupted by a sudden rumbling roar from the sky directly above them.

"Ah, this must be them now," said Crumbleceiling, jumping to his feet.

Professor McDouglass also stood up, and as the rumbling grew louder and louder, they both looked to the sky. As suddenly as it had begun, the rumbling stopped and was replaced by a deafening and drawn out HONK! And then, a gigantic swan pedalo fell from the sky and landed gently on the road in front of them.

Much like Mr Moustache, the man sat in the front seat of the pedalo was very fat. In fact, he was even fatter. But this was okay because he was a friendly and kind character, and this, along with being evil or unpleasant, was one of the circumstances where it is apparently perfectly acceptable to describe someone as being fat.

"Well, I certainly wasn't expecting anything like that," said Professor McDouglass.

Crumbleceiling ignored her. "Barry," he said. "At last, you've made it."

"One moment please." Barry turned back as though to talk to another who might have been sat behind him, but there was no one there. "Doors t' automatic n' cross-check," he said in a strong Yorkshire accent.

"Sorry 'bout delay," Barry said as he climbed off the pedalo. "There wor air traffic control strike we 'ad t' avoid, n' then we got stuck in 'olding pattern due t' spot o' bad weather."

"Well, you're here now. Do you have the boy?"

"T' lad? Ah knew ah'd forgotten summa'." Barry looked at Crumbleceiling, and then to Professor McDouglass. Off her look, he said, "Calm down. Ah'm only messin' wi' theur. Ah've got lad 'ere. Managed t' gerr' 'im out in time before wrong fowk turned up." He pulled a bundle of blankets out from within his weathered coat. "Lad calmed down n' fell asleep an 'our ago."

Crumbleceiling and Professor McDouglass leant in to look at

what was hiding within the blankets. Just visible was the head of a small baby boy, sleeping calmly. "He's an ugly child, isn't he?" critiqued Crumbleceiling. Professor McDouglass nodded in agreement and then noticed a small cut on the boy's forehead, half covered by his pitch-black hair."

"What is that?" asked Professor McDouglass.

"That," replied Crumbleceiling, "that is a trademark."

"But what is the shape?"

"Personally, I believe it resembles a dollar sign. What about you, Barry?"

Barry looked down at the boy's forehead. "Aye, it looks like dollar sign, Professor. Maybe even two."

"How long will it be there for?" asked Professor McDouglass.

"Far too long," said Crumbleceiling. "Well, we'd best be getting this over with, anyway."

Crumbleceiling took the bundle of blankets from Barry and turned towards the house.

"Professor, could ah – could ah seh t'rah f' now t' lad?" Barry asked. Crumbleceiling turned back so Barry could lean in and nearly choke the baby with his long thick beard. And then suddenly, Barry let out a scream that pieced the silence around them. "WHY? WHY 'IM?"

"Will you be quiet!" Professor McDouglass said, hitting Barry sharply in the stomach to shut him up. "If you carry on like this, you'll wake somebody up, and then they'll make phone calls. The last thing we need is for the police to be turning up."

"I don't think any of us would be in too much trouble," Crumbleceiling interjected. "I mean, we're all powerful and white. In fact, there are few people in this story who aren't."

"All the same, Crumbleceiling."

"Ah'm s-s-sorry 'bout that," Barry sobbed as he blew his nose on a tissue he'd just pulled from his pocket. "Bur it's all so sad. 'is parents dead, n' now Billy 'as t' live wi' commoner fowk."

"Yes, yes, but do pull yourself together Barry, otherwise somebody will think we're doing drugs out here."

"Well, if you're offering…" said Crumbleceiling.

"Headmaster!"

"Not the appropriate time. I've got it."

For a moment there was silence, except for Barry's continued sobs, as Crumbleceiling walked towards the front door of the Moustaches house and laid the bundle of blankets softly down on the doorstep. Pulling a letter out from the pocket of his dressing gown, he tucked it within one of the blanket's many folds. He took a step back and looked down at the bundle for a short moment, and then turned around and went back to join the other two, tripping over on the way.

"What a stupid place to put a garden gnome," he said, picking up what he had fallen over.

"Headmaster – be quiet, remember."

Crumbleceiling threw the gnome to one side. "We've done all we came here to do," he said. "There's no reason for any of us to stay longer. We may as well go get drunk."

"Aye. Ah could do wi' few," Barry agreed as he remounted the pedalo. "G'night, Professors."

There was another loud honk as the pedalo rose slowly back into the air and then sped off into the starless night sky.

"You know I caught him urinating into a staffroom draw a few weeks ago, don't you?"

"Let the man celebrate with a drink," said Crumbleceiling as they walked away from the house.

When they reached the spot where Crumbleceiling had first appeared, they turned back to look at the bundle of blankets on the doorstep.

"I'm going to manipulate you into killing yourself one day, Billy," said Crumbleceiling under his breath.

"I'm sorry, what was that?" said Professor McDouglass.

"Spoilers."

Professor McDouglass nodded uncertainly, and a second later, they had both disappeared.

As a light breeze skimmed the top of the neat grass verges that ran down the street, inside the bundle of blankets, the tiny hand of Billy Smith was closing on the letter. He rolled over in his sleep and dreamt on, not knowing that in just a few hours time he was going to be woken by Mrs Moustache screaming, nor that he would spend the next ten years of his life being abused and mistreated by his aunt, uncle, and cousin... He couldn't know, also, that at that very moment, right across the country people were celebrating and toasting to the terrible and traumatic event which had led to the death of his parents.

Chapter Two

"That Penguin Had a Business Card?"

Almost a decade had passed since the cold November morning on which Mr and Mrs Moustache had been shocked to wake up and find their baby nephew, Billy Smith, curled up inside a bundle of blankets on their doorstep, but little had changed on the street outside. The sun still shined upon the same neat front gardens that stood tidily side by side, divided only by the equally well-kept and bright green hedgerows that separated them. It still shined, too, upon the highly polished door number Mr Moustache had screwed onto the wall next to their *Beware of the Bulldog* sign. The Moustaches didn't actually have a bulldog — Mrs Moustache had allergies which made that impossible — but they had seen the sign while out shopping one morning and decided it would make their household appear much more patriotic to anyone passing by.

Inside the house, the same sun that shined brightly outside also shone through the same flowery curtains that had been there on the night Mr Moustache had sat down in his comfortable armchair by the window and watched that fateful weather report informing him there were to be freak hailstones that night due to climate change. To those people who, like Mr Moustache, were incredibly stupid, it felt as though the sun was somehow much brighter now than it had been back then. But to anyone who had even the most basic and simplistic understanding of scientific concepts — or the ability to listen to those who knew more than they did — the reality was no one had ever cared enough about the issue of global warming to actually do anything which might have avoided the continued rise in global temperatures.

Ten years ago, the mantelpiece and walls had been adorned with photo frames exhibiting photographs of what at first glance appeared to be a giant inflatable toy wearing outfits of various bright colours — but Yate Moustache was no longer the small boy he had been back then.

Taking after his father, Yate was also now very fat. Of course, he was fat. Yate was set to grow up as such an unpleasant child, he simply couldn't not be fat in a story such as this, could he? While Yate's yet to be mentioned campaign of bullying against others is something to be strongly condemned, in this world, for some reason it's as though children should be taught that bullying is only ever a problem when it is perpetuated by those deemed less attractive — or fat — by a judgmental society, and never when those same people are victims themselves. Because of this, Yate himself was apparently fair game, and this is why he wasn't only fat, but rather he was a giant hippopotamus of a child.

Mr and Mrs Moustache were both very proud of their hippopotamus-sized son, and so the photographs spread around the room now showed the giant boy getting into his first fist fight at school, getting stuck in a swing at the local playground, illegally hacking into a supposedly secure government computer system with his father before forwarding what they found to *WikiLeaks*, and being hugged and kissed by every member of his family so often that anyone else could only presume none of them were aware of the risks of such close contact were there ever to be a global pandemic.

None of the photographs in this room, or indeed any other room in the house, showed any sign there was another boy living there as well.

But Billy Smith was still a member of the Moustache household, and at that moment, he was still asleep.

The first noise of the day came from his aunt as she picked up the morning post from the doormat and screamed shrilly with the upmost disgust.

"Oh, my goodness," said Mrs Moustache in a panicked voice. "MICHAEL!" she shouted up the stairs. "MICHAEL, COME QUICKLY."

There was movement from above, as a short sequence of thuds preceded the appearance of a half-dressed Mr Moustache at the top of the stairs, and then more thuds as he attempted not to trip over his own trousers as he walked down the stairs with them still around his ankles.

"What have I told you about calling me by my first name outside the bedroom, Jennifer?"

"But Michael, they've used... they've used a second class stamp on this letter."

The thuds stopped.

"WHAT?"

"Look at it. It's all blue and there's a little number two, followed by a tiny letter N and a tiny letter D. I've seen the neighbours using them before. It's definitely authentic."

The thuds resumed, though they were lighter than before, as Mr Moustache made his way towards a scene which he hoped no one he knew would ever witness him being a part of; much like when the more respectable staff at a major publishing house are asked to attend a meeting to discuss the release of a new book by one of the country's former most-popular authors... allegedly.

"They must..." began Mrs Moustache as her husband took the letter from her.

"...think we are second class citizens," Mr Moustache finished for her. "Where did this letter come from, Jennifer?"

"It's from the television licensing people."

"DAMN IT!" bellowed Mr Moustache. What is it these communists don't understand? I will not pay for their left-wing liberal hacks to disgrace our great nation on the public airwaves. No, I won't do it. And now they have the... the AUDACITY to send us a communication in the same way poorer people buy household goods from the back of newspapers. I will not stand for it. I just won't."

"But what do we do about it, Michael?"

"Well, first, we must burn this letter in protest. And then after you've calmed yourself down over a cup of tea, made my breakfast, and done all the washing up, you should write a stern letter to our Member of Parliament to tell him exactly what I think about the matter. Yes, that will do it."

"I don't think I can even concentrate on making breakfast right now," said Mrs Moustache, her voice shaking.

"Get the boy to make it."

There were more thuds as Mr Moustache pulled his trousers up from around his ankles and then made his way along the hall towards the kitchen door. He stopped just short of the cupboard under the stairs, cleared his throat, and then slammed his fist so hard on the cupboard door that the wood might have splintered.

"BOY!"

Inside the cupboard, Billy woke with a start.

"Up! Get up and out of bed and stop being so lazy!" It was his aunt who spoke this time, as she too began banging her own hands on the door. "Right this instant!"

Billy sat up in bed.

"UP!" screamed Mrs Moustache again. Billy listened in silence as he heard her go into the kitchen and the door close behind her. He rubbed his eyes as he tried to remember the dream he had just woken up from. It had been a good dream. There had been love and acceptance for all people regardless of how they chose to identify or live their lives. He had a strange feeling he'd had the same dream before. He shook his head and laughed to himself about how ludicrous such a concept was in this universe.

His aunt was back outside the door.

"Have you got up yet?" she screeched as she began scratching at the wood as though she was a possum attempting to launch a daring escape from an animal testing facility run by one of the many immoral cosmetics companies.

"I'm getting up now," Billy replied through a yawn.

"Well, move quicker. I want you to make breakfast. And don't you dare ruin any of it. Everything must be perfect today for Yate's birthday."

Billy sighed.

"What did you just say?" demanded Mrs Moustache as she peered through the small air hole Mr Moustache had drilled into the door.

"Nothing. I didn't say anything..."

Yate's eleventh birthday. How had he forgotten about it? It was all his cousin had gone on about for weeks.

Billy got out of bed, slowed by the heavy feeling of dread he felt for the day ahead, and started to look for a clean pair of socks. He found a pair in the corner of the cupboard and, after pulling a venomous and deadly black widow spider off one of them, he put them on. Billy was used to black widow spiders because his aunt and uncle kept releasing them into the tiny cupboard where they forced him to sleep in the hope he'd get bitten one night and die, so they could claim on the life insurance policy they had set up in his name.

After pulling on an old t-shirt and pair of jeans, he left the cupboard and went into the kitchen. Mr Moustache was sitting at the table reading a piece in the *Daily Mail* about how something bad was all the fault of that young couple from Eastern Europe who had recently moved in down the street, though much of both he and the table were hidden from view by the mountain of colourfully wrapped boxes and packages that were Yate's birthday presents.

It looked to Billy as though Yate had been given many of the things he wanted: a new gaming computer, which he referred to as a set-up, a switchblade to replace the one he'd had confiscated at school the week before, a mountain bike, and a big cuddly toy to go to sleep with. Exactly why Yate wanted a mountain bike was a mystery to

Billy, because again, Yate was a wayward child who was therefore very fat and hated exercise – unless, of course, that exercise was pinning Billy to the ground and repeatedly punching him in the head as though role paying a member of the *Metropolitan Police* in a situation where they faced no threat at all. Yate's favourite punching bag had always been Billy, but it was often difficult to catch him. He didn't look it, but Billy was very fast.

Perhaps it had something to do with years of being abused by his aunt and uncle by being forced to live in the dark, damp and cramped cupboard under the stairs for most of his life, but Billy had always been generic, small, and on the skinny side for his age. It was almost as if he was supposed to be the heroically deliberate contrast to his fat cousin and other fat characters who are yet to be introduced, but will inevitably be just as bad. The clothes he wore made Billy look even smaller still, because all the Moustaches ever gave him to wear were Yate's old hand-me-downs, and Yate was, and this really can't be emphasised enough for some reason, really very fat.

Billy wasn't fat. Having been starved by his aunt and uncle on a semi-regular basis as a form of torture for him and entertainment for themselves, he was very thin. He had a thin face and thin knees. In fact, everything about him was thin, except for the paycheques he proved for those using him as cover while abusing their influence and power, and the thick black and messy hair that sat atop his head, giving him just enough fringe to reach the top of his bright blue eyes. In front of his eyes, Billy wore an old pair of glasses held together by tape after the time Mr Moustache had thrown a cricket ball at his face during a school sports day event he was about to come ahead of Yate in.

The only thing Billy liked about the way he looked was the dollar-shaped trademark on his forehead. He'd had the trademark for as long as he could remember, and the first question he could remember asking Mrs Moustache was how he had gotten it.

"From the angry swan that attacked, killed, and gobbled up your parents," she said sharply. "You're quite lucky it was full up by the time it had gotten to you. Now, don't ask me any more questions."

Not asking questions was the second rule for anyone who wanted a quiet life living with the Moustaches. The first rule was always to ensure Mrs Moustache never ran out of her edibles.

Mr Moustache put down his newspaper and looked over at Billy.

"Use a brush on that hair boy. You look as though the Prime Minister has stuck his hair into a tub of lard and gone outside on a windy day," said Mr Moustache by way of a passively aggressive morning greeting. He laughed to himself for what he felt was a witty line.

Billy was used to this. It happened at least once a week that Mr Moustache would put down his newspaper and say something about the way Billy's hair looked. The Moustaches had tried to fix what they considered a major problem by dragging Billy to the hairdressers and demanding of the person cutting his hair, that they stick to one of a limited number of Mr Moustache-approved styles, as though they were living in North Korea, but it made no difference. After all, no matter how much they might have wished they could control how others lived, Mr and Mrs Moustache didn't actually live under an authoritarian regime which punished individuality and free spirit — at least not yet, anyway. Billy's hair simply grew messy and ruffled looking, and there wasn't anything they could do about it.

Billy was coughing up phlegm into Mr Moustache's morning coffee when Yate entered the kitchen. Yate was the spitting image of a young Mr Moustache, which, as a reminder, meant he was very fat. To complete the image of Yate being unintelligent, he also had a bowl of blonde hair which sat atop his round, fat head. Mrs Moustache would often comment that Yate was the most handsome boy she had ever seen. Billy often commented that Yate was so fat each of his legs were in different postcodes, which, while actually a callous thing to say to anyone, was okay here because Billy was the thin hero triumphing over his evil cousin.

Billy brushed a little of the dandruff from his hair into his uncle's coffee to make up for a shortage of sugar, gave it a quick stir, then placed the mug down on the table in front of Mr Moustache as Yate began counting his birthday presents.

Yate's face fell.

"There's only thirty-four presents," he said, his eyes starting to fill with tears. "You got me more presents last year," he began to howl. "Why don't you love me anymore?"

"What about this one here?" said Mrs Moustache as she picked up one of the presents. "It's from your aunt. You didn't count this one."

"It's still less than last year. You've ruined my whole birthday and my whole year. I don't like having you as parents. Why did I have to have you as my mother?"

Billy, sensing some shit was about to go down, ducked just in time as Yate grabbed the nearest present and threw it across the room towards the spot where Billy's head had been a moment earlier.

"Now I've only got thirty-four presents."

Mrs Moustache, obviously remembering how sharp the switchblade they had bought Yate was, decided it would be best to try and calm the situation. "How about we buy you some more presents while we're out today? We'll buy you four more and then you'll have more than last year, won't you? How's that?"

Yate scrunched his face into a painful expression as he tried to work out what this would mean for him. "Okay then," he said after a moment.

"And we'll even buy you a frame for your *ASBO*. We know how proud you are to show off your certificates."

"Just like his father," said Mr Moustache as he finished his coffee and began choking on an especially large piece of dandruff from the bottom of the mug. "Always getting recognition for his achievements. So proud."

In the hall, the telephone ran and Mrs Moustache left the room to answer it, while Billy and Mr Moustache sat and watched Yate unwrap his presents. Alongside his mountain bike, switchblade, and big cuddly toy, Yate had also been given a remote control car, a mobile telephone, and a box set of *The Lord of The Rings* trilogy in paperback. Yate couldn't actually read that well yet, but everyone knew that *The Lord of The Rings* was *the* fantasy series to introduce young people to the wonders of reading. He was unwrapping a large bar of chocolate when Mrs Moustache came back into the room wearing an angry expression.

"It's not good, Michael," she said. "Mrs Young has broken her leg and can't look after it." She gazed over at Billy here.

Yate put down his bar of chocolate and looked at each of his parents in turn as his eyes once again began to water. Billy, meanwhile, felt a sudden uplift in his mood. Every year, Mr and Mrs Moustache would take Yate and one of his friends out for the day to celebrate his birthday, and every year, Billy was left behind with Mrs Young, a bitter old woman who lived on the next street. Billy hated it there. Her whole house smelt of bigotry, and whenever he was forced to go, Mrs Young would spend the entire time talking about how she believed people who she would refer to as *"real women"* were being cheated out of great sporting achievements by *"men who are only pretending to be women."*

"What do we do with it?" Mrs Moustache asked Mr Moustache as she gave Billy an expression that lay the blame entirely on him. Billy knew he should be feeling sorry for Mrs Young, but it wasn't so easy when he remembered all the hurtful things she had said about others over the years.

"We could always phone my sister?" Mr Moustache put forward as a suggestion.

"Don't be an idiot, Michael. She hates the boy so much she wanted to drive him to Switzerland and have him euthanized."

This was exactly how Mr and Mrs Moustache always spoke about Billy: as though he was beneath them, and they were always superior, even if he was in the room at the time, and could hear every word they were saying.

"What about your friend, you know, the one you used to go for nights out with – Andrea?"

"Currently serving a ten-year prison sentence in the Philippines for attempting to smuggle proscribed medication into their country," replied Mrs Moustache.

"Why don't you just leave me here instead?" Billy suggested with vague hope in his voice. He'd never been allowed to stay home on his own before. He'd be able to eat whatever he wanted from the fridge, use Yate's toothbrush to clean the inside of the toilet bowl before putting it back again, and maybe even use the vacuum cleaner on his face because it never stops being unexplainably fun no matter how old you get.

Mrs Moustache looked as though someone had pointed out to her that trans women were indeed real women.

"And come back to find everything we have ever worked for has been destroyed?" Mrs Moustache snarled back at Billy.

"I'm not going to set your house on fire," Billy attempted to reassure them, but they weren't listening.

"What about..." began Mrs Moustache cautiously, "if we took it with us? We could always just leave it in the car..."

"Absolutely not, Jennifer!" Mr Moustache asserted. "I've worked damned hard for that car. It wasn't easy letting those people with young families go just before Christmas, so the company would have the money to pay my annual bonus, you know! But I did it. I earned that car and I will not give it the opportunity to mess up the inside."

By now, Yate was wailing loudly. He often wailed loudly whenever things weren't going the way he wanted. Side by side, he was fast approaching the nation of Japan in terms of who did the most wailing. Unlike Japan, however, Yate's wailing wasn't for *research purposes*, but instead because he'd always been so spoiled by his mother and father, that he'd never learnt the difference between something childish and an actual real world problem, such as the rising rate of racial hate crime across all regions of the country.

"Yatey Yeti Yates, don't cry. Mummy won't let big bad Billy ruin your special day," Mrs Moustache said, flinging her arms around him as she began crying herself at the sight of Yate being so upset.

"But... I... don't... want..." Yate yelled through his sobs. "He... can't... come... He always ruins everything."

Yate stopped crying almost immediately as the doorbell rang – "Oh, goodness," said Mrs Moustache as she stood up in a fluster. "They're here already."

Mrs Moustache went through into the hall and a moment later returned behind Yate's best friend from school, a short and plain looking boy called Matthew. Matthew was smaller than Yate, though that wasn't exactly a difficult thing to achieve, because, in case you've forgotten, Yate was fat. Most often, Matthew was the one who looked out for teachers, while Yate was busy punching one of the other children.

A short while later, Billy, amazed Mr Moustache hadn't just decided to lock him out of the house for the day, was sitting in the back of his uncle's new *Volkswagen* with Yate and Matthew, on the way to the zoo for the first time in his life. Before he'd gotten in the car, however, Mr Moustache had taken him aside.

"This is your only warning, boy," he had said, leaning in so close his breath steamed up the outside of Billy's glasses. "If I see anything I don't like today, or hear anybody saying anything that makes me feel uncomfortable – even one thing – and I will call so many lawyers, you'll be wishing you were as brave as the boys I am proud to call our armed forces."

"I'm not going to do or say anything," said Billy. "But I can't stop other people. It's wrong to try and control what others do with their lives."

Mr Moustache didn't agree with Billy. He seemed to think he'd somehow earned the right to control exactly what others did with their lives, and to be the final arbitrator on what was right and what was wrong.

It didn't help Billy's case, also, that things which made Mr Moustache feel uncomfortable often happened around him, and it was always a waste of time trying to explain to his uncle that he himself was the problem.

One evening, Billy had been working on a piece of homework from school about colonisation when Mr Moustache had come into the front room and turned on the television to find a programme on that very subject had just started in a primetime slot. Mr Moustache had come to the conclusion that the school must have conspired with the *BBC* to install a doctrine of cancel culture towards the traditions of the Empire that had, as he put it, "Made Britain the greatest nation in the history of the world."

Yate had spent the hour laughing as Mr Moustache made comment after comment about how being invaded by Britain was the best thing that ever happened to any of those countries. Billy, meanwhile, didn't think killing millions of innocent people while enslaving millions more was such a funny thing, and so once the programme had finished, Mr Moustache had sent Yate out of the room before turning to Billy and telling him he should have more pride in his heritage.

On another occasion, Billy had gotten into terrible trouble when he and Yate returned from a school trip to the British Museum, and their teacher had told Mr Moustache that Billy had been asking how many of the exhibits had been stolen from other countries. But all

Billy had been trying to do (as he explained to Mr Moustache as he screamed at him in front of the rest of the class) was point out it might be time to give some of the things back to the people they were taken from. Billy supposed everyone must have been okay with stealing, so long as it was rooted in racism and justified by patriotism. Mr Moustache, on the other hand, thought it was time Billy began acting more like Yate, who believed everything in the museum had been made in Coventry and was an excellent example of British engineering.

But today, nothing was going to go wrong. After all, the hippos at the zoo hadn't been stolen, and Billy was quite sure none of the tigers had fought on the front lines in World War Two – although Mr Moustache often said he "didn't fight in the war to see all this happening to our glorious country now," and he wasn't born until sixteen years after the war ended, so Billy couldn't rule out his uncle claiming *Tigger* had been his commanding officer.

As he drove, Mr Moustache complained out loud for everyone else to hear. He enjoyed complaining about things: the way people parked on the road near junctions, Billy, the supermarket substituting an item on his home delivery order, Billy, mistakes he blamed on others even though he'd made them himself, Billy, anyone who ever voiced there was a need to do something about an injustice in the world, Billy, and the way *Volkswagen* had lied about the emissions of his new car, which he thought were too low for him to "prove a point to those hippies." On this particular morning, he was complaining about members of the LGBTQI+ community after a minibus full of people overtook them on their way to a Pride event.

"...pathetic, all of them. They should just grow out of it," he said in anger as he sped up to try and overtake the minibus – he didn't want Mrs Moustache thinking he was prepared to give way to people like that.

"I had a dream about a pride event once," said Billy, remembering something from the week before. "Love was love, and everybody was free to be who they wanted to be."

Mr Moustache slammed his fist onto the horn and nearly crashed the car as he swung around in his seat to scream into Billy's face. "LOVE IS NOT LOVE, AND PEOPLE ARE NOT BORN IN THE WRONG BODY!"

"It was only a dream," said Billy. "But knowing that transgender people exist and can be happy isn't going to affect any of our lives in any way."

Billy wished he hadn't said anything. If there was one thing the Moustaches hated even more than immigrants, it was members of the LGBTQI+ community expressing themselves or making their own choices about how to live their lives, no matter if it was nothing to do with them or even if it was in a dream – they all seemed to believe it would destroy their own identities somehow.

It was an especially warm morning, and by the time they arrived at the zoo, the carpark was nearly full. Mr Moustache parked the car in an empty disabled parking bay close to the entrance. As another family gazed disapprovingly over at him as they passed, he began walking with a sudden limp as he led the family over to the gates. Mr Moustache dropped his act as they walked by the scene of a commotion between the zoo's security team and a small number of animal rights protesters.

Mr Moustache didn't like protesters and often voiced support for proposals by the government to introduce new laws granting a single partisan politician the power to declare any protest they disliked as illegal. Mr Moustache especially didn't like animal rights protesters. It was his belief it was the animals own fault they were born as a non-superior species, and he went over to where the protesters were stood to tell them so.

Half an hour later, after the zoo's security team had repeatedly assured Mr Moustache they were perfectly capable of handling the situation on their own, they were walking by the lion enclosure when Billy started to wonder if this might have been the best day he'd ever had. His good mood was punctured, however, after listening to one of the zookeepers explain the plight of the endangered sea turtle.

Billy had been careful to walk a little behind the Moustaches to reduce the risk of anyone realising he was with them. When Mr Moustache led the family off to look at a couple of elephants, so he could tell them about how he thought an ivory stature might make a nice addition to the front garden, Billy stayed behind and slipped into the aquarium building.

A small group of tourists were gathered around one of the zookeepers who had a small baby sea turtle in his hands. Billy joined the group and listened with interest as the zookeeper explained how human actions were affecting the natural habitats of the species right across the world. When they came to the question and answer session, Billy was the first to put up his hand and ask what ordinary people like him could do to ensure the continued survival of the sea turtle.

"Well," the zookeeper had begun, "even something as simple as reducing your carbon footprint by walking instead of driving short distances, or eating a little less meat in your diet could go someway to slowing the rate at which their habitat is being destroyed."

Billy regrouped with the Moustaches for lunch, but soon wished he hadn't. Mr Moustache had shouted at him so loud for asking the waiter if they had a vegetarian menu – Billy felt if he was going to aid the plight of the endangered sea turtle he should begin right away – that everyone in the restaurant turned around to stare over at their table.

After lunch, they went to watch a live show in the penguin enclosure. It was entertaining, thought Billy, though afterwards he felt he should have known it was all going too well to last.

It was as they watched a trio of perfectly choreographed penguins jump out of the water, through a hoop held by their trainers, and then back into the water with a graceful splash, that things started to go wrong. All of a sudden, the cheers of the crowd were drowned out by chanting coming from somewhere nearby. As everyone looked around wondering what was going on, the group of animal rights protesters from that morning – now tripled in size and having found their way past security – crashed through a wooden gate and into the performance area.

The protesters' chants grew in intensity as security arrived, and began ushering the audience away from the area, so as not to give the protesters an audience, but Mr Moustache had had enough. He pushed past the security guard closest to them and made his way over to where a few protesters were now chaining themselves to some metal railings.

"NOW LISTEN HERE, ALL OF YOU..." were the last words Billy heard Mr Moustache say with any clarity before a three-way argument broke out between Mr Moustache, the protesters, and the zoo's head of security, during which everyone said a lot, but no one heard anything.

Billy stood a little back from Mrs Moustache, Yate and Matthew, who themselves were stood a little back from Mr Moustache and watching on with embarrassment. He felt something touch his hand. He looked down to see one of the penguins from the show standing by his side.

"Hello," he said, as the penguin tapped at his hand with his flipper as though shaking it. "I'm sorry your performance was ruined. I thought it was very good, though."

The penguin jumped up and down on the spot.

"Do you enjoy performing?" asked Billy, somehow not even for a moment stopping to wonder why he was talking to a penguin.

The penguin jumped up and down again.

The other two penguins from the show swam over and climbed onto the small ledge by the water's edge where Billy and the first penguin were stood.

The first penguin appeared to confer with the other two before looking back at Billy. It used its flipper to point at Mr Moustache, then to the rest of the Moustaches, and finally to its forehead in a gesture that said quite clearly: "*This happens all the time.*"

"It must be really annoying," said Billy.

All three of the penguins jumped up and down on the spot.

"Where do you all come from anyway?"

The first penguin ruffled its flipper by its side, then held it out to hand Billy a card. Skipping the penguin's *Equity* number at the top, he read aloud: "Emperor penguin. Antartica."

"Was it nice there?"

The penguin took the card, flipped it over, and then handed it back. Billy read on: "This specimen was bred in captivity."

"Oh, I see — so none of you have ever seen Antartica?"

All three of the penguins made a sad sounding noise that a moment later was downed out by shouting.

"YATE! MRS MOUSTACHE! HAVE YOU SEEN THESE PENGUINS? LOOK AT WHAT THEY'RE DOING!"

Yate came waddling — not because he was a penguin, but because he was fat — over to where Billy and the penguins were stood.

"Out of the way, you," he said, pushing Billy to one side. Caught by surprise, Billy was knocked to the ground. What came next was so unexpected that Billy wouldn't have believed it had happened if he hadn't witnessed it first hand. As Yate took a closer look at the penguins, the one which had given Billy his card swung its flipper and knocked Yate into the water with a dull plop.

There was a shrill scream from Mrs Moustache as she rushed over to help her son, but she ended up joining him in the water, slipping on a wet patch by the pool's edge and tumbling in head first.

"WHAT THE —" came the roar of Mr Moustache as he turned his focus away from the protesters.

Mr Moustache didn't slip on the wet patch, but as he knelt down by the water to help Mrs Moustache, one of the penguins, obviously disappointed that he hadn't also fallen in, turned to give Billy what he was certain was a wink before jumping onto its front and sliding into the back of Mr Moustache as though he was a giant bowling pin. "I was in *Mary Poppins*, don't you know?" said the penguin, ducking out of the way of Mr Moustache.

At the other side of the enclosure, a large sea lion which had also taken part in the performance, began clapping and making a noise that sounded a lot like laughter.

The trainers of the three penguins were hopeful the Moustaches would see the funny side of what had happened. "Our penguins do have a mischievous side," one of them had said as they made Mrs Moustache a cup of tea. "That's why we tell everybody to stay in their seats and never get too close to the water."

Damp and ruffled looking, Mr Moustache didn't see the funny side. Instead, he repeatedly demanded the zoo put all three of the penguins and the sea lion to sleep, and whenever anyone told him he was being unreasonable, he threatened to sue.

The car journey home wasn't fun. Mr Moustache was so angry with the protesters, everyone running "that mad house," and "those bloody penguins," that he even forgot to complain about Billy. That was until Billy said something he instantly regretted.

"I think they're making a good point," Billy had said after Mr Moustache voiced his opinion that every single one of the protesters should be sent to prison for fifty years.

Mr Moustache waited until Matthew had been picked up by his mother before rounding on Billy. He mustered just enough strength to say under his breath, "How dare you waste time… caring about animals when… there are patriotic and heroic veterans… sleeping on our streets…" before pushing Billy into his cupboard.

Billy tried to point out to Mr Moustache that he never did anything to help homeless veterans himself, but it was no use. Mr Moustache slammed the cupboard door shut and then went into the kitchen to pour himself a strong drink.

Billy had lived with the Moustaches almost ten years. Ten long and miserable years, ever since he'd been a baby, and his parents had died at the beak of that particularly angry swan. He couldn't remember being there when his parents had died. Though sometimes, when he strained his memory during long hours in his cupboard, he came up with a strange vision: a giant swan, a deafening honk, and a large man with a beard. This, he supposed, was the swan that killed his parents, and it must have just looked giant to him because he was only a baby. He couldn't imagine where the bearded man had come from, though. He couldn't remember his parents. The Moustaches never spoke of them, and they always got angry if he dared ask a question. There also wasn't a single photograph of them anywhere in the house.

When he had been younger, Billy had dreamt and wished someone might notice how badly he was being treated by the Moustaches and call the appropriate authorities, but it never happened. There had been so many cuts to local services, there simply weren't enough people looking out for the warning signs of child abuse. It wasn't as though his school ever noticed he often went hungry either. In fact, ever since they had introduced a new, and very cruel policy of refusing meals to any child with a lunch debt, his school was part of the problem.

Occasionally, thought Billy, or perhaps he was just imagining it, strangers seemed to know who he was. Very strange strangers they were too. One time a short man wearing a turquoise bow tie had bowed to him while he was out shopping with Yate and Mrs Moustache. As Billy pointed at the man and began shouting "stranger danger" as loud as he could, the man seemed to disappear on the spot. The weirdest thing about all these people, though, was the way they all seemed to be wearing long dressing gowns out in public and in the middle of the day.

At school, everyone knew who Billy was, but he didn't have any friends. Billy Smith was the unusual and unpopular kid who everyone laughed at for fear of being laughed at themselves.

Late that night, as Billy lay in bed half asleep, something suddenly occurred to him, and he sat up straight with purpose. "That penguin had a business card?"

Chapter Three

A Kangaroo, a Penguin, a Donkey, and an Alligator

The incident at the zoo cost Billy heavily. The next time Matthew had been around to see Yate, he'd let slip at the dinner table that he'd seen Billy talking to the penguin that had pushed Mr Moustache into the water. By the time his uncle let him out of his cupboard again, school was over and the summer holidays had begun.

Billy was glad he didn't have to get up early to go to school anymore, but he still couldn't escape Yate and his gang of friends who came over to see him every day. Matthew, William, Mason, and Liam were all easily led and impressionable — something Yate had taken full advantage of to ensure he was their leader and successfully peer-pressure them into taking up smoking by the age of eleven.

Yate and his friends were the reason Billy tried to spend as much time outside the house as possible. He wandered, almost subconsciously, around the streets, though he was careful to avoid going anywhere near the local off-licence in case he ran into Yate and his friends trying to convince an adult to buy them the sort of magazine Mrs Moustache believed needed banning because "women should never choose to do that as a career."

As he strolled, Billy thought about the end of the holidays, where he could see a small amount of hope things might get better. When September came, he would be going to secondary school, and he wouldn't be going with Yate. Yate had been given a place at a private Catholic grammar school in the next town, although the school weren't aware that Yate neither lived in that town or wasn't actually a Catholic. Matthew's parents had also lied to get him a place there as well. Billy, meanwhile, would be going to Rafbat High, a local publicly run school with a *needs improvement* rating on its last inspection. Yate thought this was very funny.

On the last weekend of July, Mrs Moustache took Yate into town to buy his new uniform, leaving Billy with Mrs Young. Mrs Young wasn't as bad as usual. It turned out that while she was in hospital, she had her leg operated on by a transgender doctor, who she was surprised to discover could actually do the job just as well as any cisgendered doctor, and as a result, she now viewed transgender people as actual humans who didn't pose a threat to her.

Later that evening, Yate paraded around the house in his new uniform so that Mr and Mrs Moustache could take photos to send the rest of the family.

There was a disgusting smell in the kitchen the next morning when Billy went in for breakfast. He looked around expecting to see his uncle sat at the table, but he hadn't come downstairs yet. He walked over to the sink and realised the smell seemed to be coming from what appeared to be old rags bathing in milky water.

"What's this?" he asked Mrs Moustache as she came into the room. She pushed him out the way and began stirring the contents of the sink with a large wooden spoon.

"It's your new school uniform," she answered.

"Oh," said Billy, looking into the sink. "I didn't know it had to be so damp."

"Don't be stupid," snapped Mrs Moustache, pushing him out of the way a second time, so she could reach a cupboard. "I'm bleaching some of Yate's old clothes white for you. I'm just glad you're not a girl. Girls have to wear red robes and white hats at Rafbat High."

Billy held his nose and stood back.

"It's a lot of work, I'll have you know," said Mrs Moustache, noticing the expression on Billy's face. "But you'll look the same as everybody else when I'm finished."

Billy doubted this, but he thought it best not to argue. He went over and sat down at the table, wondering exactly what sort of outdated and backward school Rafbat High must be to require boys to wear bright white and girls to wear red robes.

Yate and Mr Moustache sauntered into the kitchen, both holding their own noses due to the smell. Mr Moustache went to sit at the table, so he could begin reading his newspaper, while Yate went straight for the fridge.

Just then, they heard the click of the letterbox from the hallway, followed by a light flop of letters falling onto the doormat.

"Yate, go and get the post," said Mr Moustache.

"Make Billy get it. I'm eating."

"Billy, go and get the post."

"Make Yate get it. I'm eating too."

Mr Moustache stopped reading and looked into Billy's eyes. "What did you just say?" he said, rolling up his newspaper.

"Fine. I'll go get the post."

Mr Moustache unfurled his newspaper again as Billy got up from the table and went into the hallway. Four things lay on the doormat: an election leaflet from the *Green Party*, a *sorry we missed you* card from *Royal Mail*, a white envelope with an official looking logo on the front, and – a letter for Billy.

Billy picked up the letter and stared at it for a moment. No one, ever, in his whole life, had written to him. Who would write to him? He didn't have any friends, and besides the Moustaches, he didn't have any family either. Yet here it was, a letter addressed so plainly there could be no mistake he was the intended recipient. The envelope was thick and heavy, made of a cream-coloured parchment, and the name and address on the front were handwritten in neat swirls of black ink. He found it curious that there was no stamp.

Turning the envelope over, his hand shaking, Billy found a red wax seal bearing a coat of arms; a kangaroo, a penguin, a donkey, and an alligator surrounding a large letter F.

"Hurry up, boy!" shouted Mr Moustache from the kitchen.

Billy returned to the kitchen, still staring at his letter. He handed the rest of the post to Mr Moustache, sat back down at the table, and began slowly pealing the wax seal off the envelope.

Mr Moustache ripped open his own letter. "JURY DUTY!" he bellowed, slamming his fist onto the table. "Why should I have to give up my time so pathetic lowlifes can have a day out at the taxpayer's expense? I'll show them. I'll make sure every one of those thugs is found guilty and sent to prison."

He next picked up the election leaflet and said, as he tore it into tiny pieces, "You know if they really want to save the environment, they should stop printing these leaflets." Finally, Mr Moustache reached the *sorry we missed you* card. He looked at both sides and then turned to Mrs Moustache. "Jennifer, I require you to call the constabulary and report that next door have stolen our parcel," he said. "This card says it was delivered to them."

"I don't know why the post carrier thinks it's okay to give away our things just because we didn't answer the door," replied Mrs Moustache.

"I quite agree."

"Dad," said Yate suddenly. "Dad, Billy's got a letter."

Billy was about to unfold his letter, which was written on the same heavy cream parchment as the envelope, when it was yanked out his hand by Mr Moustache.

"Who'd be writing to you?" sneered Mr Moustache. "We ruled out anthrax years ago."

Billy watched as Mr Moustache unfolded his letter and read the top line. Within seconds, his uncle's usually bloated red face had gone a pale white.

"J-J-Jennifer," he gasped.

"What is it? Is it another second class stamp?"

Yate tried to grab the letter, but his father pushed him away. Mrs Moustache took it and read the first line. For a moment, it looked as though she might be sick, and then she reached for a glass of water from the table and drank it in one.

"Michael. Oh, my goodness – Michael."

"It's not a third class stamp, is it?" asked Billy. "There's no such thing."

Mr Moustache and Mrs Moustache stared at each other, seemingly forgetting that Billy and Yate were also there.

"Give me my letter back," Billy said loudly. "I want to read it as it's mine," he continued, reaching out to take the letter.

"Both of you, get out of the kitchen," Mr Moustache said weakly as he took the letter back from Mrs Moustache and began stuffing it back inside the envelope.

Billy didn't move.

"I WANT MY LETTER!" he shouted.

"I want to read it," said Yate.

Mr Moustache found his strength again. "OUT!" he shouted, grabbing them both by the collar and throwing them out into the hall. He slammed the door shut behind them. Billy and Yate had a silent fight over who would listen where. Yate won, and so as he put his ear to the keyhole, Billy picked his glasses up from the floor and then laid on his stomach, so he could listen at the gap between the door and floor.

"Michael," Mrs Moustache was saying in a shaky voice, "look at the address they've put on the envelope. They've written his cupboard – how could they possibly know where he sleeps? You don't think they're watching the house, do you?"

"It wouldn't surprise me. They're clearly freedom-hating liberals who don't think people like us should be able to tell others what to think and do," said Mr Moustache.

"What should we do, Michael? Should I put something over the microwave in case they're watching us right now?"

"Yes, do that."

Billy could see Mrs Moustache's slippers as they marched from one side of the kitchen to the other as she went to cover the microwave with a towel.

"But what about the letter? Should we write back? Tell them we don't want –"

"No. We'll ignore the letter. If they don't hear anything back... Yes, that's the best thing... We'll just ignore it and pretend nothing has happened..."

"But –"

"I will not have that nonsense in my house, Jennifer! It's unnatural. Didn't we swear when we took him in that we'd beat any sense of spirit and individuality out of him?"

That night, when he retuned from work, Mr Moustache did something he'd never done before; he visited Billy in his cupboard.

"I want my letter!" demanded Billy, the second Mr Moustache had opened the door wearing protective gloves in case there were any black widow spiders nearby. "Who's writing to me?"

"No one. Somebody had addressed it to you by mistake," replied Mr Moustache as he flinched at the sight of a small piece of fluff he mistook for a spider.

"I have burned it," he continued, looking back at Billy.

"It was not addressed to me by mistake," Billy argued. "I heard you saying it was addressed to me."

"BE QUIET!" screamed Mr Moustache, and dust fell from the ceiling as the whole cupboard was shaken by his voice. He took a long deep breath and then forced his face into a smile that made him look remarkably like Keir Starmer being forced to meet with voters in the

North of England.

"Listen, Billy — about this cupboard. I was speaking to your aunt earlier, and we were thinking... it really is a bit too small for you now... we think you should move upstairs into Yate's second bedroom."

"Why?" asked Billy suspiciously.

"Don't ask me any questions!" snapped Mr Moustache. "Just take all your stuff upstairs, now!"

The Moustache's house had four bedrooms: a spacious master suite with fitted wardrobe, ensuite bathroom, and large double-glazed windows which looked out in a southerly direction over the back of the house and benefited from all day sun during the summer months, where Mr and Mrs Moustache slept; a smaller double bedroom with a plush carpet and decorative wallpaper feature where visitors slept (but which Mr Moustache had put a filing cabinet in, so he could claim the room was an office for tax purposes), a cosy single room next to the bathroom where Yate slept, and another single room at the other end of the landing where Yate kept all the things that wouldn't fit into his first bedroom.

It took Billy only a single trip and one box to move everything he owned from the cupboard under the stairs to his new bedroom. He sat down on the lumpy bed and stared around him. Nearly everything he looked at was broken or damaged. The cuddly toy Yate had got for his birthday sat headless on a shelf, Yate having attacked it when his mother accidentally asked for the wrong sort of dip when they had ordered a takeaway one night. In the corner of the room was Yate's first-ever television, which he'd put his foot through when *Richard Osman* had appeared on yet another panel show. On top of an old wardrobe was a pile of books. They were the only things in the room that looked as though they'd never been touched, though Billy couldn't blame Yate, as they were all written by an author who signed an open letter promoting free speech, but also used their power and wealth to threaten someone into silence for accurately quoting them.

As he lay back on the bed, Billy could hear Yate screaming at his parents downstairs. "I don't want him in that room... that's my bedroom... make him get out..." He sighed and stretched out. Although he always enjoyed witnessing Yate be upset about something, he'd have gladly given up both that and his new room if it meant he could have his letter.

The next morning, breakfast was a quiet affair. Yate was still upset, but he was too exhausted to make any more of a stand. He'd cried and screamed all night long, at one point even packing a small suitcase and threatening to leave home; but he'd only made it as far as the end of the street before coming back again. Billy chewed on his toast as he thought back to this time yesterday and wished he'd just opened the letter in the hall or put it in his cupboard to read later. Mr Moustache and Mrs Moustache, meanwhile, just kept giving each other stares that seemed to say a lot between them, but told Billy nothing.

When the post arrived, Mr Moustache, who seemed to be making an effort to be nice to Billy, made Yate go and get it. They heard him banging his hand against the wall in a bad mood as he walked down the hall. Then, he shouted, "There's another letter — Billy Smith, The Smallest Bedroom —"

Within seconds, both Billy and Mr Moustache had leapt up from the table and gone to the kitchen door. As they ran down the hall, Mr

Moustache pushed Billy back. Billy responded by grabbing onto his uncle's leg, causing him to fall just short of where Yate stood, letter in hand. Yate didn't want to hand the letter over to either of them, however, and when Mr Moustache had got back to his feet, there was a short fight between the three of them. Eventually, Mr Moustache straightened himself up, short of breath, but holding Billy's letter out of reach.

"Both of you go to your bedroom," he instructed, trying to breathe deeply.

As he walked into his new room, Billy slammed the door shut in anger. But as he paced round and round on the worn carpet, he remembered something. Yate had read out the address and it had included his bedroom. Whoever was trying to write to him seemed to know that he'd moved upstairs and that he hadn't received the first letter. Maybe that meant they would know he hadn't received this one either? He had a plan to make sure he received the third.

Billy set his alarm early the next morning. When it rang out, he turned it off quickly and got dressed as silently as he could. He mustn't wake anyone else. He walked downstairs – careful to avoid the creaky step two-thirds of the way up – without turning on any of the lights.

He was going to wait for the post carrier on the corner of the street to make sure he got the letters for their house before they were put through the letterbox. His heart hammered as he tiptoed across the hall towards the front door, opened it, then stepped outside into the cool morning air.

Billy had been sitting against a small wall outside number one for nearly four hours when he wondered if there was actually going to be any post today. As he walked, defeated, back down the street after another hour, something occurred to him; a plot hole. Neither of the letters he'd been sent so far had a stamp anywhere on them, and more than that, whatever world this was he was living in, he felt certain quite a big deal was going to be made out of how people like him didn't use the ordinary postal service to communicate. It was a waste of time to wait for the post carrier.

His thinking was proven to be correct almost immediately, but being right didn't save the sinking feeling he felt as he walked into the living room and found Mr Moustache kneeling beside the fire, burning four letters that were all addressed to him.

"Good morning," said Mr Moustache in a joyful mood as he tore up the last of the letters and threw the pieces onto the flames.

On Friday, no less than eleven letters arrived for Billy, all finding some unusual way to make it into the house. A couple had risen up out of the downstairs toilet when Yate had flushed it. A couple more had been fired in through an open window attached to a flaming arrow, while another had even appeared out of the top of the toaster at breakfast, accompanied by the loud buzzing sound a fax machine might make.

Mr Moustache stayed home from work that day. After burning the letters, he proceeded to spend the rest of the day repeatedly electrocuting himself as he attempted to work out how the toaster had delivered a letter, without unplugging it first.

On Saturday, things began to get out of hand. Twenty-nine letters were delivered to the house by *Royal Mail special delivery*, and Mr Moustache was not happy about it. It wasn't the letters that annoyed him so much on this occasion – by now he had discovered they made an excellent kindling for the fire – but rather that the post carrier had delivered them at fifteen minutes past nine rather than before nine, as was the guaranteed time of the service. While Mr Moustache waited on hold to complain to *RoyalMail*, he told Mrs Moustache, who was busy tearing the letters up into small pieces, that this was simply another example of the postal service's slipping standards.

On Sunday morning, Mr Moustache sat down at the breakfast table looking tired, but relieved.

"No post on Sundays," he reminded them cheerfully as he removed the finance section from his newspaper. He didn't actually understand any of the articles within it, but he liked to pretend he did.

"No damn letters today –"

There was a light tap on the kitchen door.

"What was that?" asked Mrs Moustache, looking around.

There was another tap. And then another. And another. It sounded as though pellets were hitting the glass and bouncing off again.

Mr Moustache stood up from the table and went to open the door.

"WHAT THE –" he said as forty or fifty letters came flying through the doorframe right at him, as though they were guided missiles. Mrs Moustache and Yate ducked out the way, as still more letters came after them, but Billy, who didn't seem to be a target, reached out to grab one.

"Out! OUT!" came Mr Moustache's voice, and then, as he

noticed Billy's hand closing on a letter, "Oh no, you don't, boy."

Mr Moustache grabbed Billy around the waist and threw him into the hall. Caught off guard, Billy dropped the letter he'd caught.

"That does it," said Mr Moustache, struggling to protect Yate and Mrs Moustache from the ever growing onslaught of flying parchment. "I want all of you back here in ten minutes ready to leave. We're going away. Just pack what you need and be quick."

"But –"

"No arguments, just pack."

He looked so angry that no one dared argue, and a short time later, they were in the car speeding towards the motorway.

Yate was sat teary eyed in the back seat. Mr Moustache had hit him around the head for holding them up while he tried to pack a table, television, electrical generator, inflatable sofa, his duvet and bedlinen, and a barbecue.

Billy had also been hit around the head by his uncle, but this was because he'd asked him if he'd tried getting a good night's sleep, buying fewer avocados, eating less takeaways, and going on a nice walk.

No one knew how long they were driving for or where they were going. Mr Moustache still seemed so annoyed, even Mrs Moustache dare not ask where he was taking them. He didn't say anything to anyone, but every so often he'd take a random turn and begin driving in a different direction for a while. "This will do it… confuse them… they can't find us like this…" he would mutter to himself whenever this happened.

They didn't stop once all day. By the time night fell, Yate was complaining. He'd never had such a bad day. He was hungry, and he'd missed multiple programmes he'd wanted to watch on television. Billy tried to point out there were people feeling violence and famine — only to discover when they eventually reached safety, that privileged people were far too xenophobic and hateful to show compassion — who had it much worse than him, but Yate didn't care.

Eventually, Mr Moustache stopped the car outside a *Hampton Inn* on the outskirts of a large town. Mr Moustache went inside to see if they had any rooms available, but he returned quickly.

"Okay," he began, climbing back into the car in a seemingly more cheerful mood. "All the rooms at this hotel are being used to house innocent child refugees who have been illegally separated from their families, but the manager told me there's another hotel in the town centre with space for us."

They set off again and passed a large sign saying *Welcome to Ipswich* by the side of the road. Perhaps Mr Moustache believed Ipswich was a dire enough place no one would visit here just to deliver a letter. As they drove further into the town, Billy thought his uncle might have been right if that was his plan.

At last, they reached a second hotel and checked-in; though not before Mr Moustache had spent fifteen minutes complaining about not being offered loyalty points or free Wi-Fi because he hadn't booked direct. Billy and Yate shared a twin room. Yate lay in bed snoring, but Billy couldn't sleep. Instead, he sat by the window and stared out at the lights of passing cars thinking…

They ate breakfast in the hotel's restaurant the next morning. They had just finished when the hotel manager came over to their table.

"Excuse me, but is one of you Billy Smith? I've got a pile of these at reception."

She held up a cream parchment envelope, so they could read the address on the front. Sure enough, it was addressed to Billy the same way all the others had been. Billy made a grab for the letter, but Mr Moustache pushed him out the way and got to his feet.

"I'll sort them," Mr Moustache said, following the manager out of the restaurant.

Before long, they were back in the car, and Mr Moustache was again driving with purpose.

"Might it be easier to go home today?" Mrs Moustache asked hours later, but Mr Moustache didn't seem to hear what she said. Exactly what he was looking for, none of them knew. He kept stopping the car in the middle of large open fields, dense woods, Sheffield, and supermarket carparks, each time getting out, climbing onto the roof, and looking around before shaking his head and setting off again.

Late that afternoon, after they had been driving along a coastal road for what seemed like hours, Mr Moustache parked the car on the seafront in a small town, locked them all inside, and disappeared into the heavy rain outside.

Inside the car, Yate began to cry.

"It's Monday," he said to his mother. "I want to stay somewhere with a television."

Monday. That reminded Billy. If it was Monday – and the days of the week were one of the few things Yate ever got right – then tomorrow was his eleventh birthday. It was true his birthdays had never been fun – last year the Moustaches had cooked him a special meal using meat that had gone bad, then told him his present was the food poisoning he spent the next week suffering from – but it still wasn't every day you turned eleven.

An hour later, Mr Moustache returned, and he was in a very good mood. He was carrying a long package wrapped in very damp brown paper, and he didn't answer Mrs Moustache when she asked what was inside.

"I've found us a place to stay," he said. "Come on, everybody out of the car."

It was extremely cold outside the car, and the icy wind bit against their faces. Mr Moustache was pointing out to sea, though the torrent of rain made it impossible to make out whatever it was he was supposed to be pointing at.

"There's a storm forecast for tonight, which is good news," said Mr Moustache gleefully, "but it means we need to get a move on. This kind man has agreed to lend us his boat to get across the water."

An old yellow toothed man smelling strongly of tobacco and cheap beer came towards them with a smug smile on his face and pointed towards an old rowing boat sat on the beach below them.

"I've already got everything we need," said Mr Moustache, "so give me a hand pushing the boat into the water, and we'll set sail."

Mr Moustache didn't notice the looks on the faces of the rest of the family as he turned to the old man. "Thank you again, Nigel, and don't worry, if I encounter any of those *economic migrants*, I'll be sure to call you."

However cold it had been on land, it was nothing compared to the freezing temperatures in the boat. Sea spray, helped along by the strong wings, made them wet, and before long they were all suffering from wind chill and numb faces. After what felt like hours, they reached a large rock far enough away from the land they couldn't make out where they had come from. Sat atop the rock was an old wooden hut that looked as though it might fall down at any moment.

The inside of the hut smelled horrible. There was a puncturing damp that hit their noses as soon as they walked in through the door. The hut didn't seem to provide much shelter either, as the wind funnelled its way through gaps in the wood and down the empty chimney into the main room, where there was little more than a wooden chair by the window and a moth-eaten sofa.

Mr Moustache's idea of everything they would need turned out to be a loaf of bread and a lump of cheese. He tried to start a fire to keep them warm, but the only wood he could find was too damp to burn.

"I wish I'd brought some of those letters with me," he joked to himself.

It seemed he was in a very good mood despite the condition of the hut. Billy felt sure Mr Moustache thought no one could deliver a letter to him out here.

As darkness fell, the forecast storm arrived. The wood rattled as high waves broke over the top of the rock and crashed into the walls of the hut. Mrs Moustache found some old blankets in another room and was able to make up a bed for Yate on the sofa. She and Mr Moustache shared a single bed in the next room, while Billy was left to fend for himself.

As the night went on, the storm grew more aggressive, and the temperature inside the hut fell. He might have been tired, but Billy couldn't sleep. He sat in the corner of the room, trying to shelter as much as possible from the wind blowing its way in through a broken pane of glass in a window. He looked around for something to distract him and noticed the light from Yate's watch. It was five minutes to midnight. That meant it was five minutes until his birthday.

He watched the minutes go by as he thought about where Mr Moustache would take them all tomorrow – surely they couldn't live out here on this rock forever?

Three minutes to go. Billy heard a loud bang outside that was distinctly different to the sound of the storm.

Two minutes to go. He wondered if the letter writer would try again? If they had tried this hard already, they wouldn't give up now, would they?

One minute to go.

Thirty seconds… twenty… ten…

He thought about tipping the sofa over and blaming it on the wind.

Three… two… one…

CRACK!

Billy started as Yate woke suddenly. They both stared over at the door. Someone was outside.

Chapter Four

"Couldn't This Have Been an Email?"

CRACK! Whoever was outside was knocking to come in.

"It's the North Koreans," said Yate stupidly. "They've started a nuclear war. We're all going to die."

There was another loud bang behind them as Mr Moustache came into the room, armed with a shotgun — now they knew what he was carrying with him the night before.

"Who's there?" he shouted, aiming the gun towards the door. "I'm warning you — I'm armed."

There was a moment of silence. Then — SMASH!

Whoever was there had knocked on the door so hard it came clean off its hinges, flew a little way inside the hut, and then landed with a deafening crash upon the cold stone floor.

"Oh, bugger," they heard a voice say in a strong Yorkshire accent.

Mrs Moustache entered the room behind Mr Moustache, and they, along with Billy and Yate, watched with fear as the silhouette of a giant figure of a man appeared in the doorway. With each flash of lighting outside, the man's face was illuminated just enough for them all to see he had a long, unkept mane of hair and an even more tangled beard.

The man attempted to squeeze his way into the hut, but got stuck, as the door was at least a foot shorter than he was tall.

"Eh? Now what's goin' on 'ere then?" the man said, pushing himself free. On his second attempt, he ducked so low he was practically crawling as he crossed the threshold of the door and entered the hut.

"Ah chuffin' wish they'd mek doors a bit 'igher, y' get wha' ah'm sayin'?" he asked the room at large as he stood up straight and caught his head on one of the wooden beams holding up the ceiling. "Be nice if they'd give bit more room f' noggin n' all."

The man looked around for the door, and then picked it up and put it back into its frame. "Ah'll be wi' theur all in a mo'," he told them all as the door fell straight out again. It took at least another four or five attempts before the door finally stayed in place long enough for him to turn back and look at them all.

"Sorry 'bout that. Nah then, what's bin 'appenin?"

He made his way over to the sofa where Yate was sat frozen solid, unable to take his eyes off the giant.

"Come on, lad. Budge up. Theur dunt need all that space, do theur? Thas not that fat yet." The man looked up at Mr and Mrs Moustache. "No offence meant by that, mind. Jus' 'asn't bin mentioned this chapter n' ah wanted t' mek sure no 'un had forgot."

Yate let out a little squeal and went to hide behind his mother, who herself was hiding behind Mr Moustache.

The man looked around the room and spotted Billy sitting on the floor, staring up at him.

"Ey up, Billy, lad. 'ow theur bin? Ah've not seen theur since theur wor reight small."

Billy focused on the man's face and saw his eyes and mouth were creased into a smile.

"It must be ten-year since ah saw theur last," said the man. "Theur sure do look a lot like old man. Except f' eyes, they look nothin' like 'is or theur mother's."

Mr Moustache cleared his throat. "Sir, I hereby demand you leave this place at once," he said, attempting to sound as authoritative as possible. "You are breaking and entering."

The man turned back and stared down the barrel of the shotgun Mr Moustache was now aiming straight at his face. "Or what? They'll shoot me brain out of back o' noggin'?"

There was a small pop as Mr Moustache pulled the trigger, but all that happened was the man started to laugh at the small red flag with the word *pow* written on it that had appeared out the end of the shotgun.

"Now jus' calm down, reight. There's ain't a need t' gerr' all mardy 'bout owt, is there? This ain't America," said the man. He reached out to take the shotgun from Mr Moustache, bent it in half as easily as if it had been one of those cheap knockoff items flooding the market without meeting the required safety standards, and threw it across the room where it hit the door, knocking it back out of its frame.

"See wha' theur gone n' made 'appen now?" said the man. "Ah'm not puttin' door back again. If theur parky, theur can do it thy sen."

Mr Moustache made a rather defeated sort of noise.

"Nah then, Billy, lad," said the man, turning away from the Moustaches. "Ah ain't forgot it's theur birthday. Ah've got summa' for theur 'ere n' all."

From an inside pocket of his giant overcoat, the man pulled a large brown padded envelope which he handed to Billy. Billy began to open it… "It's a magazine," he said, looking inside and noticing a bulge of pages.

"Is it? 'old on. Must av' given y' wrong one," said the man, taking the brown envelope back. "These are… they're erm… it's me readin' material for y'know… before ah go t' bed."

He pulled another envelope, this time red, from his pocket, and handed it over. "This is yours."

Billy opened the envelope and, for the first time in his life, pulled out a birthday card. He laughed at the picture showing one candle telling another they were going out tonight.

"Oh, n' ah got y' summa' else n' all – ah mighta sat on it on way 'ere, bur it won't kill y'."

The man pulled a small, slightly squashed cardboard box from another of his many pockets and handed it to Billy. Billy opened it. Inside was a small chocolate chip muffin topped with buttercream icing. A single candle was sticking out the top.

Billy looked up at the man's face. He meant to say thank you, but the words got lost on the way to his mouth, and what he actually said was, "Does this cake have palm oil in it?"

The man sighed.

"Youth of t'day. You just 'ang around waitin' t' be offended by things. Yeh should jus' gerr' over y' sens n' get on wi' life. Too much time on *Twitter*, tha' wha' it is."

"Now you're talking sense, sir," said Mr Moustache in agreement.

"Shut it, Moustache,"

"I'm sorry," Billy began, "but the production of palm oil is one of the leading causes of deforestation across the world —"

"Listen, if theur want t' argue, argue wi' somebody who 'as time t'. Ah just want t' lead carefree life, so ah'm goin' t' seh what ah think, n' then theur should just shurrup. Ah dunt need 'ate n' rubbish at my time o' life."

He shook his head.

"Anyway, ah ain't introduced me sen, av' ah? Me name's Barry. Ah'm groundskeep' at Frogsports."

The man held out his huge hand and used it to shake Billy's whole arm.

"Nah wha' 'bout a brew or whiskey if theur got it? 'ospitality 'ere so far is like stayin' in Lancashire."

Barry's eyes fell on the cold and empty fireplace. He bent down in front of it. No one could see what he was doing, but when he got back up a moment later, a cosy fire filled the space. It lit up the inside of the hut, and Billy felt a satisfying rush of warm air flush over him.

Barry sat back down on the sofa, which creaked because he was even fatter than Yate and Mr Moustache combined (just in case you had forgotten), and began pulling things out of his coat pockets: a small thermal flash, some sausages wrapped in brown paper, a poker, a copy of the constitution for some gender critical campaign group, and a couple of broken mugs. Before long, the whole hut was filled with a homely warmth and the welcoming smell of sausages cooking. No one said anything as they watched Barry cooking, but as he slid the first sausages from the poker, Yate seemed to move on the spot a little. Mr Moustache put his hand on Yate's shoulder and said, "Don't have anything he gives you, Yate. We don't know if it's safe."

Barry laughed to himself, then made a cruel fat joke about Yate, because apparently you need reminding it's okay to do that.

He handed a sausage to Billy and said, "They're not vegetarian, mind. Ah dunt believe in any o' tha' nonsense, so theur will jus' av' t' man up f' a bit."

It was true that ever since a girl he liked told him about how the production of half a kilo of beef generates the same emissions as producing one hundred loaves of bread, and how it takes over three hundred gallons of water to produce one hamburger, he had thought about going vegetarian to impress her, but he hadn't started yet, and he was feeling hungry. He took the sausage and bit into it. He had never tasted anything so good, but he worried about what the girl might say if she ever found out. As he finished the sausage, he looked up at Barry and said, "I'm sorry, but I still don't really know who you are? Barry... who?"

The man finished his own sausage and wiped his mouth with the back of his hand.

"Well, ery'one calls me Barry 'cos that's me name," he said. "n' like ah told theur, ah'm groundskeep' at Frogsports — surely theur know 'bout Frogsports?"

"I've never heard of Frogsports," said Billy.

Barry looked taken aback.

"Never 'eard o' Frogsports?"

"Sorry," Billy said quickly.

"Sorry?" barked Barry, turning to stare at the Moustaches, who all seemed to shrink a little under his gaze. "It's them tha' should be sorry. By 'eck, ah knew theur weren't gerrin' theur's letters, bur ah never thought it would be this bad. Dunt theur ever wonder 'ow theur's parents got through life?"

"What do you mean, got through life?"

"WHAT DO AH MEAN?" Barry shouted. "WHAT DO AH MEAN? Nah wait jus' a secon'."

He jumped to his feet, his anger overpowering the warmth of the fire.

The Moustaches retreated a little into the shadows.

"Are theur tellin' me," Barry barked at them, "tha' this kid 'ere – this kid – he knows nowt 'bout any o' it?"

"I do know some things," said Billy, feeling Barry was being unreasonable. "I learnt maths and English at school." But Barry simply waved his hand.

"Ah mean real stuff – 'ow can theur understan' owt if theur can't put it in't context o' our world. Theur's world. My world. Theur's parent's world."

"What word?"

Barry looked as though he should be covered in health and safety stickers, warning he was a pressurised container that shouldn't be put near a naked flame in case he exploded.

"MOUSTACHE!" His voice made the whole hut shake.

Mr Moustache, who had gone a ghostly white, said something under his breath that sounded like, "Should read a different book sometime."

Barry stared down at Billy.

"Bur theur must know sum' o' it?" he said. "Ah mean, it's famous.

"Theur dunt know owt?... Theur dunt know..." Barry ran his

fingers through his hair, fixing Billy with a bewildered expression.

"Bur 'ow does theur understan' everythin' theur read n' see in't news?

"'ow does theur know president who separates kid from family is bad guy if theur can't compare 'im t' fictional character?

"'ow does theur understan' fight f' racial equality if theur ain't read 'eroic tale o' orphan lad who overcame evil magic man wi' dodgy nose?

"'ow does theur know t' accept fowk for who thee are if theur ain't read book series full o' straight white fowk?

"Does theur not even known wha' theur is?"

Mr Moustache suddenly found his bravery.

"No more," he said. "Just stop. I forbid you from telling the boy anything else."

"Telling me what?" asked Billy eagerly.

"NO! I FORBID IT!" Mr Moustache was panicking now.

Mrs Moustache gasped.

"Ah, shurrup, pair o' theur," said Barry. He turned to look Billy in the eye. "Billy — thas a magician,"

Silence fell inside the hut. Only the storm outside could be heard.

" — I'm a what?" asked Billy.

"A magician, 'course," said Barry, sitting back down on the sofa, which almost snapped during this periodic reminder that he's still fat. "n' ah'll tell theur wha' else, ah think it's time theur read y' letter… assumin' theur learnt t' read wi'out magic book series."

"I know how to read," said Billy. "I learnt reading *Twilight* —"

"Eh!" exclaimed Barry with a look of horror on his face. "We'll av' less o' that filth, y' little shite. If ah cop theur swearin' li' tha' again, ah'll be washin' theur's gob out wi' soap."

"I'm sorry," said Billy.

"Aye, well jus' get letter read n' we'll seh nowt more 'bout it."

Billy stretched out his hand to finally take the cream envelope hand addressed to him. He pulled the letter out and read:

FROGSPORTS ACADEMY *of* MAGICAL WHIZZING *and* KABOOMS

HEADMASTER: *Professor* R. *Crumbleceiling* E*sq.*

(*Played:* 114, *Won:* 204, *Drawn:* D*inosaur,* L*ost:* H*is calculator)*

Dear Mr Smith,

I am pleased to inform you that you have been accepted at Frogsports Academy of Magical Whizzing and Kabooms! Please find enclosed a list of overpriced books written by multi-millionaires who really don't need the money, and equipment you are required to pay full price for, because our education system is drastically underfunded and the school can't afford anything itself.

The school year begins on the 1st of September. We await your pigeon by no later than the 31st of July.

Yours, most graciously,

Professor M.C. McDouglass

Deputy Headmistress

Questions exploded inside Billy's mind, like a *TERFs'* head trying to comprehend that the *Equalities Act* isn't pick n' mix, and he couldn't decide which he wanted to ask first. After a few minutes, he looked up at Barry and said, "Couldn't this have been an email?"

"Eh, dunt start wi' environmental bullshite again or ah'll clip theur's ear."

Billy looked back at the letter and noticed another paragraph at the bottom of the page:

The views expressed in this letter are the views of the sender, and may not necessarily be views shared by Frogsports Academy of Magical Whizzing and Kabooms! Frogsports Academy of Magical Whizzing and Kabooms! takes your privacy seriously. For more information on our privacy policy, please visit our website at www.iherebyirrevocablywaivemyrighttosue.com. If you wish to unsubscribe from future communications, return the delivery pigeon with an injury, and we'll get the message.

"What do the mean they await my pigeon?"

"Bugger! Theur reminded me of summa' ah got t' do," said Barry. From yet another of his coat pockets, he pulled a pigeon — a real, live, and rather angry-looking pigeon — a long quill, and a sheet of cream parchment.

Concentrating hard and looking as though he was a cuttlefish confronted with a *Rubik's cube,* he scribbled a note that Billy could read upside down:

Dear Professor crumbleceiling,

Given Billy his letter. You were right. He's still an ugly child. I'll pay you the bet when I get back. Taking him to London tomorrow to buy everything he needs. Weather is like holidaying in Blackpool.

Hope you're well, Barry

Barry rolled the note up, gave it to the pigeon, went to the door, and threw the pigeon out into the storm. Then he came back and sat down as though this was as normal as *tweeting* your opinion on a subject you knew nothing about.

Billy, realising his mouth was wide open, closed it quickly.

"Reight, were wor we?" said Barry, but at that moment, Mr Moustache, looking angrier than Billy had ever seen him before, moved into the firelight.

"He's not going," he said.

Barry groaned.

"Reight, n' sum' great commoner li' theur sen goin' t' stop 'im?" he said.

"Commoner?" Billy questioned with interest.

"Commoners," Barry repeated. "It's wha' we call t' non-magicians like them lot."

"When we took him in, we said we'd put a stop to that nonsense," said Mr Moustache. "We swore we'd stamp it out of him. He's different to us. For all we know, he's dangerous, and we've got Yate to think about. Magician indeed."

"You knew?" asked Billy. "You knew I was a magician?"

"Knew?" Mrs Moustache shrieked out of nowhere. "Of course, we knew. How could you not be with my freak of a sister being what she was? Yes, she got a letter just like that one, and off she ran to that school, coming home every summer with her pockets full of enchanted vegetables and her head full of ideas like – like the lefty she was. I was the only one who recognised her as different – an abomination! But for your mother and father, oh no, it was always Phalaenopsis this and Phalaenopsis that, yes, they were actually proud of having such an aberration in the family."

She stopped to take a breath before ranting on. It was clear she had wanted to say all this for years.

"And then she met that Keith Smith at school, and when they left they had... relations, and then you came along, and of course, I knew you'd be just as abnormal and strange. And then they just had to go and get themselves killed by not wearing their seatbelts, so we got left with you."

Billy started to feel sick. He swallowed and said, "Not wearing their seatbelts?"

"Too stupid to listen to any of the warnings."

"You told me an angry swan ate them."

"ANGRY SWAN!" Barry roared as he got to his feet again. Mr and Mrs Moustache retreated back into the shadowy corner of the hut. "'ow could swan kill Phalaenopsis n' Keith Smith? It's slander. Scandal. Wha' do theur think theur are? Contributor to *Mail Online*?"

"But then what did happen?" Billy asked urgently. "What killed them?"

The anger left Barry's face as he looked at Billy with a worried expression.

"Ah wasn't expectin' theur t' know so little," he said, in a low soft voice. "Ah dunt know if ah'm reight person t' tell theur owt, bur thas got t' know summa' before theur go t' Frogsports. Especially when every other kid knows wha' 'appened. It's famous."

He threw a disapproving glance at the Moustaches.

"Reight, well sit theur sen down n' ah'll tell theur as much as ah can, bur ah can't tell theur everythin', mind. Ah dunt think anybody know all details. It's a great mystery, bits o' it, n' who knows when it'll be retconned," he said, sitting back down. "Well, ah guess it begins wi' guy called — by 'eck, it's incredible theur dunt know 'is name, ah thought ery'one knew it."

"Who is it?"

"Ah dunt like t' seh name if ah can avoid it. No 'un does."

"But why?"

"Why? T'rah t' jammy lass wi' parky butty f' dinner, Billy! Fowk still scared o' name, lad." He shook his head. "See, theur wor magician who went reight bad. As bad as theur could go. Worse. Worse than bin a *Conservative*. Worse than bin a *Republican*, even —"

"Worse than *Nick Clegg*?"

"Eh? That's grand point theur made there. Nah, not that bad. No 'un is as bad as that smug bastard... Anyway, 'is name wor..."

Barry gulped, but no words came out.

"Why don't you write it down?" suggested Billy.

"Can't spell it... Reight — it wor Steven." Barry shuddered as though he'd just taken part in the ice bucket challenge. "Dunt mek me seh it again. Anyway, this — this magician, 'e wor reight bad guy n' 'e started lookin' f' mates t' follow 'im. Sorta like club, theur could seh gang even. 'e certainly found members — ah guess sum' wor too scared t' refuse, bur others just wanted t' share 'is power. n' 'e wor gettin' 'imself power alight. Dark days, Billy. Dark days. Bur it wor not all bad."

Barry had a reminiscent look on his face, as though longing for the days when racism, homophobia, and transphobia were still accepted and commonplace.

"Bad things 'appenin n' 'e wor takin' over. Anybody who dared t' stand up t' 'im, 'e killed. 'orribly. Only safe place wor Frogsports.

Most fowk think Crumbleceiling wor only guy That-Evil-One wor afraid o'.

Something Billy wasn't expecting happened. There was a roar of thunder and a flash of lighting not from the storm outside, but directly above his head. Before he could look up, the cloud rained on top of him and disappeared.

Barry laughed as Billy looked up to see if he was sitting under a hole in the roof. "Sorry, should av' warned theur 'bout that," said Barry.

"Anyway, ah knew theur's mother n' old man," Barry continued, "n' theur wor the best magicians ah've ever known. Could av' gone on talent show n' won is wha' ah'm sayin'. Leader o' theur 'ouse at Frogsports, n' all. Bur 'e wanted 'em out o' way, 'e did, n' so 'e turned up in't village where theur wor all livin', ten-year ago on 'alloween – theur wor just a baby – n'... n' 'e killed 'em both."

Barry took a handkerchief from his pocket and used it to wipe below his eyes. "Sorry," he said, "bur ah knew theur's parents n' thee could av' chuffin' gone places if they'd av' just learnt t' calm theur gobs a bit n' be respectful t' older generation."

"Bur 'ere's strange thing 'bout it all, 'e tried t' kill theur too, bur 'e couldn't. Ever wondered 'bout tha' trademark on forehead? That's no ordinary trademark. That's wha' theur get from powerful, evil energy who wants t' stop fowk livin' 'appy lives by deprivin' 'em o' rights."

"A load of bollocks," said Mr Moustache. Billy started; he had almost forgotten the Moustaches were still there. Mr Moustache seems to have gotten some of his confidence back. He stared at Barry with his hands clenched into fists.

"Now, you listen here boy," he said half-angry, half-panicked to

Billy. "I accept there's something weird about you, but that's our fault for being too soft on you. Now as for your parents, well, they deserved everything they got… I'm telling you, if they'd just listened and done what they were told to do –"

Barry didn't need to say anything. His look alone was enough to silence Mr Moustache.

Billy still had thousands of questions he wanted to ask.

"But what happened to Stev – sorry – I mean, That-Evil-One?"

Barry ducked out the way of the cloud. Clearly, he was experienced enough to avoid it.

"Grand question that, lad. 'e vanished on t' same night 'e tried t' kill theur. That's why theur famous, see. Some think theur killed 'im instead. Some think 'e's still out there waitin' t' come back. Bur all anybody knows is summa' 'bout theur stopped 'im that night."

Barry looked at Billy with admiration in his eyes, but rather than feeling that same pride in himself, Billy felt sure there had to have been some sort of mistake. How could he be a magician? He'd once performed a magic routine in a school talent contest and come in last place – he'd even lost to Yate's recital of the chicken dance played in F-sharp on the ever popular ice cream tub and rubber band combo.

"Barry," Billy said quietly, "I think you're making a mistake. I don't think I can be a magician?"

To Billy's surprise, Barry started to laugh.

"Theur dunt think theur a magician, eh? Theur never made owt strange 'appenin when theur stood up for summa'?"

Billy gazed into the fire. It was as if an occult hand had reached into his head and moved his memories into an order that suddenly made sense… every single thing that had ever made his aunt or uncle angry with him had happened when he, Billy, felt strongly about something or had taken a stand… all those times Mr Moustache had told him he should have more pride in his country, he had just pointed out it's hard to be patriotic towards a nation whose entire history is built on racism and violence… and then there was the incident at the zoo when he thought the animal rights protesters had a point, hadn't he befriended three penguins who then pushed the Moustaches into the water? Billy looked back at Barry, smiling, and saw Barry was smiling back.

"Nah theur gerrin' it. Just 'old on – theur will love it at Frogsports."

But Mr Moustache wasn't done yet.

"I've already said," he began, "he won't be going to that school. He's going to Rafbat High, and he'll be grateful for it. I've read that letter, and he needs all sorts of expensive things – books, vegetables and –"

"If e' wants t' go, e'll go. Nowt theur can do will change that," said Barry. "'is name's bin down since 'e wor born. 'e's goin' t' best school for magical whizzin' n' kabooms in't world. 'e'll be around 'is own sort for once. A place that accept fowk for who they are," he glanced at Billy here, "Terms n' conditions apply, subject t' status, 'course."

"IF WE WANTED HIM TO LEARN SORCERY, WE WOULD HAVE SENT HIM TO ETON," yelled Mr Moustache.

But Mr Moustache had finally pushed Barry too far. "NEVER –" he said cooly, "OUR EXAM RESULTS ARE MUCH 'IGHER THAN AT ETON!"

Barry pulled an umbrella out from the inside of his coat and pointed it at Yate – there was a flash of bright light, a bang that sounded like a firework, and the next second, Yate had a lettuce for a head.

Mr Moustache roared in anger, while Mrs Moustache screamed in fright. Mr Moustache grabbed his wife and son and made straight for the other room, glancing back with a terrified expression on his face, before slamming the door shut behind them.

"Bugger," said Barry. "Shouldn't av' lost me temper, bur it didn't work anyway. Meant t' turn 'im completely in't vegetable, bur ah suppose 'e wor so stupid already, there weren't much left t' do."

"Barry, isn't that child abuse?" asked Billy. "And don't you work at a school?"

Barry ignored him.

"Anyway, it's gerrin' late n' we've got busy day t'morrow. av' t' nip t' London n' buy all theur stuff n' that."

He took off his heavy coat and threw it to Billy.

"Theur can kip under that. Should keep snowflake like y' warm enough."

Chapter Five

The Sino Pauper Edo Recondo Mammonas Bank

It was still early when Billy woke the next morning. He could feel the warmth of the sun shining on his face through a hole in the wooden that covered one of the windows, but he kept his eyes shut.

"None of it was real," he told himself. "It was all a dream. I had a dream that a giant man called Barry came and stood up to the Moustaches. When I open my eyes, I'll be staring up at the ceiling in my cupboard."

He heard a sudden tapping noise.

And there was Mrs Moustache coming to wake him up, he thought to himself, his heart sinking. But still he didn't open his eyes.

Tap. Tap. Tap.

"Okay," he mumbled. "I'm getting up now. I'll make breakfast."

He opened his eyes, but instead of the low cupboard ceiling he was expecting, he was staring up at the damp and rotting wooden beams that held up the roof inside the hut on the rock. He sat up and

Barry's heavy coat fell off him. The whole hut was filled with sunlight, and the sea outside was both calm and inviting. Barry was still asleep on the sofa. Presumably, the Moustaches had been too scared to come back out the other room, as none of them were in sight.

Tap. Tap. Tap.

Over by one of the windows, an enormous pigeon scratched at the glass with its beak; it had a newspaper tied to a piece of string around its neck.

Billy jumped to his feet, filled with a sense of elation like he'd never felt before. He went over to the window and swung it open. Feeling as though he was in a fairytale, he had a sudden urge to start singing, but thought it better if he didn't start parodying things from Disney, and giving their lawyers the opportunity to publicly defend hate and show they have no sense of humour either. The pigeon flew into the hut, catching Billy on the side of the face as it passed, and landed on Barry's chest to drop the newspaper. As Billy watched, the pigeon jumped down to the floor and began pecking at Barry's coat.

"Stop it, don't do that!"

Billy tried to move the coat away, but the pigeon merely gave him an angry look and continued pecking at the sleeves.

"Barry, there's a pigeon here," said Billy loudly. "It's attacking your coat."

"Aye, it'll want payin'," Barry grunted.

"What?"

"It'll want payin' f' deliverin' paper. Check in coat pocket, lad. Theur will sure find sum' brass in there."

Billy looked down at Barry's coat and noticed for the first time that it appeared to be made out of real fur. "Barry, is this coat made out of mink?" he asked in horror.

"Nah, ah dunt like feel o' mink. It's raccoon."

"But Barry," Billy began, remembering something he'd learnt at the zoo a few months earlier, "if humans keep hunting animals to use their fur for clothing, they'll go extinct. It's morally wrong. We have a responsibility to —"

"Eh! Wha' did ah tell theur last night? — If ah wanted lecture, ah'd watch *Ted Talk*. Nah gerr' on wi' payin' bloody pigeon before we die o' old age."

With disgust, Billy put his hand into one of the coat's many pockets and began pulling things out.

"Tea bags?" he said to himself.

"Aye, n' not jus' any old tea bags, neither. Those are best tea bags theur can buy. Propa' brew. Got t' av' fancy stuff wi' me in case ah find sum' place servin' own brand, see."

Eventually, Billy pulled out a handful of very strange-looking coins.

"Give it fifty cents," said Barry sleepily.

"Cents?"

"Aye, cents. We use euro in't magical world, lad. Much more stable n' valuable than sterling these days, that's f' sure."

Billy counted out five of the little gold-coloured coins with a number ten on them. The pigeon came forward and Billy put them into a small pouch around its neck. Then the pigeon flew off through the open window, leaving behind a small folded piece of paper.

Billy picked it up and unfolded it. "It's a VAT receipt," he said.

"F' me expenses," Barry explained. "Only, they dunt always remember t' give 'em out."

Barry yawned as he sat up on the sofa and stretched.

"Well, we best gerroff, lad. We've got umpteen things t' do t'day. av' t' get t' London n' buy stuff theur need f' school."

As he turned the euro over in his hand, Billy suddenly thought of something which made him feel qualmish.

"Barry," he said.

"Aye," said Barry, as he pulled on the first of his two heavy black boots.

"I don't have any money – and, well, you heard my uncle last night... how am I going to afford to go to Frogsports?"

"Theur dunt need t' worry 'bout tha', lad," said Barry, laughing to himself. "Theur mother n' old man left theur plenty o' brass when they died."

"But you said their house was destroyed –"

Barry laughed even more now.

"Please don't laugh about my parent's death."

"Ah'm sorry," said Barry. "Bur thee didn't keep everythin' in't 'ouse, lad. Nah, the first place we're off t' is t' bank."

"Magicians have banks?"

"Jus' one o' 'em – the thievin' lyin' bastards – sorry, ah mean it's called the Sino Pauper Edo Recondo Mammonas Bank – the thievin' lyin' bastards. It's run by the most disgusting, rapacious, corrupt, n' selfish people in't world."

"Who?" asked Billy curiously.

"Bankers."

"Bankers?" Billy repeated.

"Aye – so tha'd be mad t' think they're there t' 'elp theur out. Never gabble wi' bankers, Billy. It dunt matter wha' they do, they always find ways t' avoid accountability. Reight safe place, though, is Sino Pauper Edo Recondo Mammonas — the thievin' lyin' bastards. Probably only Frogsports, that's safer. I've got t' visit bank me sen anyway. Crumbleceiling wants me t' pick summa' up f' 'im. Frogsports business, y' know.

"Theur got thy stuff together? Come on, then — n' ah'll av' me euro back n' all."

Billy handed back the euro he had in his hand, then followed Barry out of the hut and into the sunlight.

The sky was a cloudless blue, and the sea shone brightly. The boat Mr Moustache had brought them out on was still tied to the rock; it looked even less safe now than it had before the storm.

"How did you get here?" asked Billy.

"Ah came on tha' boat, 'course," said Barry, pointing at a second boat, which appeared to be in considerably better condition than the first. It also had an engine.

They climbed into the boat, and Barry pulled the cord to start the engine. Moments later, they were speeding away from the rock and towards the land they could see on the horizon.

"Why is Sino Pauper Edo Recondo Mammonas so safe?"

"Tricks — bewitchments," said Barry, unfolding his newspaper as he spoke. "They even seh there's billionaires 'oardin resources kept in't most valuable vaults, n' they'll do owt t' keep 'old o' stuff, even if theur dunt need it. n' then there's all money launderin' n' tax evasion stuff in place — that dunt apply t' billionaires so much f' sum' reason, though."

Billy sat and thought about eating the rich while Barry read his newspaper: *The Riled Rag*.

"Secretariat o' Sorcery are screwin' ery'thin' up again — no change there," Barry muttered to himself.

Billy had learnt from Mr Moustache that people often filled themselves with enmity and resentment by reading the tabloids, so he thought it best to try to save Barry from this terrible fate by keeping him talking.

"There's a Secretariat of Sorcery?" he asked.

"'course, there is," said Barry. "Crumbleceiling ran f' Secretary, 'course. Bur even though 'e got most votes, there's ain't no proportional representation, n' then there's election school t' deal wi'. So old Rufets L. Flack got 'is sen elected instead."

"But what does the Secretariat of Sorcery do?"

"Nah that is bloody grand question, lad. Ah ain't got foggiest — waste our tax brass n' shun voters wishes most o' time." Barry turned the page. "It says man 'ere tried t' sue 'is airline f' losin' 'is luggage, bur 'e lost 'is case — oh, n' ah can gerr' me sen a free packet o' seeds if ah send off f' 'em."

At that moment, the boat came to a gentle stop as it beached itself on the sand. Barry folded up his newspaper, and they climbed out of the boat and walked across the beach to some stone steps which brought them out onto the street above. Barry seemed to speed up a little as they passed a rather threatening looking man complaining to a police officer that his boat had been stolen during the night.

People stared a lot at Billy as they strolled through the town. Billy couldn't blame them because when he thought it about it, to most it must have looked as though Barry was trying to abduct him. After all, here he was, an eleven-year-old boy, following a mysterious man he'd never met before on the promise of riches and a better life. Was Barry perhaps on darknet forums with the *Child Catcher, Willy Wonka,* and *Pumbaa*?

"Barry," said Billy, trying to think of something different. "Did you say there's billionaires at Sino Pauper Edo Recondo Mammonas?"

"Aye – some seh they av' successful businesses, bur most reckon they jus' exploit those less privileged," said Barry. "Blimey, ah'd love t' run me own business, though."

"You want your own business?"

"av' done ever since ah wor a little kid. All tha' financial freedom n' work life balance tha' go wi' it – 'ere we go."

They had reached the station. There was a train to London departing in five minutes, but they didn't catch it. Although he didn't understand "common money", as he called it, Barry still knew the price the man at the ticket counter had quoted him was ridiculous. "'OW MUCH?" he shouted to general approval from those nearby. "Ah could fly t' New York n' back f' that price!"

The ticket man explained that if they waited until the first off-peak train of the day, their tickets would be cheaper, so that's what they did. They had been sat waiting on the platform for nearly three hours when the nine forty-two train arrived at eleven minutes past ten – conveniently just one minute short of being late enough for anyone to be compensated for the delay.

People stared more than ever on the train, though this was probably because, despite there being plenty of empty seats, Barry had still decided to sit next to someone else, who was now squashed against the window looking uncomfortable.

"It leaves pair o' seats free f' when others come along, see," he explained to Billy. "Anyway, av' theur still got y' letter from las' night?

There's list o' ery'thin' theur need f' school in there."

Billy took the cream envelope out of his pocket. He looked inside and found a second piece of parchment he hadn't noticed the night before. He took it out and read:

FROGSPORTS ACADEMY *of* MAGICAL WHIZZING *and* KABOOMS

LIST OF UNIFORM, SET BOOKS, AND EQUIPMENT FOR FIRST-YEAR STUDENTS

UNIFORM |

ALL FIRST YEAR STUDENTS ARE REQUIRED TO PURCHASE:

1) *Four black dressing gowns for day wear*
2) *Three top hats (without rabbit) that you shall never wear and which will never again be mentioned*
3) *Two stage capes (black, silver fastenings)*
4) *One body bag (non-vinyl polyethylene or similar)*

Please note all body bags should be named and contain a copy of dental records within.

BOOKS |

ALL STUDENTS ARE REQUIRED TO HAVE A COPY OF EACH OF THE FOLLOWING:

~ 101 MODERN CARD TRICKS *by Q. Een O'Hearts*
~ MY FIRST RABBIT: A GUIDE TO RABBIT CARE *by Hare E. Foot*
~ HOW TO SAW A PERSON IN HALF *by Enid Stitches*
~ THE PRODUCERS GUIDE TO THE EDINBURGH FRINGE *by Lucky B. Stard*
~ YEARBOOK *by Seth Rogen*
~ THE WORST WITCH *by Jill Murphy*

OTHER EQUIPMENT |

~ *Enchanted Celery*
~ *One dove*

~ Three identical cups and one table tennis ball

~ Two die

~ One sparkly box with extendable legs

Students may also bring with them a pigeon OR *a peacock* OR *a hamster (or if you wish to completely ignore this, something else like a rat, or perhaps an iguana).*

As a reminder, first-year students are not permitted to bring their own space hoppers.

"Can we find all this in London?" Billy asked, looking up from the list.

"Either London or *IKEA*," said Barry. "Except f' body bag, theur will av' t' gerr' tha' from *Amazon*."

"Why do we need a body bag?"

"Oh, look, we're 'ere already," said Barry, ignoring Billy's question as he got to his feet. They had indeed just arrived into Charring Cross station.

Billy had never been to London before. Barry, meanwhile, seemed to know where they were going, even if he wasn't happy about many of the things they came across on the way. As they went down the escalator into the Underground, he complained loudly about a piece of artwork that was clearly created on *Microsoft Paint* by an artist too lazy to even fit the writing on a single line.

"It's reight daft o' Mayor t' commission multi-millionaire t' create this shite while ignorin' city's own under-represented talent," he said. "Especially at time 'e's breakin' promise not t' raise fares."

Billy didn't have time to focus on the artwork. He was too busy trying to stop himself from being sick after gazing at the new advertising screens, which gave the disorienting illusion that you were leaning forward while travelling down.

"Ah dunt know 'ow these commoner fowk deal wi'out air conditioning on Northern Line," said Barry a short time later when they came out of Tottenham Court Road station and onto a busy pavement lined with shops.

They set off down the street with Barry leading the way, passing by embassies and a *Starbucks*, theatres and another *Starbucks*, a third *Starbucks*, and *Andrew Lloyd Webber* begging passersby for money, so he wouldn't have to sell one of his many theatres (despite being worth hundreds of millions and previously having used his position and privilege as an unelected Lord to vote in favour of cuts that would severely impact the disabled and most vulnerable in society). There was nowhere that looked as though they might sell magical vegetables, though. This was just an ordinary street filled with ordinary shops. Could there really be greedy and immoral people who cared about money much more than ever doing the right thing nearby? They passed a sign telling them they were entering Bloomsbury, and Billy suddenly felt it was a little more likely.

"'ere we are then," said Barry, coming to a stop. "The Whine n' Milk It! This is us."

They were outside a small, dirty-looking pub that didn't seem to fit in with the character of the area. Billy was surprised the council had ever permitted it to be built, but as he looked at the people walking past them, he had the strangest feeling that none of them even knew it was there. It was as though only he and Barry could see it. Before he could ask, Barry had led him through the door.

For the entry point to a magical world, it was shabby and rundown inside, and the air was thick with the smell of stale urine. At a table in the corner, two *Instagram* personalities were busy influencing and discussing how tragic the menu was. As they stepped forward, Billy felt his feet sticking to the carpet, but he didn't want to think about what might have been causing that.

A man who looked to be the barman came over to them. He looked relieved to see them there.

"Oh, Barry," he said. "My best customer – am I glad to see you here. Business has been terrible. All these cases of Conjurors Condition going around – people just don't want to go out, you know? And the Secretariat isn't doing anything to help the situation."

"What's Conjurors Condition?" asked Billy.

"It's jus' this 'ighly contagious virus that's bin goin' 'round magicians," explained Barry. "Killin' us off, y' know?"

Barry looked back at the barman and noticed him glancing down at Billy.

"Oh, ah ain't introduced y' both," he said. Then he cleared his throat and said loudly enough for the whole pub to hear, "Mike, ah'd like theur t' meet Billy Smith."

This didn't seem to have the effect Barry thought it might. No one seemed to care who Billy Smith was, though someone did shout out, "Hey, boomer, the naughties called, they want their popular culture back."

"Anyway, said the barman, moving things along, "did you both scan as you came in?"

"I didn't know I had to scan anything," said Billy.

"Everybody must scan when they enter the pub. It's the law," said the barman, and he showed them both a poster on the wall with a large QR code in the middle of it. "It's to help stop the spread of the virus."

"Ah'm scannin' nowt," said Barry defiantly. "n' neither is Billy."

"Oh, well, I know you, Barry, I'm sure it will be fine. And as for your friend, I'm sure if you say he's okay, there will be no problem — you will both stay for a drink, though, won't you?"

"Can't Mike. Got stuff t' do n' things t' buy."

The barman looked disappointed.

"Yes, I understand," he said. "Maybe later or another time?"

Barry led Billy through to the back of the pub, then stopped as he passed a table where a haggard looking man was sitting alone, drinking a coffee and reading a book.

"Professor Quigley!" said Barry cheerfully. "Ah didn't expect t' run in't theur in 'ere."

The man flinched.

"Oh, I didn't see you there, Barry. How are you?"

"Ah'm doin' grand, n' y' sen?"

"Very well, thank you."

"Billy, this 'ere is Professor Quigley — 'e'll be one of y' teachers when y' get t' Frogsports."

"Billy Smith," said Professor Quigley, reading forward to shake Billy's hand. "Very pleased to meet you."

"What do you teach, Professor?"

"Vigilantism," said Professor Quigley. "I suppose you've come to buy all of your things for school? I just came to pick up this book myself," he continued, holding up his book he was reading. Billy read the cover: *Brie and Me* by Émile Arquette.

"Well, we must be gerrin' on," said Barry. "Got umpteen things t' do."

They said goodbye to Professor Quigley, then continued into a small room at the very back of the pub.

"Ah'm surprised 'e ain't talkin' wi' a stutter," said Barry.

"I'm not," said Billy. "That would just be making stuttering out to be a joke, and reducing it from something real to something evil people experience only because they're bad."

They came to a door. Barry opened it and led Billy out into a small walled garden.

"Barry, if there's a deadly virus going around, shouldn't we all be wearing masks?"

"'course, not," said Barry. "Wha' does theur figure this is? Entire rest o' world? Nah shurrup a mo' so ah can concentrate."

Barry pulled his umbrella from his coat and told Barry to stand back. Then he held it up in front of the wall and muttered a few words Billy didn't understand.

Billy expected something to happen, but nothing did.

"Eh?" said Barry. "Tha' not reight."

He went up to the wall and pressed his ear against the brickwork.

"Ain't even able t' 'ear owt."

"Barry –"

"Shurrup, ah've got n' idea," and he stood back before taking a run up and crashing shoulder-first into the wall. But it made no difference.

"Barry –"

"Wha' is it?" said Barry, getting back up on his feet.

"I think it's that wall over there," said Billy, pointing over at an archway which had just opened up in the middle of an adjacent wall.

"Oh..." said Barry, straightening out his coat. "Reight, come on then."

They stepped through the archway and into the cobbled street on the other side. As he glanced over his shoulder, Billy noticed the archway disappearing.

"Welcome, lad," said Barry, "t' Upper Lower Upper Regent Street – though, we're at top end, so officially it's Upper Upper Lower Upper Regent Street."

They began walking down the street.

Billy wised they could stop for a moment, so he could take it all in. He looked around in every direction as they passed shops he could never even have dreamed might have existed, let alone ever have seen before. They walked by a woman saying to her friend, "Bovum fimus, seventy-nine euro for seven! It's out of control…"

A soft cooing sound came from a shop with a sign saying One Stop Pigeon Shop. At the next building down, several children around Billy's age had their noses pressed against a window with space hoppers in it. "Look," Billy heard one of them say to the others, "it's the new BunnyRibbit Eleven – highest bounce ever –" There were shops selling rabbit food, shops selling spinning tops, a *Starbucks*, and more shops selling unicycles, juggling sticks, and fire eating equipment.

Next, they passed a cinema with posters outside advertising upcoming screenings of *Edward Scissorhands, Charlie and the Chocolate Factory, Sweeny Todd, Alice in Wonderland,* and all five *Pirates of the Caribbean* movies. Billy took a moment to wonder why anyone would choose that hill to die on.

"We ain't interested," said Barry, as a young man came up to offer them both his latest mixtape, and the man walked off. They didn't have such an easy time from Elmo, who continued to follow them down the street until Barry agreed to pay him ten euro just to go away.

"Here it is," said Barry. "The Sino Pauper Edo Recondo Mammonas Bank – the thievin' lyin' bastards!"

They had reached a tall white stone building that towered over the rest of the street. Sitting on the steps leading up to the bronze revolving doors, wearing the contents of a *T. M. Lewis* discount bin and eating a *Marks & Spencer* meal deal, was – "Aye, that's a banker," whispered Barry as they moved past him. Billy glanced back at the banker and noticed he had an *Audi* branded umbrella with him and a vape kit sticking out the top of his jacket pocket.

"Theur would think they might be goblins or summa' in this world, wouldn't theur?" said Barry.

"Erm… no," said Billy.

Barry came to a stop just before the doors.

"Eh?"

"Goblins would likely be lazily depicted as having hooked noses and many other stereotypical traits that ignorant hate-filled people attribute to the Jewish community in an attempt to attack them. Writing them to be untrustworthy and greedy characters who act secretive and are segregated from everybody else would only be further playing into that. It would actually all be really anti-Semitic."

Ignoring Billy's point, Barry continued through the doors.

They entered a gigantic marble hall with a high ceiling from which opulent chandeliers dangled and doors – too many to count – leading off to other rooms in every diction. A hundred or more counters lined both sides, from where they were standing all the way down to a collection of yet more doors at the end of the hall. Sat behind each of them was a banker asking someone, "Would you like a mortgage with that?" Close by, another banker was busy explaining to an armed bank robber that they needed to push (not pull) the door if they wanted to get out.

Barry and Billy made for a free counter next to one where a woman was busy checking her balance by standing on one leg as someone attempted to push her over.

"Ey up! We've come t' ten sum' brass out o' Mr Billy Smith's vault."

The banker looked down at Billy and with a suspecting voice said, "And does Mr Billy Smith have two forms of photographic identification and proof of address going back the past three years?"

"Oh, burger."

This problem took a long time to fix. But eventually, after he had filled in multiple forms, confirmed the answers to his security questions, passed a DNA test, and recited *God Save the Queen* in reverse, both in tune and out of it, the banker was satisfied that Billy could make a withdrawal.

"Oh, n' there's summa' else too," said Barry, talking more seriously now. "Ah av' t' pick summa' up from vault sixty-nine."

The banker started to laugh.

"Wha' so funny?"

"Well, it's just — you said *sixty-nine,* didn't you — "

"Oh, reight," said Barry, and he too started laughing.

"I don't get it," said Billy. "What's so funny about the number sixty-nine?"

Barry and the banker laughed even harder now.

"Anyway," said the banker, "is vault sixty-nine in your own name?"

"Ah, it ain't, no."

"Very well," said the banker. "If the account is not in your own name, I will be unable to carry out a security check, so I shall waste none of your time and have somebody take you down to both vaults straight away. Sebastian!"

Sebastian was yet another banker, though it seemed he only had the job because his parents were wealthy enough to help him buy a place at a top university. Barry and Billy followed him through one of the doors leading off the hall.

"I still don't understand what's so funny about sixty-nine," said Billy.

"Theur will av' t' ask adult when y' gerr' older," said Barry.

They were in a small grey room with a set of silver doors in front of them. Sebastian pressed a button next to the doors, and the lift opened. He gestured them both inside, then followed and pressed a sequence of buttons on a silver panel.

As the lift doors closed, light casual music began to play through a speaker above their heads. It had an agreeable medley and a pleasing drum beat, but quickly became repetitive and annoying; it reminded Billy of a UK entry in Eurovision. Then, as he sniffed, his mind was taken off the music.

"Barry –"

"It ain't me," said Barry flatly.

Barry and Billy both looked at Sebastian.

"Well, it isn't me," he said pompously.

They were all relieved when the doors opened a minute later, and they could step out into the fresh, but cold, damp, and dark stone passageway on the other side. Billy looked around; he thought they must be deep underground now. Their footsteps echoed around them as they walked.

Sebastian led them around a corner to where a dozen or so rusty metal doors stood side by side as the last line of defence protecting the treasures inside. He told Barry and Billy to stand back as he unlocked one of the doors, then moved out of the way as it opened and revealed its secrets to them.

"It's all for theur," said Barry.

Billy gasped — he couldn't believe it. There were piles of coins stretching all the way to the back of the vault, bank notes — grey fives, red tens, blue twenties, orange fifties, green hundreds, yellow two hundreds even — sticking out as though colourful flowers in a bed of gold and silver. At the side of the vault, there was a cardboard box.

"Look at tha'," said Barry. "Ah think that's y' old man's stamp collection."

"What's that next to it?"

"Oh, that's y' mother's — she used t' collect fossilised cat shit."

As Billy began filling a small bag with some of the money, Barry looked through the boxes.

"Look at this, she managed t' collect Tiddles, Fuzz Aldrin, and *Bustopher Jones* — nah, 'old on, tha' jus' a DVD o' *Lesbian Vampire Killers*."

When Billy was done, Sebastian closed and locked the door again. Then he led them back to the lift and took them even deeper underground. Billy expected it to be cooler when he stepped back out a few moments later, so he found it a surprise when the doors opened and a humid breeze hit his face. There was a strong burning smell in the air, then — he looked down the passageway and saw a burst of fire coming from something he couldn't see.

"Barry, what was that?"

It was Sebastian who answered.

"Nothing to be concerned about," he said. "It's only rocket science."

Billy remembered what Barry had told him about billionaires guarding the vaults down here.

Sebastian again told them to stand back as he unlocked the door to vault sixty-nine. As it opened, the burning smell was replaced by a strong scent of ammonia. Billy wondered where it could be coming from because the vault appeared empty. Then he saw it; a small wooden box was sitting on the floor of the vault. He leant in to look closer, but felt Barry pull him back by the shoulder.

"Barry, what is that?" he asked, pulling his shirt up to cover his nose from the smell.

Barry stepped forward to pick up the box.

"Ah can't tell theur tha', lad," said Barry, putting the box in his pocket. "*GDPR* n' all tha' stuff."

They had extra company on their way back up. Just as the lift doors were about the close, someone shouted for Sebastian to hold them. A man dressed in *SpaceX* branded shoes, a *SpaceX* branded hooded jumper, and a *SpaceX* branded baseball cap, with *SpaceX* branded sunglasses, entered the lift. Just in case they had any doubt about where the man worked, as the lift started moving, he turned to them all and said, "Oh, hey, how are you all doing today? I've had a busy morning working for *SpaceX* and now I'm just heading out, so I can call my boss, *Mr Musk*. Have you heard of *Mr Musk* before? He's fantastic, isn't he?"

The lift came to a stop, and the man rushed off ahead of them. Sebastian thanked Barry and Billy for their loyalty, then bowed them back into the marble hall. As they went to leave the bank, they passed a banker telling someone, "Yes, your balance is outstanding."

"Thank you very much," replied the woman he was talking to.

Outside the bank, a *Black Lives Matter* march came past them on the street. This seemed to make Barry feel uncomfortable all of a sudden.

"What's the matter?" said Billy.

"Well, where's white lives matter march?" said Barry. "Dunt all lives matter?"

"They're not saying white lives don't matter, they're saying black lives matter as well. White lives aren't under threat from institutional racism or a prejudiced society."

"Does theur ever shurrup?"

"Does theur ever stop being wrong?" said Billy.

"Eh! Less o' tha' or theur will gerr' y' sen a smack 'round face, lad. Respect y' elders."

"I don't think you're allowed to hit children anymore."

"Is there anythin' y' can still do these days? Theurs lot av' ruined it all f' rest o' us… can't physically assault children… can't racially abuse minorities… sexual assault is out n' all… can't fire people f' who they love… wha' ever 'appened t' freedom? – wha' next? Will we not be able t' go f' drink wi' a few friends or pick up a book?"

"Er, Barry… are you okay?"

"Ah'm grand," said Barry. "Nah, let's jus' gerr' on wi' wha' we came for!"

Barry shook his head.

"Best start wi' y' dessin' gowns," he said, nodding towards a department store a little farther down the street. "Listen, there ain't much ah can 'elp wi' in there, so why dunt ah go gerr' a few o' y' other things n' we can meet up after? Save some time n' tha'." Billy agreed, so he walked off down the street alone.

Outside the shop, a couple of assistants who were on their break were discussing the recent news that the owner had run off with the pension fund and left the whole company bankrupt. What a selfish arsehole, Billy thought to himself as he passed them and entered the shop.

As Billy scanned a rail of black dressing downs for one in his size, a woman who looked as though she worked there came over to him.

"Are you Frogsports, dear?" she asked.

"Er, yes," said Billy.

"You're looking in the wrong place here. These are all plain dressing gowns. You need the ones with the school logo on the front. They cost three times more and are much worse quality, but the school gets to keep some of the profits," she explained, leading him over to an open space where another boy around Billy's age was stood on a footstool being measured by another assistant. He had blonde hair and appeared rather uninterested in everything.

"You join this young man here and I'll get you sorted out," said the woman.

"Oh, hello," said the boy, noticing Billy was there. "Are you going to Frogsports as well?"

"Yes," said Billy.

"I'm here with my father, but he's gone to the bank while I have my dressing gown fitted," said the boy. He had a pretentious voice. "But afterwards I'm going to take him to look at space hoppers. I really don't understand why first-years aren't allowed to bring their own. I've got one at home that I'm going to try smuggle in somehow, though — have you got your own space hopper?"

"No," said Billy.

"You don't play Frogsports at all?"

Play Frogsports? What did the boy mean?

"No," Billy said again, wondering how he was supposed to play the school.

"Shame — I've played since I was six. Naturally, my father thinks I will be picked for my house team, and I'm sure he'll be right. Any idea what house you might be in yet?"

"No," said Billy, starting to wonder just how long the list of things he didn't know actually was.

"Well, nobody really knows until the sorting, do they, and they change how they do that every year. But I have a feeling I'll be in Crocodilian house, all my family has been so far — I do feel sorry for those going with a history of their family being sorted into Gluteal house, though. I mean, imagine having that little to live up to?

Billy nodded, hoping the boy wouldn't notice he didn't understand a word he was talking about.

"I say, what's going on over there?" said the boy suddenly, pointing over to the front window. Barry was stood outside, arguing with a bald man dressed as a fake monk who had just asked him to sign the book he was holding.

"That's Barry," said Billy. "He works at Frogsports."

"Oh, yes," said the boy. "I've heard of him. He's a lonely old man who lives in the grounds, isn't he?"

"He's the groundskeeper," said Billy.

"I've heard he's picked up a lot of questionable views and probably shouldn't be allowed to work in a school."

The boy had a point, thought Billy.

"Why are you with him anyway? Aren't your mother or father around?"

"They're both dead," said Billy bluntly. He wasn't sure he felt like talking about them just now.

"Oh, well, they'll live," said the boy. "But they were, you know..."

"No, I don't know."

"Nuclear?"

"I think so," said Billy, not really understanding what the boy was asking him.

"I know that what some might call, shall we say, non-traditional families are everywhere, and it's a perfectly ordinary thing," said the boy. "And I get this is supposed to be an inclusive world, and all that, but I really don't comprehend why anybody should feel entitled to expect that sort of representation in the story — at least not explicitly. Don't you agree?"

Before Billy could ask the boy what the hell was wrong with him, the shop assistant said, "You're all done, dear," and Billy, not sorry for a reason to leave, jumped down from the footstool and went over to the counter to pay before going outside to join Barry.

With the sun shining bright above them, Barry decided they should go for an ice cream to cool down. Billy was quiet as he ate, something which didn't go unnoticed by Barry.

"Wha' up wi' theur?" He said. "Theur look as though y' greyhoun' got it sen disqualified."

"Barry, what's Frogsports?" Billy asked.

"Frogsports? It's name o' school, 'course."

"Somebody asked me if I played Frogsports earlier. They can't have been talking about the school, can they?"

"Oh, nah. Theur on 'bout sport. Frogsports is magical sport ery'one follows. It wor invented at school, see, so it got named after it."

"Isn't it just lazy to name it after the school?"

"Maybe – bur perhaps writer o' book wanted t' avoid bin sued f' trademark infringement n' couldn't come up wi' anything better. Maybe they're jus' 'opin ery'one gives them break after keepin' this thin' up f' 'undred thousan' words."

"But what are the rules of Frogsports?"

"The rules? Kinda 'ard t' explain, bur there's two sides wi' eight players a piece. Six o' 'em dress up as frogs n' they bounce 'bout on space 'op. Three o' 'em try t' score points wi' rugby ball, n' they use 'ockey stick t' mek sure ball dunt 'it ground. Oh, n' there's two goal keep on each team too."

"Each side has two goal keepers?"

"Aye – front 'alf n' back 'alf." Barry explained. "O' pantomime 'orse," he continued, off of Billy's confused expression. "Goal keep av' 'ardes't job o' all as netball 'opp thee av' t' protect is suspended above water n' thee av' t' balance on inflatable unicorn."

"I really want to try playing it," said Billy. "But didn't they think it through before inventing it?"

"Not before rememberin' 'ow many chapters they'd av' t' write 'bout it later on."

"And what are Crocodilian and Gluteal?"

"School 'ouses — two o' four. Ery'one says Gluteals are a bunch o' asses, bur —"

"I bet I become a Gluteal," said Billy downheartedly.

"Better t' be a Gluteal than a Crocodilian," said Barry darkly. "That-Evil-One was a Crocodilian — oh, sorry," he added, as a cloud appeared above Billy.

Billy didn't feel like finishing his ice cream now it was covered in rainwater, so they went off to buy his school books in Pickar, Waring, Jolly & Tull; a bookshop a little way down the street. While one of the assistants went into the storeroom at the back of the shop to check if they had any more copies of *101 Modern Card Tricks*, Billy browsed the shelves in the history section. A book on Native American history caught his eye. He took it off the shelf and opened it. To his surprise, the text of the book had been entirely covered over with white correction fluid, on top of which someone had scribbled their own footnotes.

"Barry, is this book meant to look like this?"

Barry wandered over from the bargain bin.

"Wha' it called?"

Billy showed him the cover of the book.

"Aye — in this magical world, there ain't such a thin' as Native American 'istory. It's jus' a myth created by commoner fowk t' demonise those who think their fictional world is more important than real one."

"That's not how things work, Barry. Native American history

doesn't cease to exist just because somebody excludes it from their imagination.

"Dunt mind that now," said Barry. "Have y' seen this book?" He showed Billy the book in his hand: *The Art of The Deal*. "Ah think there's summa' wrong wi' it. It's got too many chapter elevens."

"Yes, it's the only thing saving it from the fiction section." The shop assistant had returned with a copy of *101 Modern Card Tricks*.

With his school books bought, they left the shop and Barry checked Billy's school list again.

"Reight, jus' y' enchanted celery t' gerr' now — oh, n' ah need t' get theur a birthday present."

Billy suddenly felt very embarrassed.

"You don't have to do that —"

"Okay, ah won't then," said Barry. "Ah'm kiddin' — ah know ah dunt av' t' get theur owt, bur ah dunt imagine y' got much livin' wi' those Moustaches. Ah'll tell theur wha', 'ow 'bout ah get y' an animal? Theur dunt want n' hamster, theur would get laughed at wi' hamster — n' peacocks would mek book more complicated t' write. Ah'll get theur a pigeon. Ery'one needs a pigeon in this world."

Half an hour later, they left the One Stop Pigeon Shop with Billy now carrying a large cage that housed a fluffy white Jacobin pigeon, looking around curiously at everything and everyone else on the street.

"Jus' Olivehandlers left — best place t' gerr' y' sen an enchanted celery, Olivehandlers, n' theur has t' av' the best vegetable theur can gerr'!"

An enchanted celery… this seemed a little unnecessary to Billy, but then you never know what someone will try trademark or claim they were the first to invent next.

This last shop was small and rather rundown looking. Old-fashioned lettering painted in gold onto the wood above the door read *Olivehandlers: Greengrocers Since 402 B.C.*, because apparently, magicians still recognised the birth of Christ. In the window, a long stick of celery lay on top of a velvet cushion.

They went inside and found themselves in a dark shop front, which was completely empty, except a tattered red rug on the floor, the counter in front of them, and a small chair which Barry went over to sit on. Billy approached the counter and pressed the top of a brass bell. He was just gazing up at the dusty chandelier above his head when –

"Cashier number one please!" said a voice from the darkness. Billy jumped, then watched as a man stood into the light behind the counter. "Good afternoon," said the man.

"Er – hello," said Billy, somewhat unsure.

"Ah, yes." The man smiled. "Billy Smith, yes, I thought I would be seeing you sometime soon. I must say, your eyes are most different to those your mother had."

Billy thought this was a strange comment for the man to make, but he didn't know what to say, so he let him continue.

"I remember your mother. Yes, she came in here one time to buy her first enchanted vegetable when she was the same age you are now. Eleven inches long, very streamlined at both ends – made it opportune for performing sorcery at speed."

As he spoke, Mr Olivehandler began pulling boxes from the shelves behind him, then placing them on top of the counter.

"As for your father, well, his was much more ordinary, though still offered sufficient capabilities for his magical needs."

Mr Olivehandler looked at Billy now, but as Billy glanced up at him, he noticed his gaze seemed focused on his forehead.

"So it really does exist," he said softly. "I feel I should apologise to you, Mr Smith, after all, I am the one who allowed that trademark to be created. Sixteen-and-a-half inches. I remember it well. Powerful, too powerful, and in the wrong environment... well, if I had known exactly what that vegetable was going out into the world to do..."

To Billy's immense relief, Mr Olivehandler now noticed Barry sitting by the window.

"Barry! How wonderful to see you again... Yes, I remember you well. Yours came from an especially good crop following a prolonged summer of rain."

"Ah remember theur tellin' me, sir," said Barry.

"Very powerful vegetable, that one. But I assume it was blended into a smoothie after you were expelled?" said Mr Olivehandler.

"Yeh, it wor," said Barry in an unusually quiet voice.

Barry had been expelled? He hadn't mentioned that the night before.

"Why were you expelled from Frogsports?" asked Billy.

Billy expected Barry not to answer, but to his surprise he said, "Well, t' tell theur truth, there wor this big problem wi' this creature goin' 'round n' killin' students back in my day, n' ah got blamed f' it all. Ah wor innocent, 'course. Bur they could never find real culprit, so ah got kicked out, see. Bur Crumbleceiling let me stay on as groundskeep'."

"A creature was killing students?"

"Now y' know why theur need a body bag!"

Mr Olivehandler brought the conversation back around to enchanted celeries.

"Now then, Mr Smith, every magician must have an enchanted vegetable with which they can channel their sorcery. In this country, we prefer to use celeries over alternatives such as carrots, cucumbers, asparagus, and spring onions; I have even heard of some especially bitter men who choose to use green beans."

Billy watched as Mr Olivehandler opened one of the boxes on the counter and took out a long stick of celery.

"Myself, I have always used the finest celery — organic, of course. And each and every stick is hand treated with a special coating that will preserve and protect the vegetable through a lifetime of use."

He handed Billy the celery, leafy end pointing down.

"Just give it a wave and say *Legalese*."

"*Brownmark Films LLC v Comedy Partners, 683 F.3d 687 (7th Cir. 2012)*," said Billy, but nothing happened.

"Ah, no, Mr Smith, you have misunderstood me. I meant for you to say the word *Legalese*."

"Oh," said Billy, nodding.

He waved the celery a second time and said, "*Legalese!*"

This time, something did happen; all the shelves with neatly arranged boxes in front of him collapsed and piled on top of each other, the counter fell apart, the chair Barry had been sat on split in half, sending him tumbling onto the floor, and the chandelier above their heads came crashing to the floor, narrowly avoiding Mr Olivehandler and sending a cloud of dust up into the air which made them all start coughing.

"I'm sorry," said Billy, panicking. "I didn't know that was going to happen."

"All damages," Mr Olivehandler coughed, "must be paid for, Mr Smith. It does say so on the sign."

"What sign?" said Billy.

Mr Olivehandler pulled out his own enchanted celery and gave it a wave. Billy stood in amazement as the whole shop repaired and reformed itself around him, leaving not even a single trace of destruction.

"That sign," said Mr Olivehandler, pointing at a notice on the wall behind the counter. Then he realised. "Ah, yes," he said, turning to face Billy. "Well, it was worth a try."

Mr Olivehandler took the first stick of celery from Billy, then handed him a second, slightly shorter piece.

"Same again please."

Billy swished the celery and said, "*Legalese!*"

This time, the glass in the shop windows smashed and flew out in all directions as tiny pieces of sand. A few people walking past outside jumped back in shock.

"Not that one either, I see," said Mr Olivehandler, taking the second stick of celery back from Billy.

"'ow the bloody 'ell does theur gerr' insurance on this place?" said Barry, brushing sand out of his hair.

Mr Olivehandler gave his enchanted celery another wave, and the window instantly repaired itself in front of them.

Billy watched as Mr Olivehandler picked up a third box from the counter. He didn't open it straight away, but instead hesitated in thought. "I wonder..." he said, seemingly to himself. "Maybe... perhaps, yes... only one way to find out..."

He opened the box and took out a third stick of celery, which he handed to Billy.

"Try this one."

This time, there was no ruined shop or smashed windows. Billy had barely finished saying "*Legalese!*" when the celery had started glowing in his hand.

"Aha! I think we have found the one for you, Mr Smith," said Mr Olivehandler with a smile on his face. "How interesting though... how very, very interesting."

"I'm sorry," said Billy, "but what's interesting?"

Mr Olivehandler gazed down at Billy.

"Well, you see, Mr Smith, it is most often the case that more than a single enchanted celery can be harvested from a single crop. Frequently, those from the same crop are best suited to those from the same family or part of the same bloodline. But it would seem that for yourself, the norm does not apply. It so happens that your own enchanted celery was cultivated during an especially difficult year and was one of only two to be collected from that specific plant. It is interesting that this should be the celery for you when the other, why, the other was used to create that trademark."

Billy paid three hundred euro for his enchanted celery, and Mr Olivehandler put it back in its box and wrapped it up in brown paper for him.

Billy thought he liked Mr Olivehandler and his eccentric manner, but as they left the shop, he overheard him muttering to himself.

"Crumbleceiling was certainly right about him. I must pay him that bet."

Back outside, the sun was now hanging low in the sky, and shops on the street were starting to close for the day. Billy had too much on his mind to talk as he followed Barry back up Upper Lower Upper Regent Street, back through The Whine and Milk It, and back onto the street outside. He hardly noticed where they were going as they trudged back past where they had encountered *Andrew Lloyd Webber* that morning – a spot now occupied by *Cameron Mackintosh* desperately searching in the gutter for his credibility – to Russel Square station, got on a train, and then spent an hour changing lines at Green Park. Eventually, they came out into Waterloo station where Barry glanced up at the departure board, then said to Billy, "'bout an hour or so until theur's train leaves, got time t' gerr' summa' t' eat. Wha' y' fancy?"

"My train? But aren't we going to Frogsports?" said Billy.

Barry laughed then said, "'course not. It's only start o' summer, ain't it. Nah, y' goin' back t' y' aunt n' uncles 'ouse f' a bit. It would really mess wi' continuity if y' went straight t' school."

They decided to buy sandwiches and then sit at a table on the upper concourse to eat them. As they went up the escalator, they passed a person meeting their destiny in quite a similar way who was going down.

"Everythin' okay wi' theur, lad?" said Barry after a few minutes of silence. "Theur dunt seem t' av' much t' seh."

Billy wasn't sure how to explain it, but eventually he said, "I just don't feel as though I fit in. I don't know anything or anybody. I don't even know what happened to my parents."

Barry smiled at him.

"Dunt worry y' sen 'bout any o' tha'," he said. "Theur will learn soon enough, ery'one does. Jus' keep y' noggin' down, learn t' shut theur gob, n' remember, adults always know best – that's why we're called adults, it because we ad… ad…"

"Yes?" said Billy.

"Never mind," said Barry, and he waved his hand. "Not sure where ah wor goin' wi' tha'."

A short while later, Barry helped Billy onto the correct train, then handed him an envelope which he put in his pocket.

"Dunt lose tha'," he said. "It's y' ticket f' Frogsports – first o' September from Euston Station – n' dunt be late!… See theur at Frogsports, Billy."

As the train departed, Billy rose in his seat and pressed his face against the window to watch Barry; the security guard from the shop where they had bought the sandwiches from had just come over to him. Next second, Billy blinked, and when he opened his eyes, the train had turned a corner.

Chapter Six

The Journey on the Rail Replacement Bus Service

Billy's last month living with the Moustaches wasn't fun. In fact, it was almost alarming. True, Yate was now so scared of him that he wouldn't spend longer than a few moments in the same room as Billy, but those few moments were always filled with him howling and screaming about how everything was unfair. His aunt and uncle, meanwhile, seemed to be making sure to ignore him as much as possible.

Still angry with him, but also terrified of what he might do to them, Mr and Mrs Moustache acted as though Billy simply wasn't there. While he thought this was in some way an improvement on before, Billy did after a while start to feel a little broken down about the situation.

Most of the time, Billy stayed out the way in his bedroom upstairs, his new pigeon keeping him company. He had decided to call her Yodel, because so far, she had done little more than annoy him and give the impression she had no idea where she was going and wouldn't be very good at delivering anything. He spent the days reading his new school books long into the early hours of the morning, Yodel flying in and out of the open window. It was a good thing Mrs Moustache never came into his room to clean up anymore, because Yodel kept bringing him packages addressed to someone Billy had never heard of, and they were starting to pile up in all corners of the room. At the end of each day, just before he went to sleep, he crossed out another day on the calendar he had pinned to the wall, then counted down the days remaining until the first of September.

When he woke on the last day of August, it occurred to Billy that he didn't yet know how he would get to Euston Station the next morning. So he decided to ask Mr Moustache if he could take him into London. Billy went downstairs to the living room where his aunt, uncle, and cousin were all watching a new *ITV* game show on the television, and talking about how they could do much better than any of the contestants, even though they kept shouting out wrong answers. Billy coughed gently to let them know he was there. As he had expected, Yate responded by starting to cry and then running out of the room screaming.

"Erm — Uncle..." Billy said cautiously.

Mr Moustache gave a grunt of acknowledgement.

"I need to get to Euston Station tomorrow to — to catch the train to school..."

Mr Moustache let out another grunt.

"Would you be able to take me into London?"

Another grunt. Billy supposed that meant yes.

"Thank you."

He was about to go back upstairs when Mr Moustache called after him.

"I'm surprised you want to go by car. I thought all you woke lefties hated pollution and wanted to take public transport everywhere instead?"

Billy didn't say anything. He had never once discussed politics with his uncle, but he knew Mr Moustache liked to call anyone a woke lefty if they had an opinion different to his own.

"Where is this school anyway? Which part of the country?"

"I don't know," said Billy. He pulled the ticket Barry had given him out of his pocket and realised for the first time he seemed not to have changed his trousers for over a month.

"My ticket just says I have to take the twelve o'clock train from *platform nine and three-quarters*," he read.

His aunt and uncle stared at him, but Billy didn't think he'd said anything unusual.

"Platform what?"

"Nine and three-quarters."

"There's no such thing as *platform nine and three-quarters*," said Mr Moustache.

"It's on my ticket."

"It must have been created because of the engineering works for HS2," said Mrs Moustache.

"Barking," replied Mr Moustache, shaking his head. "The whole project is a complete waste of money and will never have anywhere near the economic benefits people claim it will. Who actually wants to get to Birmingham half an hour quicker than they can now?"

"And think of all the natural beauty in the countryside that's going to be destroyed," added Mrs Moustache.

"Yes, well, that I don't mind so much," said Mr Moustache. "But the entire project had already gone over budget while the developers pocket billions, and I don't understand why honest and hardworking taxpayers like myself should have to pay for something in a different part of the country, especially when it's going to create jobs that people make money from — I mean, if these people want money that badly, they should work hard, get out there, and create their own jobs."

"Erm —" said Billy, hoping to bring the conversation back around.

"You just wait until it's finished. You'll see. All right, we'll take you to Euston Station tomorrow. We're going into London anyway, or I wouldn't bother."

Billy woke much earlier than he needed to the next morning, but he was too excited to go back to sleep. He got up and pulled on a pair of jeans and a clean shirt because he didn't want to walk into the station in his dressing gown — that sort of behaviour was only accepted at Victoria Station, where trains were so often delayed, commuters had begun sleeping upright in the packed train carriages because by the time they finally got home, it was time to set off again. He checked his school list a final time to make sure he had everything he needed, put Yodel into her cage, and then laid back on the bed staring at the ceiling, waiting for the rest of the house to wake up. A few hours later, Billy's heavy suitcase was loaded into the boot of Mr Moustache's car, Mrs Moustache had bribed Yate into sitting next to Billy, and they set off for London.

As usual, Mr Moustache spent the entire journey complaining

about something. Today, it was the congestion charge he would have to pay for driving into the capital.

"It's just another tax on the successful," he said. "We pay our fair share already, and we shouldn't have to pay more now just because we can afford to drive a car instead of taking the Underground. It's a matter of freedom."

Mr Moustache's rage only increased when he discovered he also had to pay an additional charge to drive into the city's *Ultra Low Emissions Zone*, because his petrol card didn't meet the Euro 4 criteria of the European emissions standards, as set out in the European Union's European Council directive *2003/76/EC* and European Council directive *2006/96/EC*, which would have exempted his vehicle from the charge.

Despite Mr Moustache spending the remainder of the journey concentrating more on complaining how disgraceful it was that as a British person, he was still being controlled by the rule of the European Union and explaining why it was all *Sadiq Kahn's* fault – even though *Boris Johnson* actually first proposed ULEZ while he was Mayor of London – than where they were going, they reached London in good time, and when Mr Moustache finally worked out how to follow the diversions around the *HS2* engineering works to the new station drop-off point, Billy had just under an hour until his train departed.

"You see," said Mr Moustache, as he and Billy got out of the car. "What did I tell you? Look at all this mess," he continued, pointing at some nearby high fencing adored with a large banner showing what Euston Station will never look like once the redevelopment is complete. "And it slowed us down. We'd have been here half an hour quicker if we didn't have to drive around it all. What's the point in the train being quicker if we lose the same amount of time getting to it?"

Billy was surprised when Mr Moustache helped him lift his heavy suitcase out of the boot and onto a luggage trolley. He was even more surprised when he appeared to want to see him off as he pushed the trolley into the station with Billy following behind.

Mr Moustache's motives soon became clear – he wanted to enjoy this. "Well, here we are then. There is platform nine and there is platform ten next to it. Your platform should be somewhere in the middle of it, but it doesn't appear to exist, or maybe we're just at the completely wrong station."

Billy looked up at the platform numbers above them. Sure enough, on one side was a large number nine, and on the other side of the tracks, a large number ten.

"Have a pleasant journey," said Mr Moustache, patting Billy on the shoulder before walking away towards the station exit with a smile on his face.

What was he going to do now? There were no signs pointing him in the right direction. He felt his mouth go dry all of a sudden. He looked around and noticed a large board advertising the opening of a new *Starbucks*, just next to the station's existing *Starbucks*, and across from an old *Starbucks* that had recently become a *Costa Coffee* after the *Starbucks* that was there had relocated to a larger unit on the upstairs concourse. Even though he needed to find his train, Billy felt he had enough time to queue up and buy a coffee priced high enough to raise questions about the ethics of the company when considering how little tax they choose to pay.

Once he'd bought his coffee, still unsure of where to go, he decided to stop a nearby person who looked as though they worked for one of the train companies. The man had never heard of Frogsports before, and when Billy couldn't even tell him where it was, he started to get angry. Feeling as helpless as the passengers boarding the eleven fifty-four London Overground service to Watford Junction, Billy asked for the train that departed at midday, but the man said there wasn't a train departing at midday. Eventually, the man walked away, muttering something to himself about how he wasn't paid enough to deal with people like that.

By now, Billy was starting to panic. According to the large clock above the main departure board, he had just ten minutes left to find the correct platform and get onto the train, but he still had no idea how to do it. He was stuck in the middle of a large station with a heavy suitcase, an overrated coffee in his hand, a pocket full of euro, and a pigeon that kept calling out to another that was pecking at the floor nearby.

He looked around. There was a large group of strangely dressed tourists getting in everyone's way as they waited to have their photographs taken in the wrong place and buy overpriced souvenirs. Barry must have forgotten to tell him something he needed to do to find the platform. He wondered for a moment if he should simply jump into the space between the tracks that served platforms nine and ten, but then he remembered something from school. An official from Network Rail had come in to give a morning assembly about staying safe on the railway, and according to them, jumping onto the tracks was one of the most dangerous things a person could do. Billy didn't know if any of the rails were electrified, and the noise of the surrounding crowds was sure to make it difficult to hear if a train was coming.

At that moment, a group of people passed behind him, and he caught a few words of what they were saying.

"— the place is as packed with commoners as ever, of course —"

Billy turned around. The person speaking was a short and rather plump woman — because describing someone as plump is nicer than calling them fat, even though they both mean the same thing — and she was leading what looked to be her sons: a large group of boys, all of who had vivid ginger hair. Each of the boys carried a suitcase similar to Billy's, and one of them had a pigeon in a cage.

"Now, there's been a last minute platform change... again... and so we all need to go over to platform four and two-thirds instead," the woman told the group at large.

Thinking he might finally find where he needed to go, Billy pushed his trolley after the group. They stopped near the ticket barriers to platforms four and five. Billy stood a little away from them, but close enough that he could eavesdrop.

"Okay, so is everybody ready?" the mother asked.

"Can I go too, mum?" asked a small girl Billy noticed for the first time. She was wearing a fluorescent gold coat, and like her brothers, she had fiery orange hair.

"You're not old enough, Gertrude. Now let us get on with his." The mother turned to her boys. "Who wants to go first? How about you, Jacob?"

What seemed to be the oldest boy stepped forward. He was wearing a top hat and a pretentious expression on his face.

Billy watched as the boy reached into his pocket, pulled out a ticket that looked just like his own, and then walked towards the ticket barriers with purpose. Billy tried not to blink, so he wouldn't miss it, but it wouldn't have mattered either way because a large crowd came walking past in front of him, and by the time they had cleared, the boy had vanished.

"And now you, Chad," the mother said.

"I'm not Chad, I'm Larry," said the boy. "Honestly, you've been our mother for thirteen years and you still can't tell us apart."

"Sorry, Larry, dear. I didn't mean to mix you up."

"I'm only joking, I am Chad," said the boy. He too pulled a ticket out from his pocket and then walked towards the ticket barriers. Just before he disappeared – seemingly into thin air – he called back for his twin. A second later, both had gone – but how had they done it?

There was nothing else for it, Billy would have to ask.

"Excuse me," Billy said to the woman, who here you again seemingly need to be reminded was fat.

"Hello," she said. "Is it your first time going to Frogsports? Ed here is new, too."

She pointed at the last and youngest of her sons. He was much taller than she was, and much thinner as well.

"Yes," Billy told her. "But I don't know – the thing is, I don't know how to –"

"To get onto the correct platform?" she asked with a smile on her face, and Billy nodded.

"Don't worry. It's confusing, isn't it?" she said, patronisingly. "Especially with the mix up and platform change. It's easy enough to find your way, though. All you have to do is hold out your ticket and then walk straight at the ticket barriers leading to platforms four and five. Don't stop and don't worry about walking into them, that's very important. If you're feeling nervous, it's best to do it at a bit of a run and then you'll be through before you know it."

Billy nodded.

"Why don't you go before Ed? Go on."

"Okay," said Billy, sounding uncertain as he tried to remember everything she had just told him.

He turned his trolley around and looked forward at the ticket barriers. They looked very solid.

He held his ticket out and then started to move towards them, gaining speed with each step. He knocked an old woman over as he passed, but thought screw her – the youth of today! Leaning forward on his trolley, he broke into a run as the barriers got closer. He was going to smash into them and be flipped over the top of the trolley, and he was sure it would probably hurt – he was only a few steps away – he wouldn't be able to stop now – he closed his eyes, ready for the impact – he felt nothing… he opened his eyes again and found he had come to a complete stop just short of the barriers.

"Ah, this sometimes happens, dear."

He looked around. It was the boy's mother speaking. She approached him and took the ticket from his hand.

"Sometimes these tickets just don't read well. Not to worry, though, there's an easy trick."

Billy watched as she rubbed his ticket on her leg as though cleaning the magnetic strip on the back of it.

"There you go," she said, handing him back the ticket. "Now why don't you try again?"

Billy nodded, then closed his eyes. He held his ticket out a second time and took another step closer to the barriers.

He felt a sudden breeze hit his face. He opened his eyes again. In front of him was an ancient looking diesel train waiting next to a platform filled with people. Billy looked up to where a sign overhead read *Frogsports Express — Delayed* and next to it another with the words *Platform Four and Two-Thirds* written in thick black lettering. He had done it.

But just as he made to move towards the train, he felt a hand close on his shoulder.

"Excuse me," said a voice, "but do you have your ticket there?"

Billy looked up at the indifferent expression on the face of a man who was clearly a ticket inspector. He was wearing a uniform in the same colours as the Frogsports Express, and a badge on the lanyard around his neck was passive-aggressively asking Billy not to abuse him.

"I'm sorry," said Billy.

"Do you have your ticket with you? I need to check you have the right ticket for this train. Tickets marked London North Western Railway only are not valid on this service, you see."

"I just had to use my ticket to get onto the platform," said Billy.

"Yes, but some people like to try and jump the barriers," the man said in an accusatory tone.

"How could I jump the barriers with this trolley?"

"Your ticket please..."

Confused about why he was being accosted like this, Billy pulled out his ticket and handed it over.

"And do you have your Railcard with you?"

"I don't know what a Railcard is," said Billy.

"Oh dear — this ticket was bought with a Railcard discount. I need to see your valid Railcard, please."

Billy looked at where the man was pointing on his ticket. The words *Railcard Discount* were indeed printed on it in tiny letters.

"I didn't know that was there. I didn't buy this ticket," Billy tried to explain, but the ticket inspector was having none of it.

"Are you telling me that you found this ticket? Or perhaps that you stole it from another student?"

"This ticket was given to me by Barry..."

Twenty minutes later, the ticket inspector finally let Billy go, but not before issuing him a penalty fare and telling him how lucky he was not to be being prosecuted for fare evasion.

It was a good job the train was delayed, thought Billy, otherwise he'd probably have just missed it. He approached the nearest carriage to see how quiet it was, but noticed in the reflection on the glass window that the ticket inspector was now laughing and high-fiving with another man dressed in the same uniform.

This first carriage was already packed with students, some fighting for seats in overcrowded compartments, while others hung out of the doors and windows to talk to their families on the platform.

Billy set off down the platform in search of a quieter carriage.

About three carriages down, he passed a short and dim-looking boy who was crying as he said to an older woman, "Granny, I've lost my hamster again."

"Oh, Josh," Billy heard the woman sigh, "You really are such a stupid boy."

Billy continued pushing his way through the crowds until he made it to the end carriage, which seemed much emptier than any of the others. He put Yodel inside the train first, then went back for his heavy suitcase. As he struggled to lift the suitcase onto the train, he slipped and dropped it onto his foot.

"Damn it –"

"Do you need a hand?" It was one of the ginger-haired twins he'd encountered at the ticket barriers.

"Yes, please."

"Oi, Larry!" the twin shouted to his brother. "Come over here and help a minute."

With the help of the twins, Billy was soon sat in an empty compartment with his suitcase in the overhead racks, and Yodel sleeping in her cage on the floor.

Billy thanked them as he wiped away the sweat on his forehead.

"What's that?" asked one of the twins suddenly, pointing at Billy's forehead.

"OMFG!" said the other twin. "Are you…"

"He is," said the first. "Aren't you?" He added to Billy.

"Who?"

"You're Billy Smith," said the twins in unison.

Billy was relieved when a voice from outside the train stopped the twins from staring at his forehead.

"Chad? Larry?"

"Coming, mother."

As the twins left, Billy leant against the window, half hidden by an old nylon curtain. He could just about hear the conversation the ginger-haired family were having on the platform.

"Where has Jacob gone?" asked the mother.

"Here he is now."

The oldest of the boys came towards them through the crowd. He was already wearing a long black dressing gown, which fell below his knees. As he watched, Billy noticed the boy had a small badge with a shiny letter L on it pinned to his chest.

"We need to make this quick, mother, dearest," he said. "The other house leaders and I have our own private carriage at the front of the train —"

"Well, of course," said one of the twins sarcastically. "We wouldn't want you having to mix with the riffraff at the back, would we?"

"Oh shut up," said Jacob.

"How come Jacob gets to go in first class?" asked the other twin.

"Because he's been made Leader of the House," their mother replied with pride in her voice. "Have a good year, dear," she then said to Jacob. "And be sure to send me a pigeon when you've arrived."

Jacob kissed his mother goodbye, tipped his top hat to the rest of the family, and then disappeared back into the crowd.

"Now, you two," said the mother, turning to the twins. "Please try not to get arrested again this year."

"It wasn't our fault," explained the first twin.

"Professor Crumbleceiling asked us if we wanted to help with something. How were we to know what he had planned?"

"Yes, well — just try to behave yourselves. And look after Edward, won't you?"

"Don't worry, little Eddie will be safe with us around."

"Shut up," said the youngest boy, looking embarrassed. "I'm tuss enough on my own!"

"Hey, guess who we just met on the train?"

Billy pulled the curtain forward a little, so they wouldn't see him watching.

"You know that kid who was stood near us at the ticket barriers? Guess who he is?"

"Who?"

"Billy Smith."

"Is he really, Chad? How can you be sure?"

"We asked him."

"Poor child – I wondered why he was alone. He was incredibly polite when he asked how to find the platform. But still, that means I owe Professor Crumbleceiling some money."

"And guess what else?"

"We saw his trademark too."

Their mother because suddenly very stern.

"Well, I forbid you to spend any more time looking at it. As if we can afford that."

"Okay, boomer, calm down."

The crowd on the platform seemed to be thinning now.

"You best all get on the train," their mother said, kissing the twins and her youngest son goodbye. As the three boys climbed onto the train, their younger sister started to cry.

"Don't cry, Gertie, we'll send you a letter every week."

"Yeah – we'll even send you a bootleg of Billy Smith's trademark."

"LARRY!"

"Only joking."

At that moment, a public announcement came from a speaker above Billy's head.

"Good afternoon and welcome to this, the twelve-hundred Frogsports Express service to Frogsports. This service will be calling at Frogsports only. We apologise for our delayed departure today, this was due to overrunning engineering works in a different part of the country. Due to a shortage of train crew being hired by the company, there will be no catering on this service."

There was a sudden jolt as the train began to move out of the station. Billy watched as the boys' mother and sister waved. A moment later, as the train entered a tunnel, they disappeared from view.

"Any passengers not intending to travel on this service today should have returned to the platform five minutes ago," the announcement continued. "My name is Christopher and I will be your conductor for today's journey. If there is anything I can do to make your journey a more enjoyable one, please do not hesitate to keep it to yourself."

The door of the compartment opened and the youngest ginger-haired boy came in.

"Do you mind?" he asked, gesturing at the empty seat across from Billy. "The rest of the train is full."

Billy shook his head and the boy sat down. "Thanks," he said.

"Hey, Ed."

The twins had returned.

"We're off to go annoy Jacob at the front of the train."

"Right," mumbled the boy.

"Billy," said the second twin, "did we introduce ourselves? I'm Larry Beaversley and this is Chad. And then this is Ed, our younger brother. See you both later then."

"Bye," said Billy and Ed together. The twins left, closing the door behind them and leaving an awkward silence as Ed stared at Billy. It wasn't until they sped through Milton Keynes half an hour later that he actually spoke.

"Are you really Billy Smith?" he asked.

Billy nodded.

"OMFG!" exclaimed Ed. "That's totally mental." He began pointing at Billy's forehead. "And have you actually got – you know..."

Billy pulled back his hair to reveal the trademark underneath.

"Wow!"

"But I don't remember getting it," said Billy.

"You don't remember anything?" said Ed, sounding disappointed.

Billy shook his head.

"So is everybody in your family a magician?" Billy asked, wanting to change the subject.

"All of them," Ed nodded.

"So you must know a lot of sorcery already?"

"The rumour is you went to live with Commoners," said Ed. "What are they like?"

"Awful – well, not all of them. But my aunt, uncle and cousin are – they're all *Daily Mail* readers."

"Oh, I've heard of that. It's sort of like a brand of toilet paper where journalistic integrity goes to die, isn't it?"

Billy nodded. "I wish I had three magicians for brothers instead."

"Five," Ed corrected him. For some reason, he looked as down as the price of a cryptocurrency following a tweet from *Elon Musk*. "I'm the sixth to go to Frogsports and I've got a lot to live up to. Two have already left – Issac got top marks and now works on a cruse ship entertaining passengers eight shows a week, and John does birthday parties. Now Jacob has become Leader of the House, too. Chad and Larry always mess around, but they're really popular and they've already signed up for a *Netflix* special. Everybody in the family expects me to do just as well, but if I do they'll just say I'm copying what they've already done. There's never anything new, either, with a family this big. I've got Issac's old dressing gown, John's old celery, and Jacob's old lizard."

Ed reached inside his pocket and pulled out a sleeping green iguana.

"His name is Scampers and he's useless. Jacob got a pigeon for being made Leader of the House, but my parents didn't have enough for — I mean, I was given Scampers to look after instead."

Ed looked suddenly out of the window. He seemed to think he'd said too much.

Wanting to make Ed feel better, Billy started telling him about his life with the Moustaches and how he'd always had to wear old clothes and was never given anything for his birthdays. This did cheer Ed up a little, because apparently he found enjoyment in other people's suffering. It even seemed to lighten Scampers' mood as he was now awake and staring at Yodel in her cage.

"... and until a month ago, I didn't even know that I was a magician, or who my parents were, or anything about Steven —"

Ed seemed to choke.

"What's wrong?" asked Billy.

"You said That-Evil-One's name!" said Ed. "Oh, sorry," he added a moment later as the cloud appeared above Billy's head.

"I'm not trying to show off by saying the name," said Billy. "I've just never learnt that you shouldn't — hold on, what's Scampers eating?"

They both glanced down at Scampers, who was chewing on something bulky in his mouth. Billy looked quickly at Yodel to check she was still safe in her cage.

"I don't know," said Ed, picking Scampers up. "But it's got a tail." He forced open Scampers' mouth and set free the hamster he was attempting to eat. Billy watched as the hamster limped out of sight under the seats.

While they had been talking, the train had taken them through the West Midlands, but as they looked out of the window to watch the fields passing by, it was hard not to notice they seemed to be slowing down.

There was a knock on the compartment door, and the dim-looking boy Billy had passed on the platform came in looking tearful.

"Sorry to disturb you," he said, "but have either of you seen a hamster?"

"Erm… no, sorry," said Ed, moving his jacket to cover Scampers.

The boy started to cry. "I've lost him again. He keeps escaping."

"I'm sure he'll turn up," said Billy.

"Yeah," agreed Ed. "He'll just be hiding somewhere, that's all."

"I hope so," said the boy through his tears. "If you see him…" and he left without finishing his sentence.

Ed waited until the compartment door had closed and the boy had disappeared, before pulling his jacket off Scampers.

"I can't believe it. He almost never wakes up, and then when he does, he goes and eats somebody's pet," Ed said in disgust. "Larry gave me a spell to turn him blue yesterday, want to see?"

"Yeah," said Billy eagerly.

Ed pulled a rather wilted looking piece of celery out of his pocket. He was just pointing it at Scampers when the compartment door opened again.

The boy was back, but this time he was joined by a girl who had already changed into her new Frogsports dressing gown.

"Has anybody seen a hamster? Josh has lost his," she said. She had a rather commanding voice, dark messy hair, and incredibly large front teeth, which gave her the appearance of a quokka trying to pass itself off as a human, just in case you'd forgotten it's perfectly acceptable to target someone's appearance in this world.

"We've already said, we haven't seen a hamster," said Ed, glancing guiltily at Billy, but the girl wasn't listening. She was staring down at the stick of celery he was pointing at Scampers.

"Oh, are you trying some sorcery? Show us, then."

She sat down and stared expectantly at Ed.

"Erm — okay, sure."

Ed cleared his throat and raised the celery. *"Jiggery-pokery,"* he said, swishing the celery down, but nothing happened except Scampers waking up and biting off the end of the celery.

"Hey," said Ed, pushing Scampers away as he came back for a second bite.

"I'm not sure that's a real spell," commented the girl. "If it is, it's certainly not a good one. I've only practised a few myself, but I've got *Alakazam, Open Sesame,* and *Hey Presto!* to work for me. I didn't think I'd be able to do any sorcery at first, though. No one in my family was a magician before me so I thought it would take ages to learn. But I've spent all summer reading our books and I guess I'm just a natural. I just hope that doesn't make anything too easy at Frogsports, but I've heard it's the best school of magical whizzing and kabooms there is, so I'm sure I'll still be challenged — I'm Elahoraella Parker, by the way, and who are both of you?"

She spoke very fast, and Billy was relieved to see Ed didn't seem to understand much of what she had said either.

"I'm Ed Beaversley," replied Ed.

"Billy Smith," said Billy.

"OMG!" said Elahoraella. "OMFG, even. Maybe even OMFG-ROTFOMFG-ing! Are you really? I know everything there is to know about you, of course — I even have a mug with your face on it."

"My face is on a mug?" asked Billy, feeling slightly creeped out.

"Oh, didn't you know? It's not just mugs. I've seen pens, phone covers, shot glasses too. I've even seen tattoos — though why grown adults want to go around with a teenage boy's face tattooed on their body..." said Elahoraella. "Do either of you have any idea what house you might be in yet? I hope to be sorted into Osphranter house, it sounds like the best," and she began jumping up and down as though to imitate a kangaroo. "But I suppose being sorted into Eudyptula house wouldn't be too bad." This time she imitated the waddle of a penguin. "Anyway," she said, sitting back down, "we'd better continue looking for Josh's hamster. You two should put on your dressing gowns, we have to change before we get arrive."

And with that, she left, taking the boy with her.

"What the hell was all that?" asked Ed. His whole face was twisted into an expression somewhere between confusion and amusement. "I just hope I'm not in the same house as her."

"What house are your bothers in?"

"Osphranter," said Ed. "My whole family has been in Osphranter house, so they all expect me to be as well."

They looked out of the window and noticed the train seemed to be slowing down even more now.

"We can't be there yet, can we?" Billy asked.

"Chad and Larry said the journey takes all day. It hasn't even started to get dark yet."

They came to a complete stop a few minutes later. Billy looked out of the window and noticed a platform sign nearby.

"We're in a place called Crewe," he relayed to Ed.

"It looks ghastly."

Billy agreed. "I wonder why we've stopped here, though."

He got his answer when a voice filled the compartment. "Good afternoon," the conductor began, "on behalf of the Frogsports Express, I wish to offer my apologies for any inconvenience, but due to a broken-down train on the line ahead, this service will today be terminating at Crewe. Please collect your belongings, exit the train, and make your way to the front of the station where staff will be on hand to help you continue your journey by rail replacement bus services."

Chaos and confusion followed. There wasn't enough room on the platform for this many students and all their luggage, and there was even less room than there might have been because of the passengers waiting for the delayed Llandudno Junction service.

By following a few of the older students who seemed to know where they were going – clearly this wasn't the first time this had happened – Billy and Ed found their way to the main road outside the front of the station where a member of staff told them that onward transport was on its way.

As they waited for the rail replacement buses to arrive, Billy and Ed continued their conversation.

"Which Frogsports team do you support?" asked Ed.

"I don't know any," Billy admitted.

"What? How can you not know any?" Ed almost looked offended. "Just you wait, you'll love it. It's the best sport in the world – and there he went, explaining all about balancing the ball on a hockey stick, how the back half of the horse was the hardest position to play because they had to balance on the inflatable unicorn without being able to see what they were doing, and describing the space hopper he'd like to buy if he had the money. He was just talking Billy through a few of the stranger rules when out of nowhere, a group of three boys pushed in front of them.

"Sorry, but we were here first," said one of the boys, glancing back at Billy. "Oh – so I guess it really is you?" Billy immediately recognised the boy as the blonde-haired one he'd met while buying his dressing gown. The boy seemed to have a lot more interest in Billy now than he had back in Upper Lower Upper Regent Street. "Billy Smith is coming to Frogsports," said the boy.

Billy glanced at the other two boys who were flanking the first as though bodyguards.

"Oh," said the blonde-haired boy, "this is Alastair and this is David," he continued, disinterested.

The other two boys looked at each other. "Are you Alastair or am I David?" one of them asked the other.

"I think I'm Austin," the second replied.

"No, I'm Austin," said the blonde-haired boy with an expression that said this wasn't the first time this had happened today. He turned back to Billy. "I'm Austin. Austin Hickinbottom."

Ed forced a cough to stifle his laugh, but it didn't work. Austin Hickinbottom looked him in the face.

"You think Hickinbottom is funny, do you?" Ed coughed again, and Austin stepped forward with his chest pushed out. "Do you want to go right now? I could have you." He pushed Ed back. "Yeah, come on. Let's go. Right here." He glanced back and noticed his two friends weren't backing him up. "What are you doing?"

"No, I think you're David and I'm Billy."

"You're both idiots."

"I thought I was Austin?"

At that moment, a couple of buses arrived, and the station staff began sorting students to board them. To their immense relief, Billy and Ed were directed to get onto the first bus, while Austin and his friends were told to board a different one.

"I hope you weren't fighting out there," said a voice as they took their seats. "You'll be in trouble before we've even arrived." Elahoraella was sat behind them.

"We didn't start it," said Ed aggressively.

"There's no need to be like that," said Elahoraella. "Anyway, I wanted to ask you a question. Do either of you notice anything about the other students?"

"No – what are we supposed to be looking for?"

"Well, I was looking around while we were waiting for the buses to arrive, and I noticed there doesn't seem to be much diversity – no one has a disability."

"Maybe somebody just figured it would be easier to pretend magic can cure anything?" said Billy. "Maybe they didn't believe they needed representation?"

"Everybody seems to be white too," said Elahoraella.

Billy looked around. Elahoraella did have a point; everyone he could see was white. But then he noticed a girl sat towards the front of the bus. "There's a black girl sat over there," he said, pointing her out to Ed and Elahoraella.

"Well, yes, that's true. But will she still be black if she becomes more important in our sixth year?"

They were on the bus for a long time, and by the time they finally came to a stop on a countryside road next to a set of tall wooden gates, night had long since fallen.

While the temperature outside the bus was much cooler than on it, everyone was relieved the journey was over. For the final few hours, there had been a strange smell coming from the toilet in the middle of the bus after Josh had used it, and it didn't help that people kept having to go in there to change into their dressing gowns.

As they looked around for some idea of where to go next, they heard a voice calling through the darkness. "First-years! First-years! First-years over 'ere!" A lantern came towards them, cutting through the black. As it got closer, Billy recognised the man holding it as Barry. "Ey up, Billy, lad – first-years!"

A group of around sixty students gathered around Barry. "Is ery'one 'ere? Grand. Nah all choose partner n' 'old 'ands wi' 'em – ah'm only pullin' theur' leg."

He led them through the gates and up a dark and narrow path. The only light came from the lantern Barry held at the front of the group, so they had to walk carefully to avoid slipping over on the wet ground.

"Theur all gerr' first look o' school jus' aroun' corner," Barry called over his shoulder before following up a moment later with, "Nah, 'old on. Maybe it's next 'un."

It was a few more minutes and many more corners before they eventually reached the shore of a giant loch, but no one had any interest in the loch. There was a collective "Oooh!" as they all gazed across the water to where a giant castle stood atop a mountain, its windows offering a glow of welcoming warmth and light.

"Reight, theur all need t' gerr' in't groups. n' dunt forget theurs' oars," Barry said, pointing towards a fleet of rubber dinghies bobbing in the water. "Ery'one ready?" he shouted once they were afloat. "n' off we nip – FORWARD!"

And they began rowing across the smooth surface of the loch, following the light Barry was still holding up in his own dinghy at the front of the group. As they got closer to the mountain, Billy looked up at the castle – there were so many towers, turrets, and battlements, he simply couldn't keep count.

"Careful now!" yelled Barry as they reached a small cave on the opposite cliff face. They continued forward into the cave until they came to a sort of marina underneath the castle. "n' 'ere we are."

Following Barry's lead, they climbed out of the dinghies and onto a damp stone surface.

"Nah 'ow many boats made it?" said Barry, and he began counting the number of dinghies. "Nine... n' we started wi' eleven." There was a pause. "Well, that's better than las' year, n' it means Nessie won't need feedin' tonight," and with that, he clapped his hands together.

But as he went to lead the group forward, he stopped. "'old on," he said, bending down to pick something up from one of the dinghies.

"Whose 'amster is this?"

"It's mine!" cried Josh, stepping forward with his hands outstretched.

"'e dunt look all that grand, does 'e? Ah can do summa' 'bout that."

"Can you?" Josh asked nervously.

"'course." And Barry threw the hamster overarm across the water. The hamster hit a damp stone wall at the other side of the cave, and then slid down into the water with a plop.

"'e's not feelin' pain no more," said Barry, patting a tearful Josh on the shoulder. "Nessie's puddin'," he then said to the rest of the group. "Come on then."

Josh remained still, as the rest of the group pushed past him to follow Barry up a slippery and moss-covered stone staircase. At the top of it, they turned a corner and were greeted by a wooden door.

"Welcome t' Frogsports," said Barry, and he reached out his gigantic hand to knock three times.

Chapter Seven

"Did She Say Live and Die?"

The door swung open to reveal a stern looking woman sat on a small wooden stool at the other side. She was wearing a long green dressing gown and had a pen sticking out of her mouth. She was so engrossed by something in the newspaper on her lap it took a moment before she realised anyone else was there.

"Oh, I'm sorry," she said, looking up at Barry and the first-years. "I was just finishing a crossword while waiting for you all – incidentally, does anybody happen to know what four down is? I thought it might have been ham sandwich, but then I looked again and noticed it only has seven letters, so now I think perhaps it might be origami – no? Never mind then."

"First-years f' theur, Professor McDouglass," said Barry.

"Yes, thank you, Barry," said Professor McDouglass. "You can hand them over to me now."

"T' you?"

"To me, yes."

"T' you then, Professor"

"To me then, Barry."

"T' you –"

"I think perhaps it would be best if you just went away now."

"Reight theur are, Professor." He turned and gave Billy a friendly pat on the shoulder. "Good luck, Billy." And with that, he left.

Good luck? What was he going to have to do that he needed to have good luck for? Billy started to feel suddenly quite worried.

"Follow me, please," said Professor McDouglass to the group, and they followed her down a tight stone passageway and up a set of stairs. When they reached another door, she pulled it wide open and led them into a giant entrance hall with a ceiling so high it could have fit twelve double-decker buses or approximately two-thousand and sixty-four *Cadbury Double Decker* chocolate bars stacked on top of each other.

The first-years followed her across the hall until they reached the middle, where they came to a stop as she turned to address them all.

"Welcome to Frogsports," she began. "I am Professor McDouglass, the deputy headmistress."

From the way she spoke, Billy got the sense that Professor McDouglass was not a teacher he wanted to get on the wrong side of, and indeed, only moments later she snapped at another boy who was too busy looking around at the flickering torches on the wall to pay any attention to what she was saying.

"... as I was saying," continued Professor McDouglass. "The start-of-year feast is set to begin shortly, however, before you can take your seats inside the Banquet Hall, you must be sorted into your new houses. While you are at Frogsports, you will live, die, and study alongside the other members of your house. Together, you will earn credits for your house, but be warned, you may also lose credits if you do not follow the school rules. At the end of the year, the house with the most credits will be given an under-catered pizza party and a pointless certificate to note down on their résumés."

"Did she say live and *die*?" Billy heard another ask their friend behind him.

"Pay attention, please," said Professor McDouglass. "The four houses are, of course, those which make up our school coat of arms. They are: Osphranter house; represented by a kangaroo, Gluteal house; represented by a donkey, Eudyptula house; represented by a penguin, and finally, Crocodilian house; represented by an alligator. Each of these four houses has a long and proud history, and each has produced outstanding magicians — well, expect for Gluteal house anyway, but they do try their best and provide some excellent comic relief for the rest of us."

There was a nervous sort of laugh among the group.

"The sorting shall begin shortly in front of the rest of the school. I ask that you all wait here patiently and quietly until I return."

She turned her back on them and went through a pair of high double doors at the opposite end of the entrance hall.

"How do they sort us into our houses?" Billy asked Ed.

"Chad told me it's some sort of contest between first-years."

Billy felt his mouth go dry all of a sudden. A contest? In front of the whole school? But he hadn't learnt any sorcery yet — what were they going to have to do? He looked around and saw everyone else looked just as terrified as he did, but he took little comfort from it.

And then something unexpected happened so suddenly that it scared them all much more than the prospect of an unknown contest ahead.

A group of about fifteen ghosts floated through the wall at the far side of the entrance hall. They had a translucent complexion to them, but were all still quite easy to spot. They seemed to be in conversation with one another. What looked to be an aged man with a sword through his whole body was saying to the ghost next to him, "I say we just hide down in the dungeons. It's too dark for him to see much down there."

"What about if we just turn ourselves invisible?"

"It's not very sporting of us, though, is it?"

A ghost wearing a top hat and a monocle noticed the first-years gazing up at them.

"I do say, new students," he said, floating down to greet them all. "Well, one would simply be most honoured to see the finest of your group meet my acquaintance later on, should you be sorted into Osphranter house – it's my own former band of brothers, don't you know?"

Even more surprising than the sudden appearance of the ghosts, the soulful rifts of a popular television theme tune started playing from behind one of the doors that led off the hall. As the first-years looked towards it, a voice started singing from the other side. "*IF THERE'S SOMETHING STRANGE IN THE NEIGHBOURHOOD, WHO YOU GONNA CALL?* – damn! The door's locked. Hold on a moment." There was a loud bang, and the door swung open to admit entry to an old man with long hair and an even longer beard. He was wearing a purple dressing gown, which seemed to compliment the colour of the star-shaped party glasses he was wearing over his eyes.

"*WHO YOU GONNA CALL? GHOSTBUSTERS!*" he finished singing as he stared up at the ghosts. "Aha! Found you – I win again."

"HEADMASTER!" said a sharp voice, and the man jumped about a foot in the air.

Professor McDouglass has returned.

"What do you think you are doing? The sorting is about to begin, and we very much require your presence in the Banquet Hall."

"Ah, yes, right you are – I knew there was something going on this evening," said the man. With a pop, he disappeared on the spot.

"Who was that?" Billy asked Ed under his breath.

"I think that was Professor Crumbleceiling," Ed replied.

Professor McDouglass shook her head, then addressed the group. "Please form a neat line," she instructed them. "We are ready to begin."

Unsure how he could still walk when his legs felt more stone than flesh, Billy got into line behind Ed, and they filed silently behind Professor McDouglass as she led them all through the double doors and into the Banquet Hall.

Never would Billy have been able to dream a place like this existed. Four long tables were set with golden crockery, which gleamed brightly in the firelight, coming from the hundreds of lit lanterns which seemed to be floating in midair above them.

Each of these tables was filled with students; Billy assumed they must have been sorted by house. At the furthest end of the hall, a fifth table ran across its width, where the teachers – all wearing top hats and dressed in different coloured dressing gowns – sat expectantly as

Professor McDouglass led the first-years down the middle of the hall towards them.

Then quite suddenly, they all began to bang into the back of each other as Professor McDouglass came to an abrupt halt halfway up the hall. "Well, where has he gone now?" she thought aloud.

There was a pop, and Crumbleceiling appeared on top of the teacher's table. "Here I am," but then he wasn't, because he'd just slipped on one of the golden plates and fallen backward off the table to hit the floor with an alarmingly echoey crash that reverberated around the hall like a sharp note being played on a didgeridoo in a zero-gravity wind tunnel.

"Oh, for goodness' sake," said Professor McDouglass. "Please somebody give me the strength."

"I'm okay," Crumbleceiling announced to the room as he got to his feet. "I meant to do that. I was only spooning down here," he said, and he picked up a tablespoon from in front of him.

As Crumbleceiling took his place in a regal throne-like chair in the centre of the teacher's table, Professor McDouglass continued to lead the first-years towards a giant inflatable surface that had been set up on a raised stage between the teachers and the students. As they formed a group by the side of the inflatable, Billy noticed the top of it had four rows of coloured dots; a row of green, a row of yellow, a row of blue, and finally a row of red.

Billy looked quickly down again as Professor McDouglass went to fetch a golden bell and placed it on top of a wooden table that stood a little away from them.

What were they going to have to do? Billy's mind began race, and he was only more confused when Professor McDouglass then placed a board with a plastic spinner attached to it on the table next to the bell. For a moment, there was complete silence. Then Professor McDouglass cleared her throat. "Students, teachers, and ghosts of Frogsports, welcome to the sorting of the students. Now, following complaints that last year's game of Ludo was not an entertaining spectator sport — and after rejecting suggested alternatives including poker, *British Bulldog*, and *The Hunger Games* — we have decided that this year, the sorting shall be conducted by the playing of a competitive game of —"

"*TWISTER!*" The whole hall burst into applause as Crumbleceiling got to his feet.

"Here we go again," Professor McDouglass told herself.

The applause only grew in volume as Crumbleceiling made his way down from the teacher's table to stand beside Professor McDouglass.

"You always have to take it too far, don't you, Headmaster?"

"So we've only got to play a game," Ed whispered to Billy. "I'll kill Larry, he was going on about how much it hurt… mind you, it sounds like it nearly could have."

Professor McDouglass stepped forward with a long sheet of parchment.

"When I call out your names, which I shall be doing in groups of three, you will join the headmaster on the board and the sorting shall begin," she said. "Once you are eliminated from the game, the colour on which you lose shall correspond to your new house."

The first game to be played was between "Jones, Eleanor", "Harrison, Helen", and "Sutherland, Lewis." Eleanor Jones and Lewis Sutherland became Eudyptulas when their heads collided on "right hand on blue," but Helen Harrison continued for five more rounds against Crumbleceiling until she finally slipped up on "left food red," and became a Osphranter. She made her way over to the Osphranter table, and Billy watched as Ed's twin brothers catcalled, because that is apparently a perfectly normal and acceptable thing to write about two men doing towards an eleven-year-old girl in a children's book, even though it should obviously not be.

"Beaversley, Edward." Ed stepped forward along with "Hickinbottom, Austin" and "Drake, Justin."

Ed went first, but fell early on "left hand red," to be sorted into Osphranter house, while Austin Hickinbottom managed two more rounds before becoming a Crocodilian when he lost his balance and slipped over on "right food on green." Justin Drake became the first to be sorted into Gluteal house, falling to Crumbleceiling in the next round. His walk over to the far left table was accompanied by jeers, which quickly turned into cheers as Crumbleceiling got to his feet and celebrated his win.

There were another three games before —

"Smith, Billy."

Silence fell across the room, save for a few whispers here and there as students asked the person next to them, "Did she just say Billy Smith?"

Billy stepped onto the game board and looked ahead at Crumbleceiling. "Ah, Billy, so glad to see that you've made it," said the headmaster. "But my god, I was right, wasn't I?"

Billy didn't know what Crumbleceiling meant about being right, but he didn't have much time to think about it, as they were soon joined on the board by an aggressive looking girl by the name of

"Allen, Makayla," and a less aggressive looking girl called "Bennett, Sophie."

Professor McDouglass called out their first instruction. "Left foot green." Billy, Sophie, and Crumbleceiling all managed it with ease, but Makayla Allen somehow managed to fall over straight away. As she sulked off towards the Crocodilian table, Crumbleceiling commented, "Slipped up on her sense of self-importance, that one."

Billy thought he was doing well as the game continued. By now, he had both hands on blue, his left food on green, and his right foot on red. Sophie Bennett was the next to fall, and she became as Eudyptula when she tried to put her "right foot on blue", but found there were no spots left she could reach.

"This is it, Billy, just you and me left," said Crumbleceiling. But try as he might, Billy couldn't keep his balance on "right foot red," and tumbled over to become a Osphranter. "Excellent game, though," Crumbleceiling said, standing up and patting him on the back. "You can be proud of that result."

Billy went off to join the waiting Osphranter table cheering for him. "We've got Smith! We've got Smith!" shouted the twins.

"Parker, Elahoraella," was up next, and she did the best yet, not only beating the other two students in her game (who both became Gluteals), but even managing after twelve rounds of sudden death to beat Crumbleceiling himself, who finally lost his balance on "right foot blue." Laughter roared out as Crumbleceiling ran off to the Eudyptula table before Professor McDouglass reminded him that he was a teacher and not a student. Elahoraella continued on her own for another couple of rounds before deciding on purpose to fall at "left hand red" and become a Osphranter.

Only three first-years were left to be sorted now. "O'Connor, Patrick," said Professor McDouglass, and a short haired boy with a freckly face stepped forward, "Jones, Simon," and a black boy took his place on the game board, and finally, "Hansen, Joshua." The boy who'd lost his hamster nervously got into position.

Patrick O'Connor and Simon Jones played well for the first few rounds, but then both fell on "left hand red" and joined the Osphranter table. Josh Hansen, however, seemed to be doing better than he'd expected. Then suddenly, he too became a Osphranter when he slipped up by making a stupid mistake on "right foot red."

Billy joined the rest of the table in cheering as Josh joined their numbers. At the front of the hall, Professor McDouglass had pulled out her enchanted celery, and with a flick, the inflatable game board and stage disappeared into thin air.

Billy could see the teacher's table properly now. At one end sat Barry, drinking from a gigantic steel tankard, while at the other end was Professor Quigley, the man Barry had introduced him to back at The Whine and Milk It in Upper Lower Upper Regent Street. He was busy talking to a very serious looking teacher.

After a brief argument with Professor McDouglass, Crumbleceiling climbed back on top of the teacher's table.

"GOOD EVENING FROGSPORTS!" he shouted to roars of cheers from all four tables. "COMING UP FOR YOU LATER, WE HAVE GOT ICE CREAM, APPLE PIE, CHOCOLATE BROWNIE, AND OF COURSE, JELLYYYYYYYY!"

Professor McDouglass appeared embarrassed to be sat so close to Crumbleceiling, but the rest of the hall didn't share in her disapproval and only cheered louder.

"BUT FIRST, IT'S TIME FOR YOUR MAIN COURSE! PLEASE PUT YOUR HANDS TOGETHER FOR HAMS, TAP YOUR FEET FOR FISH, AND OPEN YOUR MOUTHS FOR MEATBALLS!"

Professor McDouglass suddenly got to her feet, "And don't forget the vegetarian option," she added.

"Is the headmaster – a bit insane?" Billy asked Jacob, Ed's older brother, who was sitting next to him.

"Insane? Quite, yes," said Jacob conversationally, "but he's brilliant too. Are you hungry, Billy?"

Billy's mouth fell open at once. The plates on the table in front of him, which had been empty a moment ago, were now piled high with food. Everywhere he looked, he saw something different. He couldn't help but notice, however, that everything seemed to be labelled as coming from Britain.

"Not everything can be better when it comes from Britain, surely?" Billy said.

Jacob shushed him. "Don't say that out loud," he said. "You don't want to offend anybody with sensitive feelings. But yes, I know what you mean. Apparently Crumbleceiling managed to get a good deal on a bunch of stuff that was about to go bad because it was stuck in a lorry park in Kent – something about a driver from London attempting to enter Canterbury with an expired passport."

Just as Billy was starting his second helping, the ghost with the monocle and top hat who had greeted the first-years in the entrance hall appeared in front of him.

"It does smell good tonight," said the ghost in a deflated sort of voice.

"Can't you eat?"

"I haven't done so since the day I died," said the ghost. "It's not that I can't – it's just I was enjoying such a lovely meal when they came to chop my head off, and the idea of eating once more brings back such harrowing memories. Anyway, one doesn't believe I have introduced myself. I am Sir Walter Melvyn Scrivener Esq. and I am the ghost of Osphranter house. Charmed to meet your acquaintances."

"Good evening, Sir Walter," said Jacob, turning around at his voice. "How was your summer?"

"Dismal, good sir. Once more, my attempt to be cast in a touring production of *Les Miserables* was fruitless. One would think that having actually had your head removed by French revolutionaries would make you perfect for a role, but perhaps the producer believes I would just be a gimmick."

"You had your head removed?" asked Patrick O'Connor as he reached for another helping.

"Allow me to enlighten your mind –"

"Oh, please, Sir Walter, not while we're eating." But Jacob's pleas were ignored.

Sir Walter reached for a nearby pepper pot from the table, emptied a little onto his hand, then rubbed it below his nose. A moment later, he sneezed heavily, and his head came clean off the rest of his body and began rolling down the table. "Would somebody mind moving the gravy boat?" he said as his body began following after his head, "it's an awful mess to clean up if it gets in one's hair."

"Cool party trick," said Simon Jones.

"Yeah, but how do you put that on your *Tinder* profile?" Said Patrick.

Sir Walter caught up with his head and returned it to his shoulders before floating back to where they were sat.

"Anyway — I do hope you new Osphranters are going to help us get the most credits this year! We've never gone so long without winning. The Crocodilians have come in first place the past five years. Baroness Thatcher is becoming unbearable — she's the ghost of their house."

Billy looked over at the Crocodilian table and saw the ghost of a rather austere looking woman holding a handbag in her blood stained hands. She was sat next to Austin, who, Billy was pleased to observe, didn't look too comfortable about her being so close to him.

Sir Walter placed his hand on the top of his head and swung it round to look over at her. "Yes, that's her," he said.

"How did she get all that blood on her hands?" asked Patrick.

"A needless war here and there… killing a few hundred people… sowing the seeds of division and inequality… and starving some children, of course."

Once everyone had finished their main course, the plates of food disappeared and desserts appeared in the place.

As Billy helped himself to a slice of chocolate cake — skipping over the treacle tart which he thought looked repulsive — the conversation turned to their families.

"Well I'm Irish, which is why I have such a stereotypical name," said Patrick. "Me dad's straight, but me mam's a bisexual — and they say there's no diversity in these books! We've also got some family in Australia because an ancestor was transported to Van Diemen's Land for standing up to the British, but my back story is irrelevant — though maybe they'll try flesh me out a bit in the movies by, I don't know, doing something like making the Irish guy out to be the one who always makes things explode in a story set during the height of *The Troubles*."

Simon Jones went next.

"I'm black, and so is my mother and father," he said. "So that makes at least three of us, but you'll never hear about them or much about me because I'm relatively minor to the plot."

"What about you, Josh?" asked Ed.

"Well, I'm white and I'm also straight," said Josh, "so my arc will probably be essential to the narrative, and a lot of time will be spent developing my character."

There had to be more diversity than this, thought Billy. He looked around and noticed a girl of Chinese descent with a stereotypical name from the wrong part of Asia, and sat near her, a boy he thought might one day turn out to have been Jewish all along. He looked up at the top table and noticed the problem was even worse among the teachers.

In the middle of the table, Professor McDouglass was talking sternly to Professor Crumbleceiling. Next to them, Professor Quigley was still having a conversation with the serious looking teacher Billy didn't know. He was dressed all in black and had long hair that matched.

It happened very suddenly. The teacher with long black hair looked past Quigley and made eye contact with Billy. He pointed at his own eyes, then at Billy, and then finally he ran his finger across his throat as though threatening him.

"Who's that teacher talking to Professor Quigley?" Billy asked Jacob.

Jacob looked over at the teacher's table.

"Oh, that's Professor Grape. He teaches Alchemy, but he hates his job — he'd much rather have Quigley's."

Eventually, the plates of desserts disappeared, and the tables were left clean and empty. At the teacher's table, Professor Crumbleceiling got to his feet and the hall fell silent.

"Ahem — before we finish our evening, there are just a few reminders which I must give out to you all."

"First, students remain banned from entering the forest in the castle grounds, performing sorcery in the corridors, walking around the castle at night, and from reading any of the works of *Steven King*.

"Trials for house Frogsports teams will be held starting next week. Anybody who is interested in taking part should let their head of house know this week.

"And finally, I must inform you that the passageway on the second-floor is this year proscribed for all students. Take this as your warning that should you fail to adhere to this rule, detention will be the least of your concerns."

"Is he serious?" Billy asked Jacob.

"He doesn't sound like he's joking," said Jacob, looking curious. "It's strange, though. Normally he tells us why we can't go somewhere."

"And now, off to bed!"

The first-years got up from the table and began following Jacob through the crowds, out of the Banquet Hall, and up the giant stone staircase that led off the entrance hall. Billy, like the rest of the first-years, felt too tied to notice many of the things they were passing. They climbed staircase after staircase, dragging their feet as they walked. Billy was just wondering how much farther they had to walk when Jacob came to a sudden stop, and a pile up of tired first-years ensued behind him.

A *Live, Laugh, Love* t-shirt was floating on a hanger in midair ahead of them.

"Karen," Jacob explained to the first-years. "She's a poltergeist. A sort of crazy, loud, and negative spirit," he explained. Raising his voice, he said, "Karen — show yourself."

A rather privileged sort of huff answered.

Jacob pulled out a mobile phone and opened the camera app.

"Do you want me to post about this?"

There was another huff, and a short woman with blonde highlighted hair that was longer at the front than the back appeared floating ahead of them and holding up the hanger.

"I was looking at this t-shirt," she said, with the sort of entitled tone belonging to someone who really enjoyed the sound of their own voice. "But it's not my size. I'm sure you'd be able to adjust if for me, right?"

"Go away, Karen, or *TikTok* will hear about this, I mean it!" said Jacob.

"I didn't want this rubbish t-shirt anyway," and with that, she vanished, dropping the garment onto the floor.

"You have to watch out for Karen," said Jacob as they set off again. "The risk of being outed on social media is the only thing that can control her. Anyway, here we are."

They had reached the end of a long corridor where hung a portrait of a ballerina.

"We don't have a password for our common room," Jacob

explained to them. "We have a passdance instead. Allow me to demonstrate," he said, and he did a little tap dance in front of the portrait. The ballerina in the painting began twirling around on the spot, and as she did, a door appeared in the wall next to the portrait.

Jacob led them into the common room and directed them up a staircase to their dormitories where they at last found the welcoming sight of their beds. Their luggage had already been brought up for them. Yodel was sat in her cage cooing gently as she slept, while Scampers was sat on top of Ed's suitcase, eyeing her while licking his lips.

Too tired to talk much more tonight, they got changed and climbed into bed.

"The food is good, isn't it?" Ed muttered to Billy.

"Yeah," said Billy.

"Get off, Scampers! He's trying to eat the end of my celery again."

As he turned over in bed, it occurred to Billy that something quite important seemed to have been overlooked.

"Hey, Ed," he said.

"What's wrong?"

"Professor Crumbleceiling said we aren't allowed to walk around the school at night, didn't he?"

"Yeah..."

"But what about if we need the toilet? There isn't anywhere to go in the common room."

"That's a good point," said Ed. "And what about if we need to wash? Only the house leaders have bathrooms."

Chapter Eight

Anhydrous What to What?

"Is that?"

"I think it is."

"Where?"

"Look, next to the tall guy with ginger hair."

"Wearing the glasses?"

"Did you see the trademark on his forehead?"

"No, I don't have a licence."

Voices followed Billy everywhere he went from the moment he left bed the next day. As he walked down corridors, other students climbed on each other's shoulders to get a glimpse of him over the crowds, or otherwise stop him and ask for an autograph or a selfie.

While he was happy to oblige one or two requests, after a while, he began wishing they'd stop, because he was too busy concentrating on trying to find his way around to focus on much else.

There were some two hundred staircases spread around

Frogsports, and Billy had a hard time trying to work out where any of them went; it didn't help that it often changed from one day to the next. Then there were the doors, which weren't really doors at all, but would fall on top of you if you tried to open them. It was also difficult to remember where anything was when you did eventually find it, because even the walk down to breakfast each morning was disorienting enough to make you forget.

The ghosts which floated around the school didn't help much either. While Sir Walter Melvyn Scrivener Esq. was always ready to point Osphranters in the right direction, the same couldn't be said for any of the others. Karen the poltergeist whizzed around the castle, getting in the way of anyone she could, and acting as though she owned the place. She would push you out of line if you were queuing up for a lesson, threaten to call the police if you made her feel uncomfortable, throw anything she could reach at you if you told her to calm down, or sneak up in front of you, invisible, grab your shoulders and then start shaking you as she demanded to see your manager.

Even worse than Karen, if that was possible, was Kevin, the school caretaker. Billy and Ed had managed to get on the wrong side of him on their first morning, when they were unlucky enough to walk unprepared into a room where he was holding a *Neighbourhood Watch* meeting. They had stated to panic when the door locked behind them, but thanks to Billy's quick thinking, they soon worked out that all they had to do was aim for Kevin's weak spot three times. Once defeated, Kevin disappeared into a cloud of purple smoke and left behind a treasure chest containing a compass and map of the school.

The classes themselves were another experience still. Billy soon learnt there was a lot more to sorcery than simply waving around a magical vegetable and hoping for the best, even if Professor Crumbleceiling had told them that was all he ever did.

At midnight, they had to study the night skies through telescopes and track the movements of the planets. It wasn't easy either, because this was Scotland and there was no such thing as a clear night. Three times a week, they had to leave the castle and go out to a collection of greenhouses in the grounds where they were taught how to make a flower squirt water in the face of anyone who got too close.

One of their most interesting lessons was History, which they had on Tuesday afternoons. Their teacher, Professor Canisters, had spent their first lesson teaching critical race theory; a subject Billy had found both engaging and accurate. He was disappointed to find out the next day that all future lessons had been cancelled, because Professor Canisters had been fired after an ignorant parent had written into the school to complain about him teaching their son to be divisive.

Professor Millbrook, the Domestic Sorcery teacher, was a short magician who could barely see over the top of his desk. While he seemed friendly enough towards students, his habit of throwing to a commercial break whenever any of them tried to answer one of his questions became annoying after a while.

Professor McDouglass was the most alarming teacher they'd had so far. Billy had been quite right to think she wasn't someone to question or disagree with. They moment they had sat down in their first Transformation class, she had set down her rules.

"Transformation is the most complex sorcery you will learn during your time at Frogsports," she had begun. "It is the skill to transform one thing into another. It is also highly dangerous and bad behaviour will not be tolerated in my classroom. I believe that is clear enough."

Billy put his hand up to ask a question.

"Yes, Mr Smith – why, Professor Crumbleceiling was quite right, wasn't he? Next lesson, please sit towards the back of the classroom."

"Professor," Billy began, "could a girl change into a boy and a boy into a girl?"

Professor McDouglass' mouth seemed to shrink a little.

"Don't be stupid, boy," she replied. "Whatever gives you the idea that would be acceptable? No, my imagination does not stretch quite as far as to believe that girls can become boys and boys become girls. That would be preposterous and completely unbelievable," she finished, then she turned her desk into a pig and back again.

After making them write down pages of notes that Billy couldn't even begin to understand, Professor McDouglass had given them each a red passport and told them to turn the cover blue without sacrificing the national economy. By the end of the lesson, only Elahoraella Parker had made any difference to her passport, turning it a dark navy colour that looked almost black. While it wasn't exactly what she was looking for, Professor McDouglass nevertheless showed it to the rest of the class and commented how it was an impossible task that only a complete idiot would ever attempt anyway.

The subject everyone had really been looking forward to was Vigilantism, but Professor Quigley's lessons proved difficult to get to. His classroom was located in the middle of a large courtyard and surrounded by a deep moat. While there was a bridge across the moat, it was guarded by a troll who asked a riddle you had to answer correctly before being allowed to cross.

It took Billy multiple attempts, but after he eventually gave "Teach it to slalom a canoe" as the answer to "You can lead a fish to water, but you cannot what?" he was allowed to continue to class where he was relieved to find out he wasn't as behind everyone else as he'd feared. There were many people who had come from Commoner families, and they all knew just as little as he did.

Friday started well for Billy and Ed. That morning, on their way to breakfast, they had discovered two chests containing arrows and a third, rather ornate looking chest, which contained a boomerang.

As they began eating their breakfast, Chad and Larry Beaversley, Ed's twin brothers, came over to them. Larry was carrying a large piece of folded parchment under his arm.

"Good morning," said Chad, as he and Larry sat down at the table. "We've got a question for you, Ed."

"I haven't done anything," said Ed.

"We're not accusing you of anything," said Larry.

"We're just curious about something," said Chad.

"What about?"

"Well, we've got this map, see," said Larry, waving the parchment he was carrying.

"And it shows us the whole school and where everybody is inside of it," explained Chad.

"Yes, and we were looking at it last night and noticed there was a boy called Peter sleeping next to your bed."

"What?" said Ed. "There isn't a Peter in Osphranter house."

"We're only telling you what we saw, because it seems like something we would definitely notice and bring up straight away," said Larry.

"Anyway, we've got to go," said Chad. "We need to go ask Quigley why he's spending so much time with That-Evil-One – oh, sorry," he added, as the cloud rained onto Billy and Ed's plates.

"Do you think we should tell Crumbleceiling?" said Larry. "It would be the logical thing to do."

"No," said Chad. "It might shorten the story too much."

"What was that about?" asked Ed as the twins wandered off.

"I've no idea," said Billy. "What have we got today?" he asked, shaking his toast dry.

"Alchemy with the Crocodilians," said Ed. "Grape's head of their house. People say he always favours them."

"I wish McDouglass favoured us," said Billy, noticing her striding over to them. Professor McDouglass was head of Osphranter house, but that hadn't stopped her from continuing to berate Billy for knowing that trans rights were human rights.

At that moment, the post arrived. Billy was used to this by now, but it had given him a surprise on their first morning when dozens of pigeons had flown into the Banquet Hall during breakfast to deliver letters and parcels to their owners. He had also been most unfortunate to discover afterwards that it hadn't been a chocolate chip in his cornflakes.

"Ah, perfect timing, Mr Smith," said Professor McDouglass as Yodel crash-landed on the table in front of him. "I have a letter for you here that my pigeon delivered to me by mistake, and I believe yours may have my letter also." While Yodel had brought him something every day so far, none of it was yet to actually be addressed to Billy. This morning, as he took the letter Yodel clutched in her beak, he noticed Professor McDouglass' name on the front.

The swapped letters, then Professor McDouglass held up a magazine. "And do you by any chance happen to know to who this belongs? It was also delivered to me by mistake —"

At that moment, there was the clinking of a knife on glass, as Professor Crumbleceiling attempted to get everyone's attention from the top table. "Has anybody seen my reading material?" he shouted out.

"No matter, Mr Smith, I believe this particular mystery may have just resolved itself."

As Professor McDouglass made her way back to the teacher's table, Billy tore open his letter and read:

Dear Billy,

There's something I want to talk to you about. Why not come and have a cup of tea around four?

Barry

Billy scribbled his reply on the back of the letter, then gave it to Yodel, who took off again.

It was a good thing he had tea with Barry to look forward to, because the rest of the day turned out to be the worst he'd had so far.

At the feast on their first night, Billy had got the impression that Professor Grape didn't like him, but by the end of their first Alchemy lesson, he knew he'd been wrong. Grape didn't dislike Billy — he hated him.

Alchemy lessons were held in one of the dungeons underneath the castle. It was colder down here than the rest of the school, except for an area surrounding a mysterious locked door marked with the number four hundred and twenty, which led to a chamber that seemed to be producing a lot of unexplained heat. Billy thought it would have been creepy enough down here without the strange chemical scent that filled the damp and dingily lit corridors.

Grape started his class by taking the register, and just like every other teacher, he paused for a moment when he came to Billy's name.

"Ah, of course," he said slowly. "We have a new celebrity among us. Mr Billy Smith."

Austin and his friends Alastair and David laughed behind their hands. Grape finished taking the register, and then looked up from his desk to survey the class. His eyes pieced anyone who dared look into them.

"My name is Professor Grape — no relation to Professor Plum," he began. He spoke in little more than a whisper, but his very presence made certain everyone in the room remained silent enough to catch every word he was saying. "Though like Professor Plum, I did once kill many a man because I am a psychopath… even so, I am still somehow allowed to teach in this school full of children…"

A long, still silence followed this admission.

"You are here to learn the subtleties required to master the art that is alchemy," Grape continued. "There is little need to wave your blasted veg-e-tab-les in this class, and consequently, I expect many of you shall never appreciate the exact science that goes on within these walls. But if you choose to listen to what I say, then I can teach you how to trick the senses… to confuse the mind… to see something which isn't really there, even — so long as you aren't all as big a bunch of snowflakes as I usually have to teach."

A longer silence followed this speech. Billy and Ed exchanged looks of bemusement. Elahoraella Parker, however, was on the edge of her seat as though desperate to prove to Grape that she wasn't a snowflake.

"Smith!" said Grape suddenly. "What would I get if I were to mix pseudoephedrine, anhydrous ammonia, phosphorous, and lithium?"

Anhydrous what to what? Billy glanced at Ed, who looked just as confused as he did; Elahoraella's hand had shot into the air.

"I don't know, sir," answered Billy.

Grape's mouth curled into a cruel smile.

"Well, well — clearly fame is not everything, is it?"

He ignored Elahoraella's hand.

"Shall we try again?" said Grape. "Smith, where would you find me a bong?"

Elahoraella stretched her hand as high as she could without leaving her seat, but Billy had no idea what a bong even was. He tried not to look over at Austin, Alastair, and David, who were all openly laughing behind Grape.

"I don't know, sir," he said eventually.

"Did you not think about doing any reading before you came here, Smith?"

Grape stared into his eyes and Billy forced himself not to look away.

"What is the difference, Smith, between papaver somniferum and papaveraceae?"

At this, Elahoraella jumped to her feet, her hand reaching for the dungeon ceiling in a desperate attempt to be given the chance to answer.

"I don't know, sir," said Billy quietly. "Maybe you shouldn't be a teacher if you need me to tell you."

A few people around the room laughed silently. Grape, however, was not pleased.

"Sit down, you stupid girl," he snapped at Elahoraella before rounding on Billy. "For your information, Smith, pseudoephedrine, anhydrous ammonia, phosphorus, and lithium are the key ingredients of methamphetamine, along with two *Golden Globes* and twelve *Primetime Emmys* in the form of a hit series. A bong is a filtration device often used for smoking cannabis. As for papaver somniferum and papaveraceae, papaveraceae is the family of plant to which papaver somniferum belongs. Papaver somniferous also goes by the name of the poppy herb and is a common source of opium... Well? Why aren't you all copying that down?"

There was a rush as everyone went to grab parchment and ink from their bags. As grape returned to his desk, he said, "And as for you, Mr Smith, that is two credits from Osphranter house for your snark."

As the lesson went on, things didn't get any better. Grape has separated them all into small groups and set them the task of creating a Canadian by mixing the DNA of a British person with the DNA of an American. While Billy and Ed thought they were doing okay, even with Grape glaring over them every few minutes as he swept around the classroom, the same couldn't be said for Josh, who appeared close to tears again. And then, just as Grape was about to tell everyone to take in the welcoming smell of *Tim Hortons* coming from Austin's table, a bolt of lighting came from nowhere and hit test tubes in front of Josh, creating not a Canadian, but *James Corden*.

"Idiot boy!" said Grape. "Now there's two of them. *Oasis* will never get back together with twice the chance of him hosting their reunion."

As *James Corden* began handing out copies of his rider and *Googling* his own name, Grape turned his attention to Billy and Ed, who had been working on the next table.

"You – Smith – why didn't you warn Hansen about the lightning? Thought people hadn't learnt their lesson from *Jay Leno,* did you? That's another two credits you've lost for Osphranter house."

Billy opened his mouth to argue, but Ed stopped him with a well hidden kick underneath the table.

"Don't," he warned Billy. "Remember, Grape's killed a man."

"Many a man," Grape corrected him, leaning in close to breathe down their necks.

A short while later, they were ascending the staircase out of the dungeons and back into the main school. Billy's mood was low and his mind was racing. What sort of school was this place? And how were any of these people allowed to work with children?

"It could be worse," said Ed. "Chad and Larry told me Grape actually poisoned a student in their first lesson with him."

"Two students."

Grape had appeared behind them.

Billy and Ed remained still as Grape pushed past them and continued up the stairs. They waited until he'd turned a corner and disappeared from view before continuing.

"So, anyway – can I come meet Barry with you?"

After their final lesson of the day – in which they had learnt how to make an object disappear under a silk handkerchief – they left the castle and made their way across the grounds to a small wooden hut that stood near the edge of the loch.

As they approached the hut, they heard a voice shout, "Eh, gerr'off me land." They looked up. It was Barry, and he was walking a giant Labradoodle. "Oh, it's theur. Come on in f' brew."

They walked over and Barry led them inside his hut. There was only one room. A wooden bed stood along the far wall, and an open fire crackled against another. Above the fire was a sign that started with *In this house we...*

"Tek seat n' mek y' sens comfortable," said Barry. "This is Charlie." He took the lead off the Labradoodle, and it made straight for Ed, jumping on him and starting to lick his face. "Dunt worry y' sen, 'e won't 'arm theur."

"This is Ed," Billy told Barry, who was now preparing tea for them.

"Ey up, lad! Ah'm glad theur two o' y'. Ah've got summa' t' discuss."

He placed a mug of tea down a coaster which said *Let the Evening Be-Gin* for Billy, and a second for Ed on a coaster which said *It's Wine O'Clock*. Sitting down with his own mug, Barry reached for a catalogue on a nearby shelf and handed it to Billy.

"Is theur owt theur want t' buy from book?"

Billy turned the cover of the catalogue and examined the first page. There were pigeon cages on sale for half the normal price, a glow-in-the-dark toilet seat, a collection of bobble heads depicting the cast of a long-forgotten 1980s sitcom, a toaster which printed the face of Steve Buscemi on your bread, and for the garden, a life-sized statue of a zombie climbing out of the ground.

"Barry, what is this thing?" said Billy.

"It's me new business, 'course. Ah gerr' paid ery' time somebody buys summa' from book. Only, ah 'ad t' buy book in first place n' ah ain't 'ad a sale yet. Ah wor 'opin theur might buy summa' n' 'elp out."

While Ed took an interest in a nice collection of plastic food containers themed around the English market town of Stratford-upon-Avon on page two, Billy picked up a copy of the Riled Rag and read the front page:

SINO PAUPER EDO RECONDO MAMMONAS LEAK

Last night, an unnamed source inside the Sino Pauper Edo Recondo Mammonas Bank leaked that earlier this year, a high-security vault was broken into. A spokesperson for the bank has this morning commented that this information was released prematurely, and that the bank had always intended to make a public statement once investigations had concluded.

While unconfirmed at this time, sources have stated the break-in took place on the evening of the 31st of July, and centred around a single high-security vault. It is believed the Sino Pauper Edo Recondo Mammonas deposit in that vault was removed earlier that same day.

"Barry, this break-in happened the same day we were in Upper Lower Upper Regent Street. It might have been happening while we were there."

"Oh, dunt worry 'bout tha'," said Barry, avoiding eye contact as he took the paper from Billy. "Now, 'ow 'bout one o' these novelty dino noggin trophies t' 'ang on y' wall?" he continued, pointing at page three of the catalogue.

As Billy and Ed trekked back up to the castle for dinner an hour later, Billy couldn't help but think about the break-in and how eager Barry had been to change the subject. Barry had emptied a high-security vault that day. Was it the same one? Had Barry taken whatever it was the thief had wanted before they could get to it? And if he had, where was it now?

Chapter Nine

"Well, There Goes My Tenure"

Billy didn't think it would have been possible for him to meet a person he hated more than Yate, but that was before he'd met Austin Hickinbottom. He felt lucky, though, that they didn't have to see much of him, as the only lessons they shared with the Crocodilians were Alchemy. Or at least that was until they read a notice that had been pinned up in the common room one morning.

First-years would be starting bouncing lessons on Friday afternoon, and the Osphranters would be learning with the Crocodilians.

"Brilliant," said Billy, as they made their way down to the Banquet Hall for breakfast. "Just the way I wanted to end the week. Spending more time with the Crocodilians."

He had been looking forward to learning how to bounce and finding out about the rules of Frogsports considerably more than the writer of this book had been about working out what they actually were.

"Look on the bright side," said Ed, "We'll get to see Austin embarrass himself. I know he keeps talking about how great he is, but I bet he's just trying to show off."

Austin certainly spent a lot of time talking about bouncing, and he was always complaining to whoever would listen about how unfair it was that first-years weren't allowed their own space hoppers and never got picked for their house team.

He wasn't alone, though. In fact, all those who'd grown up in magical families talked of nothing but Frogsports most of the time. Ed had already had an argument with Simon Philips, who shared their dormitory, about football. Ed just couldn't understand what was so interesting about a sport that didn't have a pantomime horse as a Keeper.

Josh had never been on a space hopper in his life, and he'd never been allowed to own a hockey stick. His grandmother had always thought it might be dangerous to let him. Billy, he had to admit, thought she had a good point, because Josh was an idiot who neither knew what was best for himself or ever realised when he had something valuable in his life that was worth keeping.

The only person more nervous about bouncing than Josh was Elahoraella Parker. Bouncing wasn't something she could learn by studying from books — not that she hadn't given it a good go. At breakfast on Friday, she sat at the table reading a book she'd taken from the library called *Frogsports: A Tale of Highs, Lows, and then Highs Again*. She didn't seem to find much that would help her though, and everyone was relieved when her complaints about the book being too lily pad out with pointless facts were interrupted by the arrival of the morning post.

Billy hadn't received a single letter since the one from Barry inviting him for tea, or at least not any actually addressed to him. Today Yodel dropped two letters in front of him. The first was addressed to the Russian Embassy in Washington, D.C. — the return address on the back told him it had come from 1211 6th Avenue — and the second to a boutique shoe shop in Stavanger.

A second pigeon flew down and dropped a small package in front of Josh. He opened it excitedly as the pigeon flew off. "It's from my gran," he said, taking out a small black fly-like object from inside of it. "It's a Reflyder!" he explained. "She knows I'm always forgetting things — this helps remind you what you've forgotten. Look, you just let go, and if you've forgotten something, it bites you and you remember."

He let go of the Reflyder. It flew a lap around his head and then landed on his hand. "Ouch!" he said as the Reflyder bit him. "Potatoes, onions, and apples all have the same taste," he said. "The only difference is the smell. If you put a peg on your nose and wore a blindfold, you wouldn't be able to tell one apart from the other two."

Josh was just remembering how *Arthur Conan Doyle* (best known for creating *Sherlock Holmes*) was knighted in 1902 for his work defending the British Army's invention of the concentration camp during the Boar War, when Austin Hickinbottom, who had found an excuse to pass by the Osphranter table, grabbed the Reflyder off of Josh's hand.

Billy and Ed got to their feet, hoping for the chance to fight Austin, but Professor McDouglass appeared out of nowhere by their side.

"What is going on here?" she asked, suspiciously.

"Austin took my Reflyder, Professor."

"Hickinbottom, is that true?"

Sneering, Austin let the Reflyder go.

"I was just admiring it," he said, and he strode off.

"*Brigadier Sir Nils Olav the Third* is a penguin holding high rank in the Norwegian King's Guard," said Josh as the Reflyder landed back on his hand. "He often inspects the troops of the King's Guard and can be recognised by the military badge he wears on his right flipper."

"Are you feeling okay today, Mr Hansen?" asked Professor McDouglass.

"No one has ever witnessed an ostrich burying its head in the sand."

Billy and Ed were just taking their seats again when — "SMITH! BEAVERSLEY!" said Professor McDouglass. "Just what do you think you are doing?"

"Professor?" said Billy, unsure what he was supposed to have done wrong.

"Those croissants you're eating. Why are they bendy?"

"They came like that."

"Well, it really won't do. It's far too European. We can't have bendy croissants in this school." And she took out her enchanted celery and pointed it as the pastries. Billy and Ed watched as the croissants uncurled in front of them. "There we go. It's much easier to spread butter and jam on them when they're straight."

At two o'clock that afternoon, Billy, Ed, and the rest of the Osphranter first-years made their way out of the castle and into the grounds for their first bouncing lesson. It was a clear and warm day, but a light breeze caused waves to ripple through the grass as though the wind was being conducted to a fully orchestrated arrangement of *Himno Nacional Argentino*.

As they approached the flat plain of lawn by the edge of the loch, they found the Crocodilians were already there, and so were twenty deflated space hoppers lying in neat lines on the grass. Billy had heard Chad and Larry Beaversley complaining about the school space hoopers and how they had a habit of puncturing too easily, or how if the air inside them because too hot, they'd start screaming about being the unfair target of a campaign to cancel them.

Their teacher, Madam Webb – because apparently sport wasn't important enough to give her the title of professor – arrived. She had short, brown hair, and orange eyes with circular black pupils. Elahoraella had told the Osphranters at lunch about how Madam Webb had been a professional Frogsports player, starting her career with the *Hannover Hopscotches* before becoming captain of the *Tiverton Tadpoles* and leading them to a historic win against the *Newport Newts* – the match was said to have been so tense the team mascot, *MC Hopper*, actually passed out and had to be substituted with S*noop Froggy Frog*.

"Good afternoon," she said, moving between them. "If you could all please stand by a space hopper, and we'll get right to it."

Billy glanced down at his space hopper. The colour was faded and it had a face drawn on it that looked rather sad. Still, thought Billy, it looked better than Ed's, which was a patchy orange and sporting a toupee.

"Now, I want you all to stick both hands out as though you're holding down an invisible balloon," Madam Webb instructed them.

"Then when you're ready, say *inflate*!"

"Inflate!"

Billy's space hopper filled with air at once, the sad face on the front becoming one of instant glee. No one else had such luck. While Ed's space hopper had inflated, it had become much larger than expected, and was now making whoopee cushion noises from the unusually small mouth drawn on the front of it."

"Yours has a face drawn on it too," laughed Billy.

"That's not a real – oh, wait, it is," said Ed.

Madam Webb came over to help him. "Ah, Mr Beaversley. You've drawn the short straw I'm afraid – paper straw, that is – and become the person to show us the phenomenon we call Donald Toad." She turned to the rest of the class. "Donald Toad is what happens when you're not paying enough attention. That's why it's always important to focus on what's going on."

She took Ed's overinflated space hopper and gave him a spare one. Then she began walking between the students and helping them inflate their own. When the class were ready to move on, she showed them how to mount and grip their space hoppers.

Billy and Ed found it hard not to laugh when she told Austin he'd been doing it wrong his whole life.

"Okay, I think we're ready to start bouncing," said Madam Webb. "When I blow my kazoo, I want you all to bounce three times on the spot, and then stop again. On my kazoo then. Three… two –"

But before the kazoo had even touched Madam Webb's lips, Josh had taken a bounce forward – then another – and another – on his fourth he bounced straight over the rest of the class, but he didn't stop there. He was bouncing higher and higher, and then – SMACK! –

he bounced into the broad trunk of an oak tree and fell backward onto the grass in a heap.

"Well, there goes my tenure," Madam Webb said to herself.

She ran up to Josh and bent over him. "It's okay boy," Billy heard her say. "You've only *Ryanaired* yourself — it's all right, up you get."

She turned to the rest of the class.

"None of you are to go anywhere or do anything until I return. Not one bounce while I help this boy to the hospital wing, or you'll be hopping your way straight out the front gates."

Madam Webb led a tearful, limping Josh back towards the castle. "Come on, we'll get you fixed."

"What does she mean he *Ryanaired* himself?" Billy asked Ed.

"It's when you have a really uncomfortable journey and end up no where near where you actually wanted to go."

"I thought *Ryanairing* meant somebody also has to start clapping at the end?" said Patrick O'Connor.

"Maybe if the idiot was being bitten by this stupid thing, he'd have remembered to book with a better airline."

Billy turned around. Austin was wearing a smug expression and holding up Josh's Reflyder.

"Give that here, Austin," said Billy, fronting up to him. The Crocodilians all stopped laughing to watch.

Austin gave a quiet "heh" as he sized Billy up. "I don't think I'm going to do that."

"GIVE IT HERE!" Billy shouted, but Austin had jumped onto his space hopper and was now bouncing away from the group.

Billy grabbed his own space hopper.

"Coming to get it, are you, Smith?"

"Don't do it," said Elahoraella Parker. "Madam Webb told us to stay where we are — you'll get into awful trouble."

Billy ignored her. He mounted his space hopper and bounced off after Austin. And then he felt it — a feeling like he'd never felt before. A feeling that he could leave all his worries two inches below as he skimmed the tops of the tallest blades of grass. He felt the breeze in his hair, and his dressing gown catching the wind as though it was a parachute. This was easy, he thought to himself. This was wonderful. He pushed down hard on his next landing, and the momentum pushed him upwards to even greater heights. There was a cheer from Ed as he reached a clear five inches off the ground.

Austin stopped a little ahead and watched Billy with a stunned expression on his face.

"I said give it here, Austin," Billy called. "Or I'll put a puncture in that space hopper."

"Oh, yeah?" Said Austin, his confidence faltering slightly.

Somehow, Billy knew what he had to do. He leant forward and tightly gripped the handles of the space hopper. Suddenly he was bouncing twice as fast, and Austin only just got out of the way in time to avoid the mild discomfort of a friction burn on his lower leg. Billy made a turn, and both he and the smily face on the front of his space hopper began staring Austin down.

"No Alastair and David to help you now, Austin," said Billy.

"Have it then," said Austin, and he threw the Reflyder at Billy.

Billy could see it coming straight for his face and knew he'd need a plaster if it hit his nose. He thought about ducking out the way, but at the very last moment he bounced upwards, and on his way back down, he reached out his arm and swatted the Reflyder from its flightpath and down to the ground.

"BILLY SMITH!"

He felt himself deflate quicker than a puffer fish in a *YO! Sushi*. Professor McDouglass was running over to them. He got off his space hopper and stood waiting nervously.

"Never – in all my time as a teacher –"

Professor McDouglass seemed to be in shock, and she looked furious. "How dare you, Smith – do you have any idea? – You might have suffered whiplash –"

"It wasn't him, Professor –"

"Be quiet, Mr Beaversley. Smith, follow me."

Billy could hear Austin and the rest of the Crocodilians laughing as he followed Professor McDouglass numbly back towards the school. He was going to be kicked out, he was sure of it. He wanted to try to defend himself, to explain why he'd done it, but he didn't seem to be able to say anything. Professor McDouglass led him down corridors, through doors, up staircases, and then down another, all without saying anything to him.

Eventually, she led him to the bridge leading to the Vigilantism classroom.

"Why could the dog's owner not say exactly how long the dog had been playing for?" asked the troll that guarded the bridge.

"I don't know," said Professor McDouglass. "The owner's watch was broken?"

"Incorrect."

"Smith, do you have any ideas?" she said, finally speaking to him.

"They could only give a ball-park figure?"

"They could only give a ball-park figure?" Professor McDouglass repeated to the troll.

"Correct," said the troll, moving out the way to allow them passage.

"That was very good, Smith," said Professor McDouglass, turning back to Billy and looking impressed.

She told Billy to wait there and crossed the bridge alone. He watched as she knocked on the classroom door and then went inside.

A moment later, Professor McDouglass came back out, but she wasn't alone. A tall fourth-year boy Billy had seen in the common room followed her. The boy looked just as confused as Billy was now feeling.

Professor McDouglass led the boy across the bridge, told Billy to follow as well, and then continued down another corridor.

"In here," she said.

Professor McDouglass pointed them into a classroom which was empty, except for Karen, who was busy adjusting the validity dates on a pile of coupons.

"Out, Karen!" she said sternly.

Karen looked up at her. "I DEMAND TO SEE THE MANGER," she said, floating towards them.

"I am the manager and you are banned."

Professor McDouglass pulled a mobile phone from the pocket of her dressing gown and pressed record.

"NO – DON'T VIDEO ME – STOP VIDEOING ME." Billy couldn't understand why Karen kept moving closer to the camera if she didn't want to be recorded, but Professor McDouglass' plan seemed to be working. "YOU'RE ATTACKING ME – STOP ATTACKING MEEE..." As her voice faded away, Karen exploded into a burst of negative energy.

Professor McDouglass put away her phone and rubbed her hands together. "That is how you deal with that," said said, turning back to them with a smile.

"Now, Smith, I would like you to meet Henry Plank. Plank, you know who this is already, of course, but let me introduce you to your new Swatter."

Plank's confused expression faded immediately.

"Do you mean it, Professor?"

"Certainly," said Professor McDouglass sincerely. "The boy's a natural. I've just watched him and I've never seen anything like it. Was that your first time on a space hopper, Smith?"

Billy wasn't sure what was going on, but he didn't appear to be being expelled. "Er, yes," he said. "That was our first bouncing lesson."

"I'm telling you, Plank, he swatted that thing down as easy as anything," said Professor McDouglass. "And it was fast too – add in the sun shining in his eyes, and well, he's exactly what the team needs."

Plank looked as though he was the happiest he had ever been.

"Ever watched a game of Frogsports, Smith?" he asked.

"Plank is the Osphranter team captain," explained Professor McDouglass.

"He's the right build to play Swatter, too," said Plank. "Agile – quick – he'll need a good space hopper, though, Professor – nothing less than a BunnyRibbit Eleven or a Merry-go-Bounce, if we want him to play his best."

"I shall see what can be done about that," said Professor

McDouglass. "I've got evidence the headmaster has stealing office supplies again, so I'm sure I can convince him to loosen the first-year ban."

"You must be joking — really?"

It was dinner. Billy had just told Ed what had happened when he'd left the grounds with Professor McDouglass.

"Swatter," said Ed. "But first-years never make — you must be —"

"More important than everybody else, so these things will always happen to me," said Billy. "That's what Professor McDouglas told me."

Ed stared at Billy with admiration.

"Training starts next week," said Billy. "But Plank doesn't want anybody to know I'm on the team."

Chad and Larry Beaversley entered the hall, found Billy, and ran over.

"Good one," said Chad in a whisper. "Plank's just told us the news. We're on the team too — Bouncers."

"I think this is our year for sure," said Larry.

"Anyway, we've got to make a convenient exit so some other characters can enter. See you."

Chad and Larry had been gone barely a moment when someone far less welcome appeared: Austin, with Alastair on one side and David on the other.

"Your train home delayed, Smith? Have time for a quick meal first?"

"You seem a lot braver now you've got your little friends with you," said Billy. It might only have been a figure of speech, but if Josh's Reflyder landed on your hand, you'd suddenly remember that neither Alastair nor David were little.

"I could take you on anytime on my own," said Austin. "Tonight, if you're not too scared. Magician's duel. Sorcery only. What's the matter? Never heard of a magician's duel before, Smith?"

"Of course he has," said Ed, getting to his feet. "I'm his assistant, who's yours?"

Austin looked at Alastair, and then to David.

"David," he said, shrugging. "We'll start at midnight, if that's not past your bedtimes? We'll meet you in the security office just off the main hall."

When Austin had walked off, Billy turned to Ed. "What is a magician's duel?" he asked him.

"It's where two magicians face off by seeing who can pull the biggest objects out of the smallest hat."

"And what do you mean, you're my assistant?"

"Well, an assistant is there to go *ta-da*!" said Ed.

"*Ta-da*?"

"*Ta-da*!"

"And what if I can't pull anything out of the hat?"

Ed shrugged. "Just pull it over his head and push him down the stairs."

"Excuse me."

They both looked up. It was Elahoraella Parker.

"I couldn't help but overhear what you and Austin were talking about —"

"Of course, you couldn't," said Ed.

"— and, well, I think it's very stupid to be fighting with him. Especially at night. Think of what will happen if you get caught — and you're bound to be. Think of the credits you'll lose Osphranter house. It's very selfish of you."

"And it really is nothing to do with you," said Billy.

However annoying he might have found Elahoraella, as he lay awake, waiting for midnight to arrive, he had to admit she had a point about their chances of being caught. Chad and Larry often talked about their nighttime adventures around the castle, and none of their stories failed to include at least one close encounter with a teacher. Billy and Ed didn't know their way around as well as the twins, and they certainly had no idea where any of the hidden shortcuts or hiding places were. On the other hand, Billy wanted nothing more than to face Austin head on.

"Quarter to twelve," said Ed at last. "It's time to go."

They pulled on their dressing gowns, picked up their enchanted celeries, and made their way quietly out of the dormitory, down the stairs, and across the common room. They were just about to reach the door when a voice spoke behind them. "I can't believe you're both risking this."

Ed let out a high-pitched scream, but Billy covered his mouth before it could wake anyone up.

"Thanks," said Ed.

A light flickered on as they turned back. Elahoraella Parker was sat in an armchair.

"What are you doing here?" asked Ed.

"I'm here to stop you."

"This is nothing to do with you."

Billy couldn't believe anyone could be so interfering, but he wondered if a less negative adjective or perhaps even a heroic description might be used later on if a male character did the same thing.

"Come on," said Billy. "We need to go." He pushed open the door and stepped out into the corridor.

Elahoraella wasn't prepared to give up just yet, however, and she followed them out of the common room.

"Don't you care about the rest of our house? You'll lose so many credits if you're caught."

"We're less likely to get caught if you just shut up."

"Okay, but don't say I didn't warn you."

"Be quiet, both of you!" said Billy suddenly. "I can hear something."

Ahead of them, the sound of snoring came from the darkness.

"Do you think it's Kevin? He might have fallen asleep on guard duty."

But it wasn't the caretaker. It was Josh, and he was curled up on the floor, fast asleep. He jolted awake as they got closer.

"Oh, it's you three," he said. "I've been stuck out here for hours. I couldn't perform the new passdance to get into the common room because of my arm." And he showed them the sling supporting his left arm.

Billy pulled Josh's Reflyder out of his pocket and handed it back to him. "Here. I got this back from Austin for you," he said.

"Thanks, Billy," said Josh. He let the Reflyder go, and it landed on his hand. "Did you know that the town of Cormorant in Minnesota elected a dog called Duke as mayor for four consecutive terms?"

"Er, sure — look, Josh, Ed and I have somewhere we need to be. Elahoraella will help you get back into the common room —"

"Oh no, I won't," said Elahoraella sternly. "I'm coming with both of you so that I can tell a teacher exactly what's going on if you're caught."

"Don't leave me here alone," said Josh, getting to his feet. "Baroness Thatcher has already been past three times to call me a drain on the state."

Billy glanced down at his watch — it was now five minutes to midnight — and then glared at Josh and Elahoraella.

"Fine, come with us then. But just be quiet."

They ran along corridors and down staircases, stopping every few moments to listen for the sound of approaching teachers. At every turn they expected to run into one of the ghosts or Kevin, but they were lucky. When they reached the entrance hall, it too was empty. They ran across it and entered through the small door they knew led to the security office.

What they found inside came as a surprise. Along one wall was a large desk with at least forty computer screens set up around it, each of them showing a camera feed from a different part of the castle. They watched Professor Crumbleceiling playing air guitar atop the teacher's table in the Banquet Hall before noticing another screen where Professor Grape was looking suspicious as he carried equipment out of one of the school greenhouses. There was no sign of Austin or David anywhere.

"Maybe they're too scared to come?" said Ed.

"Or they're just late."

"Oh my goodness," said Elahoraella, pointing at one of the screens.

"What is it?" asked Billy. "Can you see them coming?"

"There are – slaves. Slaves are cleaning the school at night. I can see them on the cameras."

They both looked at where she was pointing.

"I know what they are," said Ed. "They're elves."

"I don't think we're supposed to know about this for another few years," said Billy.

"Really, Billy, is it any better to be taught about slavery as though it's a perfectly normal and acceptable thing when we're fourteen compared to when we're eleven?" said Elahoraella.

Billy thought about this for a moment – Elahoraella was right. There was something seriously messed up about introducing slavery to children by framing it as being okay so long as privileged people don't have to clean up after themselves.

And then a voice made them all jump.

"In the 1960s, the CIA attempted to train a cat to become a spy, so they could eavesdrop on conversations between Soviet operatives, but the mission failed because the cat kept ignoring instructions when it was hungry."

They had almost forgotten Josh was with them and for a moment thought Kevin had found them.

"Be quiet, Josh, or somebody will –"

"IS ANYBODY IN THERE?" This time it really was Kevin, and he was stood just outside the door.

Billy made straight for a second door which he knew led to the Banquet Hall, and waved for the others to follow. They made it just in time. As Billy closed the door behind Josh, he heard Kevin talking.

"Hiding are you?" he called out. "I know you're in here somewhere. I heard you."

"I think we'll be safe –"

He fell silent as he turned around and found himself face to face with Professor Crumbleceiling, who had just stage dived onto Ed, Elahoraella, and Josh.

"I won't say anything if you don't," said Crumbleceiling. Silently, they gave each other a nod.

Crumbleceiling bowed them all goodnight and left.

"Come on!" Billy said to the others. Scared about running into another teacher, they left the Banquet Hall, ran back across the entrance hall and up the stairs to a corridor on the second floor.

They were just catching their breath when Josh declared, "Chickens can get depressed."

"Shut up –"

"Who was that?"

It was Professor McDouglass' voice that spoke this time.

"Run!" whispered Billy, and the four of them sprinted down the corridor, not looking back to see if anyone was following – they turned the corner and ran down a corridor then another, Billy leading the group but not knowing where he was leading them to. They came to a stop outside Professor Millbrook's classroom.

"I think we're okay here," Billy panted. "I don't think anybody followed us."

"Don't the teachers ever sleep?"

"I – told – you," Elahoraella gasped. "I told you this would happen."

"We need to get back to the common room," said Ed.

"Austin tricked you," said Elahoraella. "You know that, don't you? He just wanted to get you both kicked out."

"That doesn't matter now," Billy snapped at her. He nodded at Ed and then said, "Let's go."

But no sooner had they started to run again when a ghostly figure flew past them, then stopped to block the way forward.

It was Karen, and she looked as though she'd just found her prey.

"Ooo, you're not mangers, are you? You're not even supervisors — I could get you all expelled if you don't help me."

"Go away, Karen."

Karen laughed.

"I've got a little problem you can help me with first — I've got this t-shirt, see, and it says *If you don't have anything nice to say, don't say anything at all.* But it doesn't work. People still talk to me and tell me to get over myself."

"How is that our problem?"

"Should call corporate, I should," said Karen in a superior voice. "They'd explain how it's your problem."

"Just leave us alone," snapped Ed, but he knew right away he had made a mistake.

"POLICE! POLICE!" Karen screamed at the top of her voice. "HELP, I'M BEING OPPRESSED! THEY'RE DENYING ME MY FREE SPEECH!"

Diving under Karen, they ran for it. They turned a corner and sprinted down a long corridor with just a single door at the end of it — but it wouldn't open.

"What do we do now?" said Ed, panicking. "The door's locked."

"In ancient China, owning locks and keys was a status symbol afforded only to the wealthy. The ruling class often had padlocks shaped as animals," said Josh.

"How is that helpful right now?"

Behind them, they could hear running as Kevin followed Karen's shouts.

"We're done for," said Billy.

"Oh, move over and let me do it," said Elahoraella, pushing Billy out of the way. She pulled out her enchanted celery, pointed it at the lock and whispered, "*Open Sesame*!"

The lock clicked and the door swung open – they rushed through it, closed it behind them, and then listened with their ears pressed up against the wood.

"Where are they, Karen?" they could hear Kevin asking. "Which way did they go?"

"*Excuse me*? I don't work for you. You work for me."

"Just tell me where they went."

"Are you paying me to help you? I think you'll find that it's *you* who should be telling *me* where they went."

"I think we're safe," whispered Billy. "Karen isn't telling him anything – stop it, Josh!" Josh had been pulling at the sleeve of his dressing gown. "What?"

Billy turned around – and saw, quite clearly, that they weren't safe at all.

They weren't in a cupboard as he had thought. They were in a passageway. They were in the proscribed passageway on the second floor. And now they knew why it was proscribed.

They were staring straight into the eyes of a gigantic mallard duck. A duck with two heads that filled the whole passageway.

Two pairs of black eyes that blinked curiously at them; two giant bills that could crack them in half as easily as if they were twigs. They looked down; two enormous webbed feet which could crush them all with a single step. It was as if the *Quacken* had risen.

"I'm sure there's a simple *egg-splanation* for this," said Billy.

"Do any of you have any *duck tape* with you?" asked Ed. "We could tape its bills shut."

"Why don't we distract it with food? I saw something on a *duckumentary* about that once."

"I don't have any *quackers* with me."

"What about some *quackamole*?"

"Will you stop *quacking* jokes and focus," said Elahoraella.

"We could throw a *fire-quacker* to startle it?"

It was Josh's turn. "Ducks don't normally mate for life. Most ducks seek out a new mate each year, often choosing the strongest and healthiest mate for that breeding season."

One of the duck's heads moved forward and gently nudged Ed as though checking to see if he was ripe.

"I think we should stop with the wise *quacks* now."

Billy's hand searched for the doorknob as, "QUACKKKKKK!" The duck's second head harmonised with its first. Billy found the knob and as he pushed the door open, they fell backward out of the passageway. Billy jumped to his feet and slammed the door shut before the duck could push one of its heads through.

They were grateful that nothing else happened on their way back to the common room. Kevin had obviously gone off to look for them somewhere else, while Karen must have gone to leave the caretaker a negative *Google* review.

Billy performed an out-of-breath version of the passdance and they clambered into the common room before collapsing silently into armchairs by the fire. It was some time before any of them spoke.

"That duck had a *quackitude,*" said Ed finally. "What's it doing inside a school?"

Elahoraella had got her breath back, and she was in a bad mood. "Didn't any of you use your eyes?" she snapped. "It was standing on something."

"Standing on something?"

"Didn't you see the trapdoor below its feet? It's obviously guarding something."

"Protecting something from a *robber ducky,* you mean?"

Elahoraella stood up, glaring at them.

"I hope you're both very pleased with yourselves. You could have got us all killed."

"We didn't make you come with us."

"Go *duck* yourself, Ed," said Elahoraella. And with that, she went off to her dormitory.

Ed felt Elahoraella's comment had been *fowl*-play, but as he climbed back into bed five minutes later, Billy was thinking about something else she had said. The duck was guarding something… and then he remembered what Billy had told him months earlier; *the only place more secure than the Sino Pauper Edo Recondo Mammonas Bank was Frogsports.*

It looked as though he had just found out where the tiny package Barry had taken from vault sixty-nine was now hiding.

"Hey, Billy," whispered Ed from his own bed. "This place is

seriously messed up, isn't it?"

"Yeah," said Billy. "It is."

Chapter Ten

The Ancient Egyptian Goddess Heqet

Austin Hickinbottom, Billy was pleased to see, looked incredibly unhappy at breakfast the next morning. Clearly, he was annoyed to see his plan to ensure Billy and Ed were expelled hadn't worked as well as he had hoped.

Far from being annoyed with Austin, Billy and Ed thought coming face to face with the giant two-headed duck was the most exciting thing that had happened all year, and they were eager to go out another night to discover what other secrets the castle was hiding. In the meantime, their conversation had been about whatever the duck might have been protecting. Billy was certain it had to be whatever was in the package Barry had taken from the vault at Sino Pauper Edo Recondo Mammonas.

"It's got to be something really valuable," said Ed. "If they're going this far to protect it."

"It could be dangerous," said Billy.

But all they knew for certain about whatever the mysterious object was, is that it was small enough to fit inside of Barry's pocket and had a strange ammonia-like smell to it.

Neither Josh nor Elahoraella had any interest in joining in with the speculation. The only thing Josh cared about was never going near the duck again, and Elahoraella was still so angry she refused to even talk to them. Not that Billy or Ed minded the silence, because Elahoraella was a girl, and so in this world her desire to do well in life apparently made her a bossy know-it-all, rather than an intelligent and ambitious person.

"The post is late again," said Billy, looking up at the high pigeon-free ceiling. "It's been getting later every morning."

"Didn't you hear?" said Patrick, reaching over for the toast rack. "They're saying deliveries will be much later in the day now."

"What?" said Ed.

"Why?" asked Billy.

"I don't know, but I heard it's something to do with this new postmaster that's been appointed."

"I heard that, and it will take twice as long to deliver parcels," added Simon.

"It's true," said Josh, almost tearful. "My gran is sending me a new hamster, but… but it hasn't arrived yet."

Billy spent the morning wondering exactly when the post might show up, but it wasn't until he was on his way to lunch that he got his answer.

As he and Ed came into the entrance hall from the staircase leading to the dungeons, there was a loud cooing that echoed above them. Billy looked up with the rest of the students and watched as what appeared to be a giant sphere wrapped in brown paper packaging came towards them. He was amazed to realise a moment later that the package was being carried by Yodel, but he felt confused when she ignored him and gave the parcel to Ed instead. Then she landed on the floor and began pecking at Billy's foot. He looked down, and she dropped a small card in front of him before flying off again.

"What was that about?" asked Ed.

Billy picked up the card. "Sorry I missed you. I've left your parcel with a neighbour," he read.

He took the parcel from Ed and noticed a letter taped to the top of it. It was a good thing he decided to open the letter first, because it read:

DO NOT OPEN THE PARCEL IN FRONT OF THE OTHER STUDENTS.

It contains your new BunnyRibbit Eleven, but if anyone else finds out you've got your own space hopper, they'll all want one. Henry Plank will meet your outside at six o'clock for your first training session ~ good luck.

Professor McDouglass

Billy was coming to learn that whenever people wished him luck at Frogsports, it was usually because something dangerous was about to happen, but he didn't have time to worry about that right now.

They decided to go up to their dormitory and unwrap the space hopper in private, but just then a voice called after them. "What's that you've got there, Smith?"

It was Austin.

"It's none of your business," said Billy.

Austin grabbed the parcel from Billy's hand and felt it.

"That's a space hopper," he said, shoving it back at Billy with glee in his face. "You'll be out for sure this time, first-years aren't allowed their own."

"It's not just any space hopper," said Ed. "It's a BunnyRibbit Eleven. What did you say you've got at home, Hickinbottom, a HoppityClop Four?" Ed was enjoying this. He smiled at Billy. "The HoppityClop has a good bounce, but it doesn't cushion the landing quite like the BunnyRibbit does."

"What would you know about it? I bet you couldn't even afford an old HopInTheToad."

Professor Millbrook appeared.

"Not fighting are we, I hope?" he asked.

"Somebody's sent Smith a space hopper, sir," said Austin with a cruel smile.

"Ah, yes, I'm glad to hear it's arrived," said Professor Millbrook. "Professor McDouglass was starting to worry the postal service wouldn't deliver it in time for your first match. What model did she get you?"

"It's a BunnyRibbit Eleven, sir," said Billy.

"Ah, the BunnyRibbit. Yes, I used to ride a BunnyRibbit Three when I was younger – bounced my way to victory in the *Gambol National* on one in fact."

"*Gambol National*?" Billy asked Ed as they made their way upstairs a few minutes later.

"My dad watches that. It's an annual race where magicians bounce their way around a course. I never knew Millbrook had won it, though."

Billy had difficulty trying to keep focus in lessons that afternoon. His mind kept leaping back to the package, waiting for him upstairs, or hopping off to the Frogsports stadium outside where he'd be learning the rules in a few hours. He skipped dinner that night and rushed straight up the dormitory with Ed as soon as their final lesson was over. At last, it was time to unwrap the BunnyRibbit Eleven.

"I'm going to need help unwrapping it," said Billy, unable to contain his excitement.

"Right," said Ed, "both of us together."

"One each end and steady as we go."

They ripped off the brown paper, and the scarlet red space hopper rolled across the bed.

"Wow," said Ed. "You know they fill the BunnyRibbit with pure nitrogen because it's so much better than air."

Billy didn't know the first thing about the different makes of space hopper, but he thought the BunnyRibbit Eleven looked magnificent. Unblemished with a shine all over, save for a rough path that offered superior grip on the handles. It even had an inbuilt pressure gauge measuring the air inside.

As six o'clock approached, Billy left the dormitory and made his way out of the castle to the Frogsports stadium in the grounds. He'd never been inside here before. Rows and rows of seats lined the pitch, which was as green as a shamrock in St Stephen's Green, while the water surrounding the netball nets at each end was as still as unrequited love's wilted flower trodden into the floor of a broken down lift at Heathrow Terminal 3.

Eager to bounce again, Billy mounted his space hopper and pushed up with his feet. What a feeling of complete freedom – two inches high, three inches high, four inches high – he felt a thrill of adrenaline each time he hit the ground before soaring upward once more.

"Hey, Smith, come over here!" Henry Plank had arrived. He was carrying a bulky crate under one arm. Billy bounced over to him.

"The BunnyRibbit Eleven, very nice," said Plank. "I'm only going to teach you the basics tonight, and then you can start joining team practise sessions twice a week.'

He opened the crate and took out a rugby ball from inside.

"Now then," said Plank, throwing the rugby ball between his hands. "The rules of Frogsports are easy enough to understand, even if the person who created them have no idea how they'd work in practise. Each team is made up of eight players."

"Eight players."

"Three of them are known as the Attackers."

"Three Attackers, got it," said Billy. "And they've got hockey sticks?"

"That's right — I see you've been reading up. Each of the attackers has a hockey stick which they use to hit the ball between them, take shots at goal, and make sure the ball doesn't hit the ground. The Attackers job is to get the ball through the other team's netball hoop at the end of the pitch — they have to do it from a distance, though. They're not allowed to touch the water. Five points are awarded for every goal scored."

"What happens if they drop the ball?"

"Well, it depends on the circumstances. In most cases, it's just a penalty and the other team gets possession of the ball. But things are different if the fifth Tuesday rule applies."

"What's the fifth Tuesday rule?"

"If the match is played in a month with five Tuesdays in it, every third foul awards the other team a bonus of ten points, and every sixth foul means the referee must inhale a balloon full of helium. Are you with me so far?"

"I think so – the Attackers pass the ball using hockey sticks. If they get it through the net, it's five points. If they drop the ball, it's a penalty and the other team takes possession."

"Unless –"

"Unless the fifth Tuesday rule applies."

"Yes… unless the full moon rule applies, that is."

"Full moon rule?"

"If in the week prior to the match any of the players eat poultry on a night when there's a full moon, then all fouls become fowls, and any player who commits one must play the remainder of the match with a live chicken under one arm. For the second offence, the chicken is switched for a turkey."

"What about if the player is a vegetarian?"

"Then for the first offence it's a lettuce, and for the second the lettuce is swapped with a cashier who works at *Whole Foods*."

"So dropping the ball is a penalty, unless either the fifth Tuesday or full moon rules apply?"

"Yes… unless the collided fates rule applies."

"What's the collided fates rule?"

"If the two team captains have star signs which compliment each other, then the whole match must be played in slow motion."

Billy thought it best not to ask if there were any other rules. "What are those for?" he asked, pointing into the crate.

Plank placed the rugby ball down on the floor, and then took two long blowpipes out of the crate. He handed one to Billy.

"These are used by the Bouncers – there's two on each team. Ours are Chad and Larry Beaversley."

"What are they used for?"

"I'll show you."

Billy watched as Plank reached into the crate and pulled out a small dart. He loaded the dart into the top of the blowpipe, aimed it into the distance, and gave a sharp blow. The dart flew out the end of the pipe as a blur and disappeared into the darkness where – "Ha, you missed me," came the voice of Professor Crumbleceiling.

"Now you have a go," said Plank, handing Billy a dart.

Billy loaded the end of the blowpipe and aimed towards the same area Plank had. He gave a sharp blow and – "You hit me that time…" the voice faded out and was replaced by the dull thud of a body hitting the ground.

"What's in these things?" asked Billy.

"Oh, it's just a simple sleeping draught. You come around soon enough, but usually not until after the match is over."

"So the Bouncers go around firing blow darts at the other team?"

"That's right. Most often they aim for the other team's Swatter because if they can take them out, it makes it impossible for the team to win."

"And I'm our Swatter?"

"Yes – but don't worry," he said on Billy's sudden change of expression. "The Beaversley twins are good playing Bouncer, and they can usually take out their opposite numbers early on in the game."

"So what do you do?"

"Well, each team has two Keepers who work together as one horse," Plank explained, "and I'm the front half of our Keeper. I wear the horse's head."

"How do you wear the costume while using a space hopper?"

"The Keepers don't bounce around. It's only the Attackers, Bouncers, and Swatter who have to move around on space hoppers – while dressed as frogs, of course. No, the Keepers guard the nets while using inflatable unicorns to float on the small pool that makes up each goal area."

"The Keepers float, and the rest of the team bounces. I think I've got it."

"And as captain, I also have another role. If there's a draw – that is, if both teams' Swatters are taken out by the Bouncers before the other comes around again – then it's my job as captain to duel the other team's captain to decide the outcome of the match.

"Erm – do people ever die during a match?" asked Billy, attempting to sound casual.

"Sometimes, yes. And there were a couple of serious injuries last year which required people to go to hospital. You don't need to worry about any of that, though. There's only one thing that should concern you."

Billy thought he probably did need to worry about all that, but he watched as Plank lifted a small glass jar out of the crate.

"This," said Plank, "is the platinum fly, and it's the most important part of the game. It's almost impossible to see because it's so small and extremely fast. It's your job as Swatter to swat the fly before the opposing team's Swatter can do the same. If you swat the fly, you end the game, Smith. If you swat the fly, you win the game – I mean, it pretty much renders the entire rest of the match a complete waste of time for all involved, but those are the rules. So – any questions?"

"What happens if the fifth Tuesday, full moon, and collided fates rules all apply in the same match?"

"It's rare, but it does happen. In that case, the sudden death rule would apply."

"What does that mean?"

"It means sudden death. If any player gives away a penalty, the match is immediately halted so that player can be sacrificed to the *Ancient Egyptian Goddess Heqet*."

Billy wasn't sure if he wanted to play Frogsports anymore, but Plank wasn't going to let him back out at this stage.

"Right, we won't practise with the platinum fly tonight," said Plank, putting the glass jar back into the crate. "It's getting dark, and we don't want to lose it. I've got some of these instead."

He pulled a bag of pebbles out from his pocket, and a few minutes later, he was throwing them at Billy for him to swat as he bounced around the pitch on his BunnyRibbit Eleven, a fly swatter in one hand. After half an hour, during which Billy didn't miss a single one, they called it a night.

"That Frogsports cup is ours this year," said Plank confidently as they carried the crate back up to the castle. "You play like Issac Beaversley used to, and he could have gone international if he hadn't started performing in variety shows on cruise lines."

Maybe it was because he had so little free time, what with all his homework on top of Frogsports practise sessions twice a week, but Billy could hardly believe he was coming to the end of his second month at the castle. He felt more at home here than he ever had with the Moustaches, though, considering everything that went on at the school, he wasn't entirely sure this was a good thing.

They woke on Wednesday to the smell of pumpkin pie floating through the whole castle. It was Halloween, and the teachers had gone all out to decorate the school for the occasion. Even better, at the start of their Domestic Sorcery lesson that morning, Professor Millbrook announced they were going to learn how to make objects fly. Professor Millbrook had paired them up. Billy was partnered with Patrick O'Connor, while Ed was put with Elahoraella Parker. This made the lesson very uncomfortable for both of them, because Elahoraella still hadn't spoken to Ed or Billy since the night they had discovered the two-headed duck.

"Now, don't forget the delicate movement we've been practicing!" said Professor Millbrook as the class pulled out their enchanted celeries. "Twist and jab, remember, twist and jab. And don't forget to make sure you get the words right, too. Mistakes can be very costly in sorcery — never forget the person who thought *I should tweet this* instead of *I should keep this to myself* and inadvertently alienated a large part of their fan base."

It wasn't nearly as straightforward as Professor Millbrook made it appear. Try as they might, no matter how much twisting and jabbing they did, Billy and Patrick just couldn't get the autographed photo of a well-known American daytime talk show host (Professor Millbrook had bought them as an investment before they became even less valuable than the show's production crew in the eye's of the titular star) they were supposed to be levitating to lift off the desk.

At the next table, Ed wasn't having much more luck.

"*Hocus-Pocus*," he shouted, poking the autograph with the end of his celery.

"You're not saying it right," Elahoraella snapped at him. "It's *Hocus-Po-cus*, you need to make the *ho* and *po* sound longer and clearer."

"You should me how it's done then, if you're so good at it," said Ed.

Elahoraella rolled up the sleeves of her dressing gown, twisted her celery, and said, "*Hocus-Pocus!*"

Their autograph lifted off the desk at once and began spinning in midair.

"Aha," cried Professor Millbrook excitedly. "Everybody look at this — Miss Parker has got it already!"

Even though he was able to practise on his own for the rest of the lesson, Ed still had no success. By the time the class ended, he was in an irritable mood. "She's unbearable, honestly," he said to Billy as they made their way down the crowded corridor. "No wonder no one likes her."

Someone pushed through the middle of them. It was Elahoraella, and she looked as though she was about to cry.

"I think she heard you," Billy said to Ed.

They didn't see Elahoraella for the rest of the day, but on their way down to the Banquet Hall for the Halloween celebrations, they overheard Helen Harrison talking about how Elahoraella had been crying all afternoon and was skipping the feast to catch up on the work she'd missed.

Ed looked somewhat guilty at this, but that soon went away when they entered the Banquet Hall, and any thought of Elahoraella was put out of their minds by the sight that greeted them.

The lanterns which floated above the tables had been dimmed a little, and real cobwebs had been spun against the walls to give the whole hall a spooky feel. Most of the school ghosts were getting into the spirit of the occasion by making themselves invisible, gliding up the tables, and then reappearing suddenly to frighten a student. Baroness Thatcher wasn't so high-spirited, however, and she stayed at the head of the Crocodilian table complaining that if children had enough time to celebrate Halloween, then they also had enough time to start working and building character for later life.

"Has anybody seen the headmaster anywhere?" Professor McDouglass was asking a group of Osphranters as Billy and Ed took their seats. "No one has seen him all day."

This feast was the best yet. Billy was just reaching for a slice of steak pie he liked the look of when Professor Quigley ran in through the double doors, an expression of upmost fear on his face.

Silence fell across the hall as students stopped eating to watch as he sprinted up the hall between the Osphranter and Gluteal tables. There was an audible "*Oooh, that must have hurt,*" as he tripped up and slammed his face onto the solid stone floor, but he got back up again straight away.

Reaching the table where the teachers were sitting, Quigley went straight for Professor McDouglass and collapsed onto the table in front of her before gasping, "School inspector — downstairs in the dungeons — they've got a clipboard."

And then he fell unconscious and sank to the floor without saying another word.

"Oh — bollocks," said Professor McDouglass.

There was an immediate panic across the hall, most of all from the teacher's table.

"Where is the headmaster?" asked Professor McDouglas in a

panic to no one in particular. She looked around as though he might be hiding behind her chair, but Crumbleceiling was nowhere in sight.

"We need to stop them from talking to the students!" Professor Millbrook's voice rang out from somewhere nearby.

"Yes, that. I'm on it."

Professor McDouglass took her enchanted celery from her pocket, pointed it high at the ceiling, and said, "*Abracadabra!*"

A firework shot out of the end of the celery and exploded into a flash of light above where the students were all fighting to get out of the hall. They fell still and turned to look at Professor McDouglass.

"Leaders of your houses, take your students back to your common rooms immediately. Do not talk to anybody on the way."

"You're on fire, Professor," said Professor Millbrook.

Professor McDouglass examined at the end of her celery, which was indeed on fire. "So I am." She blew the fire out and continued, "Teachers, follow me — and don't forget to bring your fake lesson plans — except for, where is he? Ah, Professor Grape, please hide yourself in a cupboard and if anybody asks, tell them you're a mature-aged exchange student from Bristol."

For Jacob, Ed's older brother and the leader of Osphranter house, it was as though Christmas had come early. While he might have felt relaxed enough to sit back and fall asleep while those around him suffered, he loved telling those same people what to do even more.

"All of you, follow behind me! Stick together and don't leave any gaps! There's no need to panic if you listen to what I say — I know what's best for you! Excuse me, I'm leader of the house!"

"Why are we having an inspection now?" Billy asked as they

began climbing the stairs.

"Don't ask me. Frogsports is a private school, they hardly ever get inspected," said Ed. "Maybe Professor Crumbleceiling forgot to make a donation to the government this month."

As they passed a group of terrified Gluteals going the other way, Billy grabbed Ed's arm and held him back.

"What is it?"

"Elahoraella," said Billy. "She doesn't know there's an inspector here."

Ed looked hesitant.

"Oh, fine," he said. "But Jacob mustn't see us."

They detached themselves from the Osphranters and merged with the passing Gluteals until they were back at the bottom of the staircase and could slip down an empty corridor. They had just turned the corner at the end of the corridor when they heard footsteps behind them.

"Quick," said Ed, pulling Billy behind a giant stone statue.

Peering around it, they saw Grape glancing around as though checking to see if anyone was watching. Believing no one was there, he crossed the corridor and disappeared from view.

"Why's he here?" Billy whispered. "I thought he was supposed to be locking himself in a cupboard?"

But before Ed could reply, he took a few short sniffs and said, "Can you smell something?"

Billy sniffed too, and a strong aroma hit the inside of his nostrils. It was a mix of cheap flowery perfume and the sort of air fresher an honest friend might buy you if they were trying to tell you something.

And then they heard it — the tapping of high heels on stone.

There was a voice too. "The school has a questionable approach to the welfare of students." Ed pointed – at the end of the corridor, they could see a shadow coming towards the light. They stepped back behind the statue and watched as it emerged.

It was a frightening sight. Five foot five, she was wearing a long skirt and patterned blouse under her jacket. On her face, she wore circular spectacles, and in her hand was a bright acrylic clipboard on which she kept scribbling notes.

The inspector stopped near the open door to the Transformation classroom and stuck her head through. "Well, access is certainly better than in some other classrooms," she said, and she went inside.

"Look," said Billy. "Professor McDouglass has left the keys in the lock. We could lock the inspector in."

"Great idea," said Ed nervously.

As quietly as they could, the edged towards the door, their hearts pounding with every step. "Some of the posters on these walls don't look very inclusive," they heard the inspector say. Holding his breath, Billy reached for the handle and slammed the door shut.

"Come on!" he said triumphantly as he turned the key. But a moment later, he wished he hadn't.

A high, petrified scream came from inside the classroom.

They looked each other in the face, both as white as the school roll.

"Elahoraella!" they said together.

Facing the inspector head on was the last thing they wanted to do, but what choice did they have? Billy unlocked the door, and together they ran inside the classroom.

Elahoraella Parker was crouched in the corner of the room,

looking as if she was about to faint. The inspector was advancing on her, asking questions as she went. "Do you think you get enough support from your teachers? Do you find your lessons fascinating and engaging? Are you provided with useful feedback from your teachers after you hand in a piece of work?"

"Confuse it!" said Billy. He picked up a thick leather bound book from a desk and slammed it onto the floor.

The inspector stopped and turned around to look at Billy. "Oh," she said, and then she made for him instead, scribbling notes on her clipboard as she advanced. "Do you feel challenged at school?"

Billy did something that was either very brave or very stupid; He ran towards the inspector, wrestled the clipboard from her hands, and threw it across the room. The inspector seemed to stall for a moment, but then she rounded on Billy again. "Do you think the school's discipline procedure is fair?" she asked, glaring at him.

As the inspector cornered Billy, Ed pulled out his enchanted celery and pointed it at the back of the inspector's head. Thinking fast and panicking, he said the first words that came into his head: *"Hocus-Pocus!"*

The inspector's glasses flew suddenly from her face and hovered above her head. "Oh," she said, "I can't see anything without my glasses."

"Do it now, Billy," Ed shouted.

Billy stood tall and screamed the words into the inspector's face. "THAT-EVIL-ONE!"

It happened immediately. A grey cloud appeared above them both. First, the thunder startled the inspector, then the lightning made her jump back. Finally, as she gazed up at her glasses, still floating above her head, rain water fell from the cloud and obscured her vision.

"Does anybody have a towel?" she asked.

Her glasses dropped to the floor, and she got to her knees to find them. But unable to discern anything clearly, she crawled into the side of table and then fell unconscious as a vase of flowers fell from the tabletop and landed on top of her head.

Loud footsteps came from outside the classroom, and a moment later, Professor McDouglass entered, closely followed by Professor Millbrook, with Professor Quigley bringing up the rear. Quigley's face was bruised and bloodied from when he'd tripped over in the Banquet Hall. He looked down at the inspector and jumped.

Millbrook bent over the inspector. "It's okay, she's still alive," he said. "I expect we might lose a few marks for this, but I'm sure it's nothing we can't make up from our boarding facilities to avoid special measures."

Professor McDouglass turned her focus to Billy and Ed. Billy had never seen her look so angry. Her lips looked as whitewashed as a government report into systematic racism.

"What on earth has gone on here?" she asked them, with fury in every syllable. Billy looked at Ed, who didn't seem to know what to say either. "You're both lucky you weren't signed up to a focus group. Why aren't you in your common room with the rest of Osphranter house?"

Then a small voice came from the corner of the room.

"Professor McDouglass, please — they came looking for me."

"Miss Parker!"

Elahoraella had got to her feet.

"I went looking for the inspector because I — I thought I'd know the right things to say — you know, because I'm top of our class."

Billy's mouth fell open in shock. Elahoraella Parker, telling a lie to a teacher's face? "If they hadn't found me, the school would probably have been given a requires improvement rating, or maybe even inadequate."

"Well — in that case then," said Professor McDouglass, staring down at the three of them, "Miss Parker, you stupid girl. We don't want the inspector to meet students like you —"

"We get more money if they think every student is underperforming, see," explained Professor Millbrook.

"That's right," said Professor McDouglass. "And we need to fix our pension deficit somehow."

Elahoraella looked guiltily down at her feet. Billy was speechless. Elahoraella was the last person he'd expect to do anything that would upset the teachers, and here she was, admitting to doing precisely that, to get them out of trouble. It was as if Grape had gone cold turkey.

And then something that was even more of a surprise than Elahoraella telling a lie happened.

With a loud pop, Professor Crumbleceiling appeared in the middle of the room wearing moose antlers on his head and holding a bottle of vodka in his hand. "Okay, bitches, who's up for beer pong?" He looked around the room at each of the faces staring at him, and then said, "Not the appropriate time. I've got it."

"Miss Parker, ten credits will be taken from Osphranter house for this," said Professor McDouglass, doing her best to ignore Crumbleceiling. "I'm most disappointed in you. If you're feeling okay, you'd better get back to the common room. Students are continuing the Halloween celebrations in there."

Elahoraella left.

Professor McDouglass turned to Billy and Ed.

"Well, I guess I should probably thank you both, you've saved us an awful lot of paperwork. You each win Osphranter house ten credits. You may go."

As they left, Professor McDouglass went over to Crumbleceiling and whispered in his ear.

"Erm – Headmaster, I know it's a personal question, but do you by any chance perhaps have a blow dart sticking out of your backside?"

As Billy and Ed entered the common room, the party was in full swing. Everyone was enjoying themselves and eating the food that had been sent up from the Banquet Hall. Elahoraella however, stood alone by the entrance, waiting for them. There was a very awkward pause. Then, without looking at each other, they all said, "That inspector did have a point about the lack of inclusivity, though," and they hurried off to join the party.

But from that moment on, Elahoraella Parker was their friend. There are some things you can't share without ending up as friends, and an epiphany about how little your school seems to care about equality is one of them.

Chapter Eleven

A Tale of Highs, Lows, And Then Highs Again

As winter began, the weather turned an icy cold. The mountains surrounding the school had become snowy, and the loch had frozen over. Every morning, students would watch from the warmth of the castle as Barry could be seen walking across the frosty grounds to grit the paths, defrost the school space hoppers, or place down warning signs reminding people not to run as surfaces may be slippery.

The change in season had also brought with it the start of the Frogsports one. On Saturday, the opening match would be taking place between Osphranter house and Crocodilian house, and it would be Billy's first ever game.

No one outside the Osphranter team had seen Billy play yet, because as their new player, Plank wanted to keep his playing style a secret from the opposition. The news that Billy had made the team seemed to have become common knowledge around the school, however. Soon Billy didn't know if it was the people telling him he'd be brilliant or those who shouted he'd be awful who were jumping to the wrong conclusion.

Billy was glad he could now call Elahoraella a friend. He wasn't sure how he'd have been able to complete all his schoolwork each night while hopping between lessons and all the last-minute training sessions Plank was arranging, without her help. Elahoraella had also lent him *Frogsports: A Tale of Highs, Lows, and then Highs Again*, which he found to be a much more *ribbiting* read than she had.

Billy learnt that there was a Frogsports World Cup which was contested every *leap year*; that there were over three hundred ways to *kermit* a foul; and that the longest ever Frogsports match had lasted for over two months, during which the referee had to be regularly substituted every time their voice went *croaky*.

Elahoraella had become much more relaxed around Billy and Ed since they had saved her from the school inspector, and because it's apparently important to allude to her being a bad and unpleasant person for not trusting them earlier, she was much nicer for it. On the Friday before the match, the three of them were outside in one of the castle's many courtyards, keeping warm by a fire another student had lit. Elahoraella had reservations about letting the fire burn on and wanted to put it out, but Ed disagreed.

"I just don't think we should be adding to global warming," said Elahoraella.

"How can global warming be real when it's cold outside?" asked Ed with the air of someone who knew much less than he let on.

Billy agreed with Elahoraella, especially since there were plenty of fires already lit inside the empty rooms of the castle, but he was too busy reading to join in their argument.

They were warming their hands on the fire when Professor Grape appeared at the other side of the courtyard and made straight for them. Billy noticed at once that Grape was limping as he walked.

"What have you got in your hands, Smith?"

Billy showed him the copy of Frogsports: *A Tale of Highs, Lows, and then Highs Again.*

"Five credits from Osphranter house. Surely you know that school books are to be kept within the school at all times?"

Grape took the book from him. Billy opened his mouth to argue, but Grape simply stared him down and said, "Many a man, Smith. Many a man."

"He's just making things up as he goes along," Billy said angrily to the other two as Grape limped away from them. "What's wrong with his leg?"

"Whatever it is, I hope it's hurting him," said Ed.

That night, the common room was full of energy. Billy, Ed, and Elahoraella sat around a table by one of the windows. Elahoraella was checking Billy and Ed's Creationism homework. No one liked Creationism very much, but the Secretariat of Sorcery had passed a new law for it to replace accurate historical facts as a compulsory subject. For some reason, they took it more seriously than saving lives, creating jobs, or protecting basic human rights.

Billy was just staring out the window at the Frogsports stadium in the grounds below when he thought it would be a good idea to check if there were any tips he'd missed in *Frogsports: A Tale of Highs, Lows, and then Highs Again*. As he reached for his bag to get the book, he remembered Grape had taken it.

"Where are you going?" asked Elahoraella as Billy got to his feet.

"I'm going to ask Grape if I can have my book back."

"Good luck," said Ed, but Billy felt confident Grape wouldn't murder him if there was witnesses nearby.

He made his way down to the staffroom on the second floor and knocked. There was no answer. He knocked again, and the door opened a little.

Perhaps Grape had left the book in there? He pushed the door open a little farther – what he witnessed scarred him for life.

Grape and Professor McDouglass were inside, alone. Grape was holding up a banana in one of his hands, while Professor McDouglass had a small wrapper in her own that Billy couldn't make out.

"The headmaster wants us to teach the students sex education?" Grape was saying.

"Well, the school inspector did say we have to take it more seriously," said Professor McDouglass.

"He wants me to show them how to put a condom on a banana."

"I used a replica of – you know – the real thing, last time, but then a student recognised it as – you know – and asked why I had it. I had to explain that even elderly magicians have their needs."

"I have just been sick into my own mouth."

Professor McDouglass removed the condom from the wrapper in her hand and helped Grape slip it over the top of the banana. "There we go," she said. "Though I must say, I've certainly seen bigger in my time."

"More sick."

"Oh, don't be like that Gallienus. I'm sure you've had relations before."

"I have only ever loved one woman, and she never loved me back. I thought I could win her over by fighting her husband after he defended her when I used a highly offensive prejudiced slur, but it didn't work. And when I found out my boss wanted to murder her and her family, I only wanted to save her life and let the man and son she loved die. And because her son survived, I now dedicate my life to making his own a miserable existence."

"Yes," said Professor McDouglass. "When you think about it, it really is messed that you're made out to be a hero in the end while all that stuff is overlooked."

There was a long silence that was eventually broken by Grape changing the subject.

"What is cunnilingus?"

"I'm sorry?"

"It was on the syllabus to teach about the risks associated with oral sexual encounters."

"Oh, yes, quite right. I have a book on that you can borrow."

Billy decided he'd heard enough. He tried to back out silently and close the door, but – "SMITH!"

Grape looked dangerous as he strode over to the door and swung it open.

"I just wanted to see if I could get my book back?"

"MANY A MAN, SMITH!"

Billy left, before Grape could get close enough to harm him. He ran back to the common room.

"Did you get it?" asked Ed as Billy sat back down at the table. "What's the matter?"

In a low whisper, Billy told them what he'd just seen.

"What?" Ed laughed. "We don't need sex education."

"Oh, but we do," said Elahoraella. "It's important to learn at our age."

Billy went to bed that night feeling as though he was never going to be able to read any of the books or watch any of the movies in quite the same way again.

He woke early the next morning, but was too nervous about the match to go back to sleep. He lay awake until the rest of the dormitory had woken up, and then joined them to go down to breakfast. People patted Billy on the back and wished him luck as they walked through the common room.

"Come on, Billy, you need to eat something," implored Elahoraella, noticing his plate was empty.

"I'm okay. I'm not hungry."

"Not even a slice of toast?"

"I don't want anything."

Billy wasn't sure he'd be able to stop himself from being sick if he ate. In just a few hours, he'd be walking out in front of the whole school, and he couldn't feel more nervous about it. And then someone said something which made him do exactly that.

"Billy, you need some food in you," said Patrick O'Connor. "Those blow darts take a lot longer to wear off on an empty stomach."

"Thanks, Patrick," said Billy, thinking it might be better if he was taken out for as long as possible as soon as the match began.

"At least have something to drink," said Ed, handing Billy a bottle.

"What is it?" asked Billy.

"*Croaka-Cola,*" said Ed. "It'll give you energy for the match."

By ten o'clock, the whole school had made their way out to the Frogsports stadium in the castle grounds. Ed and Elahoraella joined Josh, Patrick, and Simon in front of where some older Osphranter students were sitting in the stands.

Billy, meanwhile, was in the changing rooms putting on his frog costume — the technical name for which he was told was a *jumpsuit* — and blowing up his red space hopper (the Crocodilian team would be playing on green ones).

Plank came into the changing rooms from the captain's office. "Okay, this is it," he said. "This is the big one. It's the first match, and we have to win it if we're going to get off to a positive start —"

However hard Plank may have been trying to make his speech a serious one, it wasn't easy for the rest of the team to receive it as such. Plank had already changed into his kit, so to the rest of the team it appeared as if they were being given a pep talk by a horse.

"Hey, why the long face?" joked Larry.

"Yeah, come on, Plank. With a face like that, you look like a *neighsayer*," added Chad.

"Be quiet, you two. Those jokes weren't funny last year," said Plank. "This is the best team Osphranter house has had for years. We're going to win it this time, I just know —" He paused. The front half of the horse began to cough. "Daniel, I thought we agreed we wouldn't do that inside the horse?"

Plank removed the head of the costume to give himself some fresh air. "Okay," he said, after a few long deep breaths. "It's time to get out there. Good luck to you all."

Billy stood up and followed Chad and Larry out of the changing rooms and onto the pitch where they were greeted by loud boos from one side of the stadium and even louder cheers from the other.

Madam Webb would be refereeing the match, and she stood waiting for them in the middle of the pitch, trying to keep her balance on a hoverboard.

"Ah, Plank," she said, as the team approached. "Unfortunately, you and your team will not be able to take the knee before the match begins. *The Department of Digital, Culture, Media and Sport* have decided it would create too much division and banned it. But don't worry, I'm sure they'll have had time to look over their poll numbers and decide they're against racism before your next match."

"What about the –"

"Unfortunately, we are not able to light the stadium in rainbow colours either. The governing body has ruled that not upsetting homophobes is much more important than standing up to that sort of hate."

The Crocodilian team walked out onto the pitch to even louder boos than the Osphranters had. "Right then," said Madam Webb as they joined them. "I want a clean and sporting match from all…" and she was off. Her hoverboard was out of control and took her straight through the middle of the two teams, before going round and round in small circles until she finally lost her balance and fell off. "Bloody thing," she said, picking up the hoverboard and taking it back to where she'd started. "It was so much easier when we used *Segways*. Anyway – as I was saying. If you do insist on cheating, just make sure I don't see it. Do it *croak* and dagger style."

Billy attempted to swallow his nerves.

"Now get in line for the house anthems, please."

Billy joined the rest of the team as they lined up on the edge of the pitch, facing the stand where the teachers were sat. It was their anthem up first, and as the music began as though being played through giant invisible speakers, Billy sang his heart out with the rest of the Osphranters.

"Osphranters all let us rejoice,
For we love our yeast extract,
We all adore our yeast extract,
We all enjoy our yeast extract,
For breakfast, lunch, and tea..."

Clap, clap, clap-clap-clap, clap-clap-clap-clap, clap, clap.

There was an outbreak of applause from the Osphranters in the stands. Billy looked up at Professor McDouglass, who was sitting wearing a kangaroo hat next to Crumbleceiling with a tear in her eye.

"And now, the anthem of Crocodilian house," announced Madam Webb, and the music started again.

"Never smile at a crocodile..."

Neither the players themselves nor the rest of Crocodilian house sat in the stands seemed to know much more than the first few words to their anthem, so they improvised with a series of "snap, snap, snaps," that were all badly timed to the beat of the music.

With the anthems over, Plank and Daniel Foster (the back half of the Osphranter goalkeeper) went over to the team's netball net to get in position afloat, the inflatable unicorn bobbing gently on the water. Billy went over to get in place on the halfway line — Plank had won the toss for them to kick off – and looked up the pitch to where the Crocodilian goalkeeper (made up of James Carter as the front half and Felix Cole in the rear) was getting into position on their own unicorn. Billy was glad it wasn't his job to try and score, because the netball net the horse would be guarding looked a lot higher up now that he was on his space hopper.

Madam Webb made her way to the centre of the pitch – slowly so as not to lose her balance and fall off the hoverboard a second time – and opened a small jar to release the platinum fly into the open. Billy caught only a glance of it before it disappeared from sight.

"Are we ready? Three... Two... One..." Madam Webb gave a sharp blow on her kazoo, and the match kicked off with Amber Mackenzie, one of the Osphranter's three Attackers, throwing the rugby ball high into the air and hitting it hard with her hockey stick into deep Crocodilian territory.

"And that was an excellent start to the match by Mackenzie there, that won't be easy for the Crocodilians to defend," came the voice of a commentator. "But no, captain Lucas Ramsey has hit the ball right back down to the Osphranters – how will they respond? – Sydney Jenkins of the Osphranters has the ball, taps it lightly across to Mackenzie, and she balances it nicely as the Crocodilians approach – AND OH THAT WAS CLOSE! – Mackenzie showing real talent as she passed the ball back to Jenkins while narrowly avoiding two blow darts fired at her by the Crocodilian bouncers – and what's this? Jenkins is going for it, bouncing up the field with only one hand on her space hopper, the other on that hockey stick with perfect ball control – Evan Harrison makes a challenge for the ball, but no – that is a blow dart to the neck for Evan Harrison from Larry

Beaversley of the Osphranters, and he is out of the match — but don't look for too long as Jenkins is still on the attack — Ramsey bounces in but Jenkins passes it to teammate Clarissa Stewart who side bounces Crocodilian Vincent Chase, dodges a blow dart, and makes a short at the net — and, yes, James Carter makes a jump for it but his rear half just wasn't ready — OSPHRANTERS SCORE!"

Boos rang out from the Crocodilians in the stands, but they were countered by the cheers of the Osphranters.

"Ey up — move up theur lad, give us sum' room."

"Barry!"

Ed and Elahoraella bunched closer together to give Barry enough space, but the people behind them were less than pleased about having their view blocked by a man twice as tall as any other. "Selfish."

"Eh, ah 'eard that, thy little shite," said Barry. "Less o' attitude. Theur should respect theur elders — we wor 'ere first." He turned his attention back the match. "'ows Billy doin'? Any sign o' platinum fly yet?"

"None yet," said Ed.

Out on the pitch, Billy was having the time of his life as he bounced up and down on his space hopper, but there was no sign of the platinum fly yet. He'd had a rush of adrenaline a few minutes earlier when he'd given chase to something which flew past, but that had only turned out to be a wasp.

"Watch out, Billy!" It was Chad bouncing up and down behind him, his blowpipe aimed at a target past Billy's head. Billy ducked and Chad gave the pipe a sharp blow. Billy felt the blow dart race above his head, and as he looked up again, he saw it strike one of the

Crocodilian Bouncers in the chest just seconds before they could fire their own dart at him.

"And that is Anthony Cooper out of the match thanks to some quick thinking by Chad Beaversley there," said the commentator, as the Bouncer succumbed to the dart and fell unconscious off his space hopper.

It was as Caleb Anderson, the Crocodilian's other Bouncer, came to avenge his teammate that it happened. Billy had just dodged a blow dart fired by Anderson when he spotted a second coming for him. He wondered for a moment if maybe Anthony Cooper hadn't been hit after all, but as it got closer, he realised it wasn't a blow dart. And there was another one. Two sharp daggers were flying straight at his space hopper. If they hit their target, they were sure to puncture the rubber, and then he'd be out of the match. He bounced high, and they flew under him. But as he looked around, he saw a third, a fourth, and even a fifth coming after him. As Billy began bouncing for his life down the length of the pitch, the daggers followed.

The commentary continued, seemingly unaware of what was happening to Billy.

"And the Osphranters have the ball – it's Jenkins to Stewart – Stewart charging down, a nice bounce over Ramsey who misses his chance to challenge – Stewart passed to Mackenzie – Mackenzie goes for the net and – the Crocodilian's Keeper is in the water – Mackenzie scores for the Osphranters – that is one damp horse."

Elahoraella didn't join in with the cheers from the surrounding Osphranters. She'd just noticed Billy.

"What's happening to Billy?" she asked Ed with concern.

"They look like –"

"Daggers, yes. But where from?"

She looked away from Billy and over at the teacher's stand instead. "It's Grape," she said. "He's controlling them somehow."

"Should we do something?"

"I've got an idea," said Elahoraella, and she left, pushing her way past the other students.

Billy found it hard to keep ahead of the daggers now. He bounced and he bounced, but they appeared to be getting closer. Sydney Jenkins and Clarissa Stewart both helped by coming alongside him and taking two of the daggers out with their hockey sticks, but the rest were closing in.

"Hurry up, Elahoraella," Ed muttered to himself, seemingly not wondering for a moment why he was leaving it all for Elahoraella to fix and doing nothing to himself.

Elahoraella had managed to push her way across to the teacher's stand. "What on earth are you doing over here, Miss Parker?" asked Professor McDouglass. Elahoraella didn't stop to answer her, nor did she stop when she pushed past Professor Quigley and knocked him over.

Stopping next to Grape, she bent down, pulled out her enchanted celery and said "*Jiggery-Pokery!*" under her breath. Flames shot out the end of the celery and set the bottom of Grape's dressing gown on fire. She made her exit under the cover of the smoke that was now starting to fill the stand.

The cheers from the rest of the stadium told her she'd done what she needed to.

The other daggers had fallen to the ground, and Billy was bouncing as free as a bunny rabbit riding a pogo stick on a trampoline. And then he saw it. Just ahead was the platinum fly. He went after it, leaning forward and willing his space hopper to bounce faster. He held out his swatter ready to make his move, but then — he felt a sharp prick in the side of his neck and lost his balance. Falling forward, he hit the ground as his space hopper flipped over his head and rolled away from him.

Billy turned over and sat up. He noticed his teammates coming over to see if he was okay, then looked down to see the tiny platinum fly trapped under his swatter. And then, nothing.

When Billy came around again, he was lying on the bed in Barry's hut. Barry, Ed and Elahoraella were sat around the table in conversation. He sat up and looked at them.

"Billy," said Elahoraella, noticing he was awake.

"Ey up, lad. Come join us f' brew," said Barry. "Grand show out there — won match n' all."

"Ramsey wasn't happy," said Ed as Billy got up from the bed and joined them. "He kept complaining your swat shouldn't count because a dart hit you, but Madam Webb said you didn't faint until after you'd swatted."

Billy rubbed his neck. It felt sore.

"You took it right to the neck," said Elahoraella. "It looked painful."

"It feels painful," said Billy.

"Theur will gerr' over it," said Barry. "Theur not dyin'."

"What happened?" asked Billy. "Somebody was trying to throw daggers at me."

"It was Grape," said Ed. "Elahoraella and I saw him. He was

using that *Hocus-Pocus* spell to make them fly straight at your space hopper. Only, he didn't seem to be using an enchanted celery."

"Complete knackers!" said Barry, who seems to have missed everything that had happened during the match. "Why would Grape want t' deflate Billy's space 'op?"

"I think he thinks we know something about him," Billy explained to Barry. "And we do – we know he tried to get past that giant two-head duck on Halloween. It attacked his leg. We think he was tying to steal whatever it is the duck is guarding."

"Who told theur 'bout Waddles?" asked Barry.

"Waddles?"

"Yeh – 'e's me pet – bur Crumbleceiling asked t' borrow 'im t' guard summa'."

"What's he guarding?"

"Ah'm not sayin' nowt more," said Barry. "It's secret."

"But whatever it is, Grape's trying to steal it."

"Bullshit – 'e'd do nowt o' sort."

"Then why did he just try to kill Billy?" said Elahoraella, as though imploring him to see sense.

"Theur must be mistaken. Grape wouldn't try t' kill student – not after las' time, anyway."

"Last time?"

"No more. Ah've said too much. Jus' listen – theur all stickin' noses where they ain't not wanted, reight. Forget 'bout it all. Wha' that duck is guardin' is between Professor Crumbleceiling n' Émile Arquette."

"Who's Émile Arquette?" asked Elahoraella.

Barry ignored her.

Chapter Twelve

The Wardrobe to Iqaluit

Christmas was fast approaching. One morning in mid-December, they had woken up to find the whole school covered in a blanket of velvet smooth snow as white as the corporate board of the average *FTSE 100* constituent. The loch had frozen over, and the Beaversley twins were punished for telling Professor Crumbleceiling that Santa wasn't real. Snowstorms battered the windows from outside and made it near impossible for any post to be delivered. The few pigeons that did make it through had to be hidden to save them from Barry putting them out their misery.

No one could wait for term to end, and spirits were high when they woke up on their final day before the holidays. Their lessons that morning were laid back, and instead of making them do work, Professor Millbrook let them all watch *Arthur Christmas* on an old television set that was wheeled into the room and far too small for anyone at the back to see. In Professor McDouglass' class, they watched a pirated version of *The*

Muppet Christmas Carol. At lunch, they laughed and joked with Chad and Larry about building a giant snow slide on a hill in the grounds, or using the snow to trap Kevin in his office.

As they left the Banquet Hall to go to their final lesson – Alchemy – they found a giant Norwegian spruce blocking their way. The two feet they could see at the bottom of it, and the casual swearing coming from within its branches told them Barry was at the other side.

"Hi, Barry," said Ed. "Need any help?"

"Nah, ah'm grand, Ed," said Barry. "Bur while theur all 'ere, any o' theur be interested in buyin' y' sen a kayak from book? Ah only got t' sell four n' then ah gerr' entered in't contest t' win me sen an 'olibobs t' Florida, see."

"And how many have you sold so far?" Billy asked, entertaining him.

"Well… none – bur it's a reight grand kayak. Ah'll show theur." But as he went to take the catalogue from his pocket, he let go of the giant tree, and it came crashing down on the floor with a reverberating thump.

"Oh, bugger."

"Would you mind taking a little more care?" came Austin's pretentious drone from behind them. "If that thing had fallen the other way, you might have taken my head off."

"I wish it had taken your head off," said Billy, but he regretted doing so straight away. Professor Grape had just appeared at Austin's side.

"SMITH!"

"It wor jus' a joke, Professor," said Barry.

"Threatening another student is against school rules, Barry," said Grape coldly. "Ten credits from Osphranter house, Mr Smith, and be grateful I'm not murdering you instead." He turned to Barry. "And next time, if you could aim for Smith's head, that would be excellent."

Barry didn't seem to hear what Grape had said. He held up his catalogue and said, "Ah dunt suppose tha'd like t' buy y' sen a kayak, Professor Grape?"

Before Grape could say anything, a loud wailing alarm suddenly filled the entire entrance hall, seemingly coming from nowhere.

"What's that?" said Elahoraella, covering her ears with her hands.

"Oh, not now," said Grape. "It's snowing outside."

Professor McDouglass came from the Banquet Hall, ushering students forward. "Everybody outside, please. It's only a fire drill, but we need everybody to exit the building – you too, please, Sir Walter," she said, for Sir Walter Melvyn Scrivener Esq. had just come floating past.

"But one is a ghost, my dear lady. One simply cannot perish in flames that rage with the wrath of the gods."

"Everybody needs to leave. It's in the regulations."

As Billy, Ed, and Elahoraella joined the rest of the students making their way out of the castle and into the cold and frosty grounds, they could hear Karen complaining loudly behind them.

"I'm giving a one star review on *Tripadvisor* for this," she was shouting to anyone who would listen. "I was in the middle of my shower when that alarm went off."

It took a long time for the rest of the school to assemble outside, and longer still for students to sort themselves into their houses. Eventually, the teachers began moving among them and asking everyone if they weren't there. Satisfied with no one saying they were still inside, they concluded the drill had been a success.

As the whole school began rushing back to the shelter of the caste, Billy overheard Professor McDouglass asking Professor Millbrook if he knew where Crumbleceiling was. They didn't have to wait long to find out. As they came back into the entrance hall, there was a loud "WHEEE..." as Crumbleceiling entered from the Banquet Hall on an office chair being propelled forward by two fire extinguishers that had been taped to the back of it. He had just enough time to say, "Just checking they're all working, Professor McDouglass," before he flew off down a staircase.

Professor McDouglass took a moment, then turned to the students gathered behind her. "I think perhaps it would be best if we all agreed we hadn't just witnessed that," she said.

"Well, there is one good thing about all that," said Billy as they were walking down to the dungeons a few minutes later.

"What's that?" said Ed.

"We've missed most of Alchemy."

Grape wasn't yet there when they took their seats in his classroom, but that still didn't stop him from waltzing into the room five minutes later, and taking a credit from each of them for turning up an hour late to his lesson.

Billy wanted to argue, but Ed stamped on his foot.

"Wise move, Beaversley," said Grape.

Grape went over to his desk, and to his great surprise, someone stood up from behind it.

"Oh, you're not Professor Crumbleceiling," said a man wearing a while polo shirt and carrying a clipboard.

"Who are you?" asked Grape.

"My name's Brian," said the man, holding out his hand to shake Grape's. Grape didn't reciprocate. "I'm from the energy company. I just came to read your meters. Your gas is fine, but electricity consumption for this part of the school seems a little high, so we might need to check for a fault."

"GET OUT!" Grape yelled, and the man left in a hurry.

"What is going on today? Is this some sort of parody?" Grape thought aloud, and then he picked something up from his desk and held it up for the class to see. "This is a banana…"

When they left the dungeons at the end of the class, they could overhear Austin talking loudly to his friends ahead of them.

"I do feel so sorry," he said, not sounding sorry at all, "for all those people who have to stay in the cold castle over Christmas because they are simply not welcome at home."

The Crocodilians around Austin all laughed while Austin himself, obviously knowing Billy was walking behind them, turned around and sneered.

It was true Billy wasn't going back to the Moustaches for Christmas, but he didn't feel sorry about it at all. In fact, he was looking forward to the holidays and thought this would probably be the best Christmas he'd ever had. Ed and his brothers were staying at Frogsports too, because Mr and Mrs Beaversley were going on a cruse, so they could watch Issac's new stage show.

They came into the entrance hall. Barry was stood waiting, catalogue in hand.

"So, 'bout them kayaks," he said, bounding straight for them.

"We'd love to hear more, Barry," said Elahoraella, "but we've got to get up to the library before dinner."

"Theur off t' library?" said Barry. "Bur lessons av' finished ain't they?"

"Oh, we're not doing school work," said Billy. "We've been trying to find out who Émile Arquette is ever since you mentioned his name."

"Theur bin doin' wha'?" Barry looked both angry and a little worried. "Look, ah've already said, it's nowt t' do wi' you lot, so drop it, reight. Or theur will end up wi' clip 'round ear."

"We only want to know what he's famous for," said Elahoraella.

"You could always just tell us," said Billy. "We've looked in hundreds of books so far and can't find his name anywhere."

"Theur gerrin' nowt from me," said Barry bluntly.

"We'll just have to keep looking ourselves then," said Ed, and they left Barry, who turned his attention to asking a passing Professor Quigley if he'd ever considered taking up water sports as a hobby.

It was true they had been searching in books for some mention of Émile Arquette ever since Barry had let the name slip, because how else were they going to find out about something which had nothing to do with them? They'd thought about asking Karen for help, because that was exactly the sort of thing she was good at, but it was hard to convince her to do anything when there was nothing in it for her.

Not knowing what Arquette might be known for, it was difficult to know which sort of books they should be looking in. The size of the library didn't help their search either. Tens of thousands of books were piled high across hundreds of shelves, floor to ceiling, and wall to wall.

As Elahoraella continued searching row by row so as to be able to keep track of where she'd already looked, Ed went over to a random shelf and started looking inside books on subjects such as shoebills and economy stability in countries ruled by authoritarian regimes. Not for the first time, Billy couldn't help but wonder why for people who could perform sorcery, the magical community was so far behind the rest of society that they didn't even have access to *Wikipedia*. He wandered over to the restricted shelves. He had been thinking for some time Arquette might be in one of these books, but unfortunately, books on these shelves were considered too dangerous or unpalatable for most readers, and they could only be read by older students for purely academic purposes.

After another hour of finding no mention of Arquette, they gave up and went for dinner.

"You will keep looking while I'm not here, won't you?" said Elahoraella. "And send me a note with Yodel if you find anything."

"Sure, but you probably won't receive it until Easter," said Billy.

"You could ask your parents if they know who Arquette is," said Ed. "They might know something."

"They don't know anything about anything," said Elahoraella. "They watch *GB News* every night."

It wasn't easy to keep their word to Elahoraella when the holidays started the next morning. Billy and Ed were having too good a time to worry about Arquette or whatever it was that Grape was trying to steal. They had the dormitory to themselves, and the common room was empty most nights, so they were always able to get the good chairs by the window. Not having to get up for lessons the next day meant they could sit long into the early hours of the morning, plotting ways to get Grape fired – though they concluded if he still had his job at this point, he could probably murder a teacher and end up being promoted for it. When they went to bed on Christmas Eve, Billy was looking forward to the food and celebrations the next day, but he wasn't expecting to receive any presents.

When he woke the next morning, however, the first thing he saw was a small pile of colourfully wrapped packages waiting for him at the bottom of his bed.

"Happy Christmas," said Ed, as he sat up and stretched.

"Happy Christmas," said Billy. "I can't believe it. I've got presents!" he said, getting out of bed and pulling on his dressing gown.

"What were you expecting, a boxset of the field hockey coverage from the *XXV Olympiad*?" said Ed.

Billy picked up the top package. It was wrapped in thick brown paper and had a note scribbled across the top which read *To Billy, From Barry*. Inside was a gift set of *Lynx Africa* shower gel and body spray. He opened the box — it smelt like a desperate teenager's first date.

He went to pick up his second present, which wasn't a parcel, but a white envelope. He opened it, expecting a card, but instead found a small handwritten note.

We are currently under investigation for tax evasion and cannot afford to send you a proper gift. From Uncle Michael and Aunt Jennifer. Billy checked the envelope again and found a used bus ticket. On the reserve was an expired voucher offering six chicken nuggets for only one ninety-nine.

"One from Barry and one from my aunt and uncle," said Billy. "So who sent me these?"

"I think I know who sent you that one," said Ed, pointing at a package which looked similar to one of his own that he had just picked up. "My mother. I told her you weren't expecting to get anything, and — oh," he sighed, "she's made you a Christmas jumper."

Billy had torn off the paper to find a woollen, hand-knitted jumper with rows of colourful Christmas patterns.

"She makes us one every single year," said Ed, unwrapping his own, "and they're always really itchy."

There were just two presents left now. Billy picked up the larger of the two and felt it. It was heavy, but soft. He tore off the paper.

Something brown with small glints of green fell into a heap on the floor. Ed gasped.

"I've heard of those," he said in a low voice, dropping the present he was unwrapping. "If it's what I think it is —"

Billy picked the thick material up from the floor. It was rough to touch, like a well-worn fabric.

"It's a translucency tree," said Ed, a look of amazement on his face. "I'm sure of it — try it on and see."

Billy pulled the costume over his head and stood up straight, his arms outstretched.

"It is! Look in the mirror!"

Billy went over to look at himself in the mirror. There was no other way to describe it; he was dressed as a tree. Twig like cuttings were stitched to hang off the material as though fingers and toes. On his head, it looked as though he was wearing a gigantic wig made out of leaves in various shades of green.

"I don't understand," said Billy. "What is a translucency tree?"

"It's a costume that makes you unnoticeable," said Ed. "You're not invisible, just sort of unseen."

"But I can see myself, and you can see me too," said Billy.

"You already know you're wearing it, though, and I saw you putting it on," Ed explained. "But if you went outside wearing it, no one would know you weren't a real tree. You'd just sort of blend in, and they'd think you were meant to be there. It's kind of like a disguise. Makes sense when you think about it, trees are everywhere."

"So not invisible… just unnoticed," Billy repeated.

"Translucent," said Ed. "Look, there's a note," he added, pointing at a piece of parchment that had fallen from the parcel.

Billy pulled off the costume and picked up the parchment. Unfolding it, he found a handwritten note scribbled in green crayon, but he didn't recognise the handwriting.

Merry Christmas,

Your father left this with me shortly before he was murdered by an evil man who also wants to kill you – put it to good use.

There was no name.

"What's the matter?" said Ed, noticing the expression on Billy's face.

"Nothing," said Billy. But something was the matter. Who had sent him the tree costume? Did it really once belong to his father?

He put the costume and the note to one side, then picked up his final present and unwrapped it. It was from Ed.

"Ed, you shouldn't have," said Billy.

"Oh, it's nothing," said Ed.

"But really – you shouldn't have. I didn't get you anything."

Ed stopped unwrapping the package in his hand and looked up at

Billy.

"Well, this is awkward," said a third voice.

Chad and Larry had come into the dormitory, both of them wearing their own Christmas jumpers.

"Hey, look, Billy's got a Christmas jumper too," said Chad.

"And I'm sure he'll have sent something to mum in return," said Larry.

"Er…" said Billy, uncomfortably.

"Yeah," said Chad. "I mean, here's our family all poor and struggling to get by, and there's Billy with all that money and nothing and no one to spend it on but himself."

To Billy's immense relief, Chad turned his attention to Ed.

"Why aren't you wearing your jumper, Eddie?"

"I don't want to. They're too itchy."

"Come on, it's Christmas. We all need to put them on."

"Especially when mum has gone to such great lengths with the designs this year." Larry glanced at Billy here.

"Yes," said Chad. "I mean, look at Larry's here, I think it makes him look like a member of the *Conservative Party* trying to appear casual."

"And I think Chad's makes him look like a member of the *Labour Party* striving to appear professional," said Larry.

Ed pulled his own jumper over his head. "So what do I look like?"

Chad and Larry glanced at each other, and then looked tragically at Ed. Together they said, "A *Liberal Democrat*."

"What's going on here?"

"And here comes *Reform UK*," said Larry as Jacob came into the room, carrying his own Christmas jumper in his hand.

"And why haven't you got your jumper on, Jacob?"

"I find them too itchy."

"That's what I said," said Ed.

"Well, that's not good enough," said Chad, and he grabbed the jumper from Jacob's hands, then with the help of Larry, began forcing it over Jacob's head.

When they walked into the Banquet Hall for Christmas dinner a few hours later, nothing could have prepared Billy for the sight of Professor Crumbleceiling being kicked violently in the chest by a reindeer he was attempting to fit a red clown's nose on.

"Are you okay, Headmaster?" Professor McDouglass said, helping him to his feet.

"Nothing seeing that thing turned into a fireside rug won't fix, Professor McDouglass," said Crumbleceiling as she helped him limp up to the teacher's table.

Billy had never had a Christmas lunch like it. There were plates of roast turkey which they gobbled up — because for some reason, this much drier, tasteless, and all-round worse cousin of chicken is the ideal centrepiece for special occasions — and bows filled with vegetables of every variety: carrots, parsnips, roast potatoes, *TERFs*, and more. Well, almost every variety; there was a noticeable absence of sprouts, because the Secretariat of Sorcery had banned them for refusing to renegotiate a legally binding treaty.

The tables were also lined with Christmas crackers in silver, red, and green. Billy was entirely apathetic to receive a giant plastic paperclip, a set of miniature playing cards, and a fortune telling fish.

Hundreds of Christmas puddings followed the main course. Jacob nearby broke a tooth on a euro hidden in his slice, and he skipped the rest of the meal to go off and find Karen to see if she was interested in filing a group litigation order against the school. Billy, meanwhile, sat and watched Barry getting more and more drunk at the teacher's table, finally kissing Professor McDouglass on the cheek, who responded by slapping Barry in the face and reminding him that the mention of alcohol and the occasion of Christmas didn't make it any less messed up to portray sexual harassment as a joke now than it had been in Chapter Seven.

After lunch, they decided to go out to the Frogsports stadium in the grounds with some of the school space hoppers and have a snowball fight while bouncing around. A few of the teachers joined them too, and Professor McDouglass seemed to use it as an opportunity to let out a lot of unspoken feelings. She chased Crumbleceiling right around the whole pitch, using her enchanted celery to send snowballs crashing into the back of his head, but then took it too far when she also knocked over the snowman he'd spent an hour building.

Even Professor Grape had come out to join the fun, though for some reason he was wearing Hawaiian shorts and appeared much more laid back than usual. When Professor Millbrook asked him if his legs were cold, he muttered something about cool vibes and then told an anecdote about a cat video he'd seen on the internet a few days before.

As darkness fell, Billy and Ed returned to the common room alone – Jacob was busy running away from Crumbleceiling's rebuilt snowman that Chad and Larry had bewitched to chase after him, and Chad and Larry themselves had gone off to help Crumbleceiling with something — where they spent another evening sat around laughing and joking while toasting marshmallows on the fire until eventually going up to bed in the early hours of the morning.

Just as he had expected, it had been the best Christmas Billy had ever had. Even so, neither the good food or the snowball fight on the Frogsports pitch, nor the fireside conversations could distract him enough to forget about the thing that had been on his mind since that morning: who had sent him the translucency tree?

He was about to ask Ed if he was also creeped out by the fact a complete stranger had come into their dormitory during the night to deliver presents while they were asleep, when he heard snoring.

Well fed and with nothing playing on his own mind, Ed had fallen asleep quickly, but no matter how tired he might have felt, Billy couldn't do the same. He laid back on his bed thinking. The note had said the costume had once belonged to his father. And then he thought about what else the note had said.

Put it to good use.

Had Ed been correct when he described what it did? Would it really allow him to go anywhere he wanted, not invisible, but unnoticed? He had to find out now. He jumped off the bed and grabbed the costume from under it. Slipping it over his head, he looked at himself in the mirror again. He could still tell it was him, but then, he thought, he knew he was wearing it.

Put it to good use.

Suddenly, Billy felt wide-awake. The whole castle was open to him while he was dressed as this tree. Ideas flooded him. If Ed was right, he could go anywhere he wanted, and no one would ever notice he was there.

Ed let out a loud snore. Billy thought about waking him, but something held him back – Ed was still bitter about Billy not buying him a gift – and besides, this had been his father's tree costume – he felt this time, he wanted to use it alone.

He left the dormitory, walked down the stairs and across the empty common room – careful not to trip over any of the roots protruding from the bottom of the costume – then exited out onto the hallway outside.

Where should he go? He stopped. Thoughts were racing through his head and his heart was pounding. He could go anywhere he wanted. He could sneak into one of the other houses' common rooms and look around, or break into one of the chambers down in the dungeons that Professor Grape had forbid students from entering. He could even visit Grape's personal office and mess it up if he wanted. But then it came to him. He wasn't going to do anything fun or exciting, he was going to go to the library and look at some books. He'd be able to read for as long as he liked, until he was able to find out who Émile Arquette was. He'd even be able to look at the books on the restricted shelves.

He set off and was lucky not to come across anyone on the way.

The library was pitch-black and very quiet. Billy lit a lamp that had been left near the door. He made sure to hold the lamp a little ahead of him; he wasn't sure how flammable a tree he was.

The restricted shelves were at the far end of the library. He made his way over to them and held up the lamp, so he could read the spines. He knew these were the books considered to contain material too inappropriate, offensive, or even dangerous for most students, and as he read the titles, he could understand why.

There was a copy of *Piers Morgan's* autobiography, an entire shelf dedicated to biographical accounts of *George W. Bush's* time as President, and a book titled *Liberal Privilege*; the man on the front cover looked as though he was having an uncomfortable time trying to pass a kidney stone.

Billy picked a book off the shelf at random, opened it to the first chapter, and started reading: *And such was he, of whom I have to tell* — He stopped. He could hear footsteps nearby that weren't his own. And then a voice.

"Is that you, Karen?" It was Kevin who spoke.

Panicking, Billy dropped the book and it slammed onto the floor.

"What was that?"

Billy looked over at the entrance to the library. Kevin was walking towards the restricted shelves, his own lantern in hand, checking each row as he passed them.

It was now or never, thought Billy. It was time to test if the translucency tree really did work. He stepped out into the open, held one arm high and the other low, and waited for Kevin.

"That's funny, there's only this tree here," said Kevin, walking up to him. "I could be sure I heard something."

Billy held his breath, rooted to the spot, as Kevin held up the lantern to examine his face.

"You are just a tree, aren't you?" asked Kevin.

Doing his best impression of a giant sequoia, Billy replied, "I am just a tree."

"I thought so." But as Kevin went to walk away, he turned back and asked, "You haven't seen anybody come this way, have you, tree?"

"They went that way," said Billy, pointing off into the distance.

"Thank you," said Kevin, and he wondered off into the darkness.

Unable to believe his luck, Kevin's stupidity, or that the tree costume had actually worked, Billy made straight for the door. He wasn't ready to return to the dormitory just yet, though, and he decided to take a detour to see what else he could find.

He was just walking past Professor McDouglass' classroom when he heard two sets of footsteps ahead, and then to his horror, Professor Grape's voice.

"What is it, Kevin? Why are you rushing?"

"There's a student out of bed, Professor. They were looking around the library."

"How do you know?"

"I asked a helpful tree, and they pointed me in the right direction."

"What do you mean, you asked a tree? There are no trees in the library. And trees can't talk."

"This one did. He answered my questions."

"Trees don't grow in libraries."

"Well it was either a tree, or a performing arts student exploring their emotions."

"Frogsports doesn't have a performing arts department. The Secretariat cut our funding for that last year."

"That's how I know it was a tree."

"You idiot! That probably was the student dressed as a tree."

"No, it was definitely a tree. I asked it."

Worried the costume might not work on Grape, and feeling certain Kevin would recognise him as the same tree he'd just seen in the library, Billy held his breath and backed away from them as quietly as possible, taking care not to let his roots drag along the floor. He passed by a door that stood ajar. It was his only chance. To his great relief, he was able to make it through the gap without the door creaking, but he did so just in time. He felt a draft as Grape and Kevin passed down the corridor outside. Billy took a few deep breaths as he listened to their footsteps fading away. That had been too close, he thought to himself.

Billy wasn't sure exactly where he was. He thought it might have been McDouglass' classroom, but there were no posters on the walls promoting membership of any religious cult-like organisations which only pretend to care about children. Rather, it appeared to be an unused classroom. The tables had all been pushed up against the walls, and the chairs were stacked on top of one another. And then, he noticed something standing in the middle of the room that didn't seem to belong there.

It was a giant ornate oak wardrobe at least twice Billy's height, and had detailed patterns and drawings etched into the wood. At the top of the wardrobe was a carved inscription: *Los que traducen tienen demasiado tiempo libre.* With no sound of Grape or Kevin, curiosity replaced his panic, and he approached the wardrobe.

Billy reached for the door handle, expecting the wardrobe to be locked; but to his surprise, it wasn't. He pulled the doors open and felt a sudden blast of cold air hit his face, but he wasn't sure where it could have been coming from. He was staring at a collection of thick coats. He was so intrigued by the mysterious wardrobe that he didn't even stop to worry about whether they were made out of real fur. He wasn't sure why, but somehow he knew he had to step forward into the wardrobe. And then he took another step. And another. He thought he should have hit the back of the wardrobe by now, but no. Another step, but this time his foot didn't land on wood. He'd stepped onto snow.

For a moment, he thought he might have just stumbled upon a secret passageway out of the castle, but he couldn't be in the grounds. It was daytime, and he knew Frogsports didn't have this may adults; nor a motel, bank, or *7-Eleven*. He was stood on a street corner, but he hadn't any idea which street corner.

It wouldn't hurt to look around, he thought to himself. After all, he hadn't technically left the school. He set off down the street and came across a small coffee shop. Feeling hungry all of a sudden, he went inside and ordered himself a plate of Belgian waffles served with sides of bacon and maple syrup. It wasn't until his plate was empty, that he realised wherever he was probably didn't accept euro as payment. To his surprise, when he explained this to the owner of the coffee shop, they said, "Oh, don't worry about it, eh!" and then invited Billy to join them and their family to watch the game, whatever that was.

The game turned out to be a lot like Frogsports in that the players had hockey sticks, but there was much less bouncing and more ice, as well as no blow darts, but a lot more violence. It was good, thought Billy, but he couldn't help feeling it could still be improved somewhat by the inclusion of a pantomime horse wearing ice skates.

It was starting to get dark outside when the game had finished, and Billy thought he better hurry back through the wardrobe before Ed woke up and noticed he wasn't there. As he hurried out of the unused classroom and up to his dormitory, though, Billy knew he had to come back again.

"You should have woken me up," said Ed, through a mouthful of toast. It was the next morning, and Billy was telling him about what he'd found.

"I'm going back tonight, you can come with me," said Billy. "I want to show you this place."

"And I want to see this mysterious snowy land you've discovered by walking through a wardrobe," Ed said eagerly. "It sounds just like —" A loud beep came out of nowhere and censored the end of Ed's sentence.

"That was strange," said Billy.

"Yeah," said Ed. "Anyway, have some toast or something, why aren't you eating? You're not jet-lagged, are you?"

Billy couldn't eat. He wanted to save room for some more Belgian waffles that night.

As they left the Banquet Hall at the end of breakfast, they passed a determined looking Professor Crumbleceiling wearing shorts and two giant gloves coming the other way. "I'll show that reindeer," he was attempting to say through a mouthguard.

"Headmaster, this isn't what they mean by Boxing Day," Professor McDouglass was saying, trailing after him.

It took a long time to reach the room with the wardrobe in that night. With Ed also hiding under the translucency tree, they had to move slowly, so they wouldn't trip. Billy was surprised there was enough room for two of them in the costume, but it did seem to be just big enough because of course it did.

"It's freezing down here," said Ed, as they opened the door to the unused classroom.

"You'll be a lot colder in a minute," said Billy.

They closed the classroom door and pulled off the translucency tree.

"Is this it?" said Ed, walking around the outside of the wardrobe. "But how does it work?"

"I don't know," said Billy. "Are you ready?" He pulled open the doors of the wardrobe, and they were greeted by the same cool blast of air Billy had experienced the night before. With Billy leading the way, they walked between the fur coats and out onto the snow-covered street on the other side.

"Weird," said Ed, looking around. "It's the middle of the night, but it's light here."

"That's what I thought," said Billy. "We can't still be at Frogsports, but I don't know where we are."

"We could go ask at that visitor centre," said Ed, pointing at a nearby building.

"We don't have time for that now," said Billy. "I want to show you something," and he led Ed to the coffee shop he'd eaten at the night before. After two helpings of waffles, they went back outside to explore the town until it got dark, when they decided to go back to school.

"Cool place," said Ed, as they climbed out of the wardrobe and back into the castle. "Do you reckon it's real or just an illusion?"

"I don't know. I don't think people like that exist in real life, do they?"

The snowstorm outside the castle had cleared a little the next day.

"Want to go out to the Frogsports pitch with some space

hoppers?" asked Ed.

"No," said Billy.

"We could go find out more about those kayaks from Barry?"

"You can go if you want."

"I know what you're thinking about, Billy, that wardrobe. You shouldn't go back tonight."

"Why not?"

"I've got a bad feeling about it – you don't even know where that place is. What if you end up trapped there?"

But Billy wasn't interested in listening to Ed. He had only one thought on his mind that day, and it was to go back through that wardrobe as soon as night fell, because for some reason, even though he had nothing else to do all day, he still had to wait until night.

He found his way down to the correct classroom quicker that night, and didn't meet anyone on the way.

He swung open the wardrobe doors, pulled the fur coats to one side, and there it was; the perfect town waiting for him. He stepped through and went over to sit on a bench overlooking the water. There was nothing to stop him staying here as long as he wanted, except an overly complicated immigration system and –

"It's a nice view, isn't it, Billy?"

He looked to his right. Professor Crumbleceiling was sat next to him wearing his usual purple dressing gown.

"I didn't see you there, Professor," said Billy.

"It's strange how being dressed as a tree can make that happen." Billy was relieved to see he was smiling.

"So," said Crumbleceiling. "I see you have discovered the wonders of the Wardrobe to Iqaluit."

"I didn't know that's what it was called, Sir."

"But I expect by now you have worked out where it takes you?"

"It – well – we're not inside Frogsports, are we?"

"No, we are not. But perhaps you should have taken your friend Ed's advice to visit the local visitor centre."

"How do you know? –"

"I don't have to dress as a tree in order to go unnoticed," said Crumbleceiling. "I can simply make myself invisible whenever I choose."

"Sir, do you mean to say that you made yourself invisible to spy on two of your students during the night?"

"Yes, I suppose that is what I'm saying."

"That's really creepy."

"You know, when I think about it, I suppose it really is," said Crumbleceiling. "Anyway, let us not dwell on another, shall we say, disturbing fact of this world. Tell me, Billy, can you think what the purpose of the wardrobe is? Why it brings us here?"

Billy shook his head.

"Allow me to explain. Somebody wishing to see the world as it should be – I mean to say, the sort of world where *Tony Blair* never became Prime Minister and *Simon Cowell* never appeared on television – would step through the wardrobe and discover a place that met their vision."

Billy thought. Then he said, "So it shows us a better place…"

"Yes and no," said Crumbleceiling. "The wardrobe transports us to a place where things are better than even our wildest dreams. A place where people care about one another. In short, it takes us to a place where things are as they could be at home, were we so inclined to make it so. We are in the city of Iqaluit in Nunavut. However, it is very important to remember that the wardrobe does not transport us to a place of possibility, but rather false hope. People have wasted away wishing for the chance to move to such a place, often having to settle upon retiring somewhere like Adelaide instead.

"The wardrobe shall be moved by tomorrow, Billy, and I have to ask you to promise you will not go searching for it once more. It does not do to dwell on how much better things could be if people simply cared a little more about their fellow citizens — it all gets rather depressing after a time."

"Sir — Professor Crumbleceiling? Can I ask you something?"

"You may," said Crumbleceiling, smiling.

"What are you doing here?"

"I? I am here to pick up some legally sourced marijuana to help soothe the injuries I received from riding an office chair down a flight of stairs and coming off worse in a fight against Rudolph.

Billy stared.

"I find that which can be found on this side of the wardrobe to be just a little safer than some local sources."

It was only when he was back in bed that it struck Billy how little sense it made for politicians not to legalise cannabis for recreational use in this country. No one would be forced to smoke it, but for those who chose to, it would make it much safer if the supply was controlled and regulated. And then there was the good that could be done with all the tax revenues. It also wasn't as though there weren't plenty of studies showing it was much safer than alcohol of tobacco.

Chapter Thirteen

The Full Moon Rule

Billy kept his promise to Crumbleceiling not to go looking for the Wardrobe to Iqaluit again, and for the rest of the Christmas holidays, the translucency tree remained folded up underneath his bed. Billy wished he could forget about what he'd seen on the other side of the wardrobe. He kept being distracted by thoughts of *what if?* What if people in this country treated asylum seekers with respect and dignity? What if this country didn't think sacrificing children and the vulnerable was a reasonable price to pay so they could visit a pub? What if this country had strategic reserves of maple syrup, an annual bathtub race, and had been in an ongoing war with Denmark for over ninety years, which is fought using bottles of whiskey or schnapps to stake a claim to territory?

"Crumbleceiling was right, it's hard not to think about how things could be different once you've seen it for yourself," said Ed, when Billy told him about these thoughts.

Elahoraella, who had come back the night before term started, had a different view on things. She was torn between interest in what Billy had seen ("Maybe we don't have to accept how things are at the moment? Change is always possible!"), and disappointment that he hadn't been able to find out who Émile Arquette was.

They had almost given up entirely on their search for Arquette in any book now, even though Billy was certain he'd heard the name somewhere before.

For Ed and Elahoraella, the start of lessons the next day meant having less time to search, but for Billy, it meant having almost no time at all because Frogsports training sessions were now being scheduled nearly every night.

Plank was working the team incessantly. Even the endless days of rain weren't drowning his spirits. Chad and Larry Beaversley kept saying Plank was becoming obsessed, but Billy was on Plank's side. The Osphranters were in second place behind the Crocodilians on the table, but if they won their next match against Eudyptula house, they would move ahead.

Despite Plank's insistence they also started fitting in extra training sessions before breakfast, so they could spend more time getting used to bouncing on a wet pitch, the whole team was in good spirits about the upcoming match. Then, during one particularly wet training session, Plank gave the team some bad news.

"Will you stop doing that!" he yelled at Chad and Larry, who were attempting to bounce high enough on their space hoppers to complete a backflip in midair. "That sort of messing around is exactly the sort of thing that could lose us the match. Grape is refereeing this time, and he'll be looking for excuses to give penalties wherever he can."

Larry Beaversley stopped mid-backflip and fell headfirst into a muddy puddle.

"Grape?" he said, through a mouthful of dirt. "But when has Grape ever refereed a Frogsports match?"

The rest of the team joined in complaining.

"I'm not happy about it either," said Plank. "And neither is Professor McDouglass – you should have heard her. She asked me to help her move some bananas earlier, and she wouldn't stop complaining about it the whole time. But she said it was on Professor Crumbleceiling's orders and there was nothing she could do about it."

"But he's not going to be fair to us if we could overtake the Crocodilians."

"It gets worse too," said Plank. "I checked a calendar this morning and there are five Tuesdays this month. Not only that, either. There's a full moon the night before the match, so none of you eat anything with chicken in on Friday."

"There's no collided fates, is there, Henry?" asked Amber Mackenzie, the Attacker.

"Thankfully, no. I've checked with the Eudyptula captain, and we don't compliment. So we're not playing under that rule or sudden death – but may we still play in tribute to Marcus Sullivan."

"He was out Swatter last year," Chad explained to Billy. "Committed a foul during a sudden death match."

"Yes, and it cost us the game," said Plank bitterly. Mackenzie coughed. "But that doesn't mean we shouldn't honour his memory."

While the rest of the team hung back after training to share memories of Marcus Sullivan, Billy headed straight up to the common room to find Ed and Elahoraella.

"What's wrong with you?" asked Ed, as Billy sat down between them. "You look terrible."

Speaking quietly enough to stop anyone from eavesdropping, Billy told them about Crumbleceiling appointing Grape as referee for the upcoming match.

"You mustn't play," said Elahoraella at once.

"You can't play," said Ed.

"Grape's killed a man, Billy," said Elahoraella.

"Many a man," added Ed.

"I've got no choice, I have to play," said Billy. "If I don't, we'll have to forfeit the match. The only other Swatter we have was sacrificed to the *Ancient Egyptian Goddess Heqet* last year."

At that moment, Josh came into the common room. It was lucky the passdance had recently been changed to a waltz, because that was all his legs appeared to be able to do. With no control over where he was going, Josh danced into a table and fell over, his legs still moving around in the air as though he was a turtle someone had turned on its back.

Elahoraella got to her feet and pulled out her enchanted celery. With a quick flick towards Josh, his legs stopped moving, and he was able to get to his feet. "What happened?" Elahoraella asked him, leading him over to where they were sat.

This might have been a simple question, but giving an answer was anything but. For some reason, it also seemed Josh could only talk in limericks.

"Outside a classroom, Austin was on a hunt. He pulled out his celery, it looked rather blunt. Then he muttered a word, that could barely be heard, and I danced away from that —"

Elahoraella waved her celery just in time, and Josh fell silent.

"Oh — I can talk normally again. Thanks, Elahoraella," he said.

"You need to go to Professor McDouglass," said Elahoraella. "Report Austin."

Josh shook his head.

"He'll just come after me again if I do that," he mumbled.

"He goes after everybody, Josh," said Ed. "It's what he does. He doesn't care about anybody's feelings or emotions, and he never takes the time to consider how his actions hurt them."

"And that's why we've got to stand up to him," said Billy. "We'll do it with you.'

"Thanks, Billy," said Josh, and he seemed to cheer up a little. "I guess it's like Émile Arquette says: *allow the ecumenical mountain goats to establish the true circumference of the flan pudding.*"

"What did you just say?" said Billy.

"I didn't say anything," said Josh, but Billy, Ed, and Elahoraella were giving each other meaningful looks, which all said: *"The first bit, not the crap he said after that."*

"At least Austin didn't steal this from me this me," said Josh, pulling his Reflyder out from his pocket. He let the Reflyder go, and it landed on his hand. "Émile Arquette is a famous magical fromager born 1411 in Montpellier. He is best known for his work on pataphysics with his partner, Richard Crumbleceiling, and for maturing the only known Bewitched Brie."

Something very strange happened. Without realising they were doing it, all four of them sung together, *"This is cheese as cheese should be. The Bewitched Brie is the cheese for me. HEY!"* They ended by waving their hands in the air.

"What just happened?" asked Ed.

"I don't know," said Billy.

"I think I'm going to go to bed now," said Josh, sounding scared.

As Josh left, the three of them leant in close to whisper.

"I've conveniently just remembered something," said Billy. "Professor Quigley told us about Émile Arquette in our first lesson."

"Oh, I've just conveniently remembered that too," said Ed.

"And I've just remembered something else," said Elahoraella. "I've conveniently been carrying around the correct book all this time."

She pulled a giant leather bound volume from her bag and just happened to open it to the correct page first time.

"What is this book?" asked Ed.

"It's called *Brie and Me: All About What I'm Famous For* by Émile Arquette," said Elahoraella. "It's part of his series called *Fromage and Friends.*"

"That's convenient," said Billy.

"Yes, it is," said Elahoraella. "But listen to this…" and she began reading from the book. *"Following my success in maturing my famous Clairvoyant Caerphilly, the only cheese known to give the person eating it the ability to temporarily see into the future and thus warn of an approaching Englishman, I wanted to go further than ever before to discover the true power of fermented milk. Next, I created the Parapsychological Parmesan and the Philosophical Philadelphia. While the first of these was considered a delicacy, the second spread easily. I didn't experience a real breakthrough in my studies, however, until I created the Bewitched Brie."*

It happened again. *"This is cheese as cheese should be. The Bewitched Brie is the cheese for me. HEY!"* They put their hands down.

"I don't think we can say the name of the cheese without singing," said Elahoraella.

"Weird," said Ed.

"Hold on, there's more in the book." She read on. "The – cheese – has many mythical properties which are released upon consumption. The exact effect experienced is determined by the method of serving. Eaten cold, the Brie will grant a person infinite wisdom. Eating on a baguette will allow a person to speak fluent French. Baking the Brie first will render the person eating it immortal."

"Immortal," said Ed.

"It means you never die," said Elahoraella.

"I know what it means."

"I'm sorry, but some people struggle with that."

"I think we know what Waddles is guarding now," said Elahoraella. "It's the Bewitched Brie."

"This is cheese as cheese should be. The Bewitched Brie is the cheese for me. HEY!"

"Can you stop saying the name!" said Ed.

"No wonder Grape is trying to steal it," said Billy. "Who wouldn't want to learn French that quickly?"

"And the immortality," said Ed.

"And whoever bakes and eats this cheese will never die, even after just one bite?" said Billy. "They don't have to keep eating it?"

"After just one bite, yes," said Elahoraella. "If they kept having to eat it, then it wouldn't be immortality. Émile Arquette must have known somebody wanted to steal it, and he's asked Crumbleceiling to help protect it." She looked back at the book. "It says right here they know each other."

"Did you say there's a whole series of these books?"

"Oh yes – as well as *Brie and Me*, there's also *Chatting with Cheddar; Fraternising with Feta; Colluding with Colby; Having a Nice Chat with Monterey Jack; Perusing with Provolone; Dancing the Fandango with Grana Padano; Getting Ethical with Emmental; Having a Friend Over for Gorgonzola* –"

"How many more are there?"

"Quite a few – *Having a Clean With a Slice of Gubbeen; Scream a Little Louder for Here's Some Gouda*..."

At dinner on Friday, Billy and Ed were still talking about what they'd do with the Bewitched Brie if they had it. It wasn't until Ed said he'd sell it and get himself the best space hopper money could buy – The Bullfrog – that Billy remembered Grape was refereeing his match the next day.

"I've got to play tomorrow," said Billy, reaching for a chicken wing. "If I don't, all the Crocodilians will think I'm too scared to face Grape. But I'll show them... it'll really –"

"BILLY! NO!"

Plank was shouting at him from down the table. But it was too late. Billy had bitten into the chicken wing.

"There's a full moon tonight, remember?"

"What does that matter?" asked Elahoraella.

Billy looked down at the chicken wing in his hand with horror. "Oh no! The full moon rule."

"Excellent," said Chad, clapping his hands together. "Always makes for a more interesting match when bouncing around with a live turkey under one arm."

"Still, at least we're not vegetarian," added Larry.

They looked down at Sydney Jenkins, who was starting at Billy with a look that quite plainly, and quite sarcastically, said: *"Thanks."*

Billy knew, when they wished him good luck outside the changing rooms next to a pen filled with poultry being watched over by a teenager wearing a *Whole Foods* uniform the next afternoon, that Ed and Elahoraella were wondering if this whole thing was starting to get out of hand. This wasn't what you'd call comforting, with another four chapters left to go.

Too nervous about what Grape might do to stop the Osphranters from winning, Billy hardly heard a word of Plank's pre-match pep talk as he put on his frog costume. But before they went out to the pitch, Plank took Billy to one side.

"I don't want to put any pressure on you, Smith, but we could do with an early swat in this match. We need it over before Grape can show too much favour to Eudyptula house."

Billy couldn't help himself. He looked into the face of Plank's costume and said, "Don't worry, Henry, I won't horse around."

Out in the stands, Elahoraella was still telling Ed about cheese based books written by Émile Arquette.

"There's *Measuring Wattage With a Tub of Cottage; Someone Will Sue Me For My Halloumi…"*

"Elahoraella —" said Ed.

"… Everyone's Hotter Holding Ricotta; Shouting Fore! With Montebore —"

"Look, they're coming out," said Ed, pointing over to where Plank was leading out the Osphranter team to join the waiting Eudyptulas and their captain, Swatter Rachel Miller, in lining up in front of the teacher's stand.

As the house anthems player, Billy thought about he'd want you all to know that no chickens, turkeys, or indeed *Whole Foods* employees were harmed in the playing of this sport.

Eudyptula had won the toss to kick off, so with the anthems over, Billy went over to the middle of the Osphranter half of the pitch to get into position.

It didn't take long once grape had blown his kazoo for things to get contumacious.

Within seconds, he'd blown the kazoo a second time to award the Eudyptulas two penalties after the Beaversley twins both started the match by aiming a blow dart at him.

"Don't worry, this always happens to Chad and Larry," Amber Mackenzie told Billy as the match was stopped, so the twins could each be given a live chicken to hold for the remainder of the game.

"Well, this does make things much more *egg-citing* for those of us watching," said the commentator, as Grape blew his kazoo for play to restart. "They won't be trying that again, though, or they'll be required to *egg-sit* the match and be *egg-spelled* from Frogsports quicker than Karen the *poultry-geist* can speed dial your line manager.

"And play resumes — Sydney Jenkins has the ball for the Osphranters and passes it to fellow Attacker Amber Mackenzie — Mackenzie to Clarissa Stewart now — what an *egg-cellent hen-semble* of players this Osphranter team has — certainly high *egg-spectations* for their performance today after all that training around the *cluck* — they really are a high *hen-durance* team — if you're laughing at any of these, your sense of humour is *im-peck-able,* by the way – Stewart back to Mackenzie then back to Stewart to avoid the Eudyptula Attacker there – they'll have to set their alarm cluck earlier than that to catch Mackenzie – Stewart *bok-bok-bocking* down the field now, a clear run ahead of her – will she set up her shot on goal or just *wing* it? – here she goes – STEWART SCORES! – five points to Osphranter house and yes, there's an *egg-plosion* of cheers in the stands – they'll be celebrating that one until half-past *hen* on *Fry-day*!"

"Taking a risk with Snøfrisk; Resting My Head on a Pillow Next to My Quesillo; 'ello 'ello 'ello, What's All This Brin? –"

"Aren't you watching the match?" said Ed. "We've just scored.

Back on the pitch, the situation was starting to resemble opening time of an electronics store on Black Friday.

Grape had blown his kazoo again to award a second penalty against Larry Beaversley, this time for aiming at the commentator. Unlike his shot at Grape, this one was on target, and the commentary fell silent to cheers from all sides of the stands.

After the chicken under Larry's arm was replaced with a turkey, play restarted, but it didn't last long. It was clear that despite having to inhale a balloon full of helium after every sixth penalty he awarded, Grape felt the risk of sounding like a cackling Ricky Gervais watching a poacher being attacked by a lion was worth taking if it meant he could punish the Osphranters.

This time he was awarding a penalty against Plank and Daniel Foster, and as far as Grape was concerned, there being two of them meant it counted as two penalties, and they both had to skip the chicken and go straight to the turkey. This made it considerably harder to move around inside the horse costume, and consequently, the Eudyptulas got on the scoreboard.

Half an hour later, there was still no sign of the platinum fly, and the score was eighty points to Eudyptula house and ninety-three to the Osphranters, though no one was quite sure where the three had come from. By now, most players on both teams were carrying poultry, while Sydney Jenkins, the vegetarian Attacker, was bouncing around, giving a piggy back to the *Whole Foods* cashier. Grape, meanwhile, was now higher than an out-of-work comedy writer.

And then Billy saw it. The platinum fly came straight past him. He turned around on his space hopper, taking care not to let go of *Bernard Matthews* under his arm, and gave chase. But then he heard something. A low buzzing from something electrical was behind him. He turned and saw Grape following, his enchanted celery in hand, ready to attack.

Billy leant forward to bounce quicker, but in doing so, he lost his grip on the turkey, and it flew off behind him, hitting Grape in the face and knocking him off his hoverboard. But he didn't have time to watch now, the platinum fly was just ahead… he reached out his swatter and — yes, he hit fly to the ground.

"In Penny Lane, There is a Barber Showing Photographs of Every Curd He's Had the Pleasure to Know, and finally, Encyclopaedia L'Explorateur," said Elahoraella.

"Are you done now?" said Ed. "The match is over."

"Oh, what happened?"

Billy bounced over to the rest of the team, his swatter held high in victory. He'd done it — they were now ahead of the Crocodilians. As the rest of Osphranter house spilled onto the pitch, he noticed Grape struggling to fend off the turkey with his enchanted celery. The turkey stepped forward and grabbed the celery in its beak – then Billy felt a hand close on his shoulder, and he looked up into Crumbleceiling's smiling face.

"Excellent performance," said Crumbleceiling quietly, so no one else could hear. "I see you picked up a few tips from watching the ice hockey during your time in Canada."

Sometime after the match had ended, Billy left the changing rooms alone to return his BunnyRibbit Eleven to the storage hoppers. He couldn't ever remember feeling like this before. Osphranter house were now top of the table. And even better than that, Grape hadn't been able to murder him.

But speaking of Grape…

Billy could see a hooded figure striding out of the castle. Clearly wanting to avoid being seen, it disappeared swiftly around a corner. Billy recognised the limp; It was Grape, sneaking out of the castle while everyone else was inside the Banquet Hall eating dinner – what was going on? Billy jumped back on his BunnyRibbit Eleven and bounced after him.

When he turned the corner, Grape had disappeared behind, he couldn't see him anywhere. But he could hear voices coming from the other side of a nearby wall. He bounced up to the wall and stopped.

"I don't know why you wanted to talk this evening, Gallienus…"

"Oh, I thought we should have a little catch-up to see how things are going," said Grape, his voice cold.

Billy began bouncing on the spot until he was bouncing high enough to see over the wall. Professor Quigley was stood facing Grape, and he looked terrified.

Billy gasped.

"What was that?" said Grape, but before he could look up and see Billy, he'd fallen back below the wall.

As Billy bounced back up, he noticed Grape looking around, suspicious.

"We can't be overheard, can we? Students aren't supposed to know about the Brie, after all."

Grape turned back to Quigley.

"Have you found out how to get past that two-headed duck yet?"

"But, Gallienus, I –"

"It is much easier to be on the same side as me, Quigley," said Grape, steeping towards him.

"Now you're starting to sound like That-Evil One –"

"Don't say that!" said Grape, panicking. But it was too late.

Just as Billy had come to expect by now, a small grey cloud appeared above Grape's head, but what came next, he wasn't prepared for. As the water rained down on him, the colour of Grape's hair seemed to run, and a moment later, he didn't have black hair, but strawberry blonde instead.

"You idiot!"

"I – I'm just saying, Gallienus, I don't see why anybody but he would want to steal the Bewitched Brie."

"This is cheese as cheese should be. The Bewitched Brie is the cheese for me. HEY!"

With his hands forced upwards to wave, Billy lost his grip on the space hopper and fell to the ground with a thud. He thought Grape and Quigley might have been too distracted to have heard him, but decided not to wait and find out.

"Billy, where have you been?" said Elahoraella as he walked into the common room a short while later.

"Yeah, come on," said Ed. "You're missing the party."

"Never mind celebrating now," said Billy. "I need to tell you about something..."

He led them over to a quiet corner of the room, looked around to check no one was standing too close, then told them about what he had seen and heard.

"Grape is a natural blonde?"

"That's not important, Ed," said Elahoraella. She turned to Billy. "Is he really, though? Did you see it?"

"Yes," said Billy. "But don't you see what this all means?"

"He's polluting our waterways every time he dyes his hair black?" said Elahoraella.

"No – well, yes, that as well. But this means we were right about what that two-headed duck is guarding. Grape asked Quigley if he knew how to get past Waddles – but it can't only be the duck that's protecting the Brie, can it?"

"That duck could stop anybody," said Ed.

Billy shook his head. "Barry kept him as a pet, he can't be that threatening – I think there have to be other things protecting it too. Loads of sorcery, probably, and Quigley must have helped put things in place which Grape needs to find out how to get past –"

"So you mean Quigley is the only thing standing between Grape and the Bewitched Brie?" said Elahoraella with worry in her voice.

"This is cheese as cheese should be. The Bewitched Brie is the cheese for me. HEY!"

"It'll be gone by the end of next week," said Ed.

Chapter Fourteen

An Exciting Opportunity To Transform Your Life

However worried they might have been about Quigley, in the weeks that followed, it seemed as though they didn't need to be. While Quigley did appear to be looking more and more ill as the days went on, Grape strolled around the school with even more hostility towards any student who wasn't in his own house than usual, which surely had to mean Quigley hadn't given in and told him what he wanted to know yet.

Whenever they passed nearby, Billy, Ed, and Elahoraella would take a small detour, so they could press their ears up against the door to the proscribed passageway and check that Waddles was still on the other side, guarding the trapdoor.

Elahoraella was worrying about a lot more than just the Bewitched Brie, however. Their exams were fast approaching, and she had decided now was the time to start writing up all her notes and planning out her revision for the weeks ahead.

"It's only two months until our exams," she told Billy and Ed one evening when they asked her why she was spending so much time doing school work. "You should both be doing the same."

Unfortunately for Billy and Ed, all their teachers were thinking the same way as Elahoraella, and they now never failed to finish a lesson without giving them all extra homework first. On the last day before the Easter holidays, they had been given an extensive list of subjects likely to come up in their exams and told to spend their two weeks off doing extra research on their own. This meant that rather than going out to the Frogsports pitch with Chad and Larry, as they had planned to do, Billy and Ed found themselves spending every day from breakfast until dinner in the library with Elahoraella, failing to keep up with her pace of work.

"This is pointless," said Ed, pushing away the book he was reading. "They can't possibly fit all this in one exam, it'd be a week-long."

"It wouldn't be a very good exam if they told us exactly what was going to be in it, would it?" said Elahoraella.

"Why not? Are they supposed to be testing our memory or how adept we are at the actual subject? If it's just about remember things, teachers shouldn't be allowed notes or answer books," Ed countered as he sat back in his chair and gazed longingly out the window at the welcoming clear blue sky outside.

Billy, who was reading about the best way to shuffle a deck of cards, didn't look up until he heard Ed say, "Barry! What are you doing up here?"

"Don't shout, Ed, or we'll get kicked out," said Elahoraella.

Barry walked over to them, hiding a book under his arm. As

usual, he was wearing his giant coat, but for some reason his hair seemed much neater and cleaner than usual. As if to imply that people like him didn't have the intelligence to read books, he looked as though he didn't belong in the library.

"Ah wor jus' lookin' summa' up in a book," he said in a voice that made them all feel certain he was up to something. "Wha' all theur up t'? Ah 'ope theur workin' n' not still lookin' f' stuff on Émile Arquette."

"Oh, we've already found out who he is," said Ed casually. "We know what that two-headed duck is guarding on the second floor as well. It's Arquette's Bewitched Br –"

"Dunt finish tha'!" said Barry, panicking. "Does theur want 'ole library t' start singin' song?"

Ed apologised.

"There were a couple of things we wanted to ask you about actually," said Billy. "We were wondering what else is guarding the Brie other than Waddles –"

"Shurrup!" said Barry, loud enough that a few of the people sat at nearby tables looked over at them. When they had all turned back to what they were doing, Barry leant in and whispered, "Come n' see me later, reight. Ah'm not promisin' theur owt, bur we can't talk 'ere – theur not supposed t' know owt 'bout this. People will think ah've told theur."

"We'll come and see you after dinner then," said Billy.

Barry walked off shaking his head.

"I wonder what he's trying to hide under his arm," said Elahoraella, as she watched Barry leave the library with an inquisitive look on her face.

"I'm going to go see which books he was looking at," said Ed, and he got up and walked over to the shelves Barry had appeared from. After a moment, he returned with a handful of books and dropped them onto the table.

"Multi-level marketing," he whispered. "Barry was looking stuff up on multi-level marketing. Look at some of these books: *Recruiting Downline for Beginners; Is It a Pyramid Scheme?; Inside The 2016 Presidential Election; and Running Your Own Business Made Easy.*"

"Barry's always wanted to run his own business, he told me so the first time I met him," said Billy.

"You don't think he's taken this whole catalogue thing too far and joined a pyramid scheme now, do you?" said Elahoraella.

"He can't have done, it's against the law," said Ed. "And he'll end up in even more trouble if he starts trying to recruit students to join him."

"But what else could he be up to?" said Billy.

As they walked across the castle grounds towards Barry's hut that evening, they thought at first he had all his curtains shut. But as they got close, they saw that piled high on the other side, and completely blocking the view, were what appeared to be brown cardboard boxes.

When they knocked on the door, Barry seemed reluctant to open it until he first knew for certain it was them. He looked through a tiny gap to check they were alone, then hurried them inside and quickly closed the door behind them.

Even though it was still light outside, the inside of the hut was dark. Cardboard boxes weren't just piled up in front of the windows, but also in the usually lit fireplace, under the bed, next to the bed, and even on top of the bed. They were also taking up most of the space on the chairs, forcing Billy, Ed, and Elahoraella to perch on the edges as Barry made them all tea, seemingly oblivious to their discomfort.

"So – theur said y' wanted t' ask me 'bout summa'?"

Billy decided to waste no time. "We were wondering what else is guarding the Bewitched –"

"Dunt seh name o' it in 'ere," said Barry. "Ah dunt want t' knock owt over."

"We were wondering what else is guarding the Brie other than Waddles?"

Barry frowned at them all.

"Even if ah knew me sen – which ah dunt – y' know ah couldn't tell theur owt 'bout tha'," he said. "n' anyway, by sound o' it, theur all know too much already. Ah still dunt know 'ow theur foun' out 'bout thin' in first place. Ah suppose y' worked out why it's 'ere, though? Nearly got stolen from Sino Pauper Edo Recondo Mammonas – the thievin' lyin' bastards!"

"Oh, come on, Barry, you must know. You helped protect the Brie when it was moved to Frogsports," said Elahoraella, smiling at him. "We don't want to know exactly what the protections are, just who else was responsible for helping put them there."

"Well, ah guess if tha' all theur want t' know ah dunt see no 'arm in telling theur… let's see… Crumbleceiling did most, 'course, n' then 'e borrowed Waddles from me… n' then it wor other teacher who did rest o' it… Professor McDouglass… Professor Millbrook… Professor Quigley… oh, n' Professor Grape did summa' too."

"Grape did something?" said Billy, a little more aggressively than he meant to.

"'course 'e did – good magician is Grape," said Barry, then, off their expressions, he continued, "Theur dunt still reckon e's' out t' steal it do theur?"

They didn't answer.

"None of the teachers know how to get past anything any of the other teachers did, though, right?" said Billy.

"None of 'em even know wha' t'others did, except f' Crumbleceiling."

"And no one knows about Waddles, do they?" said Elahoraella.

"Couple o' teachers 'elp me t' feed 'im, bur other than tha', nah. No 'un knows 'ow t' gerr' past 'im anyway – well, except f' me n' Crumbleceiling."

"Well, that's good at least," Billy whispered to Ed and Elahoraella. "Barry, why is it so dark in here? What are all these boxes for?"

"Oh, they only jus' arrived this mornin'," said Barry. "They're me 'air products."

"Your what?"

"Me 'air products. Ah washed me 'air wi' 'em earlier t' test 'em out."

"We can see," said Elahoraella.

"But why do you need so much of it?" asked Billy.

Barry laughed.

"It ain't all f' me sen," he said. "Nah, ah got it t' sell on t' students."

"To sell to students?" said Elahoraella, sounding shocked. "But where did it all come from?"

"It came from me distributor, 'course."

"Your distributor?"

"Yeh. Ah wor down in village las' week 'avin a drink, n' ah got talkin' t' this stranger, n' ah asked 'im if e' might want t' buy his sen a kayak from me book, because ah've only sold the one, see. Anyway, 'e said 'e knew summa' much better than sellin' from book if ah wanted me own business, n' so 'e signed me up as downline distributor for 'im. Offered me good price on all this stock t' gerr' me goin' n' all."

"Barry, are you sure he hasn't just signed you up to a pyramid scheme?" said Elahoraella.

"Ah thought tha' me sen at first, bur 'e said it ain't a pyramid scheme, jus' a scheme that's pyramid shaped."

"Pyramid shaped?" said Billy.

"Yeh, bur ery'thin' is when theur stop n' think 'bout it, ain't it? Ah mean, tek school f' example – that's pyramid wi' students at bottom, then teachers above 'em, n' Crumbleceiling reight at top."

"But what are you going to do with all this stuff?" said Elahoraella.

"Ah already said, ah got it t' sell t' students."

"But what are students going to do with it? Even if everybody bought some, there's enough here to last until Christmas."

"Well, they ain't goin' t' use it, are they?" said Barry, laughing to himself. "They become distributors n' sell it on t'other students f' profit."

"Barry, this is definitely a pyramid scheme."

"Nah. It's an exciting opportunity f' all involved – maybe theur would be interested in becoming part-time independent distributors y' sens? Ah mean, 'aven't theur always wanted financial freedom?"

"Barry, we're eleven," said Billy.

"Never too early t' start livin' lifestyle theur deserve. Tell theur wha', give me a couple minutes o' y' time n' ah'll tell theur 'ow this could transform y' lives…"

Half an hour later, they had eventually got away by promising Barry they would consider it, but as they walked back up to the castle, Elahoraella tuned to the other two and said, "I don't care what he says, Barry has definitely joined a pyramid scheme."

Over the next few days, they did their best to avoid Barry whenever they could. This wasn't too difficult during the week when they had lessons, and most of their leisure time was taken up with revision, but at meal times they had to make sure to keep a low profile and eat quickly, so they could avoid him noticing them and coming over to talk. By the weekend, however, it became simply impossible to ignore him any longer.

At breakfast on Saturday, Yodel had brought Professor Millbrook a note addressed to Billy. It was a good thing Barry had made sure to fold the note before sending it, because when Millbrook gave it to Billy, it read:

I understand you might not be interested in the hair products. But I've got something else that I think you'll love and will sell really well. Come and see me about it, and I'll tell you about some of the other benefits.

Barry

"Do you think he's ever going to stop?" said Billy, handing the note to Elahoraella, so she could read it too.

Billy looked up at the teacher's table where Barry was sat waving at them. He gave a half-hearted wave back.

"At least he's only asking us and not any of the other students. He'd be in real trouble if they reported him to one of the teachers," said Elahoraella, passing the note to Ed.

"Yeah, but how long until he does start asking other students if we keep ignoring him?"

"Maybe we should go see him?" Ed suggested.

"We don't have the time, Ed," said Elahoraella, as though this was a ridiculous idea. "We've got revision to do today, remember."

"We've been working late every night this week," said Ed. "It's the weekend, surely we can have a little time off? We can make up for it tonight or tomorrow."

"But what are we even going to say to him? We don't want to join his stupid pyramid scheme."

"Finding out more couldn't hurt –"

"Shut up!" Billy whispered to them.

Austin was walking past, but he had just stopped dead to listen. How much had he overheard? Billy didn't like the look of the smile on his face.

After breakfast, Ed and Elahoraella continued to argue all the way up to the library ("But Ed, you won't make any money from it unless you sign up other students!"; "But I could sign you up, and Billy would do it too, wouldn't you, Billy?"). Eventually, Elahoraella agreed to go down and see Barry with the other two during lunch, if only so she could tell him she definitely wasn't interested in signing up.

It wasn't easy for Barry to let them in when they knocked on his door. The number of boxes seemed to have grown since their last visit, and they had to squeeze their way through a small gap to get inside his hut. There was now only one chair that wasn't being used as a shelf, so Billy and Elahoraella shared it while Ed sat on the floor.

"Ah'm glad theur all came – that's it, mek y' sens comfortable," said Barry without a single shred of recognition that this couldn't have been any less possible.

"Listen, Barry," Elahoraella began, "we have thought about, but I don't think we'd have any time to do any selling or sign anybody else up. We've got all our school work to do, and our exams are coming up. And besides that, if anybody found out, we'd all be in a lot of trouble, and so would you."

Barry didn't seem to be listening to anything Elahoraella was saying, and Ed wasn't helping her by humouring Barry and showing interest in the product list he was now showing him.

"So theur see, this is all t' stuff theur can get. There's 'air products n' facial creams, tha' sort o' thin', bur also 'ealth stuff like shakes n' bars. Bur if theur want summa' a bit different, y' can currently gerr' some o' these on special offer."

Barry reached into the nearest box and pulled out a souvenir mug with a drawing of the Loch Ness Monster on the front.

"Ah know it ain't completely accurate n' tha' – Nessie 'as a bigger nose n' it's pierced in real life, n' they missed out 'er mohawk – bur ah reckon students might like 'em as summa' they can send back t' family at home, see, n' teachers could use 'em in staff room."

"Barry, how many of these have you bought?" said Billy, looking around and trying to count the boxes.

"Ah got twelve boxes, n' there's summa' like 'hundred in each o' 'em."

"You've bought over a thousand of these mugs?" said Elahoraella, doing the maths.

"Aye, bur ah got me sen best discount ah could o' got on 'em, so ah can mek good profit when ah sell 'em on."

"Oh, but Barry, who are you going to sell them to? There aren't even a thousand students at Frogsports."

"Ah explained this t' theur before – students buy more than one n' then they sell 'em on."

"This is definitely a pyramid scheme."

"Complete cobblers! It's nowt o' sort."

"But what do you do with the mugs you can't sell?" said Billy. "Are you able to send them back?"

"No returns allowed. Bur ah dunt mind keepin' 'em f' me sen. Tiptop quality n' all, n' they'll go grand wi' the Nessie planes, glasses, n' table mats ah've got comin' t'morrow."

"You're going to keep them?" said Elahoraella. "But how will you ever make your money back if you can't sell them or return them?"

"Easy," said Barry. "When ah bought all these, they counted as unencumbered units, see, so ah became an 'igher ranked distributor. It means next time ah can buy more cheaper than normal, n' mek more profit when ah sell 'em on."

Elahoraella was shaking her head, she couldn't believe what Barry was saying.

"Never mind 'bout numbers anyway," said Barry. "av' y' sen a look at quality o' printing on these mugs."

"I'm sold," Ed joked.

"Grand," said Barry, not noticing Ed's tone. "So 'ow many mugs do ah put theur down f'? These will all be encumbered units f' theur, 'course, so they won't contribute t' theurs' distributor rank. Anyway, mugs cost me six euro each n' they sell f' ten, so 'ow 'bout theur buy five 'undred off me f' eight euro each, n' theur can mek y' sen n' easy thousan' straight away..."

"Barry –"

"Ah'll even throw in fifty f' free —"

"I was joking," said Ed."

"Oh, ah see," said Barry, sounding downhearted. "Well, why dunt theur all tek a mug each n' use 'em on trail basis f' a bit?" He handed them each a mug. "Theur can see if anybody says owt n' wants their own."

Over the next week, they took it in turns to spend what little free time they had trying to convince Barry to quit before he was caught out, but Barry wasn't interested in hearing anything any of them had to say. Instead, he just kept getting more and more things delivered until his hut began resembling a warehouse rather than a home. On Thursday night, Billy and Elahoraella were sat working in the common room, waiting for Ed to return. It had just gone eleven o'clock when the door opened, and Ed came in wearing Billy's translucency tree. He was in a bad mood.

"Look at this!" he said, showing them his hand, which was bright red and covered in blisters. "He's got this new hand cream, and he told me to try it out, only he put it on my hand before I could say anything, and now I've come out in a rash. I'm telling you, none of that stuff is safe. This feels like I've spilt acid on it."

There was a sudden tap on a window behind them.

"What's that?" said Elahoraella as they all turned to look.

"It's a pigeon," said Ed. "But it doesn't look like Yodel."

"What's a pigeon doing here at this time?" said Elahoraella.

Billy rushed over to the window and opened it to let the pigeon it. It landed on the table where they were sat and dropped a note in front of Elahoraella.

"It's from Barry," she said. "Ouch – it bit me."

As she had gone to pick up the note, the pigeon had attacked her hand, then started pecking at an ink stamp on the bottom of the note that read: *Reverse charge postage, recipient to pay.*

"I can't believe Barry," said Ed, pulling a coin from his pocket and giving it to the pigeon.

Once the pigeon had flown back off through the open window, Elahoraella picked up the note and read it aloud. *"You were right, I need to do away with everything. Quickly."*

"What's gone wrong?" said Billy.

"It doesn't say," said Elahoraella.

"But how can he just discard everything?" said Ed. "His whole hut is full of boxes. Even if he tried to use it all himself, it would take years to get through that much."

Billy looked down at the mug he'd been drinking water from all night; it was one of the mugs Barry had given them as a sample. Then it came to him. "Nessie," he said quietly.

"What?" said Ed.

"Nessie."

"What about her?"

"That's the answer. We can just dump all those boxes into the loch. No one will ever find them in there. They'll be too scared of Nessie eating them to search."

"And what if Nessie eats us while we're trying to put them there?"

"We'll just have to use a boat," said Billy. "And we can wear the translucency tree to make sure no one sees us doing it."

"Trees can't row, though," said Ed.

"We can do it at night then," said Billy. "Saturday would be good.

There are no lights on the loch, so even if somebody looked out of a window right at us, they'd never make us out."

Ed was sold on the idea, but Elahoraella had reservations ("It's going to cause a lot of pollution in the loch, and what if Nessie tries to eat any of it? It could make her very ill!"). Even so, she eventually agreed to help, because as Ed said, what other ideas did they have?

Next morning, to Billy's surprise, it was Ed, not Elahoraella, who backed out of the plan. The rash on his hand had now spread up his arm, and worse than that, both his hands and face had gone puffy. It looked as though he was allergic to whatever had been in the hand cream. He managed to make it to the end of breakfast before deciding he needed to go up to the hospital wing and get it checked out.

At the end of their final lesson, Billy and Elahoraella rushed to the hospital wing to check Ed was going to be okay, and to deliver the news that Professor Grape was taking five credits from Osphranter house because Ed hadn't had the courtesy of at least dying if he was going to be ill enough to miss his class. After reassuring Ed they would be fine on their own, they went down to visit Barry and explain Saturday's plan to him.

"Ah won't let theur in," he said through a crack in the door. "There ain't a lot o' space in 'ere at mo'."

When they told him about their idea to dump everything in the loch when it's dark, he nodded and said, "Well, ah guess it's f' best — maybe ah should tek up crypto or summa' like tha' next time."

"Barry, why do you want to throw everything away anyway?" said Billy. "You didn't say anything in that note you sent us last night. What changed your mind?"

"Oh, theur dunt need t' know details o' it. Wha' matters, is we av' plan t' fix it."

"I'm still worried, though," said Elahoraella. "What if Nessie tries to eat any of it? I mean, look at what's happened to Ed, and that's just from getting it on his hand."

"Dunt worry y' sen 'bout tha'," said Barry. "Nessie will be fine."

"But how can you be sure?"

"Well, she's a fictional creature f' one thin'," he said. "So it's jus' magic, ain't it? Anyway, speaking o' Ed, theur do promise not t' tell anybody wha' really 'appened dunt they? Seh it wor Grape or summa' — y' always saying ow' theur dunt like 'im anyway."

"What do you think changed his mind?" Billy asked Elahoraella as they walked back into the castle five minutes later. "Barry doesn't seem to want us to know."

"I don't know," said Elahoraella, "but it doesn't matter right now. We just need to do away with everything tomorrow night, and then all this will be over."

Some brushed past them. It was Austin, and he turned back to give them both a knowing smile, then — SMACK!

Too busy glancing back at Billy and Elahoraella to notice where he was going, he had walked head first into one of the Banquet Hall's double doors.

"Do be careful where you're going, Mr Hickinbottom," said a passing Professor McDouglass.

"How much do you reckon he just overheard?" said Billy, once Austin had continued into the hall.

"I don't know," said Elahoraella. "But we can't change the plan now. If we don't get this done on Saturday, Barry might change his mind before we get another chance."

Billy agreed, and they went for dinner.

Once the common room had emptied on Saturday night, Billy and Elahoraella pulled the translucency tree over their heads, then set off down to Barry's hut. They didn't come across anyone else on the way until they reached the entrance hall, where the sudden noise of footsteps made them stop dead.

A moment later, Professor McDouglass appeared from the staircase that led down to the dungeons, but she wasn't alone. Looking annoyed about something, Austin was following behind her.

"Detention for you, Mr Hickinbottom," she said, sounding just as angry as he looked. "And I think we shall have fifty credits from Crocodilian house as well. There is no reason for you to be wandering around at this sort of hour —"

"But Professor, you don't understand. Billy Smith is coming down here — he's trying to destroy evidence of something."

"And that shall be another fifty credits for your havering. How dare you try sproutin' aye ma auntie! Come on, and make no mistake, the headmaster will be hearing about this — well, he will when I work out where he is this evening anyway."

Billy and Elahoraella held their breath as Professor McDouglass stopped as she passed by. She looked at them for a moment, then said to herself, "I see the trees are migrating back outside for the summer early this year," and continued walking.

They waited until Professor McDouglass and Austin's footsteps had faded away before continuing. Elahoraella seemed to move with a new-found joy in her step.

"Austin's got detention!" she said gleefully. "And all because he thought he was on to us."

Laughing about Austin all the way, they left the castle and made for Barry's hut where they could see he'd left them a rowing boat by the water's edge. They pulled off the translucency tree, then folded it up and placed it in a small nook under the hut for safe keeping.

"Ah've got all boxes ready f' theur," said Barry, as he opened the door. "n' ah've also added a bit o' weight t' sum' of the lighter boxes t' 'elp 'em sink a bit quicker, y' know?"

"Aren't you going to help us?" said Billy.

"Can't lad, ah've 'urt me arm. Doctor said ah ain't t' do any 'eavy liftin'."

"When did you have time to see a doctor?"

"Well, ah seh doctor, bur ah mean ah *Googled* it. Bur it also said ah only got three week t' live, so gerr' on wi' job before ah find me sen six feet under."

As Billy and Elahoraella began loading the heavy boxes into the boat, it was difficult not to wonder if Barry might not have been telling the truth about his arm.

"I think we'll have to come back for the rest," said Elahoraella once they had loaded half the boxes. "If we take too many at once, the boat might sink."

"Agreed," said Billy, and he helped her push the boat out onto the water.

They climbed aboard, then began rowing until they reached what they thought was the middle of the loch.

"I think this is the spot," said Elahoraella. "The loch must be at its deepest here."

Billy leant over the side of the boat to look at his own moonlight reflection staring back at him. Crumbleceiling was right, he thought – he must remember to pay him that bet.

He sat back up and nodded to Elahoraella. "Let's do it."

Box by box, they began throwing the evidence overboard. They had to admit, the extra weight Barry had added to some of them was doing its job. The moment they hit the surface, every box disappeared into the watery depths.

"That's all of them," said Billy, dropping the last box into the water. "Let's go get the rest."

When they returned to the shore, they were in for a surprise. Perhaps it was because he had just been thinking about him, but when he climbed out of the boat, Billy found himself face to face with Professor Crumbleceiling. He had to be imagining things. Maybe he was just hallucinating because of how tired he was.

Billy blinked. Crumbleceiling was still there. Now they were in trouble, he thought.

"Professor…" Billy began with panic in his voice, "we were just –"

"Never mind what you're doing now," said Crumbleceiling. "I came over to ask if I could borrow your boat? My kayak just sunk," he continued. Crumbleceiling pointed over to the edge of the loch edge where a couple of stacks of paper were standing a little ahead of where the top of a kayak was sticking out the surface of the water.

"Er… sure," said Billy.

Billy helped Crumbleceiling load his papers onto the boat, then climbed aboard.

"Ahoy there, matey!" Crumbleceiling said to Elahoraella as he joined them on the boat. Then he shouted out, "Weigh anchor and hoist the mizzen!"

"Are you going to help us row, Professor?" said Billy.

"I'm afraid I can't, dear boy. I hurt my arm earlier."

"Did he have to come on the boat with us?" Elahoraella whispered to Billy. "He's just adding extra weight"

"Well, I couldn't say no, could I? He's the headmaster."

"We're like pirates, aren't we?" said Crumbleceiling as they started rowing back out to the middle of the loch. "Shall we sing a sea shanty?"

"Let's not," said Billy.

"Aye, aye, Captain!"

They stopped in roughly the same place as before, then began dumping the rest of the boxes overboard.

"Professor, what are all these papers for anyway?" Billy asked as he threw Crumbleceiling's cargo into the water.

"Oh, just some old records the school no longer has any need to keep," said Crumbleceiling. "We do pride ourselves on our data protection practises at Frogsports."

Once they had thrown the last box over the edge, they saw a head appear above the water a little distance away. They watched as the head splashed back down as though toasting their cunning before it swam off to the other side of the loch, its mohawk giving it the appearance of a shark involved in the punk rock scene.

Back on dry land, there was another surprise waiting for them, but this one wasn't so friendly. They had just pulled the boat out of the water when Kevin's lantern-lit face appeared in the darkness ahead of them, and Billy felt a sudden need to swab the poop deck.

"Oh dear," said Kevin, making no effort to hold back the smile on his face. "We do have some explaining to do, don't we?"

"Shiver me timbers! It's a scurvy dog," said Crumbleceiling. Then he turned to the other two and continued, "Let's cleave him to the brisket and feed him to the fishies. Dead men tell no tales!"

Chapter Fifteen

Consequences and Contradictions

Billy felt certain they were both about to be expelled.

They followed silently behind Kevin — who seemed to be in a very good mood for once — as he led them all back up to the castle, and then to Professor McDouglass' office where they were told to stand in front of her desk and wait. There was a cold draft coming from the empty fireplace, but Billy thought it was more likely his nerves that were making him shiver as he did. He knew there wasn't a single excuse in the world Professor McDouglass would accept, but that still didn't stop him from desperately trying to come up with one. There was no good telling the truth, either, as that would only get Barry into trouble as well.

Billy was just thinking that things couldn't possibly get any worse, when getting worse is exactly what they did.

Professor McDouglass entered the room with Josh following behind her. He looked petrified.

"Stand over there," she told him, pointing next to Billy.

"I'm sorry, Billy," Josh whispered. "I couldn't find you in time – I was trying to warn you about Austin. He was trying to catch you, he said you were –"

"Enough talking," snapped Professor McDouglass, and she glared down at them all looking angrier than Billy had ever seen her before. "Kevin tells me he caught you rowing a boat out on the loch. It is the middle of the night, for goodness' sake. Explain yourselves – all of you!"

Billy and Elahoraella looked at each other, both hoping the other might know the right thing to say, but neither of them spoke. Then –

"It was all their idea," said Crumbleceiling, pointing at them both.

"I think I already have a fairly accurate idea of what has been going on tonight," said Professor McDouglass. "All the pieces are there. You have been trying to get Austin Hickinbottom into trouble by luring him out of bed during the night. I've caught him already and I assure you that he is in just as much trouble as you both are. As for Mr Hansen here, I can only assume you find it even funner that he has been caught up in this little game of yours, as well."

Billy glanced at Josh and tried to give him a look to tell him this wasn't the case at all, but he wasn't sure he'd pulled it off. Josh looked close to tears again – all he'd tried to do was help them, and now not only was he in trouble for it, but he thought Billy and Elahoraella found it funny he'd been caught.

"And as for you, Headmaster, Professor McDouglass continued. "Have you been embezzling funds from the school accounts and trying to destroy the evidence again? You promised the authorities that you wouldn't be doing it again after last time."

"I needed the money to invest in this wonderful hair product I have discovered. I could tell you more about it, if you'd like? All I need is a few moments of your time and I may be able to completely transform your life —"

"Now is not the appropriate time for this, headmaster."

Professor McDouglass shook her head and looked back at Billy, Elahoraella, and Josh.

"I am most disappointed in all of you," she said sternly. "I honestly cannot believe it — four students out of bed in just one night! Sure, I may have lived through the rise of That-Evil-One — oh, do stop fussing so much, Hansen. It's only a bit of rain — witnessed students being murdered by the evil monster which lives within the bowels of the school, and been a teacher during *Michael Gove's* time at the *Department for Education*, but I can assure you, in all my time here I have never seen anything so shocking or disturbing, quite like four students out of bed while it is dark outside. The school is very dangerous at night, especially these days."

For a moment, Billy thought about pointing out that if the school was too dangerous for students to walk around, this might be something the teachers should be fixing as a priority, but he didn't think he dared just now.

"You will all be receiving detention for this," said Professor McDouglass. "And to ensure the message gets across, fifty credits will be taken from Osphranter house."

"Fifty?" Billy repeated in shock — she couldn't be serious?

"Fifty credits each," said Professor McDouglass.

"Professor — please — you can't —"

"It is now one hundred credits each, Mr Smith — nothing gives any student the right to wander around the school at night."

Billy was about to ask if she meant even for Astronomy lessons when Professor McDouglass said, "Yes, what is it, Headmaster?"

"Am I also in detention?" asked Crumbleceiling.

"No, of course, you are not in detention," said Professor McDouglass. "You are a teacher, not a student. Unless you wish me to place you in detention?"

"I'm good," said Crumbleceiling. "But I was hoping to get the chance to use this," and from his pocket he pulled a *get out of jail free* card which he'd taken out of a *Monopoly* set.

Professor McDouglass shook her head again. "Now, all of you back to bed, and know that should I ever catch you wandering around the school at night again, you will be expelled."

All things considered, it hadn't been a good night; but the next morning, things got even worse. Losing three hundred credits has wiped out the lead Billy had won in the last Frogsports match, and Osphranter house had gone from the top of the house table to the bottom. At first, no one seemed to know what had happened, but when Professor McDouglass started fielding questions from curious students, she wasted no time in informing them all exactly who was responsible. Billy thought briefly about telling everyone the truth about how it had all been Barry's fault. But when he mentioned this to Barry, he simply shrugged his shoulders, pointed out all the evidence had been destroyed, then started pretending he had no idea what Billy was talking about.

Overnight, Billy had gone from being one of the most popular students in the school to one of the most hated. The only people who didn't seem to have any problem with him were the Crocodilians, who kept stopping to pat him on the back and thank him for helping them reach the top of the table. It wasn't even as though they were annoyed with Austin, either. In Alchemy on Monday, Grape had started the lesson by awarding Austin one hundred credits simply for turning up on a day when he must still be feeling tired from his nighttime stroll.

It might have been too late to fix the situation now, but Billy vowed to himself that he would never get involved in anything that wasn't to do with him again.

Ed was the only person standing by him.

"Don't worry about it. Chad and Larry have lost Osphranter house loads of credits while they've been here, and they're both still popular. And anyway, you'll earn them back at the next Frogsports match."

But Billy wasn't even sure if he wanted to play in the next match. He had gone to find Plank at lunch to offer his resignation from the team, but Plank had refused it. Even so, training had lost its fun. None of the rest of the team would speak to him, and during their warmups where they passed the ball between themselves, they always made sure to miss Billy out.

Things weren't much better for Elahoraella or Josh, but not being known by face to many students meant they were left alone most of the time. Fellow first-years had been ignoring and talking about them, though, and Elahoraella had started sitting at the back of every class and making no effort to answer any questions.

Billy was starting to feel glad the exams were getting closer. His workload kept his mind off everything else and meant they didn't have as much leisure time, during which the rest of the house could glare over at them while muttering harsh things to their friends. He, Ed, and Elahoraella spent every evening working late into the night at a far table in the corner of the library.

Then, less than a week later, Billy's new plan not to get involved in anything that didn't concern him faced its first challenge. As he walked back to the common room on his own one afternoon, he heard three voices coming through the open door of a classroom as he passed it. He recognised two of the voices as those belonging to Grape and Quigley. Was Grape making another attempt to get the information he sought from Quigley? If so, it sounded as though he might have help this time.

Billy stopped short of the door and peered through a gap by its hinges. Inside the classroom, Grape and Quigley were sat on chairs opposite each other, while a woman Billy had never seen before was sat between them as though mediating or refereeing almost.

"I want to start by thanking you both for coming here and seeing me this afternoon," said the woman, smiling at one of them, then the other. "My name is Sharon and I'm from human resources. It's my great pleasure to empower you both to seek a mutually agreeable resolution to your workplace conflict today. I hope that you find this experience a rewarding one."

Since neither Grape nor Quigley looked as though they were going to say anything, Sharon went on.

"Why don't you begin by telling me about the problem you are currently experiencing? How about you first, Gallienus?"

"My name is Professor Grape," said Grape flatly.

"Okay, and does using your title and surname when talking to other adults make you feel better? Does it make you feel like a bigger person perhaps?"

Grape was biting his tongue, so she turned to Quigley instead.

"And what about yourself? What do you feel is the cause of the breakdown in the relationship between yourself and your colleague?"

"He keeps asking me questions."

"I only want to find out if he knows how to get past all the protections on the second floor."

"And you obviously have some reservations about sharing this information," Sharon said to Quigley. "Why don't we discuss those?"

"I really don't think it's any of his business."

"Okay, but do you understand why it might be better to share this information? Communication between colleagues is a vital ingredient in the great big pie that is an efficient and happy workplace."

Billy had heard enough, and besides, Grape looked as though he might be about to storm out of the room at any moment, and then he'd discover Billy had been eavesdropping in on the conversion. He rushed up to the common room where Ed and Elahoraella were busy reading through their Transformation notes from that morning. They stopped as Billy sat down at the table and told them what he had just witnessed.

"Grape still doesn't know yet then," said Elahoraella. "That's something."

"Yeah, but it sounded as though Quigley might be close to breaking. I reckon another few days, and he'll have given in."

"There's still Waddles, though, and Barry said he hasn't told anybody how to get past him, except Crumbleceiling."

"Maybe Grape already knows how to get past Waddles without Barry's help," said Ed. "I know it's got two heads and everything, but it's still only a duck. It can't be that hard to get past. I bet there's a book somewhere in the library telling you exactly how to do it – with the amount we're being forced to read, I wouldn't be surprised if it's on our list. What do you think we should do, Billy?" he finished, a sense of adventure in his voice.

It was Elahoraella who answered.

"Go to Crumbleceiling," she said. "That's what we should have done the first time. If we had done, we could have stopped all this by now. And besides, Professor McDouglass has already made it clear that she'll expel me and Billy if we're caught out at night again."

"We don't have any proof, though," said Billy. "We haven't got anybody to back us up, and who do you think Crumbleceiling will believe, us or a teacher? And don't forget, students aren't supposed to know about Waddles or the Brie. We'll be in even more trouble if we have to explain how we found out about them, and so will Barry – not that I mind so much right now, but I don't want him to lose his job over it."

Elahoraella agreed, but Ed wasn't convinced.

"What about if we just did a little –"

"No," said Billy plainly. "We know too much already."

The next morning, Yodel delivered notes addressed to Billy, Elahoraella, and Josh to Chad and Larry, who were sat a little further down the Osphranter table.

"What's that?" said Ed as they came over to deliver the notes.

"It's our breakfast," said Chad.

"I didn't know you could get fast food at Frogsports."

"You can't," said Larry. "We ordered this through *Ural Eats*."

Billy looked at the note:

Your detention will take place tonight at midnight. Wear something warm and meet Kevin outside the front door.

Professor McDouglass

"I understand why we've got detention," said Elahoraella, looking up from her own note, "but if the school is so dangerous when it's dark, isn't it just irresponsible to give us a detention at midnight?"

"Best not to think too much about all the contradictions," said Chad. "It makes your head hurt after a while."

At a quarter to midnight that evening, they left Ed — who had said he would wait up until they got back — in the common room and went down with Josh to meet Kevin outside the castle. They had just reached the top of the staircase leading down to the entrance hall when a voice shouted after them.

"What are you all doing there?"

They turned around. It was Professor McDouglass, and she looked furious to see them.

"You three again? I thought I made myself very clear when I said you would all be expelled if I ever caught you walking around at night again. Did you not learn anything from your detention?"

"Er, Professor..." Billy began.

"I hope you have a very good explanation for this, Mr Smith."

"Well, it's just, we're on our way to detention now," Billy continued. "You told us to come at this time."

Professor McDouglass seemed stumped for a moment, then she said, "Oh, yes, that's right. I remember now. Do carry on."

As Professor McDouglass walked off, they continued down the

stairs, across the entrance hall, and through the main doors of the castle where they found Kevin waiting for them in the cool air outside – Austin was there too. Billy had forgotten Austin had also been caught by Professor McDouglass.

Kevin gave the three of them a cruel smile, then with a snide pleasure in his voice, said, "Come on then, time to get this over with." He lit the lantern he was carrying in his hand and began leading them out across the grounds.

"You won't be rushing to break another school rule after tonight, I can tell you that." Kevin seemed to be enjoying this a lot. "Shame the Secretariat banned some of the traditional punishments, though… it wasn't so long ago that you'd have found yourself being forced to watch reruns of *The Apprentice* or listen to the music of *Kanye West* on repeat for a few hours… and even before they loosened the rules for that, it wasn't much better… could lock you up in the dungeons for a week or dangle you from the battlements by chains around your wrists."

None of them was sure where they were being taken, but it seemed Kevin was leading them over to a light they could see in the distance. As they walked, Billy could hear Josh snivelling beside him.

"I'm going to tell my father about this," said Austin arrogantly. "I'm not allowed to do anything unless he approved of it first."

"Is that a threat?" said Kevin.

"And what sort of lonely old man gets pleasure out of watching children be tortured?"

"Barry," Kevin called out, ignoring Austin.

Billy's heart gave a sudden leap. Maybe things weren't going to be so bad after all.

They heard a voice shout back to them.

"Kevin? 'urry up, ah've bin waitin' f' theur all."

Kevin looked down at them and seemed to notice the expression on relief on Billy's face because he said, "You think detention won't be so bad if you're with that blunderer? He's not going to make it any better for you, boy. You're all off into the forest."

At this, Josh whimpered, but Austin stopped dead.

"The forest?" he said. "But we can't go in there – there are creatures in there – it's too dangerous –"

"That's not my problem, that's yours," said Kevin, his voice rising until he was almost cackling with joy. "This is what happens when you break the rules at Frogsports."

"But students aren't allowed in the forest – you're forcing us to break the rules."

"Well, that's what you don't understand about the rules, isn't it? They're more a set of *ministerial codes* than anything else – for teachers they're entirely discretionary."

As they got closer to the light, they found it was coming from a lantern Barry was holding in his hand. Charlie was stood next to him, and he clutched a shortbow in his other hand. A quiver of arrows was hanging off his belt.

"Sorry 'bout this," he said to Billy and Elahoraella. "Bur it'll be over soon enough, n' until then, jus' think o' it as an adventure."

"There's no point in being friendly to them, Barry," said Kevin. "Don't go forgetting they're all here as a punishment."

"Tha' explains why theur all late then. Theur bin givin' 'em all a little talk, av' theur? Not theur's job t' do tha', is it?" He looked at Kevin and held up his shortbow. "Ah can mek it look like accident, y' know!"

Kevin seemed to swallow something hard.

"I'll be back at first light," he said, then giving Billy an ornery smile, he added, "For whatever is left of them."

As Kevin started back up to the castle muttering to himself, Barry put down his shortbow, then handed each of them a bright yellow life jacket. "Reight, put these on, all of theur. Come on. They've got whistle n' light on f' attracting attention if any o' theur gerr' in't trouble."

"Why do we need to wear a life jacket?" said Austin.

"There are ponds n' streams, n' stuff in tha' forest, lad."

Although somewhat bewildered, Billy, Ed, and Josh all put their life jackets on without a fuss. Austin, however, was still hesitant.

"I'm not going in that forest," he said, a definite sense of fear in his voice.

"Theur ain't got no choice 'bout it," said Barry fiercely. "Theur done summa' wrong, n' now y' facin' consequences of y' own actions — it's called accountability."

In the back of his head, Billy suddenly remembered something Barry had once told him.

"Barry, have you ever considered a career in banking?" he said.

"Eh?... Oh, very funny. Anyway," said Barry, "y' all need t' listen t' me carefully. Ah won't lie to theur, wha' we're doin' could be dangerous, bur that dunt mean ah want any o' theur takin' more risks than necessary. Follow over 'ere a mo'."

He picked his shortbow back up off the floor, then led them over to the edge of the tree line, where a small gap gave way to a dirt track leading deep into the forest. They all felt uneasy as they followed it with their eyes to the point where it vanished into the darkness.

"Barry, what's that?" said Elahoraella, pointing down at something on the floor. Billy, Josh, and Austin had all noticed it too.

"T' luminous stuff?" said Barry, and Elahoraella nodded. "Tha' wha' we're 'ere for. It's unicorn blood. It means there's a unicorn in 'ere tha' bin hurt by summa'. Keeps 'appenin a lot recently. Ah even found one dead t'other day. Now, it might be tha' we av' t' put this one out o' its misery when we find it."

"How can there be a unicorn?" said Austin. "Unicorns don't exist."

Barry shushed him. "Dunt seh tha' out loud, lad. Ery' time somebody says that, a unicorn dies."

"But you just said you might have to kill it anyway."

"That ain't the point."

"Barry, what if whatever did this to the unicorn finds us first?" said Billy, trying, but failing, to sound braver than Austin did.

"Tha' why their got y' whistle n' light," said Barry, as though this was obvious.

They set off into the trees, Barry leading the way with his lantern lighting the track ahead, and soon, they couldn't see the edge of the forest behind them when they looked back. They didn't speak again until they came to a fork in the path, and Barry stopped them.

"Reight then, we need t' split up 'ere," he said. "Got more chance o' findin' unicorn if we av' two parties lookin' f' it. So, Billy n' Elahoraella can come wi' me one way, Austin n' Josh, go t'other way."

"Fine, but I want Charlie," said Austin, sizing the dog up and thinking he might offer some protection.

"All right, bur ah'm telling theur, e'll run away at first sign o' trouble," said Barry. "Now, if anybody gerr' in't difficultly, jus' blow on y' whistle n' we'll all come find theur — n' remember t' stick t' path — off we go then."

So they split up with Barry, Billy, and Elahoraella taking the track that forked left, and Austin, Josh, and Charlie following the track to the right.

The forest was dark and still. They walked in silence, keeping their eyes to the ground, so they could make sure they wouldn't trip over a fallen branch or inadvertently stray off the track and into a ditch.

"It couldn't be an erlking that's attacking the unicorns, could it, Barry?" said Elahoraella. "I heard there are some in the forest."

"Aye — there's 'undreds o' 'em in 'ere, bur they dunt attack other creatures. They only go after children like y' sen n' Billy," said Barry, as though they were supposed to find this reassuring somehow.

They continued following the trail of luminous unicorn blood further into the trees. Billy could hear running water close by; he rested his hand on the toggle of his life jacket just in case.

"Barry," said Elahoraella after a few minutes silence. "You never told us. What did change your mind about the pyramid scheme?"

"Oh, tha," said Barry, and he seemed to snivel a little. "Kinda 'ard t' share, y' know."

Billy looked up at him and noticed Barry looked as though he was about to cry, and then he did.

"What's the matter?" said Billy. "No one will ever find out you were part of it. We've destroyed all the evidence."

"It ain't tha'," said Barry through his tears. "It's me... me... me CEO — he got his sen arrested f' insider tradin' n' bribery... bur he wor like family t' me."

"Have you ever actually met him before?" said Elahoraella. "Or even spoken to him?"

"Well, no, bur that ain't wha' it's 'bout, is it — 'e treated all us distributors like 'is own family, n' now e's off t' prison n' 'is 'ole company is under investigation."

Billy and Elahoraella wanted to laugh, but now didn't seem the appropriate time. Then, they heard something which brought them all back to where they were.

They had just walked into a small moonlit clearing when they heard something shuffling among the trees ahead of them. Barry pushed Billy and Elahoraella back, then reached for an arrow and got it ready to fire.

"What do you think it is, Barry?" said Elahoraella.

"Ah dunt know," said Barry. "Who's there?" he shouted out. "Ah'm warnin' theur, ah'm armed 'ere!"

There were footsteps, two pairs of them, then into the clearing came — Billy didn't know. It had the palomino body of a horse, with a long tail flowing behind it, but there was no mane to match. Instead, above the waist was the body of a man with orange hair and skin, giving him the appearance of someone who had spent too long on a sunbed.

"Oh, it's only theur, Brie Brie Neigh Neigh," said Barry, returning the arrow to its quiver. "Ah thought y' might av' bin summa' else f' a mo' then. Grand performance wi' fourteen forty at 'amilton Park, by the way, won me sen 'undred euro on tha' race."

He stepped forward and shook hands with the creature.

"I trust you are well, Barry," said Brie Brie Neigh Neigh. "Were you just about to shoot me with an arrow?"

"Oh, well, not now ah know it's theur," said Barry. "Though, y' ain't got any injuries av' theur?"

"No injuries, no. But I have been thinking recently that maybe we should begin shooting our owners and trainers whenever they break a bone themselves. I mean, it's only fair, isn't it? I'm sure nobody will care too much if we just pretend it's humane and for their own good."

Barry noticed Billy and Elahoraella staring up at Brie Brie Neigh Neigh, both with an expression of shock on their face.

"Oh," said Barry, "yous two, this is Brie Brie Neigh Neigh — 'e's a centaur."

"We'd noticed," said Elahoraella.

"n' this is Billy Smith n' Elahoraella Parker," Barry then told the centaur. "They're students up at school."

"Good evening to you both," said Brie Brie Neigh Neigh. "Smith, did you say? Have you heard about the new study to discover why there's so many Smiths in the phone book? Scientists concluded it's because they all have phones."

"Er —"

"Anyway," said Barry. "Ah'm glad we've run in't theur, Brie Brie Neigh Neigh, y' might know summa' — there's an injured unicorn 'bout, y' ain't seen owt strange aroun' place av' t'day?"

Brie Brie Neigh Neigh didn't reply straight away. He gazed upwards as though addressing a crowd, then said, "I'm currently producing a play about sweet things. I've already caster sugar."

"Yeh," said Barry, "bur ah'm wonderin' if theur might av' seen owt earlier?"

"I saw a squirrel worshipping French fries earlier."

"Eh?" said Barry.

"It was a chipmunk."

A rustling in the trees nearby made Barry reach for an arrow again, but it turned out only to be a second centaur, this one white-bodied with pale skin and greying hair. It looked much more feral than Brie Brie Neigh Neigh.

"Ey up, Horsey McHorseface," said Barry. "Ah wanted t' av' word with theur. Ah won me sen 'undred euro bettin' on Brie Brie Neigh Neigh's las' race, bur then ah lost it all bettin' on theur's own. Placin' third? Wha' tha' all 'bout?"

Horsey McHorseface stepped forward.

"Good evening, Barry," he said. "Have you heard the one about the fisherman from Weymouth who couldn't get a signal on his television? It was because he couldn't find tuna in the channel."

"Sure," said Barry. "Look, ah jus' asked Brie Brie Neigh Neigh 'ere, y' ain't seen owt unusual t'night, av' theur?"

Horsey McHorseface walked over to stand next to Brie Brie Neigh Neigh. "Do you know I got asked for proof of age when buying cheese the other day?" he said to his friend. "I never knew that was what they meant by extra mature."

"Well, if either o' theur find summa', do let us know, won't theur?" said Barry. "See theur 'round, then."

Billy and Elahoraella followed Barry back into the trees, unable to stop themselves glancing back at Brie Brie Neigh Neigh and Horse McHorseface until the trees blocked their view.

"Never," said Barry frustratedly, "try t' get y' sen a straight answer out o' a centaur. If they're not racin', then they're always rehearsin' their bloody stand-up comedy sets."

"Are there many centaurs in the forest?" said Elahoraella.

"A good number... they dunt cause too much trouble, though. Jus' a bit annoyin' t' av' conversation wi'."

The continued walking and eventually came to another clearing where they found a Charlie bear's picnic. Billy started to think they should have come in disguise, but the bears were perfectly welcoming and offered them all a glass of lemonade and a *Jammie Dodger*. Once they'd finished, they apologised for distributing the party, then continued back into the trees.

They had just passed a bend in the dirt track when two bright lights appeared ahead of them through the trees."

"Barry! Look!" said Elahoraella. "I think there's other people over there. They've got lanterns... but Josh and Austin didn't have lanterns, did they?"

They didn't have much time to think about the lights, because just then, they heard a sharp whistle cutting through the air. Billy was surprised it was loud enough to reach them, but —

"AAARGH!" Austin screamed out.

They had turned around to find Austin, Josh, and Charlie stood next to them. It seemed they had all been walking close by, but hadn't noticed each other.

"What theur blowin' whistle f'?" said Barry. "Theur will frighten ery'thin' away."

"There are lights ahead," said Austin, pointing over at them. "I think something is there."

"Do you think that's what hurt the unicorn, Barry?" said Billy.

Barry squinted over at the lights.

"Er — nah, ah think tha' might be couple of doggers, actually," said Barry, guiding them all in the other direction. "Best t' give 'em privacy."

"Doggers?" Austin repeated. "Do you mean people out with their dog? Like you and Charlie?"

"Summa' like tha', yeh," said Barry. "Reight, we still ain't found anythin' so we best split up again —"

"I want to come with you," said Josh at once. He sounded terrified, so Barry agreed to change the groups.

"n' Billy, y' can go wi' Austin this time," he said, then he leant in and added in a whisper, "Sorry 'bout this, bur we av' t' gerr' it done."

And so Billy set off further into the forest with Austin and Charlie. They were walking for nearly an hour until they had no choice but to leave the track they were following if they wanted to continue forward; it seemed to just come to an end in front of them. They kept pushing forward through the trees, taking care to walk even slower now. As Billy looked to the ground, he thought there seemed to be more blood here. There were drops of it on the barks of trees and leaves of bushes, as though something had come through here lashing around in pain. Ahead, Billy could see another clearing.

"Look at that —" Billy whispered, holding out his arm to stop Austin.

Ahead of them, something bright white lay slain on the ground. It was definitely the unicorn, and it was bleeding heavily from the neck.

Billy rushed over to it and knelt down beside, then he began chanting, "I do believe in unicorns, I do, I do! I do believe in unicorns, I do, I do! Come on, I need you to join in, I saw this in a film once," he said, turning back to Austin. But Austin was preoccupied by something else.

A shadowy hooded figure was coming towards them as though stalking its prey. As he observed, Billy noticed more luminous unicorn blood dripping down the front of its cloak, giving it the appearance of a vampire at a disco.

"AAAAAAARGH!"

Austin screamed even louder this time and made a break for it – Charlie followed close behind. The figure turned its attention to Billy now and began moving towards him as though it was gliding gently over the forest floor.

Then Billy felt something he had never experienced before; a burning sensation emanated from the trademark on his forehead and made his whole body fill with an agonising pain. Blinded by what he was feeling, he took a step backwards and tripped over. The figure moved closer still, but then it seemed to hesitate for a moment, as though expecting something else to have happened by now.

"RAHHH!" it said, though its voice faltered a little; it didn't sound at all as though it was trying to be frightening.

It moved closer again, looking around wildly.

"HA HA HA!... ROAR!... CUCKOO CUCKOO!... Moo!... Woof!... Meow..."

Then, most surprising of all, the figure looked down at its wrist as though checking the time on a watch. Finally, it looked up at Billy and seemed to shrug its shoulders.

This time, the figure moved in for the kill.

The pain in Billy's trademark worsened. He couldn't keep his eyes open. Then he heard hooves galloping somewhere behind him. Something large jumped clean over his head and began attacking the figure.

It took a moment for the pain to pass, but when he could open his eyes again, the figure had gone. A third centaur was standing over and looking down at him; this one had a dark chestnut body and long black hair.

"Billy Smith," said the centaur. "I am sorry I was so late, but I injured my leg on the way here." Billy noticed he did seem to be limping slightly. "Did it cause you any harm?" he continued, helping Billy to his feet.

"No, I'm okay – thank you – but what was that thing?"

The centaur didn't answer, but instead said, "You should get back to Barry as soon as you can. The forest is unsafe at this time – most of all for yourself. Are you able to ride? We can make it much quicker this way."

"My name is Clip Clop Doing a Mic Drop," he added, lowering his body so Billy could climb up onto his back.

As he stood back up to his full height, more galloping suddenly came from nearby. Brie Brie Neigh Neigh and Horse McHorseface burst through the trees into the clearing.

"Clip Clop Doing a Mic Drop!" Horsey McHorseface roared. "What are you doing? That human on your back is not wearing his morning suit or even a top hat! And look at his shoes, they're casual! Do you have no shame?"

"Do you not realise who this boy is?" said Clip Clop Doing a Mic Drop. "This is Billy Smith. He is not safe in this forest, and the quicker he leaves, the better."

"Have you been telling him our secrets?" said Horsey McHorseface. "Remember, no human must ever find out why the chicken really crossed the road!"

Brie Brie Neigh Neigh did a little tap dance with his front legs, then said, "I bought myself a new thesaurus the other day, but it's not very good. It's also not very good."

"Your joke is not very good, Brie Brie Neigh Neigh," said Clip Clop Doing a Mic Drop.

Horsey McHorseface raised his front legs in fury.

"Clip Clop Doing a Mic Drop! What are you saying? You know we centaurs do not critique another of our kind's punchlines like that."

Clip Clop Doing a Mic Drop raised his own front legs to counter Horsey McHorseface. Billy had to hold on tight around his neck to avoid slipping off.

"And do you not think that might be why we spend all our time rehearsing and none of it performing?" Clip Clip Doing a Mic Drop roared at Horse McHorseface. "When was the last time you or any of us actually had an audience? Yes, I dare say it might be a good thing if we begin challenging each other to be better, Horsey McHorseface, and maybe humans can offer us the help we need. As the saying goes, we cannot set-up a microphone without thumbs!"

And with that, Clip Clip Doing a Mic Drop reared around on his hind legs, and with Billy hanging on as best he could, galloped off into the trees, leaving Brie Brie Neigh Neigh and Horse McHorseface behind.

Billy had no idea what had just happened.

"Why is Horsey McHorseface so angry with you?" he asked. "And what was that thing you saved me from anyway?"

Once they were a little distance from the cleaning, Clip Clop Doing a Mic Drop slowed to a walk. He told Billy to duck out the way of low hanging branches, but it was another few moments before he said anything else.

"Billy Smith, are you aware of what the meat of the unicorn can be used for?"

"No," said Billy, wondering why he was being asked such a strange question.

"It is a most terrible crime against nature to slaughter a unicorn," said Clip Clop Doing a Mic Drop. "It is not something which most would ever consider doing, even those who may have committed other monstrous acts in the past. The meat of a unicorn will ensure you stay alive, even if you are, but moments from death, however, it comes at a high cost. Taking the life of a unicorn is an act so terrible that from the moment it takes its final breath of life, your own becomes a cursed one – an existence which will ensure you may never forget the despicable deed you committed in order to save yourself."

Billy thought for a moment about the obvious plot hole created by Barry's willingness to shoot a unicorn dead with one of his arrows.

"What sort of person could be that desperate to survive?" Billy then thought aloud. "A cursed life has to be worse than a peaceful death, doesn't it?"

"It does," Clip Clop Doing a Mic Drop agreed. "But what if the purpose of consuming the unicorn is not to continue to live, but simply to survive long enough until you are able to find something else – something which does not have any conditions attached – something which will ensure you are never able to die.

"Billy Smith, do you know what is being hidden in the school at this very moment?"

"The Bewitched –"

"It may be best if you refrain from saying its full name just now, you may cause yourself to fall from my back. But yes, the Brie."

"But I don't understand who —"

"Can you really not think of anybody who may be interested in obtaining the powers the Brie could provide for them? Somebody who has been waiting for many years to return to strength and regain their former control over this world?"

It suddenly came to Billy.

"Do you mean to say," he said, fear rising in his voice, "that the thing you saved me from — that was Ste —"

"Billy! Billy, is that you?"

Elahoraella was running towards them, Barry following close behind her.

"Billy, are you okay?" she said.

"I'm fine," said Billy. His mind was too focused on other things to say much else. "The unicorn, it's dead, Barry," he continued. "It's in a clearing back there."

"We say goodbye to one another here. You are safe now," said Clip Clop Doing a Mic Drop, and he lowered his body again so Billy could climb off. "I hope you will leave me a five-star review for your journey."

Barry watched the centaur struggling to stand up again, then, reaching for his quiver, he said, "Everythin' okay with theur, Clip Clop?"

"It's just a sprain. It will heal itself in time," said Clip Clop Doing a Mic Drop. "Good luck to you, Billy Smith," the centaur continued. "I feel sure we may meet again one day."

"Theur sure ah can't do owt f' theur?" said Barry.

"I'm fine, Barry. I do not need you to shoot me dead at this time."

"Well, if theur 'as change o' heart, let me know n' ah'll be reight over."

When they returned to the common room, they found Ed asleep with his face in a book. They said goodnight to Josh, then when he'd gone up to bed, they went over and shook Ed awake.

"No, I don't think you can cook carp in a toaster," Ed said sleepily.

"Ed, are you okay?" said Billy.

Ed stretched and yawned.

"I think I was dreaming," he said. Then he stared up at Elahoraella and began pointing at her. "You turned my shoe purple. Why did you turn my shoe purple?"

"I think you might have been dreaming that as well," said Elahoraella.

"Oh… yeah… I think you're right."

Once Ed had remembered what was going on, Billy and Elahoraella filled him in on what had taken place inside the forest.

"So we were wrong," said Billy finally. "Grape isn't trying to steal the Bewitched Brie —"

"This is cheese as cheese should be. The Bewitched Brie is the cheese for me. HEY!"

"Don't say its name," said Ed.

"Sorry," said Billy, then he continued, "Grape isn't trying to steal it for himself. He's trying to steal it for Steven — he's out there right now waiting for Grape. I saw him."

"But what can we do?" said Ed.

"Nothing," said Billy. "There's nothing we can do. We just have to wait for Grape to steal the Brie, and then Steven will be able to come after me... I imagine he'd have finished me off tonight if I hadn't been saved by Clip Clop Doing a Mic Drop."

Elahoraella looked scared, but she did at least have something reassuring to say.

"Billy, you're forgetting about Crumbleceiling. I know he an —"

"Idiot?" said Billy.

"Yes, that," said Elahoraella. "But he's one of the strongest and most intelligent idiots around. And everybody has always said Crumbleceiling is the only person That-Evil-One —"

"Don't say that either," said Ed, moving his book out the way of the cloud. "The library charges a fine for water damage, you know?"

Elahoraella continued.

"Everybody has always said Crumbleceiling is the only person Steven has ever been scared to face. So long as Crumbleceiling is around, you're safe. Steven can't harm you while you're at Frogsports."

Billy nodded.

The sun had risen by the time they finally went up to bed. But the night still had one last surprise waiting for Billy.

When he pulled back his bedsheets, he found the translucency tree neatly folded up underneath them, waiting for him. There was a note scribbled in green crayon pinned to the top of it: *I hear Canada is nice this time of year.*

As he climbed into bed a minute later, Billy reckoned he finally knew where the tree had come from.

Chapter Sixteen

Police Aux Frontières

Billy would never be quite sure how he managed to get through all his exams when he was half expecting to be murdered if not by Steven coming through the door at any moment, then by Professor Grape, who seemed to have become much more aggressive towards him since the last Frogsports match. Could Grape possibly have found out that he, Ed, and Elahoraella knew what he was up to?

It was stifling hot and humid around the castle, most of all in the Banquet Hall where they had to sit their written exams. As the teachers lined them up to check they weren't trying to cheat (Josh was caught attempting to smuggle in a water bottle that had notes written on the inside of the label), the first-years complained to each other about how this sort of weather might have been nice on holiday, but never in this country.

"What's going on?" said Patrick O'Connor. "I thought this was supposed to be Scotland? They should give us the day off when it's this hot inside — I heard they have to!"

"I don't think that's true," said Elahoraella.

"I heard if somebody faints during an exam, then we all pass it," said Simon Jones.

"That's not true either."

In addition to their written papers, they also had practical exams. Professor Millbrook called them all one at a time into his classroom to see how much profit they could generate by making coins appear behind a small child's ear. Professor McDouglass, meanwhile, asked them all to transform a pile of soiled rags into a colourful chain of handkerchiefs protruding from their sleeve — marks were given for how long the chain was, but taken away if a second small child worked out how they did it and started crying that their birthday party had been ruined.

On Wednesday afternoon, they took it in turns to hold their breath underwater for as long as possible while playing dead, so as not to give away that they were a magician and face being burned at the stake.

Their final exam was Fringe Production, which took place on Friday and consisted of three parts. First, they had a written exam where they spent two hours writing down the wittiest comebacks to unoriginal heckles shouted out by drunk audience members. Next, they had to perform their best magic tricks to an audience made up of three rowdy teenagers and an old couple who had wandered in by accident, all while avoiding a career breakdown on stage. The final part of the exam took place in the afternoon, and it too was practical. One by one, they had to demonstrate all the ways they had learnt of handing flyers to passersby who were trying to avoid eye contact, while at the same time arguing on the phone with a landlord about a security deposit.

This last exam turned out to be the hardest; not because of what they had to do, but because they first had to pay thousands of euro for the privilege of taking the exam, and then complete it after being deprived of sleep the night before. It was also the only exam where it was impossible to get full marks, because no matter how they did, the teachers would take thirty-five percent of their score for themselves.

The only person who felt confident about how they had done was Elahoraella.

"That wasn't as difficult as I thought it was going to be," she yawned as they joined the rest of the first-years who were walking out into the sunny grounds. "I managed to guess the old man's card correctly on my first attempt, and once I'd finished, both he and his wife told me they'd had a wonderful day out."

"They fell asleep before I could get to my card trick," said Billy.

"They walked out of my show and demanded a refund," said Ed. "It was pay-what-you-want!"

Elahoraella always liked to go through their exams afterwards, but Billy and Ed kept asking her not to; it made them both feel uneasy about how they might have done. They walked over to the shade cast by an enormous oak tree on the edge of the loch and sat down on the grass. Out on the water, Crumbleceiling was wakeboarding behind Nessie.

"No more lessons and no more exams," Ed signed as he stretched out and laid back on the grass. "You could look a bit happier about it, Billy. We've got the whole summer ahead of us before we get any more work to do."

Billy was scratching at his forehead and looking as though he might be sick.

"It's not the exams," he said. "It's my trademark – it's irritating me."

"We all feel like that sometimes," said Ed.

"It's like it's burning."

"Go to the hospital," Elahoraella suggested. "You don't look well."

"I'm not ill," said Billy. "I think this is some sort of message… it means something is going to happen, but I don't know what…"

Maybe it was because they knew they were both too important to the plot to kill off, but Ed and Elahoraella didn't seem as worried about the Bewitched Brie as Billy. The idea of Steven returning certainly frightened them, but they both thought nothing would happen so long as Crumbleceiling was around.

"Billy, you're worrying about nothing," said Ed. "Elahoraella was right before, the Brie is safe so long as it's under Crumbleceiling's protection. Anyway, you saw Grape earlier, did he look as though he's found out how to get past Waddles?"

It was true that after a Eudyptula first-year had given him a flyer as a joke, Grape had threatened to use it as a weapon if they ever dared do it again, but that was no different to how Billy would have expected Grape to react. He just couldn't shake off the feeling that there was something else going on.

"That's just the stress from this week," said Elahoraella when he tried to explain this feeling to her. "You'll be feeling like this until we get our results back."

But whatever it was that was making him feel this way, Billy felt quite sure it wasn't the stress of his exams. He looked over towards

Barry's hut where he could see Barry sat outside with Charlie, who was sunbathing on his back with all four legs up in the air and a pair of sunglasses on his face.

Only Barry and Crumbleceiling knew how to get past Waddles… Barry would never tell anyone else… never… but –

Billy had just realised something. He jumped to his feet.

"Billy, where are you going?" said Ed.

"We need to go see Barry straight away."

Confused, Ed and Elahoraella both got up and followed him. They had to walk quickly so they could keep up.

"Billy, what's going on?" said Elahoraella. "Why are we rushing?"

"I'll explain in a minute."

As they got closer to the Barry's hut, Charlie noticed them and started to bark.

"Ey up!" said Barry, looking up to see what Charlie was barking at. "Theur exams all over? Fancy a brew?"

"Yes, please –"

"We don't have time to stay," Billy told Ed. "Barry, I need to ask you something important. That night you joined the pyramid scheme, what did the man who signed you up look like?"

"Ah dunt know," said Barry, conversationally. "He 'ad 'ood covering' 'is head."

He noticed a sudden look of shock spread across their faces.

"Nowt strange 'bout tha', though," he said. "After all, 'ole thin' turned out t' be illegal. Probably jus' wanted t' 'ide 'is face in case somebody wor already on t' 'im."

As Ed scratched behind Charlie's ears, Billy sat down on a stump next to Barry.

"What did you both talk about? Did you mention Frogsports at all?"

"Ah think it came up, yeh," said Barry, straining to remember. "e' asked wha' ah did, n' ah said ah wor groundskeep' 'ere at Frogsports."

"And what did he say to that?"

"Well, e' said ah can't be making much doin' tha', n' ah told 'im 'e wor right, which is why ah started sellin' stuff from me book… tha' wor when ah asked if 'e wanted t' buy him sen a kayak… 'e said he ain't interested, bur 'e knows sum' way ah can mek me sen much more money… tha' wor when 'e brought up all 'air products n' tha'… bur 'e said it can be 'ard work, n' so 'e wanted t' mek sure ah could 'andle it… n' then ah told 'im, ah said, after Waddles, ah can 'andle owt tha' gerr' thrown at me."

"And was he interested in Waddles?" Billy asked, trying to sound casual.

"'course 'e wor. Not ery'day theur 'ears 'bout a two-'eaded duck now, is it? Anyway, 'e asked wha' it's like t' keep 'im as pet. It's easy, ah said — Waddles falls asleep whenever e' 'ears opera, see."

"So do I," joked Ed, but then he realised what Barry had just said.

Barry himself seemed to know he'd just said something he shouldn't, because in a panic he added, "Forget ah said owt. Theur not t' know 'bout tha' stuff — 'old on, where theur all goin'?"

Billy, Ed, and Elahoraella didn't speak to each other as they rushed back up to the castle. When they stopped in the entrance hall to catch their breath, Billy turned to the other two and said, "Barry told that strange how to get past Waddles, and I bet it was Grape under that hood."

"But Billy, that doesn't make sense," said Elahoraella. "In the previous chapter, you said you didn't think Grape had found out yet, and that was after Barry had already met this stranger."

"Never mind that plot hole now," said Billy. "We have to tell Professor Crumbleceiling."

"Do you think Crumbleceiling will believe us?" said Elahoraella. "Barry will get in trouble if he backs us up. He might lose his job."

"Barry wouldn't lie to Crumbleceiling," said Billy, or so he hoped, he thought privately to himself. "Where is Crumbleceiling's office anyway?"

They looked around as if hoping to see a door with his name on. They had never been told where to find Crumbleceiling, and they didn't know anyone who had ever been sent to see him — none of the teachers seemed to think the headmaster would be very good at keeping discipline.

"We could try the staff room?" Ed suggested.

Billy and Elahoraella agreed, so they set off to the second floor at a run. But as they passed by the Transformation classroom, a voice called after them.

"What are you three doing inside, and why are you running?"

They stopped and turned around. Professor McDouglass was standing there carrying a pile of books.

"We're looking for Professor Crumbleceiling," said Elahoraella. "We need to talk to him."

"You wish to talk to Professor Crumbleceiling?" said Professor McDouglass, as though she couldn't understand why this was something anyone would ever choose to do voluntarily. "Why on earth do you need to speak to the headmaster?"

Billy tried to think of something to say, but all he could come up with was, "I don't think we can tell you, Professor." He knew right away that he had said the wrong thing; Professor McDouglass suddenly looked both angry and suspicious.

"I am sure that anything you need to say to the headmaster you can share with me instead, but seeing as though you do not seem to think I am important enough – you just missed him, Professor Crumbleceiling left the school five minutes ago," she said, sounding offended. "He received an urgent message from the Secretariat for Sorcery and left immediately for London. He even cut his wakeboarding session short for it."

"He's left?" said Billy. "But Professor… this is important…"

"More important than the Secretariat of Sorcery?"

There was nothing else for it. Billy swallowed. "Professor – this is about the Bewitched Brie –"

"This is cheese as cheese should be. The Bewitched Brie is the cheese for me. HEY!"

With her hands forced into the air to start waving, the books in Professor McDouglass' arms fell to the floor, but she made no effort to pick them back up again.

"Come again?" she said.

"The Bewitched Brie…"

"This is cheese as cheese should be. The Bewitched Brie is the cheese for me. HEY!"

"One moment please," said Professor McDouglass. Then she went back into her classroom, leaving the three of them standing there with her books at their feet.

"What is she doing?" said Elahoraella.

Professor McDouglass returned with a bottle of water in her

hand.

"One more time, Mr Smith, if you wouldn't mind."

"It's about the Bewitch –" Professor McDouglass held up her hand to stop him. He paused as she unscrewed the top of the bottle, filled her mouth with water, then replaced the cap. She gestured for him to continue. "It's about the Bewitched Brie –"

Shocked, Professor McDouglass spat out the water into Billy's face.

"This is cheese as cheese should be. The Bewitched Brie is the cheese for me. HEY!"

"But – how can you possibly know about the Brie?" she coughed, choking on the last bit of water in her mouth. "And do not worry yourself, Miss Parker, this bottle is one hundred percent plant based," she added to Elahoraella.

"Professor, we think – no, we know – somebody is going to try and seal the Bewitched –"

"Please do not say its name again, Mr Smith. I am sure that by now you have all worked out it has its own jingle, which all who hear the name are forced to sing?"

"Professor, I have to talk to Professor Crumbleceiling immediately," Billy finished, wiping water out of his face.

Professor McDouglass eyed him with suspicion.

"But who are you suggesting could possibly steal the Brie while it is here at Frogsports?"

For a moment, Billy thought about being honest and saying Grape, but then he decided revenge would be better. He looked Professor McDouglass in the eye and said, "That-Evil-One."

Elahoraella watched with horror, while Ed bit his tongue to stop himself from laughing. Billy expected Professor McDouglass to be angry with him, but as the cloud disappeared from above her head, she brushed her wet fringe to one side and said, "Touché, Mr Smith.

"As for Professor Crumbleceiling," she added finally. "The headmaster will be back tomorrow afternoon, at which time I shall inform him of your concerns. But for now, be assured that nobody can possibly steal the Brie while it is at Frogsports. It is too well protected, and if I may say so, I am fairly confident that nobody will be able to get past my own enchantment. It would take powerful sorcery like *Bibbidi-Bobbidi-Boo* to break through that barrier — good afternoon, Professor Quigley," she added, for Quigley had just walked past them scribbling notes on his hand.

"Oh — yes, good afternoon, Professor McDouglass," he said, seemingly shocked that anyone had noticed him.

"But what if they already know that, Professor?" said Billy.

"How could anybody possibly know that, Smith? You are worrying about things that do not concern you. Quite unnecessarily, I might add," she finished shortly. "Now, I suggest now your exams are over, you all go outside and enjoy the weather." She bent down and picked up her books.

Professor Quigley had returned.

"How exactly do you spell *Bibbidi-Bobbidi-Boo*?" he asked.

"Oh, it's quite easy," said Professor McDouglass, and without another word to three of them, she and Quigley strode off down the corridor.

"It's today," said Billy, once he was certain Professor McDouglass couldn't hear them. "Grape is going to steal the Brie today. He knows how to get past Waddles, and now that Professor Crumbleceiling isn't here, there's nothing standing in his way."

"But what can we do about – what?" said Ed, for Elahoraella had just gasped.

"Good afternoon."

Billy and Ed turned around. Grape was stood there, looking down at them all with an even colder smile than he usually wore.

"And what might you all be doing inside when there are no more lessons or exams taking place? Surely you cannot be studying for your second-year already?" His eyes narrowed on Billy. "I mean, you don't even know if you will make it yet."

"We were only –" Billy began.

"Only looking for –" said Elahoraella.

"Yes, Mr Smith? Miss Parker?"

At that moment, Professor Quigley came past them again. This time he was showing the way to a Pavarotti tribute act. He almost jumped out of a window when Elahoraella said, "Good afternoon, Professor Quigley."

"Oh – yes, right – yes – good afternoon, Miss Parker."

As Grape turned his head to watch Quigley out of sight, the three of them took it as their chance to leave, but as they reached the end of the corridor, Grape called after them."

"I'm warning you now, Smith – if you spend any more time wandering around this castle at night, I shall be forced to personally murder you. Good day."

Once Grape had marched off, Billy turned to the other two.

"What do we do now?" said Ed.

"We have to keep a watch on Grape," said Billy. "He's gone off to the staff room. One of us should wait outside and follow him if he leaves — Elahoraella, you'd better do that."

"Why me?"

"No one will be suspicious if you're waiting for a teacher."

"And what should we do?" Ed asked Billy.

"Camp out by the door to the proscribed passageway and just hope we can do enough to slow him down if he shows up."

It didn't take long for their plan to fall apart. Billy and Ed had only been standing outside the door to Waddles for ten minutes when Professor McDouglass showed up carrying a giant loaf of bread, and this time, she was angry from the start.

"Enough of this!" she said, glaring at them both. "Do you think you're both more of a threat than the duck or the rest of the teacher's enchantments?"

"I don't think you're supposed to feed ducks bread, Professor," said Billy. "I read it in a book once."

Professor McDouglass ignored him. "If I hear either of you have come anywhere near this door again, you will both be in detention for the rest of the year!"

Billy and Ed returned to the common room where they found Elahoraella waiting for them.

"I'm sorry," she said, as they sat down beside her. "Professor Millbrook came past and while he was talking to me, Grape came out the staff room and strode away. I wasn't able to follow him."

"Well, that's it then, isn't it?" said Ed.

"No, there's got to be something else we can do," said Billy, a look of determination in his eye.

The other two stared at him.

"What are you thinking of?" said Elahoraella.

"I've got to do it," said Billy. "I'm going to wait up here all day and give Grape the chance to go steal the Brie now, then tonight I'm going to go after him hours after he could already have left."

"You can't," said Ed.

"What about Professor McDouglass?" said Elahoraella. "If she catches you, you'll be expelled for sure."

"WHAT DOES THAT MATTER?" Billy shouted. "If Grape gets to the Brie, Steven is coming back! He wants to kill me. He killed my parents. Don't you understand?"

It was Elahoraella's turn to shout. "NO, DON'T YOU UNDERSTAND, BILLY?"

Billy was taken aback.

"You're not the only person whose family Steven has murdered. You're not the only person he's tried to kill. You're not the only person he would try to kill again if he came back. Not everything is about you just because it's your name on the front of things, Billy. Don't you ever think about that?"

"She's got a point, you know?" said Ed. "Doesn't everyone else matter just as much?"

There was an awkward silence. Bill glared at them both.

"I'm going out here tonight, whether you're with me or not," he said eventually. "I'll use the translucency tree."

"But will all three of us fit inside it?" said Ed.

"All – all three of us?"

"We're with you, Billy," said Elahoraella. "You're not going to do this alone."

"But if anybody catches us, you'll both be kicked out too."

"I don't think that's going to happen," said Elahoraella with a smile on her face. "Professor Millbrook told me I got extra marks in our exam today for thinking to stick flyers to the top of people's umbrellas in the rain. He said it's one of the best techniques he's ever seen. They don't even teach it."

They went for dinner, then returned to the common room and sat apart from each other. Elahoraella was busy reading *Brie and Me*, checking to see if there was anything written in it that might be of some use to them. Billy and Ed sat in silence, occasionally giving the other a nervous glance across the room.

Slowly, the common room began emptying as their fellow Osphranters went off to bed. Finally, after a group of sixth-year students went up to their dormitory, Ed turned to Billy. "Time to get the translucency tree," he said. Billy nodded, then ran upstairs to pull it out from under his bed.

"We should try it on here to make sure it's big enough to fit all three of us," said Elahoraella when Billy returned.

"It's going to be big enough," said Billy.

"How can you be sure?"

"Magic."

As Billy pulled the costume over his head, a voice suddenly spoke from the other side of the room.

"Where are you going?"

Billy stood frozen as Josh stepped out from behind the chair nearest the door.

"Nowhere," said Ed, speaking too quickly to sound innocent.

"Where's Billy? I heard his voice. And why is there a tree in the common room?"

"Er — it's to brighten the place up," said Elahoraella, thinking quickly.

Josh stared at them.

"You're taking it somewhere, aren't you?" he said.

"No, we're just watering it," said Elahoraella. "But we don't need any help now, so why don't you just go up to bed, Josh?"

"You can't leave the common room," said Josh. "You'll get Osphranter house into trouble again. We'll lose even more credits if you're caught."

"You don't understand, Josh. This is important —"

But Josh clearly had no intention of giving in. He moved back and stood in the doorway to block their way out.

"I'm not letting you leave," he said. "I'll fight you both if I have to!"

Billy glanced up at the clock. Every moment they were stuck here wasting time with Josh gave Grape more time to escape.

"We need to go," said Billy.

"The tree..." said Josh. "The tree spoke."

"Can't you do something?" Ed said desperately to Elahoraella.

"I'm sorry for this, Josh," said Elahoraella. She pulled out her enchanted celery and pointed it at him. *"Hippity Hoppity You Should Fu..."* Ed coughed, *"... Offity!"*

Josh fell silent at once, then he turned around to face the nearest wall and advanced into it face first. Next moment, he was lying back on the floor unconscious.

Billy, Ed, and Elahoraella rushed over to him.

"Is he okay?" said Billy.

"He will be. He'll come around in an hour or so," said Elahoraella. "But that felt so good."

"Felt good?"

"Come on, haven't you both wanted to do that to him all year? He's an idiot!"

Billy and Ed both thought about this for a moment, then nodded in agreement. "It was brave of him to stand up to us like that, though," Billy admitted.

"When I stood up to you like that, you called me interfering and annoying," said Elahoraella. "It really is quite sexist, you know?"

"That's not our fault," said Ed. "We didn't write it into the plot."

Ed and Elahoraella joined Billy under the tree costume, and the three of them carefully made their way out of the common room and into the deserted corridor outside. Feeling as nervous as they did, they couldn't help but jump at every shadow or expect to run into a teacher whenever they turned a corner, but they were lucky. It wasn't until they reached the corridor leading to the proscribed passageway that they met anyone else. Karen was busy trying to trip over a loose bit of carpet in front of a security camera.

"Who's there?" she said, looking up at the sound of footsteps. Her eyes narrowed on the tree. "I don't like trees. Why does everybody always talk about saving the trees? Don't all plants matter?"

Billy had an idea.

He coughed, then said, "Bing-bong – could the owner of the white ninety-nine *Lexus RX* with the *Costco* air freshener and *In This Car, I'm the Manager* sign in the back window, please return to your vehicle as it is illegally parked over the white line."

"No. No. This is tyranny," shouted Karen. "You're disrespecting me! It's unacceptable!"

"That is the owner of the white *Lexus* with the *The Closer You Get,*

The Slower I Drive bumper sticker, please return to your vehicle as it will be towed — thank you."

"This is inconveniencing me!" And she flew off down the corridor screaming about how she would never shop there again.

"Brilliant," said Ed.

"How did you know that would work?" said Elahoraella.

"It's what they all drive."

They continued forward, and a moment later, they were outside the door to the proscribed passageway. As they had expected, it was already open.

"It looks like Grape has already got past Waddles," Billy whispered to the other two. But there was no need for him to talk so quietly. Waddles' heavy breathing carrying through the gap in the door was enough to muffle their voices.

"If you want to turn back here, you can," said Billy. "I won't need the translucency tree anymore."

"We've come this far," said Ed.

"We're not going to leave you now," said Elahoraella.

Billy nodded his appreciation, then gently pushed the door open with his foot.

They entered the passageway. Waddles was sleeping with one of his heads leaning over the open trapdoor. Then, a voice from behind them made them all jump.

"Is somebody there?"

Having presumed they were alone, the shock made them yell out. Waddles stirred a little.

They turned around. The face of the Pavarotti tribute act who had walked past them that afternoon was gazing over at them from behind a pillar. He looked terrified.

"That's funny," he said. "There wasn't a tree there before."

They pulled off the translucency tree, and the man yelled out just as loud as they had done. Waddles stirred some more.

"Oh, thank goodness you've found me," said the man, realising they weren't going to attack him. "I was brought up here to sing this duck to sleep — I didn't want to take the job, but it was either this or selling car insurance — and I couldn't find my way back out. The man I was with fell down that trapdoor over there," he continued, pointing at the trapdoor. "He probably needs — needs —"

"What's wrong?" said Elahoraella.

Next to her, Billy already knew what was wrong. He had just glanced back at the trapdoor and noticed Waddles' head was no longer hanging over it. And then they heard it.

"QUACKKKKKK!"

Waddles was awake again.

They turned back and looked up at the duck's two giant heads. They were both gawping down at them all with a curious expression.

"You need to start singing again," Billy told the tribute act.

"I can't," he said. "It wouldn't be a union contact. They'd kick me out if they knew."

"HAVE YOU GONE MAD?" Ed bellowed. "We're all about to be killed!"

"I really need some sort of contribution. You know, times are hard enough for performers like me."

"We don't have any money with us," said Elahoraella.

"That's okay," said the man as he pulled a small device from his pocket. "I accept credit cards."

"JUST SING!" said Billy.

Glancing up at Waddles was enough to spur the man's voice. The effect was immediate. No sooner had the notes hit the air than Waddles seemed to calm, then lay back down again. With a few moments, the duck was asleep.

"Now, about payment —"

Billy turned to him. "Elahoraella," he said. "What was the sorcery you used on Josh?"

"Hippity Hoppity You Should —"

"How about you just tell me the way out, and we'll forget about the money?"

After giving the tribute act directions back to the entrance hall from where they were, Billy, Ed, and Elahoraella turned their attention back to the trapdoor, which, thankfully, no longer had one of the duck's giant heads dangling over it.

Billy knelt down and looked through the door.

"Can you see anything?" said Elahoraella.

Billy shook his head. "It's too dark, I can't even work out how deep it might go."

"Is there a ladder?"

"No. We're going to have to jump. I'll go first," he said, standing up again.

Billy turned to the others. "If I don't shout back that it's safe, don't follow me — go straight back to the common room and use Yodel to send a letter to Crumbleceiling."

"Okay," said Ed.

Ed and Elahoraella stood back and watched as Billy lowered himself into the hole until he was only holding on with the very ends of his fingers. He looked up at them and said, "I can't feel the bottom."

"Be careful," said Elahoraella.

Billy let go. He felt cold, damp air rush past his face as he fell. Above him, the trapdoor was getting smaller and smaller, then — "Ouch!" he shouted out. He'd landed onto stone.

"Billy, are you okay?" Elahoraella shouted down.

"I think I've broken something, but it's okay. There's a magic potion down here that we can use to recover our health."

"Save some for us."

Ed jumped down next, landing next to Billy. Elahoraella followed, but had her landing cushioned by falling on top of Ed.

They were in a small circular room lit by a single torch on the wall. The way forward was behind a wooden door, and next to it, just as Billy had said, was a bright red potion bottle sitting atop a small table. Billy reached out for it and picked it up.

"Let Ed use it first," said Elahoraella. "He's the most injured."

She wasn't wrong. Ed's whole body was flashing bright red on and off like a broken Christmas tree light, and he couldn't stop mimicking the sound of his heartbeat. "Ba-dum, ba-dum, ba-dum, ba-dum-tsh!"

Billy handed Ed the bottle, and he drank a third of it.

"Thanks," said Ed, as his body seemed to recover. He handed the bottle back to Billy. "Well, there's no turning back now," he said, staring up at the trapdoor high above them. "How do we get out of here when we're done?"

"We'll have to go up there," said Billy, and he pointed to a staircase at the other side of the room with a fire exit sign hanging above it.

When Billy and Elahoraella had drunk their share of the potion, they stood up and went through the door. They found themselves in another passageway. This one was longer and narrower than the one Waddles was guarding above. Ahead of them, a troll blocked their way. They recognised it instantly as the one who normally resided under the bridge to the Vigilantism classroom, but it didn't look as friendly as it usually did.

As they approached, the troll watched them. Then, when they were only a few steps away, it said, "You have three guesses." This was different, they all thought. Normally they had as many guesses as they needed; it often took Josh the whole lesson to think of the correct answer.

Billy nodded to the other two, then said to the troll, "What's the riddle?"

"Who let the dogs out?"

"Who?" said Billy.

"Who?" said Elahoraella.

"Who?" said Ed.

"Who?" said Elahoraella.

"Who?" said Billy.

The troll glared down at them all menacingly. "Incorrect," it said. "Two guesses left."

"Barry?" said Ed, assuming he was the obvious answer; Barry was the only person at Frogsports who owned a dog after all.

The troll gave them a cruel smile. "One guess left," it said.

They were starting to panic now. They looked up into the troll's hideous face and felt sure that if they didn't get the correct answer on their next attempt, they would have bigger problems than simply not being allowed to pass.

Billy was thinking hard, but before he could give an answer, Elahoraella said, "Prince Michael of Kent during an official visit to *Battersea* last March."

Billy and Ed braced themselves for something bad to happen, but to their great surprise, the troll scratched the back of his head and said, "Oh… yeah, that's right that is."

As the troll moved to one side to let them continue, Ed turned to Elahoraella.

"How the hell did you know that?" he asked.

"I went there on a school trip last year and they had a photograph of his visit on the wall."

As they continued down the passageway, the echoing sound of their footsteps was joined by a gentle drip of water coming from the gaps in the stonework above their heads. Billy figured they must be somewhere under the loch now; there was a damp smell in the air. Eventually, the passageway began sloping downwards. Ahead, it looked as though it was about to open into a bright chamber, but before they could reach it, they all froze mid-step as though forced into suspended animation.

Although unable to move his head, Billy could move his eyes. He focused on the chamber ahead of them, where he could see flickers as objects began populating the room.

Then, as suddenly as they had stopped, they were all able move again.

"What just happened there?" said Ed. "Do you think that was McDouglass' enchantment?"

"It can't be," said Billy. "Grape will already have disabled that one."

"I think the next room just needed time to render in," said Elahoraella.

They continued forward into the chamber and took a moment to survey the room around them. The way forward was visible ahead of them, but between them and the door they needed to reach were three precarious stone platforms floating not on water or in the air, but rather — for absolutely no logical reason — a river of lava flowing across the width of the room.

"This is ridiculous," said Ed.

"Maybe the developers just got lazy," said Billy.

Cautiously, they stepped forward. They could smell sulphur in the air and feel the warmth on their faces now.

"Do you reckon these platforms will be strong enough for us to jump across?" said Ed.

Billy looked around to check if there was anything they had missed.

"I don't think we've got any choice but to find out," he said. "There's no other way to get across."

He told the other two to stand back, then took a run up and jumped onto the middle platform. It took a moment for him to find his balance; the whole platform had started moving as though surfing on the lava.

"Billy, are you okay?" said Elahoraella.

"It is strong enough," said Billy. "But it's not easy to stand on."

He took a moment to ready himself, then jumped again, this time across to the solid ground on the other side.

"Just take it slow," he said, turning back to them.

Elahoraella went next. She jumped onto the platform, then across to Billy.

"Are you okay?" he asked her.

"Yes, I'm fine. Come on, Ed."

Ed was steady on his feet as he jumped onto the platform, but as he went to jump again to safety, the stone platform started to crumble beneath him, and he fell into the river of lava below.

"NO!" shouted Billy and Elahoraella together, then –

"What are you shouting for?" said Ed.

Somehow, the moment Ed touched the lava, all three of them had been transported back to the start of the chamber.

"That was weird," said Billy.

On their second attempt to cross, they had more luck. By each using a different platform, they reached the door without any of them falling in.

As Elahoraella reached for the door, though, she couldn't help but notice there was something different about Ed.

"Ed, have you got taller?" she asked.

"Oh, yeah," said Ed. "I think I just levelled up."

By now, they were all starting to think that nothing they might come across next would surprise them, but even so, the next chamber still came as a shock. They were in a vast hall filled with rope lines that led to a row of counters at the other side of the room. Billy wondered for a moment if they had somehow ended up in Sino Pauper Edo Recondo Mammonas, but it couldn't be the bank; this room looked far too sterile.

Ahead of them was a sign that pointed EU citizens one way and non-EU citizens the other. They looked over to the counters and noticed another much larger sign hanging above them, which read *Police Aux Frontières*. It seemed they had reached the French border.

"Of course," said Elahoraella, "this all makes sense."

"Does it?" said Ed.

"Yes, it does. Think about it. The Brie has come from France, hasn't it? That's where Émile Arquette lives, it says so in one of his book. But it's too difficult to bring anything through customs anymore, so Crumbleceiling must have just given part of the castle to France and decided to keep the Brie in there."

"What sort of idiot would come up with that as a solution to anything?"

"You'd be surprised," said Elahoraella.

"But that doesn't make any sense," said Billy. "The Brie was being held at Sino Pauper Edo Recondo Mammonas before it was moved to Frogsports, and the bank isn't in France. How can you explain that?"

Elahoraella shrugged.

"Magic," she said simply.

They pulled out their passports and began snaking their way up and down the rope line until they encountered their first problem. As they got close to the counters, a border agent, noticing their passports were British, shouted at them and directed them back again; they had accidentally joined the line for EU passport holders only.

"How is this a benefit?" said Elahoraella as they now entered the line for non-EU citizens.

This time when they reached the counters, an aggressive looking man called them forward. A moment later, they all jumped when suddenly the man started beating them for approaching together instead of one at a time.

"What is the purpose of your visit?" the border agent asked Billy when he then approached alone.

"I'm here to stop Steven from coming back and murdering me!"

The agent typed something on his computer and said, "I'll put business trip." Then he stamped Billy's passport and let him continue.

Elahoraella was called forward next.

"What is the purpose of your visit?"

"I'm here to stop Grape stealing the Bewitched Brie!"

"This is cheese as cheese should be. The Bewitched Brie is the cheese for me. HEY!"

With a stamp in her passport, Elahoraella was free to join Billy on the other side of the counters.

Finally, Ed was called forward.

"Er — whatever they just said," he answered when asked why he was visiting.

The border agent looked at his passport, then up at him, then back to his passport.

"No," he said. "You cannot enter."

"What?" said Ed. "But you let both of them through."

"Your passport, it is not valid for six months."

"Come on, Ed," said Billy, we need to go. "Grape's ahead of us, remember."

"He won't let me through," said Ed, gesturing at the border agent. "He says my passport doesn't have more than six months validity left on it."

"But you aren't actually leaving the UK," said Elahoraella. "You're just going into a part of it that's now treated as France for some reason."

Ed tried explaining this to the border agent, but it was no use.

"There's got to be something we can do," said Billy. "What about an emergency passport application?"

Ed shook his head.

"There isn't time for that," he said. "This is one of the sacrifices we have to make for the freedom to visit fewer places and do less things — you have to go on without me."

"But —"

"Do you want to stop Grape stealing the Brie or not? If you don't hurry up, he'll already have gone."

There was no other choice.

Billy and Elahoraella left the immigration hall without Ed and continued into yet another passageway. This was the strangest they'd been in yet. As they advanced, Billy was sure they kept passing by the exact same plant pot, window, vase, and creepy portrait with moving eyes that followed them as they went by. They were just wondering how long this passageway could possibly be when they came to another door.

This next room appeared empty, but that didn't stop them from treading carefully, just in case.

"What do you think this is?" said Billy.

"I don't know, but I have a bad feeling about it."

They relaxed a little when they were able to make it across to the opposite door without anything happening.

"This must have been where McDouglass' enchantment was," said Elahoraella. She tried the door, but it was locked. "Have a look around," she said. "There must be a key hidden somewhere."

But Billy had just noticed some writing that was etched into the wood.

"Hey, look at this," he said, pointing this out to Elahoraella. He read aloud, "Say the magic word, and I shall open."

"The magic word?" said Elahoraella. "But what's the magic word – I've got it." She pulled out her enchanted celery and pointed it at the door. *"Open Sesame!"*

Nothing happened.

"That's strange," she said. "But those are the magic words to open locked doors."

"Maybe it's something different here?" said Billy. Then he pulled out his own enchanted celery and started listing all the magical words he could think of.

"Legalese! – Hippity Hoppity! – Alakazam! –"

"Billy, I need..." Elahoraella tried to say over him.

"Hocus-Pocus! – Abracadabra! – A La Peanut Butter Sandwiches!"

"Billy, I need to think, can you please –"

The door swung open at once.

"Oh," said Elahoraella. "The magic word was *please*."

She glanced around the room, then said to no one in particular, "Thank you."

The door swung shut again.

"Er... *please*," she said again, and the door swung back open.

"After you," said Billy, gesturing for her to lead.

"Thank you –"

"PLEASE!"

They went through the door and found themselves in what Billy was sure had to be the final chamber before the Brie. There was no puzzle to solve or creature to defeat in this room. Instead, a giant black chest stood alone in the middle of the room. Behind it, opposite where they were standing, was the way forward; a high stone double door covered in chains running from all four corners into a giant golden lock that was hanging in the middle of it. As his eyes moved down to the chest, Billy thought he knew exactly where to find the key they needed.

"I reckon this is it," he said to Elahoraella. "I think Grape is on the other side of this door."

He walked forward.

"Be careful," said Elahoraella, but nothing happened.

Billy knelt down beside the chest and opened it. He was right; the key for the lock was inside it. He stood back as the key floated out of the chest, then came towards him through the air. As it started spinning in front of him, he pulled out his enchanted celery and gently tapped it on the edge of the key.

"What are you doing that for?" said Elahoraella.

Billy shook his head, then grabbed the key.

"I don't know," he said. "Dramatic effect, probably."

With the key in hand, he went over to the double doors and placed it into the lock. Immediately, the sound of mechanical clicking filled the room, then the lock started spinning in front of their eyes. Next moment, the chains dissolved into nothing, and the lock fell to the floor at his feet with a thunderous crash that caused the torches on the wall to flicker.

With the way forward unlocked, he turned back to Elahoraella.

"I need to do this alone," he said. "It's too dangerous –"

"But, Billy –"

"No, listen – go back and find Ed, then go up that fire escape and use Yodel to send a letter to Crumbleceiling. He's the only person who can stop all this. I might be able to slow Grape down, but he's stronger than me really."

"But Billy, what if he's got Steven with him?"

"Then I'll just have to challenge him to a magician's duel, and before Grape can say ta-da, I'll pull the hat over Steven's head and push him down the stairs."

Elahoraella looked scared.

"Billy — you're a great magician, you now," she said. "Even if you haven't actually performed even one bit of sorcery since you arrived at Frogsports."

"I'm not that good," said Billy. "Not like you are."

"Me," said Elahoraella. "Reading books all the time?"

"Why are you talking like that?"

Elahoraella shrugged.

"I'm supposed to play down my achievements and talents, and instead support you as the white male hero who saves everybody."

"But you're always learning more when you read."

"I've only read seven books this month! And there are more important things — decency, acceptance, understanding, and knowing the difference between your imagination and the real world."

"They don't teach any of that at Frogsports."

"No, they don't," Elahoraella laughed. "And they never will.

"Good luck, Billy."

She turned to leave.

"Oh, and Billy," said Elahoraella, turning back to him. "Don't forget to save our progress before you continue. That way we won't have to do everything again if you die in there."

"Er — sure," said Billy.

Elahoraella left.

Alone, Billy faced the double doors.

"Here I come Grape," he said to himself, and he pushed them open to reveal the path forward. He took a few minutes to prepare himself, then took a deep and stepped through into the final chamber.

But to his great surprise, Grape wasn't there.

Chapter Seventeen

This Is Cheese as Cheese Should Be

No one was.

Instead, a decorative stone pedestal stood alone in the middle of the chamber, and on top of it, a small wooden box which quite unmistakably had the Bewitched Brie inside of it; even from here Billy could smell it.

Billy moved forward to take it, but as he got close –

"Oh, damn," he heard a voice say. "I wasn't ready for you."

To Billy's great surprise, it wasn't Grape, but Professor Quigley who stepped out of the darkness and approached him.

"I didn't know how long you were going to be, so I was reading a book – *Getting Past a Giant Duck With Two Pounds of Doolin and a Little Bit of Luck* by Émile Arquette, have you heard of it? – anyway, would you mind stepping outside and coming in again? Just so we can do this properly.

Perplexed, Billy went along with his request and left the room. He waited a moment, then entered again. Quigley was now stood facing the pedestal, a sinister figure under the shadows cast by the light of lanterns falling against the giant plinths that lined the chamber.

As Billy stepped forward, Quigley slowly turned around to face him.

"I was wondering when you might – actually, it would be much better if I had one of those revolving chairs and perhaps a cat like they have in the movies, you know? Never mind, there's no time to find a cat now."

"Do you want me to do the entrance again?" asked Billy.

"Would you? I don't want to put you out, but that's very kind."

Billy left, waited a moment, then entered a third time. As before, Quigley was stood facing the pedestal, and again, as Billy approached, he began turning slowly to face him. Billy stopped and thought for a moment. Then he took a few steps back, and Quigley turned back towards the pedestal. Then he walked forward and Quigley turned back to him. A few steps back, and he turned back to the pedestal again. After amusing himself by walking forward, then backward for a while, Billy finally approached.

"I was wondering when you might show up here, Billy Smith," said Quigley in a cold and calculating voice. "I was starting to get bored with waiting here all day instead of taking the Brie and making my escape long before anybody could stop me."

"You!" gasped Billy.

Quigley smiled, but it wasn't a welcoming smile.

"Not who you were expecting, Smith?"

"I thought – Professor Grape –"

"Grape?" Quigley laughed. "Yes, I suppose Grape does seem the type, doesn't he? It certainly is helpful to have somebody like him walking around with all the suspicion he casts upon himself. It takes the attention away from me, see."

Billy couldn't believe it. Quigley was the last person he expected to find stood in front of him.

"But I thought Grape wanted to kill me?"

"Oh, he does. He thought he had the perfect plan at your first Frogsports match, but your friend Miss Parker put a stop to that when she set fire to the teacher's stand. Another few moments and he'd have succeeded."

"So he sent those daggers after me?"

"Of course," said Quigley cooly. "And he was ever so disappointed it didn't work. Why do you think he wanted to referee your next match? He wanted to have another go at finishing the job, but then he got that turkey to the face. He found out Crumbleceiling had bribed the school inspector to overlook a few irregularities, and so he used it to blackmail the headmaster into appointing him the match official. He did make himself unpopular with the other teachers, though. They all wanted to force the headmaster into giving them a raise instead."

"But I don't understand," said Billy.

"Don't you?" said Quigley, going to stroke a cat in his arms before remembering he didn't have one. "It really is quite straightforward. Grape was at school with your mother and father. He despised your father, but your mother, oh how he loved her. She didn't love him back, however, so naturally he went on to murder many people and become a servant to evil as though to imply it was all her fault for rejecting him. But never mind any of that, I suppose. He gets his redemption, of course."

Billy's mind was racing. He couldn't believe what he was hearing. What sort of person's mind comes up with these sub-plots?

"He put all that effort into executing his revenge on you this year, but for what? When I'm going to be the one to kill you tonight."

Quigley pulled his enchanted celery out of his pocket and gave it a flick. At once, cans of silly string appeared out of nowhere and began spraying themselves onto Billy until he was bound so tightly he was unable to move.

"You're far too nosy for your own good, Smith."

As Billy stood there helpless, Quigley strode over and whispered into his ear. "But what would be the fun in killing you now when I could waste time until you've found a way to escape instead?"

He went back over to the pedestal.

"Now, wait quietly, Smith. I need to examine this cheese board."

Quigley reached out to touch the box, but quickly recoiled in pain. "Heh," he laughed. "Trust Crumbleceiling to come up with something like this. He's made it impossible to simply reach out and take the Bewitched Brie."

"This is cheese as cheese should be. The Bewitched Brie is the cheese for me. HEY!"

Billy felt his arms move, but bound as he was, he couldn't wave his hands in the air.

"Don't say its name, fool!" said a new, third voice.

"I'm sorry, master," said Quigley, his own voice faltering.

"Who was that?" asked Billy.

Quigley quickly regained his cool. "We'll come to that soon enough," he said. "But first, this sorcery of Crumbleceiling's…"

All Billy could think to do was keep Quigley talking, to stop him concentrating on the pedestal.

"Crumbleceiling knows somebody is trying to steal the Brie tonight."

And then Billy heard something. Was that Crumbleceiling now? He looked up and Yodel flew into view. In one sweep, she dropped a letter in front of him, and then ploughed hard into one of the stone pillars and fell back.

Quigley picked up the letter and scanned the front. Then he started to laugh.

"It appears the headmaster does not know after all."

Quigley held up the letter for Billy to see. It was unmistakably addressed in Elahoraella's handwriting, but stamped in red ink at the top was *Insufficient Postage: The recipient declined to pay the fee due. Return to sender.* Billy's heart sank.

"But enough of this messing around," said Quigley, returning to the pedestal. "Crumbleceiling has set up some sort of barrier… but how to break it?" He flicked his enchanted celery, but nothing appeared to happen. "Of course, not," he muttered to himself. "That would be far too simple."

Then Billy saw that something had happened. As he looked beyond Quigley, he noticed a second pedestal that hadn't been there a moment before.

"The boy sees…" It was the mystery voice speaking again.

Billy tried to avert his gaze, but he wasn't quick enough. Quigley had seen where he was looking, and now he saw the second pedestal too.

"He always has to play his little games."

Quigley went over to the second pedestal and picked up the object that was sat atop it. He laughed again, then walked back over to Billy with the object in hand.

"So simple, really," he said. "Yes, this must be the way to break the barrier." He held up a large small medium-sized pebble with a cheese knife sticking out the top of it. He tried pulling the knife out, but it wouldn't come loose.

"Master, Crumbleceiling is playing a game with us. I cannot remove the knife from the pebble."

The voice spoke again.

"Use the boy to remove it…"

"Of course," said Quigley, rounding on Billy. "The headmaster will not have felt the needed to protect the Brie from students."

Quigley clicked his fingers, and the silly string binding Billy dissolved into nothing.

"Come here, Smith."

Billy walked slowly towards him.

He thought Quigley was probably right, but he mustn't show it if he was. I must be gentle, he thought to himself. Just make it look like I'm trying to pull the knife out, that's all.

Quigley held out the pebble. Billy reached out and closed his hand on the wooden handle of the cheese knife. It was smooth. It gripped well in his hand. The quality was good, too, thought Billy. For a moment, he wondered if a full set of these knives was available for three easy payments of twenty-nine ninety-nine plus shipping and VAT. Then he remembered where he was.

He moved his hand the tiniest amount he could without Quigley noticing. The knife was loose. If he pulled any harder, it was sure to come straight out of the pebble.

"Well?" said Quigley impatiently. "Can you pull it out?"

Billy summoned all the courage he had as he let go, then looked up to stare at the expectant yet frustrated expression on Quigley's face.

"No."

Quigley swore loudly.

"Move out of the way," he said, pushing Billy to one side. Billy lost his balance and fell to the floor. As he pulled himself back up, the voice returned.

"The boy lies… he lies…"

"Smith!" Quigley shouted. "Tell me the truth. Can you pull the knife from the pebble?"

"Let me speak to him… face-to-face…"

"Master, you do not have the strength."

"I have the strength for this…"

"But…" said Quigley, seeming to panic a little. "I'm… I'm shy —"

"Let me speak!"

Billy couldn't move. Terrified, he watched as Quigley began unbuttoning the front of his shirt from top to bottom. What was going on? The shirt fell open, and it took Billy a moment to realise what he was looking at. He wanted to scream, but seemed unable to make any sound. He was staring at a face. The most terrible face Billy had ever seen. It was a ghostly white with piercing red eyes and an entirely flat nose. The hair on Quigley's chest gave it a beard, quiff, and eye brows.

"Bill Smith…" the face whispered. "I see the headmaster was right about you. I must pay him for a bet."

"Steven," said Billy.

"You dare to speak my name? How very gallant of you, but still, it is unwise."

Billy tried to move back, but he couldn't.

"Do you see what I have become?" said the face. "I do not live, but merely exist. I do not possess my own body, but instead I –"

"You're living on his chest," said Billy.

"Yes, I am living on his chest, but what did you expect? Did you expect me to be living on the back of his head and hidden under a turban, perhaps? That would be cultural appropriation. That would be lazily taking advantage of offensive racial anxieties and implying that turbans are worn by the evil to hide evil."

Billy thought about this for a moment, and it struck him how amazing it was that no one had thought to change it for the adaptation.

"What happened to your nose?" asked Billy.

Quigley looked scared now.

"Halloween," he said quickly. "I tripped over in the Banquet Hall and –"

"You squashed my nose," said the face.

"But how do you smell?"

"Awful – this man does not shower often enough."

"Master, please accept my forgiveness."

"Be quiet, fool! Steven does not forgive. But you, Billy – you can help me. All I require is but a single bite of that cheese, and then I will be free of this body… Now… why don't you pull that knife from the pebble for me?"

So Steven knew he could pull the knife out. Sensation returned suddenly to his legs, and feeling as though he could move again, Billy stepped backward.

"There's no point in trying to run," sneered the face. "You are better off by joining me… Help me return to my own body, and you may walk alongside and share my power."

"NEVER!"

Billy made for the door, but Steven screamed, "STOP HIM!" and next second, he felt Quigley's hand close on his arm. At once, he felt a sharp pain across his trademark. He screamed out. Then suddenly the pain went away. Quigley had let go of his arm. Billy looked around to see where Quigley had gone, and saw him staring down at his hand, no longer fleshy and alive, but solid grey stone instead.

"STOP HIM!" shrieked Steven again, and Quigley held out his stone hand and went for Billy's neck – his trademark was burning from pain, but Quigley was screaming out too. The stone was spreading.

"Master, I cannot – my arm – it's stone!"

Quigley let go and fell back.

"Then kill him and have this over with!" shouted Steven.

Quigley raised his enchanted celery in his other, non-stone hand, but then an idea came to Billy – "You'll never get your hands on the Bewitched Brie!" he said, and all three of them beginning to sing.

"*This is cheese as cheese should be. The Bewitched Brie is the cheese for me. HEY!*"

As his hands were forced up to wave, Quigley let go of his enchanted celery and threw it behind him.

"Master, my celery –"

Billy knew what he had to do. He stood up, grabbed Quigley's arm, and didn't let go. Quigley screamed and tried to kick him away, but Billy didn't loosen his grip — he wasn't sure which of them was screaming louder — all he could see was black — all he could feel was burning in his head — he heard a voice, "Billy! Billy!"

He felt his grip loosen, but there was nothing he could do.

Billy heard a voice speaking from somewhere close by.

"I see you were correct, Headmaster. You must remind me to pay you that bet."

"I did tell you all."

He opened his eyes. Someone was looking down at him, but it wasn't Quigley or Steven. It was a woman he'd never seen before.

He sat up and saw Professor Crumbleceiling sat in a chair in front of him. Noticing Billy was awake, Crumbleceiling smiled and put down the magazine he was reading.

"Good afternoon, Billy," he said. "Have you met the school doctor? Allow me to introduce Madam Pepper," and he pointed at the woman who stood over him.

"I will leave you to it, Headmaster," said Madam Pepper.

"Thank you, doctor," said Crumbleceiling.

As Madam Pepper left, Crumbleceiling looked back at Billy.

Billy stared back at him. Then he remembered: "Sir! It was Quigley! He's taken the Bewitched —"

"Please calm yourself," said Crumbleceiling, raising his hand. "Best not to finish that off just now, your arm being how it is. I can assure you, however, that Quigley does not have anything."

Billy looked down at his arm. It was in a thick cast. Then he looked around him and realised he must be in the hospital wing. He looked across to the next bed where Yodel was laying with her wing in a sling, a thermometer in her mouth, and a tiny cool pack on her head. At the other side of the room, Madam Pepper was now tending to an injured reindeer. He stared back at Crumbleceiling.

"I was just reading about two priests who visited South America," said Crumbleceiling, picking up his magazine and showing Billy the cover. "It's amazing what they think people will read in hospital."

Billy read the title of the magazine: *Roaming Catholics*. Then he noticed the table next to Crumbleceiling, which was piled high with boxes of fresh cooking ingredients, foreign chocolates, ethical snacks, jars of sweets, shaving kits, and more.

"Ah, yes," said Crumbleceiling. "It would appear that you didn't have the chance to cancel a few free trials while you've been here, and they all seem to have renewed at once. Though I believe your teammates, Chad and Larry Beaversley, did attempt to send you four kayaks. No doubt they thought it would amuse you. Madam Pepper, however, felt they were a little unnecessary for hospital."

"How long have I been in here?"

"A little over a week," said Crumbleceiling. "Your friends Edward Beaversley and Elahoraella Parker will be delighted to hear you have woken up, they have been extremely concerned."

"But sir, what about the —"

"I see you are not going to relax until you know what has happened. Very well, the… shall we call it the fromage to save your arm the effort of waving? Professor Quigley did not manage to take it. I arrived in time to prevent that, and to stop him from taking your life."

"You got there? But Elahoraella's letter, it was returned."

"Yes, but the extra fees they charge for incorrect postage are simply ridiculous. I'm not paying those," said Crumbleceiling. "Nevertheless, I was able to read what the letter said before it was sent back to you, and as soon as I had finished in London, I returned to the school."

"You — you didn't come straight back? Even though you knew I was in danger?"

"Well, of course, Billy. I may have read the letter, but I did not pay to do so. It would have been immoral for me to have acted upon the information it contained, would it not?"

Billy stared at Crumbleceiling.

"But by chance, it turned out I was not actually needed at the Secretariat of Sorcery, and I was able to return to the school sooner than expected, which coincidentally, just happened to be at the right time. I am sure that had I been needed, however, I would still have conveniently arrived at precisely the right moment no matter what — I think it is safe to assume that you shall never be in any real peril at Frogsports, Billy. There are too many people getting rich from you to ever let you die… Or to ever take a meaningful stance against hate, apparently."

"What happened to the… fromage?"

"It has been destroyed."

"Destroyed?" said Billy. "But your friend — Émile Arquette —"

"Oh, you know about Émile?" said Crumbleceiling. "Have you read his latest book, *Making Things Better With My Sidekick Filetta*? — anyway, Émile and I have spoken about things, and agreed it was for the best. He said he was starting to prefer truffle anyway."

"But that means he'll die, doesn't it?"

"I can see why you may conclude that, but no, he will not die.'

Crumbleceiling smiled.

"Immortal means you can never die, no matter the circumstances", he explained. "If you had to keep consuming something to survive, that wouldn't be immortality."

So Elahoraella was right, Billy thought to himself.

"The funny thing is," Crumbleceiling went on, "I think after all this time, Émile may actually be starting to wish he wasn't immortal. After all, when one has lived their life, *to die would be an awfully big adventure* — or perhaps something that sounds a little less obviously stolen straight from the work of *J.M. Barrie*. You know, the fromage was really not such a wonderful thing. Living forever and having enough money to do whatever you want? The two things that stop you from being able to appreciate what and who truly makes your whole life worth living in the first place."

Billy lay there, lost for words. Crumbleceiling smiled again.

"Sir?" said Billy. "What happened to Professor Quigley?"

"Ah. I'm afraid to say he has not come out of the whole situation quite as well as you have yourself."

Billy eyed Crumbleceiling questioningly.

"He has turned to stone," Crumbleceiling explained. "I must say, though, it's nice to know I was right about him all along. I knew he was up to something this year. That's why I asked Professor Grape to keep a watch of him."

"But why did he turn to stone?"

Crumbleceiling shrugged his shoulders. "Magic," he said simply.

"What about Ste — hold on, did you just say you suspected Quigley all along?"

"That's right," said Crumbleceiling.

"And you put everybody in danger by never doing anything to stop him?"

"I'm glad to see you're following along. Now, you wanted to ask me another question..."

Billy decided to move on.

"What about Steven? What happened to him?"

"It is very thoughtful of you to use his actual name. I do not appear to have an umbrella with me," said Crumbleceiling. "But to answer your question, I'm afraid he will have survived. Not having a soul, he cannot die. He will find a way to carry on, perhaps find another body to share. We shall just have to wait."

Crumbleceiling now glanced over at the injured reindeer, who was giving him a death stare.

"And there's something else," said Billy.

Crumbleceiling gave the reindeer a nervous wave, then turned back to Billy.

"Quigley said Grape knew my mother and father, and that he went on to murder a man —"

"Many a man, Billy."

"Yes, many a man — but Quigley said he did that and now hates me because my mother once rejected him. Is that true?"

"Well, yes, when I think about it, I suppose it is true. But you are forgetting one small detail."

"What?"

"Professor Grape is a cis-gendered white man, and so naturally, his problematic past carriers neither scrutiny nor consequence."

"Isn't it messed up for anybody to write him like that?"

"Yes..." said Crumbleceiling thoughtfully. "Funny, the way

people's minds work, isn't it? In my opinion, it's almost as if they pick and choose what is right or wrong based on convenience rather than anything tangible."

Billy attempted to make sense of this, but it made his head pound, so he stopped.

"And sir, there's one more thing…"

"Only one?"

"Why was I able to lift the cheese knife from the pebble?"

"Ah, now, I'm glad you've brought that up. The whole knife in the pebble thing was one of my better ideas. You see, I thought it best if only those who wanted to protect the fromage would be able to lift the knife. I knew that would be you, and so upon casting the sorcery, I made it so that for yourself, the knife was merely resting in the pebble."

"You knew I was going to protect it?"

"Naturally, Billy. I've known what you've been up to all year."

"And you still let me advance into a situation where you knew somebody wanted to kill me?"

Crumbleceiling ignored him. Instead, he turned to the boxes on the table and said, "Enough questions for today, I think. You need to relax and make a start on some of these."

As Crumbleceiling opened a box of chocolates, Billy caught on to something else he had just said.

"Sir, you described Grape as cis-gendered. But the term cis-gendered would imply the existence of non-cisgendered people, wouldn't it?"

"I believe some would prefer if that wasn't the case," said Crumbleceiling. "But in the real word, things don't cease to be how they are simply because they make insecure people feel uncomfortable."

Madam Pepper was a compassionate woman, but she was also meticulous and very strict.

"Please, just ten minutes," Billy pleaded with her.

"Absolutely not. You need to rest."

"But I am resting, see. I'm in bed and everything. Oh, go on, Madam Pepper..."

"Oh, very well then," she said, sighing. "But only ten minutes."

And she let Ed and Elahoraella in to see him.

"Billy! We were so worried – we thought you might –"

Elahoraella seemed lost for words.

"Good to see you," said Ed.

"Crumbleceiling wouldn't tell us anything," said Elahoraella. "What actually happened?"

Ed and Elahoraella sat and listened as Billy told them everything that had happened with Quigley, and how he had been hiding Steven all this time.

"So the Brie is gone then?" said Ed finally. "Does that mean Émile Arquette is just going to die?"

"That's what I thought, but – that reminds me," said Billy, turning to Elahoraella. "You were right all along – Crumbleceiling told me that immortal does mean you never die. Arquette doesn't have to keep eating anything."

"I knew it," said Elahoraella. "If you had to keep consuming something to survive, that would make it a medicine, not a source of immortality."

"Do you think Crumbleceiling meant for you to face Quigley?"

said Ed.

"That is entirely a ridiculous suggestion," said Elahoraella.

"No, it isn't," said Billy. "Crumbleceiling knew we were on to something all year, and he never stopped us. He even knew Quigley was behind it all from the start."

"Well then, he should be struck off the teacher's register and never be allowed to work with children again."

"She's got a point, you know?" said Ed. "Maybe you should sue."

They decided to change the subject.

"You missed the final Frogsports match," Ed told him. "But the results ended up being void – something about Crumbleceiling tricking the Gluteal team to take part in match fixing. Anyway, you've got to come to the feast tomorrow. The Crocodilians have topped the table, of course, but that doesn't mean the food won't be good."

"What are you staring at?" Billy asked Elahoraella, noticing she was looking over at Madam Pepper.

"I was just wondering, why doesn't Madam Pepper have her title in her name?" said Elahoraella. "I mean, she is a doctor, isn't she?"

Billy pointed to the trademark on his forehead and Elahoraella nodded.

"Yes," she said. "That makes sense."

The next morning, Billy felt much better. Now that he was conscious, Madam Pepper was able to fix his arm almost straight away, and after a good night's sleep, his head had stopped hurting too.

"I can go to the feast tonight, can't I?" he asked her when she came over to see how he was feeling.

"The headmaster has said you are to go," she said stiffly. "But before you do, we have the small matter of the bill to sort out."

"The bill?" said Billy.

"This is a private school, Mr Smith. You didn't really think the headmaster wouldn't outsource our hospital to an American corporation, did you?"

It it wasn't for the risk of it increasing further, Billy's recovery would have stalled when he saw the amount he owed. He tried to argue that he couldn't possibly have agreed to any of these charges while he was unconscious, and eventually, Madam Pepper agreed to discount the balance by fifty percent.

"If you're able to discount the amount owed, you're clearly making too much profit to begin with," said Billy, but Madam Pepper ignored him.

"You've got another visitor," she said.

"Who is it?"

Barry came through the door as he spoke. He sat down on the chair next to Billy, took one look at him, then began crying.

"Ah'm sorry," he sobbed, his face in his hands. "It's all me fault. Ah told 'im 'ow t' gerr' past Waddles."

"It's okay, Barry," said Billy. "It's over. Steven can't get the Brie."

"Theur could av' died n' everythin'."

"But I didn't die. I'm perfectly fine. The only person who died was Professor Quigley — what's wrong?" Billy asked, for Barry seemed to be crying harder now.

"Quigley — 'e agreed t' buy summa' from me book, but now 'e's dead…"

That evening, after agreeing a payment plan to settle the bill and packing his things up, Billy left the hospital wing to go down to the Banquet Hall and join the rest of the school. As he walked out the door, he passed an ongoing argument.

"I want to see a doctor!"

"For the last time, Karen," Madam Pepper was saying, "you are a ghost. You can't get ill or be inured. And besides that, hurt feelings don't require medical attention."

"You're just discriminating against me," said Karen, defiantly.

Madam Pepper pulled out a phone and held it up.

"No... No... Aaaargh..." And Karen flew off down the corridor.

Held up by Madam Pepper's insistence that she give him one last check-up, by the time Billy made it to the Banquet Hall, the tables were already full of students talking and laughing with each other.

The whole hall had been decorated in the green and silver of Crocodilian house to celebrate them coming top of the table for yet another year. Above the teacher's table hung a giant banner depicting the Crocodilian alligator.

Billy tried not to draw any attention to himself as he made his way up the hall and slipped into an empty space between Ed and Elahoraella at the Osphranter table. Unfortunately, once one person had noticed he was there, it wasn't long before the whole hall had fallen silent to look over at him.

To his relief, Crumbleceiling limped into the hall on crutches moments later and everyone's attention turned to him instead.

"Me and that reindeer have unfinished business," he said to Professor McDouglass as she came over to help him make his way over to a podium in front of the teacher's table.

Professor McDouglass put his crutches to one side, and

Crumbleceiling turned to address the school.

"Another year is over!" he began cheerfully. "But before we can begin our end-of-year feast, I understand there is the small matter of the house table to attend to. In fourth place, Osphranter house, with three hundred and eighty-two credits; in third place, Eudyptula house, with five hundred and ninety-six credits; second is Gluteal house, with eight hundred and fifty-five credits; and in first place, Crocodilian house, with nine hundred and ninety-two credits."

Cheering broke out from the Crocodilian table as they began stomping their feet on the floor and banging their fists on the table.

Billy looked up at the teacher's table where Grape was doing a bad job of trying to hide his smug glee from the other teachers.

"Yes, well done, Crocodilian house," said Crumbleceiling. "But there are some recent events which must be taken into account."

The room fell silent and the smile on Grape's face faltered a little.

"First – to Mr Edward Beaversley..."

Ed went bright red.

"... for showing true loyalty to his friend and standing by his side as he faced danger, I award Osphranter house two hundred credits."

The whole of Osphranter house began cheering. At the teacher's table, Professor Millbrook whispered something to Professor McDouglass. Eventually, silence fell again and Crumbleceiling continued.

"Second – to Miss Elahoraella Parker... for demonstrating true patriotism by reciting the diary of a member of the Royal Family while under pressure, I award Osphranter house two hundred credits."

There was no cheers this time. People seems to know that

Crumbleceiling had more to say and they held on to his every word expectantly. "Third – to Mr Billy Smith..." said Crumbleceiling. "... as full and final settlement for any damages he may attempt to claim from the school, I award Osphranter house two hundred credits."

Talk was breaking out between those who could add up quickly enough to work out that Osphranter house now had nine hundred and eighty-two credits – just ten behind the Crocodilians.

Billy noticed a smile on Professor McDouglass' face. Did she know Crumbleceiling had more?

Crumbleceiling raised his hand and the room fell silent once more.

"There are many differences in this world," he said, as everyone listened expectantly. "But perhaps none are greater than the way in which men and women are treated for doing exactly the same thing. While when Miss Elahoraella Parker stood up to her friends it was considered interfering and annoying, Mr Joshua Hansen's equal actions can only be described as heroic and courageous. I therefore award Mr Hansen nine credits."

There was a long moment of silence, and then –

"What the *fuck*, Richard?" said Professor McDouglass, giving him a dangerous look as boos rang from every table except the Crocodilian's.

Crumbleceiling raised his hand for silence.

"Sometimes life just isn't fair," he said, and cheers erupted from the Crocodilian table.

Despite Crumbleceiling's last-minute surprise, it was still one of the best evenings Billy had ever had. Better than winning at Frogsports, or Christmas or anything... though Jacob did keep reminding him he didn't have to accept the settlement if he didn't want to, and he could recommend an excellent lawyer that Karen had given him the number of.

Billy had almost forgotten they still had exam results to come, but come they did. The only problem was none of them knew what they actually meant. To their great surprise, Elahoraella had failed everything, while Billy and Ed had both got top marks in Alchemy. Somehow, Josh had come top of the year. Thankfully, Professor McDouglass visited the common room to explain that the Secretariat of Sorcery had decided to try out a new way of awarding grades through the use of algorithms this year, but it hadn't gone quite as planned. Elahoraella felt a bit better after being told she could appeal and have her marks fixed, though she was frustrated she would have to pay for the privilege.

Before they knew it, their dormitories were empty, their suitcases were packed, and they were walking down the road that led to the station where the Frogsports Express was waiting to take them all back to London. A couple of students who lived in a nearby town were complaining that they still had to take the train because their parents had forgotten to sign the permission slip allowing them to be picked up from school, but otherwise the mood was good.

To Billy's great surprise, he found Professor Grape waiting for him on the platform.

"Deliver this to your aunt," he said, handing Billy a package wrapped in brown paper.

"What is –"

"Do not ask questions," said Grape cooly. "Just deliver the package."

Billy, Ed, and Elahoraella shared a compartment with Chad and Larry on the journey home, and they laughed and joked together as they sped through towns and countryside. To their great relief, there was no broken down train in front of them this time, and they pulled into platform four and two-thirds at Euston Station just twenty-four minutes late.

It took some time for all the students to leave the platform. The ticket inspector who had stopped Billy on the day they had left for Frogsports was demanding everyone showed him their tickets before being allowed to pass, even though they had already been checked on the train.

"You must come and stay this summer," said Ed. "Both of you —"

"I don't think we'll be able to," said Elahoraella.

"Why not?"

"This feels like it's a one-time thing to me."

Billy, Ed, and Elahoraella passed through the ticket barriers together and found Ed's mother and younger sister waiting to greet them on the other side.

Mrs Beaversley smiled at them all.

"Good year?" she asked.

"Busy," said Billy. "Thanks for the jumper, Mrs Beaversley."

"Oh, it was nothing, dear," she said, smiling. "And thank you for sending me — I spent a lot of time making that jumper, you know!"

"Ready yet?" said another voice.

Billy looked around. It was Mr Moustache, and he looked incredibly uncomfortable to be surrounded by so many happy young people, not to mention people who owned *Oyster cards*.

"You must be Billy's uncle," said Mrs Beaversley, reaching out her hand to shake his.

"Yes," he said bluntly, ignoring her hand. "Come on, boy, we've got to go." He walked off.

Billy said goodbye to Elahoraella and the Beaversleys – apologising to Mrs Beaversley and promising to make it up to her next Christmas – and then followed after his uncle.

On their way out of the station, they passed by a bookshop. In the window was a large poster advertising that a special edition book celebrating the twenty-fifth anniversary of a popular franchise was now available to pre-order. Billy stopped in front of him. He looked at the author's name, then he laughed to himself and said, "Nah, she can go eat shit!"

CPSIA information can be obtained
at www.ICGtesting.com
Printed in the USA
LVHW090416290921
698990LV00003B/299

9 781739 932022